PRAISE FOR *Any Known Blood:*

"*Any Known Blood* is a remarkable achievement. Here is an immensely readable novel, populated with sympathetic yet realistic characters. It deals sensitively, yet often humorously, with one of the most compelling issues of our time in North America—the ever-shifting, ever-problematic relationship between the races. Lawrence Hill is a wonderfully talented writer, and *Any Known Blood* will be one of the talk-of novels of the year."

—Joyce Carol Oates

"Almost unique in Canadian fiction, this is a black family chronicle. . . . *Any Known Blood* is a strong, brave book, one alive to the full complexities of any life."

—*The Hamilton Spectator*

"In this ground-breaking novel, the author plows a shrewd furrow between the minefields of history, commerce and art."

—*The Vancouver Sun*

"The novel, based on actual events and real people, is filled with humour, insight and intelligence."

—*The London Free Press*

"A considerable achievement in which an intelligent, compassionate writer manages to achieve what American feminist poet Adrienne Rich calls the 'imaginative transformation of reality.' That he manages to do so with such grace and humour is a tribute to Hill's maturity as both a writer and a human being."

—*The Ottawa Citizen*

"*Any Known Blood* is a witty, wry, well-crafted story told on a Dickensian scale."

—*Winnipeg Free Press*

"Outstanding—Hill's narrative is consistently compelling and readable, and his characters are wonderfully drawn."

—*Quill & Quire*

"Lawrence Hill masterfully threads the history of the five generations . . . into an engaging commentary of changing times. . . . Colourful dialogue and rich flashes of subtle humour abound."

—*Toronto Star*

"Lawrence Hill is on to something new: a literary examination of psyche and bones and flesh. History and the imagination of this young author surge vibrantly to define, over generations, the true meaning of life. *Any Known Blood* becomes more than a history of lives that might normally be lost, and is instead its new interpretation."

—Austin Clarke

"This is what novels were meant to be—harrowing, hilarious, hugely inventive and utterly convincing, the kind of book you'll live inside and never want to leave. *Any Known Blood* spans oceans, continents and generations—from West Africa to Virginia to the north shore of Lake Ontario—and maps them all in the contours of a single human heart."

—Oakland Ross

"*Any Known Blood* is all about love. It is a large and large-hearted novel full of tragedy and hope, and sadness and laughter. Lawrence Hill truly captivates the reader in this wonderfully boisterous account of five generations of a black family."

—Paul Quarrington

Any Known Blood

Any Known Blood

Lawrence Hill

HARPER PERENNIAL

Originally published by HarperCollins Publishers
Ltd in hardcover: 1997
First HarperCollins Publishers Ltd trade paper-
back edition: 1998
First Harper Perennial trade paperback edition: 2007
This Harper Perennial trade paperback edition: 2011

HarperCollins Canada
2 Bloor Street East, 20th Floor
Toronto, Ontario, Canada M4W 1A8

www.harpercollins.ca

Map of Oakville appears courtesy of the National
Archives of Canada, Document #NMC 4226.
Reproduced from a water-colour drawing by
Edward B. Palmer.

Library and Archives Canada Cataloguing in
Publication information is available upon request

ISBN 978-1-44340-910-0

Printed and bound in the United States
RRD 9 8 7 6 5 4 3 2 1

To my grandparents,
May Edwards Hill and Rev. Daniel G. Hill Jr.,
who lived and loved with dignity and passion

Everybody having a known trace of Negro blood in his veins —
no matter how far back it was acquired — is classified as a Negro.
No amount of white ancestry, except one hundred per cent, will
permit entrance to the white race.

Gunnar Myrdal
Vol. 1, *An American Dilemma*, 1944

My old man died in a fine big house
My ma died in a shack
I wonder where I'm gonna die,
Being neither white nor black?

Langston Hughes
"Cross," in *Selected Poems*, 1959

The Cane Family, 1828–1995

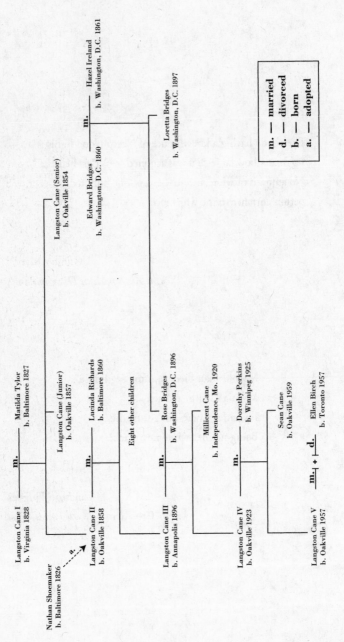

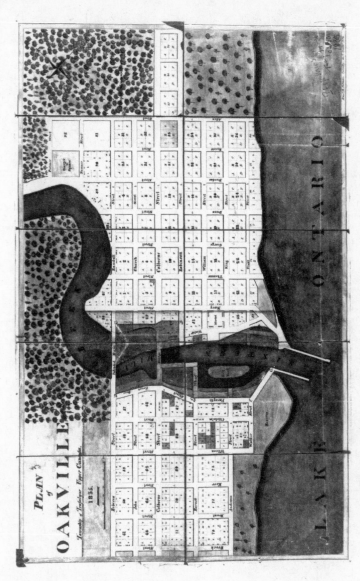

PLAN OF OAKVILLE, TOWNSHIP OF TRAFALGAR, UPPER CANADA, 1835

Prologue

SHE CAME TO HIS ROOM after darkness fell, confident that nobody had followed her. He lived alone, in a room above a dry goods store. The yellow moon hung fat and full, so low that it shone through his window. It threw their shadows against the wall as they came together, touched lips, touched tongues. She unfastened the buttons of his pants. He drew up her dress, peeled back her under-garments, and discovered her already wet. Her knees buckled. She almost fell back onto the bed. But he caught her, and righted her, and they pulled apart just enough to undress each other.

He had turned out the gas lamp before she came to him, and there were no candles burning. There was only the moonlight, and the undulation of moon shadows above his bed. Clothes pooled around their ankles. They remained standing, running fingers over bone, muscle, soft places, hard places. They turned to observe their own shadows cast against the wall. Neither spoke. He ran his middle finger down from the crown of her head, between her eyes, along the thin bridge of her nose, onto her lips. She drew her palm across his shoulder, around his pectoral muscles, down to his navel. They watched their shadows, and, to see them better, stood slightly apart. They saw his erection and one of her breasts profiled on the wall, they watched their own hands joining, and they noticed that the shadows revealed nothing of her whiteness, or his blackness.

They eased onto the bed and continued with their slow and patient lovemaking. When she finally guided him into her, he held still to relax and extend their pleasure. She lay back, closed her eyes, and tightened and relaxed and tightened herself around him, feeling him grow harder inside her, the very thought of it quickening her breath.

He raised his upper body. They locked together in a rhythmic and rocking motion, while their lips joined and parted and joined and parted. She thought, *My God, I love this man,* and he thought, *I can die now and I won't care.* She cried out his name three times, and he felt a wave of gratitude as she shuddered and pulsated and ground her pelvic bone against his. She eased back down on the bed, still until he began to move again, faster and faster. As he felt the muscles in his groin tighten, and as his quickening arousal ignited within her an unexpected new fluttering of pleasure, voices from the street — the voices of two or three young men — assaulted them. *You will die, nigger. You will die soon.* A grapefruit-sized rock smashed his window and struck the side of the bed.

Chapter 1

I HAVE THE RARE DISTINCTION — a distinction that weighs like a wet life jacket, but that I sometimes float to great advantage — of not appearing to belong to any particular race, but of seeming like a contender for many.

In Spain, people have wondered if I was French. In France, hotel managers asked if I was Moroccan. In Canada, I've been asked — always tentatively — if I was perhaps Peruvian, American, or Jamaican. But I have rarely given a truthful rendering of my origins.

Once, someone asked, "Are you from Madagascar? I know a man from Madagascar who looks like you."

I said: "As a matter of fact, I am. I was born in the capital, Antananarivo. We moved to Canada when I was a teenager."

Another time, when a man sitting next to me in a donut shop complained about Sikh refugees arriving by boat in Gander, Newfoundland, I said: "I was born in Canada and I don't wear a turban, but I'm a Sikh. My mother is white, but my father is a Sikh, and that makes me one, too." The man's mouth fell open. I paid the waitress to bring him twelve chocolate donuts. "I've gotta go," I told him. "But next time you want to run down Sikhs, just remember that one of them bought you a box of donuts!"

I tried it again at the next opportunity. A woman at a party said Moroccans were sexist pigs, so I became a Moroccan. Then I started claiming I was part Jewish, part Cree, part Zulu, part anything people were running down. My game of multiple racial identities continued until eighteen months ago, when my wife left me. It was the lowest point of my life, so low that I didn't much see the point in living, even lower than when my son died in the womb. Shortly before Ellen moved out, I saw an advertisement for a speech writer for the Ontario Ministry of Wellness. A line ran across the bottom of the advertisement: "As part of an active effort to promote employment equity in the public service, this position has been designated a Category Three job. Only racial minorities need apply."

I filled out an application. I could have told them the truth — that I was black, or at least partly so, having a white mother and black father. I wanted the job, but I also wanted to test my theory that nobody would challenge my claim to any racial identity. So, in the letter that accompanied a résumé and some writing samples, I explained that I was of Algerian origin. I got an interview. They asked if I was actively involved in the Algerian community. I said the Algerian community was small in Toronto, but that I did spend time with my brothers and sisters and with family friends.

They gave me the job. I still have it. They still think I'm Algerian. I have had to explain that my father changed his name when he came to Canada, and that his original name was Allassane Mamoudy. I have even had to deny any relation to my father, who is well known in the city and most definitely not Algerian.

It has been said that I have come down in the world. Down from an unbroken quartet of forebears, all, like me, named Langston Cane. A most precipitous descent, my father mumbled, when he heard about my latest job. I write speeches for a politician I tried to knock off the ballot. Usually, I handle ribbon-cutting affairs. *I'm delighted to join you on the occasion of your . . . I admire the years of time and effort you have invested in . . . something in which I share profound personal conviction . . .* I almost quit after the first week. But I stuck it out. I had little choice. Years have passed since I've had the courage to write — or, more properly, to re-create — my family history. And the list of occupations for which I'm ill-suited appears to be expanding. So, I stuck with the government job, and initially did well at it. That's not bragging. Speech writing does not require one to scale peaks of creativity. It does demand a certain control of the nuts and bolts of grammar and the rhythm of speech. One must attempt at all times to adopt natural human language, even if one is writing for politicians. As well, a speech writer must not feel wedded to his own convictions. The best thing is to have no convictions at all.

Convictions ruled the lives of my ancestors. They all became doctors, or church ministers. By my age — thirty-eight — they already had their accomplishments noted in the *Afro-American,* the *Oakville Standard,* the *Toronto Times,* or the *Baltimore Sun.* I will admit that it takes a certain discipline and boldness to throw oneself into high-minded professions. But it also takes something to fall from the treadmill of great accomplishments, to fail, even at the tasks of being a husband and a potential father and a writer, to march to the gates of middle age and look ahead and accept that you will not change the world.

This can't go on. I'm going to have to leave this job. I have some money saved up and nothing to spend it on — no wife any more, no children, and no outlay exceeding the four hundred dollars a month for my one-room flat above a fur store in downtown Toronto. I can leave, with no fear of having to return to my father, palm upturned.

I grew up with four family legends — one about each of my direct paternal ancestors. Every year, my father would add another tantalizing detail, but refuse to go any further. I would plead in vain for more, and for information about my father's sister, Mill. Sean, my brother, would say, "He's not telling us any more, because he doesn't know any more, and most of what he's told us probably isn't true anyway." But I ignored Sean. When my father got going, it was like being at a seance. Every drop of his hand, every rise and fall of his tone, every whisper and shout, I felt in my bones.

My father was born in Oakville, Ontario, in 1923. He returned to the States as a young boy, with his parents and sister, served as an American soldier in World War II, and moved back to Canada in 1950 to study medicine at the University of Toronto. While there, he met and fell in love with Dorothy Perkins. Other than myself, my father is the only one in the long line of Canes to marry a white woman. The only difference is, he stayed married.

Boycotting weddings seems to be a genetic trait of the Cane family. As far as I know, none of the Langston Canes managed to pull off a wedding without some key family member refusing to attend.

In the case of my parents, of course, boycotts were expected. And they were duly delivered. My mother has never confirmed this, but I happen to know from my father that my mother's mother reacted to the wedding news by proposing a brief but enforced stay for my mother in a psychiatric institution. So the mother of the bride was a no-show. And my father has never confirmed this, but I happen to know from my mother that my father's sister, Mill, let it be known that by marrying out of the race, my father was betraying black women. Her brother's wife was not to take it personally, but Mill had no intention of attending the wedding or meeting her sister-in-law.

My mother was from Winnipeg, and my father had been living in Baltimore before moving to Canada. The choice of a wedding site reflected the kind of compromise that has always characterized my parents' relationship: when my mother moves six miles, my father accommodates her by moving six inches. Accordingly, they married in Washington, D.C. The year was 1954. The season: spring. April 5, to be exact. D.C. looked like a greenhouse. There were eucalyptus trees, cherry blossoms, magnolias, and tulips from top to bottom of Chain Bridge Road, where my father's parents lived. I can imagine what the road looked like that day because I saw it many times as a boy.

D.C. in the spring was like a wall of heat, which is the way seventy-five degrees Fahrenheit always felt after shoveling snow in Ontario. I remember my grandmother Rose's vegetable garden, which took us nearly a minute to run around. I remember visiting the Howard University chapel, where my grandfather served as the minister at my parents' wedding.

I have heard so many stories about the wedding that I feel as if I attended it. When someone retells an old story, I can point out errors. It is inaccurate, for example, to say that my mother's father, George, told a joke about black people. Actually, he told a joke about a Mexican who was mistaken for black in a restaurant that served whites only.

I wish I'd been there to hear George laughing at his own joke. I wish I'd been there to see everybody freeze until my father laughed and slapped George's back and gave him a glass of vermouth and walked him onto the subject of golf. As a rule, I dislike weddings — because of the pomp, because somebody's always in a snit over something, and because I have never looked good in a jacket and tie — but that one would have been worth attending.

It had rained early in the morning, and then turned sunny and stayed that way. Outside the chapel, the lawns were wet and sparkling. It was the finest Wednesday that spring.

Wednesday?

That idea came from my mother, Dorothy Perkins. They couldn't afford a large reception. But they wanted all their friends to see their act of courage — or social deviance, as my mother, then a sociologist-in-training, joked.

To which my father replied, "We are a deviant couple, my dear, but on our wedding night, I would suggest that we converge."

"Why don't we converge our ideas on the matter at hand?" my mother said. "Let's marry on a Wednesday, at two in the afternoon. Only a quarter of our friends will be able to make it. That way, we can plan a small reception and still invite everybody."

My parents went ahead with their plans. But almost everybody came. A hundred guests squeezed into a chapel for fifty people. As my father has said, "It looked like the most popular wedding in D.C. And two conspicuous absences weren't too bad at all."

My father opened up a medical practice in Oakville, and became well known for his civil rights activities in Canada. He had two sons. One of them has a growing reputation as a first-rate criminal lawyer. That's Sean, my younger brother. They should have named him Langston. But they didn't. They gave the name to me, the first born of the fifth generation.

Chapter 2

ABERDEEN WILLIAMS CAME TO MY OFFICE the other day. I wasn't expecting him. Over the last year or so, having received my divorce papers and pretty well severed contact with my father, I have seen Aberdeen more than usual. Since he is eighty-eight, I go to him. One Sunday every month or two, I take the commuter train to Oakville, meet him at a local café called The Green Bean, and listen to his stories. He tells me about Oakville in the 1920s, when he lived with my grandparents and helped raise my father and aunt. He doesn't say much about my Aunt Mill, but the little I do know comes from him. He tells me about a Canadian wing of the Ku Klux Klan, which came after him in Oakville in 1930. He shares his theories about how black Africans in small boats crossed the Atlantic to America a thousand years before Columbus.

But I missed our last rendezvous. Completely forgot about it. Spent most of the Sunday in a downtown Toronto laundromat, thinking about leaving my speech-writing job. Aberdeen didn't call to complain that I had forgotten about him. He simply turned up at my office.

He's a short, thin man. He's jet black, has lively, inquisitive eyes, and looks about twenty years younger than he is. He still has hair, and keeps a narrow, finely trimmed salt-and-pepper mustache.

"You look good, Aberdeen," I said, and got up from my desk. We shook hands. "I can see why they used to call you 'Dark Gable.'"

He laughed. I asked how he had come to my office. He said he had taken the train, and the subway, and the elevator, like any other normal person.

"But you're not normal, Ab. You're a thousand years old."

"Maybe, but I've got a better memory than you," he said.

I stared for a minute. Then it hit me. "I'm sorry. The Green Bean. Last Sunday. I forgot all about it. But you didn't have to come in all this way."

"Actually, I'm bringing a message. From your father."

I hoped that the stiffening of my back and neck wasn't visible. At that moment, my friend and boss — a failed aristocrat named Alfonso de Altura Jr. — stepped into my office.

I introduced him to Aberdeen. They chatted for a moment, and then Alfonso turned to tell me that a delegation of business leaders from Algeria would soon be visiting our ministry. Could I meet with them?

I nodded, and started to say that I was just heading out for a coffee with Aberdeen. I was hoping to talk about the Algerian delegation when I came back, alone. But Alfonso kept going. When the man had something on his mind, he was like a high-speed train.

"They'll be delighted to meet you, being an Algerian and all. Imagine their surprise at meeting somebody of Algerian origin here. Do you speak Arabic, by any chance?"

"No," I said. "Give me half an hour, and I'll come talk to you."

Alfonso said that would be fine, and stepped out of my office.

Aberdeen's head was lowered. Slowly, he raised his eyes to meet mine. "Algerian?"

"It's a long story," I said.

"You told your boss you were Algerian?"

"I can explain it to you, Aberdeen."

"You've always been good with words, Langston. When you were in school, I thought you would become a lawyer. You can explain anything. But your explanation would just make things worse. I don't want to hear it."

Aberdeen pushed on his armrests and hovered, bent, a few inches out of his chair. I scooted around my desk to help him, but he waved me off.

"I just need a minute," he said. "I'm a bit slow in the morning."

"Where are you going?"

"Can't stay long. Your father had a message. He asked me to give it to you."

"Surely, he didn't expect you to come all the way into Toronto to deliver it. Why didn't you just call me?"

Aberdeen put his hand on mine. I could feel the calluses all around his palm, at the root of each finger, from years of gardening and working as a handyman. Aberdeen's grin drooped into sadness. "If I hadn't come into Toronto, how would I have discovered that Langston Cane the Fifth had become an Algerian?"

"That was just a silly game that got out of control. I told them I was Algerian to get the job. I wanted to see if they'd buy the story."

"When you were a little boy," Ab said, "I used to look after you. Do you remember that?" I nodded. "I know I told you about how your grandfather saved my life." I nodded again. "And I told you about your great-great-grandfather, Langston Cane the First."

I remembered that, too. My great-great-grandfather had

escaped slavery in Maryland and had come up to Oakville on the Underground Railroad. I had heard, from Aberdeen and from my father, that Langston the First had been helped by Quakers along the way. I don't believe I would be around to tell this story had it not been for Quakers here and there. Anyway, Langston the First arrived in Oakville in 1850, found a wife, had three kids, and then slipped out of town nine years later and was never seen again. According to family legend, he left Oakville in a horse-drawn carriage, seated next to John Brown, who just a few months later led an attack on the U.S. weapons arsenal in Harpers Ferry, Virginia. The link between my ancestor and John Brown seemed farfetched, but it had always fascinated me.

I walked with Aberdeen to the elevator. I got in with him and rode down.

"There are a lot of things you don't know about your own family," Aberdeen said. "There are things your father doesn't even know." My old friend cracked a smile. He still had all his teeth. Aberdeen stepped out of the building and into the wind. I followed him and asked what my father had wanted him to tell me.

"He wants you to come see him. You are his flesh and blood, Langston. I never had any children — so I know what that means. He says it's time to end the standoff."

"I'll think about it," I said.

Aberdeen grabbed my hand. "Do you love me, young man?"

"I'm hardly young any more."

"From where I'm standing, you look young. I asked if you loved me."

"You know the answer to that."

"You've loved me since I changed your diapers. You'll love me until the day I die. When that happens, there won't be anybody putting me in any history book. But will you love me — or love my memory — any less because I never amounted to much? Because I never made history?"

I gulped and stared into his big brown eyes. He was smiling.

"Your family has had some born achievers, son, but you don't have to do what they did. I know you're interested in who your people were. Why don't you write about them? You told me years ago that you wanted to do it. Write, Langston. Go write. Go do the one thing that all the achievers in your family were too busy and too important to do."

It was freezing outside, and I had left my jacket in the office, but I walked Aberdeen to the Bay subway station. I walked him down the stairs to the turnstiles and fished through my pockets and tried to give him a token.

"Don't waste your money. I've got tickets at a senior citizen discount."

I told Aberdeen that I would think about what he had said. He pushed through the turnstile and walked ahead. The moment before he took an escalator down out of sight, he turned and called out: "One of these days, you'll have to tell me all about Algeria."

I didn't set out to get fired, or to see my name in the Toronto newspapers. I have enough on my shoulders as it is. So I was not out looking for trouble. But trouble blew in with the wind, at the very moment that I had been wondering about my great-great-grandfather, and about the family legend of his demise alongside John Brown while trying to strike a blow against slavery.

The trouble began in earnest when my boss asked if I wanted to see a confidential government document.

Alfonso, like me, is one of the walking wounded. He, too, senses that he's been a failure in his father's eyes. A few years ago, he discovered that his divorced father had remarried, had another child — a boy — and given him the name Alfonso de Altura Jr. "I didn't turn out the way he wanted, so he figured he'd start again from scratch," Alfonso told me.

On the day of my undoing, Alfonso urged me to read a secret report that had somehow landed on his desk.

"No, thanks."

"Guess what our illustrious government is about to ban."

"Sex?"

"Nope."

"Sex in public places?"

"Nope."

"Sex in saunas?"

"Langston, you gotta get yourself a woman friend. But put those thoughts aside, if you can. This government is about to kill anti-discrimination legislation and junk the provincial human rights commission."

"Let me see that thing."

I spent an hour or so reading the proposal that had been sent forth to Cabinet. We certainly had entered an era of government downsizing. First, they downsized welfare cheques by about 20 percent. Then, they downsized the need for meat inspectors, elevator inspectors — just about any kind of inspectors, for that matter. Foreign investors sure as hell wouldn't be interested in putting money down in Ontario if they had to work in a climate where a company could be put out of business for selling bad meat or letting elevator cables unravel. According to this document, it was now the turn of the human rights commission and the Ontario Human Rights Code. They were obsolete and antithetical to good business practices. They had served a need years ago, thank you very much, but this was the nineties. Minorities didn't require special treatment any longer. Like other Ontarians, minorities knew businesses couldn't compete in the global economy without treating all employees fairly. Or so the document said.

I imagined having to craft a minister's speech about how eliminating human rights legislation would contribute to Ontario's positive business climate. But I knew the minister's spin doctors wouldn't allow the term "human rights legislation" in the speech. They would insist that all speeches refer to the old legislation as "the job quota law."

I have written a lot of trash on the job. But I didn't think I could write that speech. I imagined my great-great-grandfather, Langston Cane the First, shaking his head as he watched me work.

There was nothing happening in the office on the morning that Alfonso gave me the secret document. I thought about catching a noon-hour movie — but there was nothing worth seeing. I stepped out of the office at eleven, bought a hot dog and a root beer from a street vendor, strolled outside for five minutes, and returned to my desk — only to have the minister's communications aide pounce on me.

Alfonso was out at a dentist's appointment. Almost everyone in the minister's office was out that day. But the minister had a sudden problem. He had been putting in time in the legislature, snoozing through committee meetings, when he was ordered by the premier to stand in for him at a speaking function that same afternoon.

The event was scheduled to take place at a downtown hotel at one. It was now eleven-fifteen. Could I get a speech to the minister's office within an hour? Write anything, I was told, just get the minister through a ten-minute speech to the Canadian Association of Black Journalists without making a fool of himself.

In leaving, the minister's aide said, "Hey, this is kind of up your alley, isn't it? You're Algerian or something, aren't you?"

I nodded. Yes, I told him, this was right up my alley.

I know the secret to grinding out pages under tight deadlines —
write as fast as possible without thinking. So I switched on the
computer and started writing. I swear upon the memory of my
great-great-grandfather that I did not set out to get the minister
fired. Nor did I immediately conceive of the idea to write two
speeches — one straightforward version for the minister's office,
and one podium copy with a curve ball.

Had I spent weeks planning a way to trick a minister into
revealing details about a confidential document to a crowd of
journalists, I could never have pulled it off. I will admit to a
number of character faults. Unlike my ancestors, I seem to have
difficulty seizing life by the horns. Regretfully, I have shown the
capacity to be unfaithful at a critical time to the only woman I
have truly loved. But the one thing that I am *not* is conniving or
deceitful. I would be the last person in the world capable of planning a crime. My face would betray me from the very start.

I knew what I was doing, of course, when I doctored the
minister's podium copy. But it was certainly not "a brilliantly
planned, courageous blow against the Ontario government and
its right-wing agenda," as one of the newspapers said later. It was
simply a speech that fell into place with the help of chance —
namely, the minister had no knack for public speaking. His
verbal abilities were so limited that Alfonso and I had nick-
named him Pilot, for his unswerving adherence to any speech
placed before his eyes. We speculated that Pilot had probably
hired a freelancer to write the thank-you speech for his wedding
reception.

It took me twenty minutes to write the speech. It acknowledged
that blacks had contributed to life in Canada, suggested that they
wanted opportunities for their children, and claimed that the

government was paving the way for long-term prosperity by creating conditions in which businesses and investors would thrive.

I brought the speech to the minister's aide and sat with him while he scanned the pages. He caught a typo and made two edits in style. I promised to bring back a clean copy for him, as well as a podium copy for the minister.

I always prepared the minister's speaking copy in twenty-four-point type. He liked his lines triple-spaced, with no page more than two-thirds full, for easy reading from the podium.

I ran back upstairs, printed out a clean copy for the aide, and proceeded to doctor the minister's podium copy. The copy from which the minister would read was essentially the same speech that had been approved by the aide — with one exception.

My so-called "courageous blow against the Ontario government" began about three-quarters of the way through the podium copy. It began at the point where the minister would feel confident that all was going well. It began at a point of no return, where Pilot would know only how to gallop forward, like a horse going back to the barn. It began precisely after Pilot recognized that black people wanted rewarding job opportunities and a solid economic future.

"Ladies and gentlemen," I wrote for Pilot's benefit, "I understand that if people are to give fully of themselves when participating in our economic and social life, they need to feel respected. They need to feel wanted. And they need to feel that they are being treated fairly.

"Black people have had a history of challenges and of victories in this province. Ontario's long history of protecting human rights dates back to our first anti-slavery legislation in 1793.

"I am committed to upholding that history. I know that if you want to reap the harvest of a thriving social and economic climate, you have to sow the seeds ahead of time.

"So I am telling you that I will be leading the way in opposing a proposal, recently reviewed by Cabinet, to eliminate human rights legislation and to dismantle the human rights commission. Such a proposal would move Ontario thirty years backward in the step-by-step struggle to create a tolerant and diverse society."

After that part of the speech, I bridged back to the conclusion in the vetted version. I slipped the doctored speech into a large envelope marked *Minister's speech — Podium Copy* and the approved speech into another envelope made out to the communications aide, and delivered them both.

According to media reports, the minister didn't immediately realize that he had just leaked a secret government document. He read the speech verbatim, and seemed momentarily puzzled when he got a standing ovation three-quarters of the way through his remarks. But he smiled, and swallowed, and waited for everybody to sit back down, and then just kept reading to the bottom of the last page.

Later on, I heard that fifteen minutes after the minister gave the speech, a reporter for the *Toronto Times* — a black reporter, by the way, whose name was Mahatma Grafton — called the premier's office for comment. The premier's office called the minister's office. The premier met the minister, reviewed the speech, and told the minister that he was out of a job.

The reporter called every office he could think of to find out who had written that speech. He asked the premier's aide, who didn't know. He tried people in the minister's office, but they hadn't yet decided what to say, so they said nothing. He got hold of a government phone directory and found my name listed as senior writer, communications branch, Ministry of Wellness, and left a message on my answering machine at work.

Under normal circumstances, I would have returned the call promptly. But I was about to pay the price for bringing an elected official into disrepute. I was about to be the first person in five generations of Langston Canes to depart so unceremoniously from a place of employment. I was about to start wearing my very own scarlet letters — FWC, for Fired With Cause.

I learned of my imminent dismissal while visiting the men's room. Alfonso was considerate enough to catch me alone in there. His words came out slightly slurred, because he had two new fillings and his mouth was still frozen.

"Langston, they're about to fire you. I've got to hand it to you. You're a revolutionary under that placid exterior. What you did took a hell of a lot of courage." He leaned over and whispered: "You won't tell anybody where you got that document, will you?"

No, I assured him, I would not.

Alfonso sighed deeply. He was a portly forty-year-old with thick hands and roving eyes. I'd heard him sigh like that just the other week, over lunch, as a waitress sashayed away from our table. He considered her in the way that a child would study a double-decker ice-cream cone. He let out that long breath, and declared himself ravenously heterosexual and unjustly deprived.

In the men's room, Alfonso settled into position beside me. I was standing, feet splayed, midway through expelling the root beer, feeling about as content and relieved as I ever felt those days. Alfonso said we had to go straight to a meeting with the personnel director.

"How much time are they giving me?" I asked.

"Thirty minutes." Alfonso said that after our meeting with the personnel director, I was to remove my belongings from the office. "I admire you, Langston. I know you've been hurting badly about Ellen divorcing you. A lot of people would have cracked up.

Become alcoholics, or worse. It's to your credit that the wildest thing you've done is leak a confidential document by putting it in the minister's mouth."

"Yeah."

"This is a sign. Don't just find another job as a hack. Change your life. Somewhere out there in the real world, you'll find a use for your prodigious writing talents."

I snorted. "Nobody with prodigious talent writes speeches for the Ontario Minister of Wellness."

"Anybody capable of producing two speeches in an hour, one that will fool a communications aide and one that will knock a minister out of Cabinet, has writing talent to spare."

"Are they really going to fire the minister?"

"Looks like it. But let's get back to business. Can you give me a copy of that speech before we go into that meeting? And I'm not supposed to tell you this, but a security guard will check your bags when you leave the office. Don't take anything that's not yours."

"No dictionaries, no paper clips."

"You don't have to be funny with me, Langston. You must be in shock."

I turned to wash my hands. "That sure was a lot of root beer," I said.

When you miss the carrot and slice open your fingertip on the chopping board, the pain doesn't set in right away. It waits at least long enough for you to see what you've done. After coming out of the meeting with Alfonso and the personnel director, the pink slip didn't feel too bad. It felt like a liberation. Like a kick in the pants, saying, "Okay, you're off! Don't waste this opportunity." The high lasted while I sat at my desk and began removing personal matters from the drawers. I took down my Fowler's *Modern English Usage* — which was left over from the time I dreamed of becoming a writer — and I removed my government telephone directory. Then, chin up, I reversed the decision. The government directory went back on the shelf. It was time for a clean break.

The feeling of liberation and rejuvenation lasted while I removed an extra pair of socks and a container of dental floss from my bottom desk drawer. It stayed with me as I found a want-you-back letter that I'd never mailed to Ellen. I turfed old tax forms, pay stubs, bank statements, memos. The feeling lasted as I finished at the desk, switched off the fluorescent light, and swiveled in my chair to face the computer. The feeling lasted through all the rituals of office cleaning until an imposing male voice — a voice of authority, a voice accustomed to getting what it wanted and getting it immediately — filled the reception area:

"Excuse me. I'm looking for Langston Cane the Fifth."

My father! Except for the rare telephone call, I hadn't heard his voice for more than a year. It vaulted over the partitions separating me from the receptionist. This is what I heard next:

Receptionist: "I beg your pardon, sir?"

Father: "Langston Cane, please."

Receptionist: "He's four desks down on your left."

Father: "Which way, did you say?"

Footsteps slapped along the cool government carpet. Footsteps that could belong to none other than my friend Alfonso.

Alfonso: "Excuse me, sir. How may I help you?"

"I'm looking for my son."

"Your son, sir? And who might that be?" Here, I imagined Alfonso smiling with his thick lips, roving with beady eyes over his protruding brow, and twitching pudgy digits behind his back.

"Langston Cane the Fifth."

"Langston! Your son? You are *the* Langston Cane, are you not? Dr. Cane?"

"Yes. The Fourth."

"Certainly, certainly. This way, sir."

My father looked well. The strands of dark hair — on the sides of his head only — were brushed back. His eyes were the color of coffee beans, and carried an impish smile that suggested, *So! I found you.* His fingers were still long and brown and smooth around the knuckles. He saluted me with his cane. It was made of red oak, and had squares of inlaid silver. He never went out without it, although he didn't need it — except to point at things, or to win the attention of salespeople, receptionists, and the two or three hundred people in the city he had served at one time or another, over the last four decades, as a sort of guru.

My father tapped my shin with his cane.

"Hello, son, don't you rise from your chair to greet an old man?"

Alfonso backed out of sight and parked a few steps away. I could tell because I heard his asthmatic breathing. And then the breathing stopped. The bastard was holding his breath so as not to miss a word. Staying in my chair, I looked up into my father's eyes.

"Aberdeen gave me your message. I had been planning to come to visit you and Mom soon."

"But you haven't done it yet. What's the matter? You ashamed of me? You trying to pass for white?"

He laughed at his own joke. It was the same laugh I'd heard as a child at countless Sunday breakfasts, when he had told stories of light-skinned blacks trying to pass as whites in the States. Stories of evasion and discovery had always been among my father's favorites.

"Very funny. Why did you come here?"

"Do I have to have a reason to say hello? You are my son, you know. Langston Cane the Fifth, in case anybody is asking."

"A few people may be asking, as a matter of fact. Give me two minutes to finish something here. Then we can go get a coffee."

"Coffee. You sure love that stuff."

"It's just a figure of speech. It's a generic term for having milk, or mint tea, or apricot juice, gazelle blood, what have you."

"I, personally, have nothing against caffeinated libations. Taken in moderation, coffee is a fine thing. Stimulates the cerebellum. Rustles the digestive tract. And it falls squarely in the African American tradition of imbibing hot fluids to sustain the soul."

"Pipe down, would you? Give me two minutes, Dad, and we'll clear out."

"Want to get me out of here, is that it?"

I turned away from him, flicked on my computer, and inserted a floppy disk. My final, office-closing act was to transfer personal files from the computer to a disk.

"Just wait a second," I said. "I'd tell you to sit down, but as you can see I only have the one chair in this office."

"Office? You call this an office? It's a water closet. A coffin. At best, a measly nook in a rabbit warren. Son, can't you do any better than —"

Alfonso reappeared, with a chair.

"Thank you," my father said. "You obviously know something about the finer arts of civility and hospitality. What did you say your name was?"

"Alfonso de Altura Jr."

"A fine name, if I do say so myself. I like polysyllables in a name. Polysyllables are a fine and distinguishing trait. So is alliteration.

Alfonso de Altura Jr. Polysyllabic, alliterated — yes, it's quite distinctive. It traces back to noble European blood, no doubt?"

"Oh, Doctor," Alfonso sputtered, "I'm afraid that any nobility has been sadly diluted. But I must say, sir, that I find your presence here today both spectacular and riveting."

"What, precisely, is so spectacular and riveting?"

"That you and Langston are father and son."

"Spectacular? Does this lad not let his roots be known?"

"Well, not to me, anyway. Dr. Cane, may I ask you, is there any Algerian component to your family history?"

"Algerian? None whatsoever! Wherever would one get such an idea?"

"I really don't know. I must have been confused. But tell me, what are you up to these days, Dr. Cane? Your name still surfaces all the time around here. The Cane report on blacks in the media; the Cane report on police and racial minorities. The organizations you founded over the years."

"Oh, nothing much. Just my family practice in Oakville — and I've scaled it down considerably. I'm in partial retirement now."

I finished with my computer, retrieved the disk, and swung around to face the two of them.

Alfonso started up again. "Dr. Cane, I have one of your publications in my office. Would you be good enough to autograph it for me?"

"Certainly."

"Be right back." Alfonso stepped out.

I slung my bag over my shoulder, turned off the computer, and took my father by the arm. "Let's go."

"But that portly gentleman has requested my autograph."

"You can give it to him on your next visit here."

We got as far as the elevator, but were still waiting for it when Alfonso caught up to us.

"Here you are, good sir. If you could just sign here on the title page. You can make it out to Alfonso. That's A-L . . ."

"I can manage the spelling, thanks very much." My father signed the book, handed it back, and stepped into the elevator. Alfonso held the elevator door with one hand and shook my hand with the other. He leaned close to me. "Kick some butt out there, Langston. You can do it." He let go of my hand and the door.

The elevator door closed. My father asked: "Is it common practice for you to leave the office before five?"

"Alfonso is my boss, and he knows I'm leaving. At any rate, leaving early is a minor infraction. Last week, I took a two-hour lunch to catch a movie."

My father guffawed. "Very good, son. That's funny."

Just before we left the building, a black man entered through the revolving doors. He looked as if he was in a big hurry, but he stopped when he saw my father.

"Dr. Cane."

My father was used to being stopped by people he didn't recognize. He loved it.

"Yes. What can I do for you?"

"I'm Mahatma Grafton. The *Toronto Times*."

"Oh yes, I remember you now. How goes the battle?"

"Fine," the reporter said, with a quick grin. He was focused entirely on my father — I felt confident that he wouldn't notice me. "I'm in a rush, but can I ask one quick question?"

"Fire away."

"I've just learned that the government plans to scrap human rights legislation and the human rights commission. What do you think of that?"

"I think that would be an abomination," my father said. "It's hard to believe that even this government would stoop so low in its craven desire to please business."

I watched Mahatma whip a small notepad out of his jacket pocket and scribble madly. He was slender and tall and about my age. He had a brown complexion.

"That good enough for you?" my father said.

"That's great, Dr. Cane. You always come through with a good quote. By the way, are you any relation to the Langston Cane in the government phone directory?"

"Sure am. He's my son. Right here. Langston — meet Mahatma Grafton, an upstanding journalist for the *Toronto Times.*"

We shook hands.

"I left a message on your machine," he said.

"Actually, I don't work for the ministry any longer."

"That's bizarre. They haven't even got rid of your voice-mail message. Anyway, do you know about this speech the minister gave, or who wrote it?"

I managed a sympathetic smile. "Afraid I can't help you with that."

"Well, thanks anyway. Gotta run."

Mahatma ran to catch an elevator, and my father and I moved toward the door.

"Son, you should never lie to the media. Once your credibility's gone, it's gone for good."

"When did I lie?"

"You told that brother you didn't work for the ministry."

"I don't."

"As of when?"

"As of today."

My father shook his head in confusion. "You're telling me that was your last day at the office?"

We stepped outside. It was a cold, windy March day. It seemed that all the buildings on Bloor Street were sucking down the wind and aiming it at us. Three cars had collided in the middle of the intersection at Bay and Bloor. Cars were jammed in all four directions. People honked and shouted.

"This place is insane. Now you see why I raised you in Oakville."

"Let's go to a café. I'll tell you why this was my last day on the job."

"No time, son." My father took in a measured breath and expelled it slowly. "I am going to visit Dr. Norville Watson."

I grabbed his arm. "Dr. Watson? *The* Dr. Watson?" The news made me forget my own problems. "What for?"

"A time comes for everything. I'm not getting any younger. It's time to make peace with the man."

"I have to hear how your meeting goes."

"Of course. That's why I came to see you. Come out to Oakville this evening. I'll invite Sean, too. I'll tell the two of you and your mother all at the same time. And you can tell me what's going on at the office."

I did not want to go to my parents' home. I had avoided the place for a year and a half, and that wasn't long enough for me. My father, under his own roof, was intolerable.

"How about if I wait in a café? You can come tell me what happened. It'll save me the trip to Oakville."

"Can't do it, son. After I see Watson, I'm meeting your mother. We want to beat the traffic home."

"Well, I'll see about coming out tonight."

"Good. I'll see you there." My father tapped a fire hydrant

with his cane and said, "Keep your chin up, son. The Canes come from a special mold."

He headed west on Bloor Street. Norville Watson's office, I knew from countless family stories, was in a distinguished low-rise fronted with stone pillars. Norville Watson had opened a medical practice there shortly after he had denied my parents rental accommodation in 1954.

Chapter 3

I TOOK A TABLE at the back of the Old Petersburg Café, nursed a mint tea, snapped a bowl of taco chips into a heap of crumbs, and decided that if one had to lose a job, childless and divorced was the best way to go. It had felt strangely comforting to be escorted from the Ontario Ministry of Wellness by my own father. He had an unnerving way of dropping in on people. According to my mother, since going into semi-retirement he had begun traveling downtown with her. When she drove to Toronto to work as a volunteer at Amnesty International, he would often come along — usually with nothing planned. Usually that meant grabbing an espresso and dropping in on somebody who owed him something.

His latest target, according to my mother, had been Winston Carruthers, a household name during my childhood. Some twenty-five years ago, when he was a second-rate boxer from Nova Scotia who had never been anywhere and — as my father said — would never get there, Carruthers elevated himself to celebrity by kayoing a six-foot-three bouncer at the Venus Club. The Venus was a private club that required all its patrons to be members — and proceeded to waive that requirement for all but black people.

It did let in famous blacks. Any black well known in sports or entertainment was considered an asset to the establishment and was plied with free drinks. But, as my father put it, if you happened to be a run-of-the-mill nigger without a cup to drink from or a pot to piss in, then you had no place at the Venus. The job of intimidating blacks without halos fell to Jack Adams, the bouncer. If you rounded off Adams' weight to three hundred pounds, you'd be rounding down. Adams had a reputation for going hard on black men who tried to come in with white women. A week before the incident that got Carruthers on the front page of the *Toronto Times*, Adams had shoved a black man. Knocked him to the floor as he walked in with his date. "Sorry, little fella, didn't see you there," Adams said. Carruthers got the same treatment on the famed night. He took one step inside with his white date, and found himself kissing the floor. He picked himself up, turned back to Adams, and ordered him to apologize.

"For what? For not seeing you?"

Carruthers kicked Adams in the groin. Adams gasped and bent over. Carruthers hit him in the eye with a left hook, the jaw with a right, the same eye with another hook, and the same jaw with a final right. Carruthers broke two fingers in the process. But he damaged the retina in Adams' right eye and broke his jaw.

He was arrested, charged with aggravated assault with a weapon — his fists were judged to be a weapon, since he'd been a professional, although a lousy, boxer — and handed an eighteen-month jail term.

The black community was outraged, and the media had a field day. My father was quoted countless times about the incident. "Jack Adams is known to bait and bully black men. He abused his size and his position to humiliate and intimidate them. He admitted in court to having shoved Carruthers. Yet he becomes the only victim in this incident."

My father's quotes must have made it into a news clip sent by the wire services to American newspapers. My Aunt Mill, whom I had never met and whom my father refused to discuss, read about it in the *Afro-American*. And she took it upon herself to scribble an angry missive to my father: "Why'd you get your shorts in a knot over that no-account boxer? Serves him right for tomcatting with white women."

Carruthers served half his time, got paroled early, did a few media interviews, and faded quickly from the public light. He couldn't get a job. His boxing career was over and he had no other skills. He came out to Oakville one night to see my father.

I sat by the television, pretending to watch *Gunsmoke*, while my father poured coffee for Carruthers.

"What do you take in your coffee, Winston?"

"Whatever you got, Doc."

"What exactly do you mean by that?"

"I meant rum or whiskey, but I was just fooling."

I heard my father scrape a chair back from the table. "Have you been drinking?"

"Not too much. I have a beer at lunch, and maybe bum something off somebody in the afternoon, and I like my glass of wine or two with dinner, and I won't say no to rum or brandy in my coffee at night, but I never overdo it."

"Why'd you come to Oakville?" my father asked.

"I need a job."

"I can get you a job. But you have to promise me you won't touch another drink."

"I will never drink again, Doc."

"I want you to become my chauffeur. And I won't have any

man driving me if he's got a drop of alcohol in his blood."

My father didn't need a chauffeur. But for the entire summer of 1964, he paid Winston Carruthers a hundred dollars a week to drive him around Oakville and Toronto. Winston became a competent chauffeur. He dressed in a suit and tie every day. "He drives with confidence and maturity. He knows all the rules of the road, and prides himself on his punctuality. I would recommend him most highly for a position with the Ontario government." This is what my father wrote to the Ontario government's first black deputy minister, who let it be known in September of 1964 that he was looking for a chauffeur. Carruthers' new career was launched. He kept that job until the deputy was fired for fudging his travel expenses. Carruthers picked up a new job driving a minister, and held on to it for several years. He drove other government ministers and deputies until he became the chief hiring officer and trainer for government drivers — a position he holds to this day.

Oddly, my father never rejoiced in the news of Carruthers's successes over the years. One time, I heard him mumble: "I gave that man his first break. But do I ever hear from him? A thank-you note, or even a Christmas card? Nothing!"

My father holds approximately two hundred Torontonians in a similar kind of debt. Younger doctors whom he helped get into med school, receptionists who got their first job working in Dad's office, human rights activists whom he advised over the years — and he drops in on at least one unlucky debtor every week. I heard later that after escorting me from my job and visiting the office of Dr. Norville Watson, Dad picked on Winston Carruthers.

Carruthers, who is now in his mid-fifties, has an office in the Manulife Centre on Bloor Street. He earns $54,000 a year. He wears a suit and tie to work.

"Mr. Carruthers, please," my father said to the receptionist.

"He has a meeting in five minutes. Is he expecting you?"

"Please inform him that Dr. Cane is here to see him."

"I'll take down your name and number and have him call you back."

My old man leaned forward. He lowered his voice, obliging the receptionist to strain to hear him. "The name is Cane. Dr. Langston Cane. That is C-A-N-E. Mr. Carruthers would want you to let him know I'm here."

She rolled her eyes and picked up the telephone and spoke briefly into the receiver. According to my father, Winston Carruthers was out of his door in three seconds flat.

"What a pleasure, what a surprise, please come in. Coffee? As I remember, you like good coffee."

They sat around for ten minutes in Winston Carruthers' office, drinking good coffee that somebody had to run out to buy. Meanwhile, the receptionist had to stall three new drivers who had come for a meeting with their boss. My father saw them waiting in the lobby and smiled.

"You've done well, Winston."

"Couldn't have done it without your help."

"How many drivers work for you now?"

"Eight."

"Did you train 'em yourself?"

"Sure did. And what have you been up to lately?"

"Oh, not much. Not much at all. Just enjoying my semi-retirement."

Winston Carruthers shifted in his chair. He glanced at his watch. He looked at my father expectantly. What did the old bastard want?

"Well, Winston, you're a busy man, and I've got to be running. Wonderful cup of coffee you serve."

Carruthers smiled. "I haven't touched any funny stuff since you and I had that talk in your kitchen."

"You're a good man, Winston." They shook hands. Carruthers remained on edge until the old man walked out the door.

"I don't want anything from him," my father later said to my mother. Actually, he did want something. He wanted Carruthers to bend down and kiss his feet.

I really don't know what drove my father to try to see Norville Watson. Father was growing tired of his own mythology — the Norville Watson story, after all, was the story from which all other stories of his activism sprang. Over the years, I have heard many versions of the Norville Watson story, Round One. The following version is the one I choose to believe. It's one of my father's earliest versions — or, at least, one of the earliest versions that I remember hearing.

After my parents' honeymoon in Quebec City, they decided to move out of their rooming house and rent a flat together. Dad was in his last year of medical school, and my mother had finished her studies and taken a job with the Toronto Labor Committee for Human Rights, and it fell upon her to head out on her lunch hour to find a place for them to live. They both wanted to rent part of a house.

After rejecting a few flats that had cockroaches or that demanded princely rents, Dorothy found the perfect flat on the second floor of a house on Palmerston Boulevard. Langston could walk to the university in twenty minutes. There were shops all along College Street, and Kensington Market was close by. As an added plus for Langston, there was even an Italian coffee bar just a few blocks west on College. The flat itself was perfect. Clean, small, cozy, well lit, and on a quiet street. Trees outside the front and back windows. It was advertised for fifty-five dollars a month, which they could afford on Dorothy's salary and Langston's GI money — $75 a month, plus all tuition and book costs, for having served as a private and then as a non-commissioned officer in World War II.

The landlord was Norville Watson, and he lived on the first floor. He was a tall blond man, only five or so years older than Langston. He had a habit of pulling at his slender fingers and speaking in endless sentences. He informed Dorothy that he was a graduate of the University of Toronto medical school, and that he was on the verge of completing his residency in urology. A tad pompous, Dorothy decided, but who cared? He seemed impressed when she let it slip that her husband was a medical student, also at the University of Toronto. They agreed on the rent. Dorothy offered to pay for the first month then and there, and to take the key and come back the next day with her husband and their possessions.

"I don't usually like to rent until I have met both tenants," Watson said.

"My husband, as you can appreciate, doesn't have much time on his hands these days. He's preparing for —"

"Yes, of course, of course. I'll tell you what. I'll hold the apartment for you. Come back tomorrow, and we'll sign the contract and exchange the keys for the first month's rent. You have my word. I'll hold it for you."

"All right, then. Tomorrow at seven in the evening?"

"Fine."

They shook hands.

The next day, Dorothy parked her 1946 Plymouth on Palmerston Boulevard. As she walked with Langston up the steps to the house, Dorothy noticed the red and white For Rent sign still on the door.

"How come that's still there?" she said.

"Not a good sign," Langston said. He rang the bell. Watson opened the door and stepped out onto the porch. He had to bend his neck to meet Langston's eyes. Langston extended his hand and introduced himself.

"Well, we're here," Dorothy said. "We'd like to sign the contract, pay you, and bring our things in from the car."

Langston watched the man open his mouth, close it, stop, pause. People had looked at Dorothy and him in the streets — in fact, people looked at them every day — but this was the first time that they had tried to rent a place together. Langston instantly knew that they would not get the flat. The coming refusal was as certain as the sunset — but Langston sensed that it would come in a distinct way. This wasn't the United States. Nobody would swear at him, or wave a gun. Langston waited for the refusal, Canadian-style.

"I'm so sorry," Watson said, looking only at Dorothy, "and I hope you haven't been overly inconvenienced, but I have made other arrangements. A retired couple came by yesterday, after you left. They needed a quiet place, and they were prepared to take out a two-year lease, and I'm sorry, but I couldn't refuse them."

"Yes, you could have," Dorothy shot back. "And you still can. You can simply tell them that you had given me your word — your word, I remind you, Dr. Watson — that the flat was mine. Ours."

"And you had given me your word, madam, that your husband was a medical student at the University of Toronto."

Dorothy raised her voice. "I'll have you know, Dr. Watson —"

Langston put his palm on Dorothy's forearm. "If I understand correctly, Dr. Watson, you would prefer not to rent to us."

"Preference has nothing to do with it. I have entered into an agreement with another couple."

Dorothy could not restrain herself. "Then why haven't you taken the sign off the door, you asshole?"

"Oh, nice," Watson said. "Very nice. Quite elegant. A medical term acquired, no doubt, from your husband. At any rate, forgive me for leaving the sign up. It escaped my thoughts." Watson removed the tack from the door, took down the sign, and stepped back inside.

"Good luck with your apartment search," he told Dorothy. "And," he said, meeting Langston's unmoving eyes, "with your studies."

Dr. Norville Watson closed the door.

"I can't believe you stood there and said nothing," Dorothy screamed at her husband. "I can't believe you just —"

"Shh," he said. "Come on, let's go."

"No! I'm not moving off this goddamn step. That sonofabitch is a blatant —"

He squeezed her arm and whispered, "I have an idea. Come on."

They drove south on Palmerston, turned left on College, parked at Bathurst, and walked to the Mars Café. Stella and her husband, who were tenants in the Pembroke Street rooming house, worked in the café. It was the best greasy spoon in the area. Langston liked it because they knew him well in there. During his first year in Toronto, he had made it his breakfast haunt. From Monday to Friday, between six and eight a.m., they had an all-you-can-eat scrambled eggs, toast, and coffee special for seventy-five cents. Plus, they had unbeatable bran muffins. Stella had served him there a hundred times — and undercharged him whenever the owner wasn't looking over her shoulder.

Stella came up to their table. "You two look good together. Real good. So what'll it be for the newlyweds?"

"I'm too pissed off at him to eat right now," Dorothy said.

"First fight?"

"You've got to hear this," Dorothy said. And she told Stella about it. Stella's husband came over to listen.

"We can help you find a place," Stella said. "Harry and I know some landlords who don't discriminate."

"I don't want to find another place quite yet," Langston said. "I want to make this guy uncomfortable. I want to make him regret what he did for a long, long time."

"You know, Doc, they'll lift your license if you start busting kneecaps."

"That's not quite what I had in mind."

An hour later, Dorothy and Langston drove by the house. The sign was still off the door.

"Maybe he really did rent it out," she said.

"I doubt it."

They drove by another hour later. The sign was back up.

An hour after that, Stella and Harry Williams skipped their usual dinner break. "Shouldn't we go home and get some nice clothes on?" Stella asked.

"No, it'll be better this way," Langston said. "More convincing." Langston and Dorothy drove them to the corner of Palmerston and College and had them walk to the house from there.

Stella rang the bell. Watson answered it. *That man's so tall it's unnatural,* she said later. *He must have to request a special bed every time he sleeps in a hotel.*

"Excuse us for troubling you, mister, but my husband and I noticed your sign. We're just on our break. We work over at the Mars Café, you know, Bathurst and College."

"You're interested in renting the flat?"

"Yes. Could we see it?"

"Sure. Why not?"

They viewed the living room, which looked out onto Palmerston, and the kitchen, which gave out onto Ulster Street. They checked the bedroom. Stella even flushed the toilet. "Hope you don't mind. I like to make sure a place is in good working order."

"My wife," Harry said. "She's picky. But she's neat. She's a real neat freak."

"I am not a neat freak," Stella shot back. "I just don't like dirt. I don't like filth, I don't like dust, I don't like dirty floors or anything like that. If he didn't have me," she said to Watson, "he'd live like an ape."

"The apartment is fifty dollars a month. I also require a twenty-five-dollar damage deposit, which will be returned to you when you leave if nothing is broken or damaged."

"Damage deposit," Stella said. "I've been renting for eight years and I've never had to pay a damage deposit before."

"Well, I require it."

"Stella, he said he'd give it back when we left."

"All right. Who lives downstairs?" Stella asked.

"I do."

"You don't have children, do you?"

"No."

"That's good. They make a lot of noise. How about pets? Do you have a dog?"

"I find it odd that you are inquiring of me what I have in my apartment. I should be asking these things of you."

"I don't like dogs, or cats, you don't have to worry about that. It's just that I have allergies. Lots. So if you had a dog or a cat, I'd like to know."

"No, I don't."

"Good. Can I ask you what kind of people live in this neighborhood? Sometimes I have to walk home from work at night, and I need to feel safe."

"This is a very safe neighborhood. My family has owned this home for the better part of thirty years, and I don't recall ever hearing of anybody being troubled or harassed on the street."

"What about immigrants?" Stella asked.

"Some Italians and Portuguese live around here. But they're the best neighbors you could ask for. I will say that they tend to shout and to hold all sorts of family functions. But they're the first ones to call the police if they see someone trying to break in your house. They give you wine at Christmas and Easter. They treat you like one of the family. You won't have any trouble with Italians or Portuguese. And I can reassure you that I know of no neighbors who are Negroes. I would draw the line there. As a matter of fact, a Negro posing as a medical student tried to rent this apartment today, and I would have nothing to do with it."

"Good," Stella said. "That's what I wanted to hear. Is that what you wanted to hear, Harry?"

"Yeah. Great."

"I don't have my cheque book with me, or a lot of cash. Can I just give you twenty dollars to hold the apartment, and you give me a receipt? We'll come back tomorrow to take care of everything."

"Fine. That will be fine."

Back at the Mars Café, Langston told Stella to write it all down. To put every detail on paper. But she was too excited, so Dorothy, who knew shorthand, took down Stella's statement.

The two couples returned to Watson's house an hour later. Langston rang the bell.

Watson opened the door. He stared at the four of them for a minute.

"Howdy," Stella said with a grin.

"What is going on here?" Watson said.

"Dr. Watson," Langston said, "you refused to rent us that flat on the basis of my race. You told our friends as much. If you give them back their twenty dollars, and you give my wife and me that apartment, I'll consider the matter settled. But if you don't — "

"You'll what — call the police? This is my house. I can rent to anybody I want. Take your money, you clowns." Watson threw a twenty onto the porch. "Now get out of here before *I* call the police."

"Good-bye, Dr. Watson. You can expect to hear from me again. The name is Cane. Langston Cane the Fourth."

Norville Watson slammed the door.

Dorothy slipped her arm around her husband's waist. "That's the man I married," she said. "Now what?"

"I don't know, exactly. Let's sleep on it."

Stella giggled. "Langston Cane the Fourth. That's quite the name."

Chapter 4

I TOOK TEN EMPTY BOXES from a food store, piled them into a taxi, and directed the driver to my flat on Dovercourt Road. I asked the driver to tune in to a radio news station. The top local story was that Ontario wellness minister Anthony Weston had revealed that the government might scrap human rights legislation. The report said Weston had opposed the proposal in a speech, but had refused further comment when approached by the media. It ended with a quote from the communications aide to the minister, who said in a voice that shook with anxiety, "There's been a mix-up. The minister didn't plan to say those things. We'll get to the bottom of this."

The taxi driver chuckled. "Looks as if somebody will be pounding the pavement." I caught his eyes in the rearview mirror, smiled, and tipped him when he let me out.

I packed up my dishes, my books, my stereo, threw out seven garbage bags of junk, came to a quick arrangement with the landlord, and called Move and Store. I was lucky — the company was hungry for business. For five hundred dollars, it agreed to move my stuff out within two hours and store it for a year.

I was on a roll. I wanted to be finished in time to leave the next day. All I needed were traveler's cheques, health insurance, and a car. The first two didn't take long, so I quickly moved on to find a car. The Langston Canes who preceded me were genetically incapable of car repairs, and I had acquired the defective gene. My father always said we were mechanical idiots because our slave ancestors had passed along an aversion to manual labor. It made sense to me. Checking windshield fluid was as mechanical as I could get, so I needed a reliable car.

I took a cab to the nearest Volkswagen dealer. A salesman came up and said his name was Barry. I told him I wanted a good used car.

He asked what I wanted to drive.

I said: "Let's do this in an unorthodox way, because I'm an unorthodox guy. I'm thirty-eight, divorced, no kids, just fired for sabotaging a speech for a government minister. I have lots of savings, am able to buy today with cash, and have to travel tomorrow. I need something very reliable. I want to look at it, test-drive it, settle on a decent price, and be out of here in an hour with the keys in my hand."

Barry grinned. "In a hurry, are you? That's cool." He led me out to the car lot. I saw something that was light green and had all four wheels attached. It was clean. Looked nice. Four doors, but small.

"What's that?"

"A Volkswagen Jetta."

"Cost?"

"Ten thousand dollars."

"Reliable?"

"It's the best. It's a diesel."

"What does that mean?"

"Diesel. It's a kind of motor. It takes diesel fluid, not gas. Burns fuel very economically. Has the longest life of any car motor."

"How old is this car?"

"Two years."

"How many kilometers?"

"Fifty thousand. You can get another two hundred thousand kilometers from this engine, if you treat it nicely."

I gave it a test drive. It was a manual. I hadn't driven a manual since I was a teenager, but I got the hang of it quickly enough. It drove fine. Seemed to work. Didn't make funny noises. There were no ice-cream bars or candy wrappers on the floor. It had a radio — the radio worked. When I pressed the accelerator, the car went faster. When I used the brakes, it slowed down. We returned to the dealership.

"I'll give you seven thousand for it," I said.

"Sorry. I'm can't take an offer that low to my manager."

"This feels like shopping. I don't like that feeling."

He grinned. "I can't make a deal that low."

"What did you say this model was?"

"A 1993 Volkswagen Jetta. Turbo diesel. It's a turbo. That means the engine has extra kick."

I noted the details down on a piece of paper. "Okay, thanks for trying. That's the car I want. I guess I'll have to buy one elsewhere."

"If you find one at the price you want, don't buy it. There's bound to be something seriously wrong with it."

"I'll keep that in mind." I walked to the door. I hit the pavement and wondered what I would do now. I wandered out to the sidewalk, hailed a taxi, and was about to climb in when Barry tapped me on the shoulder.

"Let's talk some more."

"Seven thousand, three hundred," I said.

"That's too low. It really is. I'll give it to you for nine thousand."

"I'll take it for eight."

The taxi driver turned around to look at me. I still had one leg inside his back door. "Would you get the hell out of my taxi if you're buying a car?"

"Eight thousand, Barry?"

"Yeah, yeah, eight thousand."

I stepped out of the taxi. "You're a good guy, Barry. You're the first good thing that's happened to me today."

"Did you really get fired for screwing up a speech for the minister? I heard about that on the news."

"Honest to God." Why I said that, I don't know. I'm an atheist.

"Well, good on you. I don't think I've ever sold a car to a speech writer before. Matter of fact, I haven't even met one before. But anyway, now that you're actually gonna buy this car, why don't we have a coffee and talk about what it is you're actually buying?"

"Let's get the papers on the sale moving, first. I really am in a rush."

Barry put his people on the forms and then brought me coffee. "So what can you tell me about this car?" I said.

"Take your time getting to know her. Listen to what she wants."

"If it doesn't work out for you in sales," I said, "you ought to try marriage counseling."

Chapter 5

MY FATHER THINKS THAT IT'S ALL RIGHT for a woman to live off a man's income. But let a man, or worse, a son of his, stoop to such depths, and see what Dad says.

On the drive to Oakville in my newly acquired Jetta, I thought about what Dad had said eighteen months ago, the last time I had gone out to the house. I thought about the bit of conversation I had overheard as I'd let myself in the back door. Of course, if I had been leading the life that he wanted for me, such a conversation would never have taken place. If I had been leading the life he wanted, I would have been visiting his house with children, and I would have brought my wife, and I would have been settled in a profession, and I would have owned a car that would have sounded like a giant rolling pin on their driveway of white stones and would have alerted them to my arrival.

But eighteen months ago, I was not traveling with my wife, for she would soon leave me, and I had no car, and I alerted nobody as I walked over the stone pebbles and let myself in the back door as I had always done as a child — and, in doing so, I overheard the words that have kept me away all this time.

"I don't know what Ellen sees in him," my old man had said.

"For one thing, she sees that Langston loves her," Mother had answered. "He's still affectionate. She told me he still hugs her the way he used to do, years ago."

"Humph! I'd hug, too, for free rent."

The Jetta worked just fine, and got me to Oakville in half an hour. I needed to breathe deeply before entering my parents' home, so I parked on Sumner, walked over to Trafalgar, and headed south. Fog blurred the street lamps as I got closer to the lake. I stopped on the sidewalk to admire the imposing, unpredictable shapes of the houses. They were like masked faces in the dark. Each one hinted of movement, personality, family history. There's nothing more humbling than family history. A Great Dane rose up to eye me from inside a living room window. I crossed Lakeshore Boulevard and continued toward the water. It frothed and spat and splintered the moon's reflection. A cold wind slapped at me. The faintly sour odor of the lake rose up to greet me. It made me think back to the last time I had lived in Oakville, twenty years ago, when I was eighteen and assumed I could do nothing but rise in the world.

Oakville's so boring, I had complained to my father when I was a teenager. *Why did you move here?* He said, *I wade into chaos every day, but I like to sleep outside it. Also, I like to put my head down at night knowing the lake is there. What do I like about water? It offers itself up like a bridge for people to move between countries and continents. Water, my son, was an escape hatch for some of your own ancestors.* I said, *I think it stinks of dead fish. And I heard that rats get into the big houses closest to the lake. Is that true?* He said, *Son, you've got a way of plugging your ears like no Cane who came before you.*

I walked back up to my parents' house and stood on the stones of their driveway. They were small, rounded stones, like miniature golf balls, which seemed in keeping with Oakville's image as the golfing capital of Canada. My brother Sean and I used to joke about the town's reputation.

"It's not even safe to walk the streets any more."

"That's for sure. Our neighborhoods are declining."

"You never know when you might get hit by a golf ball."

The stones rubbed and clicked under my shoes, and I looked up, through the branches of the oak tree in the front yard, and I saw shimmering blue in my father's window, hanging, vibrating. Within seconds, the blue collapsed into pink, then purple, then blue, then green.

The old man was watching TV, no doubt. I recalled one time years ago, watching it with him when my mother stepped into the room and asked how his work had gone that day. He complained that Oakville attracted second-rate specialists, and said the town needed a new breed of medical men. *Men,* my mother sniffed. *Men is not a catch-all noun, dear husband. Some of those "men" are women, you know.* And he said, *You and I both know some of them are women, and you and I both know what we're talking about.* And she said, *You only care about things that affect you personally. When anyone makes a dumb remark about black people, you're on their back before the words are out of their mouth. But women? Gays? The disabled? That's not really serious.* He cut her off: *I'm a bad, dirty-dog husband who's been doing you wrong since the day we married. Now, how about a kiss?* Mom said, *Don't patronize me.* Dad said, *I'm not patronizing anybody. I just want a kiss.* But she didn't feel like giving him a kiss at that moment.

I glanced up again at the light in my parents' bedroom window. My father knew all about gunfights. He could tell you how many men Wyatt Earp took down in the O.K. Corral. He groaned with disgust every time some two-bit flick showed a sheriff killing eight men with a six-shooter. I found myself hoping that he had fallen asleep in front of the television.

On display at the front of the house was an Oakville Historical Society plaque that said *Robert Wilson, Ship Captain, 1815 – 1869.* Wilson was the first owner of my parents' 180-year-old house. Sean and I heard about him many times in our childhood. Wilson made a good living ferrying timber and grain to New York State and returning with coal and manufactured goods. Clocks. Armoires. Horse carriage parts. But he ferried something else back with him — fugitive slaves. He hid them in his schooner and helped them get started in Oakville.

I took the path beside the house to the back door, which my mother opened. Dark-haired, light-skinned, angular face, snub nose, hazel eyes — everyone said we looked alike. She reached up to kiss me. As her chapped lips pricked my cheek, I heard my old man's snores float down the stairs.

"I thought you'd still be up," I said.

"Why not? It's not even midnight."

"Some things don't change. Dad's sleeping?"

"Yes, but you know him. He'll probably get up and come downstairs. He was expecting you earlier. And Sean couldn't make it earlier, but he's here now." She hugged my arm, and then slipped hers through it. She was a very short woman. I remembered my surprise at discovering one day, as a teenager, that I was taller than my mother.

"I take it you know what happened today," I said.

"Just that you aren't working there any more. I tried calling you at home this evening. I got a message saying your line had been disconnected. So I started to worry."

"Why?"

"I called your landlord, who said you had paid him to the end of the month and moved out in a hurry. He also said reporters had been coming by and asking for you."

"You would have been a good reporter," I said.

"Being a contented little mousewife is far more challenging," she said, laughing. "And as for being a mother — well, you ought to try that one day."

Yes, yes, being a mother, being a parent — maybe that would have saved me from self-obsession. I had come close. I loved that little boy who had died in Ellen's womb. Loved him and loved her.

I draped my jacket on the doorknob. Mom whisked it up and slipped a coat hanger into it and put it away. From the vestibule, she led me up the six wooden steps to the kitchen. For a moment, she held my arm tightly.

Sean stood up from the kitchen table. "Brother," he said. "Long time, et cetera, et cetera."

He gave me a hug, too. They were being dispensed my way like pretzels. This family of mine really was worried. And my brother! The man was too generous, too uncomplaining, too good-hearted, and too bloody successful. Just by being good to me after all I'd put him through, he made me feel guilty. Guilt is one of my defining — and most useless — traits.

Sean sat down and used a knife and fork to slice a piece of his buttered raisin toast. Ever since he had dated a Dutch woman and visited the Netherlands, he wouldn't eat bread and toast with his hands.

Mom swept a handful of ledger sheets off the table.

"I was doing your father's bookkeeping," she said. "This is the only time I can get any work done. He never lets me alone during the day. Sometimes, in the middle of the day, I get so fed up with his pestering that I stick a book in my purse and some ledger sheets in a briefcase and go off to the library. But, of course, I couldn't tell him that. He'd be offended that I was escaping. I have to tell him I'm going shopping. He never questions that. I come back a couple of hours later, having read another fifty pages or finished up another month of his accounts, and he'll say, 'So what'd you get, Dottie?' And I'll tell him, 'Just little things. Some things on sale. Women's things.' And he'll pat me on the shoulder with that big brown hand of his and give me a big hug and say, 'You go right ahead and shop for those little things any time you want.' Of course, I'll say right back, 'Well, thanks for your permission,' but I'll be happy to see him like that. How many seventy-year-old men do you know who still light up with pleasure and hug their wives when they come in the door, even if their wives have only been gone for two hours?"

Mom poured water into the kettle and got out mint tea bags, cups, and saucers. She launched into a description of her latest strategy for dealing with sleeplessness. She didn't fight it any more. Didn't force herself to stay in bed, tossing, turning, kicking off sheets, pulling them back up, checking the clock, burying her head in the pillow, sitting up, blowing her nose, lying back down again. She said all that was too enervating. The more she couldn't sleep but tried to force it, the more of a failure she felt. So now she got up when she couldn't sleep, and drank warm milk, and stretched, gently, on the living room rug.

Mom sipped her tea, ran a hand through her long, straight hair, and looked at me. Sean smiled. My brother's face was acorn brown. Unmistakably brown, which meant that he was indisputably black, and didn't have to worry about it, or think about it, at all.

"So how come you're up at this hour?" I asked him. "Aren't you usually in court first thing in the morning?"

"I haven't been sleeping for a month," Sean said.

"Not at all?"

"I get tired around three in the afternoon. Like Mom."

"This is new, isn't it?" I asked.

"Damn right, older bro. I've finally hit the big leagues."

"So what do you do, when you finally get tired?"

"I go to the King Edward, next door to my work. I take no papers, no work, accept no phone calls. I sleep there. Actually, I sleep amazingly well. I get in there so tired I can barely walk straight, and I undress and fall into bed and the next thing I know it's seven-thirty at night. I sleep like a dead man, but I always wake up at seven-thirty."

"Have you tried sleeping at home?"

"Can't do it. Can only sleep in the King Edward. They always give me the same room. I've never turned on the TV. Never opened the curtains. The only thing I do is undress and sleep and dress and wash my face and get out of there. It's my sleep sanctuary. So far, I'm feeling okay. I must be getting quality sleep."

"Don't delude yourself," Mother said. "If you're getting four hours, and it's in the late afternoon or early evening, the first hour, and the last half hour, you're probably not getting any rapid eye movement at all, so it's not deep sleep. If you're lucky, you're getting two hours of quality sleep. The rest is filler. But that's okay. The main thing is to stay calm, and to try to feel okay. You can start worrying about it when you stop feeling okay."

I nodded at the sound of the old instructions. My head felt as if it was filled with warm water. Sean watched my mother pour mint tea. "So, brother," he said, "I take it things have been happening today?"

"A wee bit."

Sean lounged in his chair. He made a point of not staring at me, sliced into his toast, kept his tone offhand. He wore corduroy slacks, a blue cashmere sweater, and loafers, but every inch of his face and of his manicured hands broadcast the fact that he was a lawyer. He was doing his best not to look like someone who pulled in six figures annually, and certainly didn't want to emphasize the fact around me, but Sean couldn't help it. He couldn't hide his success at all.

Sean looked at me and smiled. We knew each other too well.

"I got fired and I moved out of my apartment," I said.

"Oh, Langston." This was my mother. She was hovering around the antique oak table that had come with the house forty years ago.

"I tried to tell Dad that I'd gone off to see a movie while on the job last week, but he thought I was joking."

Mother sat opposite me. "But that's not why you were fired. You were just fired today. It had something to do with your minister giving that weird speech. Your name was mentioned on the radio tonight."

"You're kidding."

"No. Some government official named you as the one who had slipped the minister a trick speech. The same person was quoted as saying you'd been fired." Mom put her hand on mine. "You must have been wanting this to happen. You must have been looking for a way out."

"It's true that I have been wanting for a while to get on with some things, but I can't say that I set out in a planned way to bring down the minister."

Sean asked how I did it. I told him. He laughed and said it was the sneakiest way he'd ever heard of leaking a confidential document. "Pretty clever, brother. So what was that movie you went out to see last week?"

"You don't want to know."

"Sure I do. Spit it out."

"*The Bodyguard.*"

Sean laughed. "Hey, that wasn't a bad flick. I kind of liked it."

"Yeah," I said. "You would."

"What, you have the patent on good taste, do you?"

Ah, my brother. What a guy. He even tried to get me into a fight to make me forget myself and feel better. "Sean, you're a great brother and I've heard you're great in court, but you ought to be incarcerated for bad taste. You drive a Corvette — a Corvette, for Christ's sake, is for grease balls — and you like leather couches and for all I know you've got a real estate agent hunting for a house in Oakville."

Sean removed a spoon from his tea and dropped it on the table. "You and I didn't do so badly here. It gave us an education. Good sports, too. Outdoor activities. Parks. The lake. Nobody beat us up or dealt heroin in the school yard. So what's wrong with Oakville?"

"It's terminally pleasant."

"You know what your problem is?" Sean said. "You think too much. You're too goddamn cerebral. If you were a few degrees stupider, you'd be a helluva lot more successful."

I stared at him.

"I'm sorry," he said. "I didn't mean it like that."

"Sure you did. It's okay. I guess, somehow, I don't really want to be successful."

"Yes, you do. You're dying for it. You just want to be successful on your own terms."

I heard my old man coming down the stairs. He made slow

progress. His feet were so swollen that he could only wear running shoes. He drummed the tip of his cane down on each step. The cane had been used by his father, before he died, and when my father banged it about, he was announcing to the world, or at least to those parts of it that cared to listen, that he had important ancestors. Langston Canes all of them, and the Langston Canes and their women and children weren't ordinary people!

Down he came, and reached the bottom, and turned to come our way. He filled the hallway with his bulk. "You folks make enough noise to wake up an army." He limped forward. "Good to see you, men," he said, entering the kitchen. His big hand on my shoulder felt kind. It felt sincere. I looked up and tried to smile, but Dad had moved on. "And you, Sean! What are you doing up at this hour? You haven't become one of the sleepless, have you?"

"Looks like it, for now at least."

"Nip it in the bud. See a specialist. Get the right pills. Don't let it become a habit."

"Yes, Dad," Sean said.

I felt closer to Sean, hearing his sarcastic obedience. Then Dad turned to me. My shoulders stiffened.

"So, Langston, when did you get out here?"

"I got to Oakville about an hour ago."

"An hour ago? I was up an hour ago."

"I walked down to the lake before coming in."

"That's the trouble with night owls. They never hurry. They've got their own pace, day and night, and there's not a damn thing anyone can do about it. So what brings you out here, Langston?"

"Stop it, Lang! You invited him." Mother got up, tapping Dad's shoulder with her knuckles. "Who wants peach crumble? Sweetened only with fruit juices."

We all decided to have some, except for Dad, who asked for coffee and took it black.

"What happened when you saw Watson?" I asked.

"He wasn't in."

"Why did you want to see him?"

"That's what his receptionist asked. I told her to tell him that Dr. Cane had come calling, and that I would drop by another time."

"But what did you want?"

"Nothing in particular. What's wrong with a simple hello?"

Sean jumped in. "Did Wellington say hello to Napoleon? Did Wolfe shake hands with Montcalm?"

"Just like a lawyer to get hyperbolic," Dad said. "I don't aim to kill Watson, and he doesn't aim to kill me."

"Why are you looking him up after all these years?" I asked.

"As I said, no particular reason. I just felt like it."

"You always cut stories off like that. It's the same way you've never really told us why you left the States, or why you don't communicate with Mill."

"I hear about her from Aberdeen," Dad said. "In fact, she phoned him today."

"Everything sure has been happening at once," I said. "And now you say Mill called. Why did she phone?"

"Apparently, she told Aberdeen that she wants to come up here for a visit sometime. But she doesn't take airplanes. And she doesn't care for buses or trains, either. So I doubt we'll see her here in this lifetime. But that's enough about my sister. Langston, did you really get fired today?"

"I did."

"Are those stories on the radio true?"

"Probably. I haven't heard them all."

"Is this an act of tilting at windmills?" Dad asked. Mom elbowed him.

"Could be," I said. "I haven't analyzed it."

"I've got to hand it to you for embarrassing the government. But what you've done won't really change anything. It'll be in the news for a day or two, but the government will move along as planned."

"I didn't really do it to change anything," I said. "I did it because it felt like the right thing to do."

"So, what are you going to do now?" Dad asked.

"I've been thinking about it."

"Try thinking about taking a job and not getting fired."

My mother shoved my father. "Langston. Quit it."

I could feel my heart shutting down. My soul walked out the back door of the house.

My brother, the lawyer, did his best. "I don't think this is a productive avenue of discussion, Dad."

"Good God, son," Dad said to him. "Didn't I teach you not to talk gobbledygook? *Productive avenue of discussion!* If you have something to say, say it! You want me to shut up? Is that it?"

Sean planted his palms on the table. "All three of us want you to shut up. Is that clear enough?"

I felt a cloud lift out of my head and unveil my own desire. It was time to move south and start to write.

"Well, I won't shut up," Dad said. I blinked. Batten down the hatches, I said to myself. Dad turned to me again. "What exactly are you doing to do?"

"I'm going away for a while."

"Not Africa again?"

"No. Not Africa. Africa's over."

"Good. Africa doesn't need you, and you don't need it. Where, then?"

"The States."

"Jesus Christ."

My mother slapped her hand on the table. "Husband of mine, would you give our son a chance? Would you let him finish, at least?" She turned to me, waiting.

"I'm going to Baltimore."

"No, you're not."

Sean stood up. "Don't take this, Langston. Let's go. You need a lift somewhere?"

"I have a car. Just got it today." I cupped my chin in my palms and looked at my father. His eyes were unmoving.

"They'll eat you up in Baltimore. I know what you want down there. Family roots. Forget that nonsense. Your life is here and now. You've got no more links to Baltimore, son, than I have to China. Anyway, you don't go to a place like Baltimore to hang out. I can help you get another job. Stay with us in Oakville until you get back on your feet."

"I'm leaving tomorrow," I said.

"Your cranium is made of metal," Dad said. "You'll come back here out of money, out of luck, and out of the job circuit. You're just hiding from your own life."

"I'm not going to talk about this any more. Good night, folks."

Dad just kept on going. "Baltimore! Where are you going to stay?"

"I'll work that out. Bye."

"Don't bother Mill. The last thing my sister needs is to have to bail you out of trouble." I stood up to go. "I'm warning you, son. Stay away from Mill."

Mom walked me to the door. She said I had years still in front of me, that I was still young, that things were sure to get better if I listened to my heart and kept my head. Over her words, I heard Sean arguing with Dad. They were talking about me, but I couldn't make out the words, only the slow monotone of my father, and the argumentative higher pitch of my brother.

"Dad still thinks I'm looking for free rent," I said.

"He loves you so deeply. But he doesn't know how to act when he's upset. So he acts aggressive."

Sean joined us in the vestibule. He invited me to spend the night at his place. I accepted, let my mother kiss me, parked my jacket on my shoulders, stepped out into the early morning fog, and followed Sean's Corvette to Toronto. On the way, I thought about how my father had cheated me. He had gone out of his way to visit me in Toronto, and to invite me out to the family house — and when I got there, he had gone on the attack. It was bizarre that Dad never picked on Sean. My brother had no family, and never would have one. I suspected that my father was terrified of the possibility that Sean was gay — which he was — and dealt with the problem by talking only about Sean's success as a lawyer, and my lack of success at everything.

We drove to my brother's Harbourfront condo. Sean didn't ask a lot of questions. He gave me a towel, a facecloth, and bed linen. He said he had to go to sleep — or to try, at least. "You don't have to run, brother. You can stay here a few days. It'd be good to see you. We wouldn't get in each other's hair. I don't get home until evening and I leave early."

Sean made me tea and toast in the morning. He sat down at the table and ate with me. I hadn't eaten breakfast with somebody in a long time. He tightened the knot of his purple and red designer tie and waved from the door. "See you tonight, I hope. Key's on the table."

When he left, I showered, read Mahatma Grafton's article in the *Toronto Times*, scribbled *thank you* on a napkin, went out to my Jetta, baptized it Sarah, and turned toward Baltimore.

Chapter 6

I TOOK THE ADVICE OF THE CAR SALESMAN, and took it easy on Sarah. We needed time to get acquainted, and I was in no hurry to get to Baltimore. I stopped in Batavia for lunch, drove another hour or so southeast, and called it a day in Naples, New York.

Naples was in the Finger Lakes district, and had been mentioned by my father as a town into which Langston Cane the First had arrived, exhausted. A Quaker had sheltered Langston the First until the fugitive had been able to continue his trek north.

I drove along Main Street, looking for a place to stay. It was sunny and unusually warm for the month of March. High school girls swung their hips in miniskirts along the sidewalk. Two old men drank coffee on their front porch, which gave onto the street. A barber had one man in his chair and two others waiting. I saw a hand-painted sign for the Hilltop Bed and Breakfast, admired the house, painted white with big windows on the second floor and a widow's walk on the roof. I parked, got out of the car, and noticed a historical plaque describing the building as a safe house on the Underground Railroad in the 1840s and 1850s. This was the place for me.

The sixty-dollar nightly rate seemed a bit steep, but the room was big and well lit and quiet, and complimentary scones and tea were waiting for me in the kitchen, and the best hamburger joint in the county was said to be just a hundred yards down the street. I snacked and prepared to take an afternoon nap and thought, as I climbed into bed, how long it had been since I'd made love. A year and a half? More, because there had been a long period of coldness between Ellen and me before she had moved out. I had been celibate for nearly two years. I tried not to think about it, and fell asleep under a down comforter.

An hour later, I awoke and wandered downstairs to chat with the owner, Sandy Ingram, who was making dinner for his wife and children.

"According to a family legend," I told him, "one of my ancestors — a fugitive slave — holed up for some time in this town. What's your connection to the Underground Railroad?"

"Quakers owned three safe houses in this town. This was one of them. I have no idea if your ancestor stayed here, but I can show you the hiding spot."

In the backyard, beside a carport that had once been a barn, Sandy lifted a square plank to reveal a hole about three feet wide, four feet deep, and five feet long. I saw a mouse scurry out of sight.

"Damn! I thought we'd caught all those mice," Sandy said.

"Where'd that mouse go?"

"Into the side hole. It used to be a lot bigger." A coffin-sized tunnel had been carved out to one side, apparently. Fugitives would slide in there, face up, and the hole leading out to the side would be covered with a thin board, which was in turn hidden behind earth. Next, the ground-level hole was covered by a trap door, which was hidden under straw and dirt. On one occasion, a man hunting for his fugitive slave had come upon the trap door and opened it, but had not noticed the side tunnel. "I think he would have noticed it," Sandy told me, "but for a dead rat just inside the trap door. He was so taken aback by the sight of the rat that he failed to notice the side tunnel inside."

"Does any record exist of the fugitives who came here?"

"They didn't exactly leave their names behind," Sandy said, chuckling.

"I suppose not," I said. My great-great-grandfather must have been thick-skinned and mule-headed. To escape as he did, hiding underground with mice and rats, sleeping — if he was lucky — beside cows to stay warm, walking barefoot through the hills of Maryland, Pennsylvania, and New York, getting into Canada only to turn around nine years later and go back. Why? Could he possibly have joined John Brown's raid? It was hard to imagine a fugitive slave settling comfortably in Oakville and then turning around and heading right back south into slave territory.

At the hamburger joint down the street, I got myself a Naples Special — a quarter pound of ground beef topped with blue cheese — and returned to bed at the Hilltop. I fell asleep before nine p.m. and didn't wake up before seven. I hadn't slept so long and so hard for years.

After the war, which he later said was enough to make any black soldier hate America, my father left the United States and came to study at the University of Toronto.

He traveled north from Washington, D.C., on a Greyhound bus. It was cheaper than the train, and not much slower, and the only inconveniences were that his clothes and hair reeked of cigarette smoke by the time the bus arrived in Toronto, and that he awoke with a stiff neck after sleeping for six hours with his head against the window.

He had fallen asleep in Pennsylvania and snored through New York State and across the Canadian border, where they waved the bus through, and along the Queen Elizabeth Way by St. Catharines and Hamilton and Oakville. He stirred only as the Greyhound headed north on Bay Street in downtown Toronto. He awoke with a cough, stretched his arms, cracked his fingers, and looked at the woman sitting to his left.

She was a white woman, about fifty, with gray hair and with blue eyes.

"You're a deep sleeper," she said.

"I was meditating," he said, grinning.

"Sure," she said. "Since when do meditators snore?"

"Me? Snore? Never!"

"Mister, you snored until the cows came home and then you snored again."

Langston smiled. He wondered if a white stranger had ever called him "mister" before.

"You're an American, aren't you?" she said.

"How'd you know?"

"I could tell. And it's not 'cause you're a Negro, either, so don't think I'm prejudiced. I could tell you were American because you're friendly. You talk to people. Canadians don't talk."

"You're talking. And I presume you're Canadian. And it's not 'cause you're white, either."

"Very good," she said. The bus rolled to a stop in the Elizabeth Street terminal. Her name was Betty Sears, and she said she ran a rooming house at 117 Pembroke Street, in case Langston was looking for a place to stay.

"I've got a place lined up. But thanks for asking. Where I come from, colored bus passengers don't often get offered accommodation by white strangers. Matter of fact, they don't sit together on buses."

Langston drew two quick conclusions as he entered the bus terminal.

Toronto could do with a few more colored people. It also needed trees. Some eucalyptus. A smattering of sycamores. Cedars and oaks and magnolias. Langston looked out at Bay Street and found hardly a tree in sight. He did find a telephone booth, dropped a dime in the slot, and dialed the number for an acquaintance of his father, who had promised to put him up.

No answer. He tried fifteen minutes later. Still no answer. Langston found a newspaper and read the local stories and then tried the line again and still got no answer. It was seven p.m. He hadn't eaten since lunch. He had forty dollars, and it had to last until his GI money came through. He wondered how long it would take to reach this acquaintance of his father's. Maybe tonight. Maybe next week.

Langston opened the telephone directory, but couldn't find a listing for B. Sears on Pembroke Street.

Damn, he muttered to himself, she called it a rooming house. She doesn't live there.

Langston shouldered his army duffel bag and headed out on Dundas Street. He bought two hot dogs and asked the vendor, a boy of fifteen or so, where Pembroke Street was.

"Tell me slow," Langston said. "I'm not from these parts."

"Walk east on Dundas till you hit it."

"Which way's east?"

"The way that streetcar is going."

"Much obliged."

"You're American, aren't you," the kid said.

"How'd you know?"

"Your accent. I can hear it clean through that hot dog. Also, you're friendly. Canadians aren't like that."

"I met a Canadian woman an hour or so ago. She invited me to stay in her rooming house, and she didn't know me from Adam. And here you are telling me exactly how to get to Pembroke Street, taking your time to make sure I get it right, and you don't know me, either. So, by my reckoning, Canadians underestimate themselves. They'll help out a colored stranger, and that's already going some distance. How much do I owe you for these hot dogs?"

"Thirty cents. Pembroke is fifteen minutes that way. It goes both sides of Dundas. The lower numbers are to the south."

"Thank you kindly! If you ever need a doctor, look me up."

"No way! I almost gave you one of those hot dogs for free. You look like you're out of money."

"I am out of money. And I'm not a doctor yet. But I will be in a few years."

"If you're gonna be a doctor, how come you're out of money?"

"I won't have any spare cash until the American eagle shits."

"Till what?"

"Till I get my GI money from the U.S. government for having been a soldier."

"And when they pay you, you say the eagle is shitting?"

"It's a long story. You sort of had to be in the war to understand."

"What's your name, anyway?"

"Langston Cane the Fourth."

"Never heard a name like that before."

"It has been around, this name. At the very least, three people had it before me. Now — one more question before I'm on my way." Langston lowered his voice. "This Pembroke Street. Is it in a colored neighborhood?"

"What do you mean by that?"

"Forget it. Thanks for the hot dogs."

The Pembroke Street rooming house wasn't clean, or quiet, or well lit. You could poke a pencil through holes in the wall. My father took a room with a dresser, a bed, a desk and chair, a rug, a washbasin and hot plate, and a view of the street. Langston used a quiet but unrelenting poor-student routine to get Betty Sears to drop her rent to thirty-five dollars a month and to let him delay the first month's payment until the eagle shat.

Pembroke Street was downright seedy, and the rooming house was no less so. A prostitute lived in one of the rooms. A string bassist lived in the basement. He practiced till one or two every night and never got up before noon and subsisted on crackers, sardines, cigarettes, and beer. Two of the residents were on welfare. Winos slept on benches down the street. Langston concluded that in Baltimore or in D.C., Pembroke Street would have been a black ghetto. But here in Toronto, Pembroke Street was predominantly white. There were a few blacks, but they didn't seem any more beaten up than the others. So where did black people live, anyway?

Langston had no money for streetcar fare, so he walked everywhere. Every day, he headed up Jarvis Street and along Wellesley to the university — and he walked a good deal farther in search of black neighborhoods. The only one he could find ran west of Bathurst, between King and Queen streets. It was by no means a black area, but Langston was likely to bump into one or two black people as he walked there. On Bloor or Yonge, however, he could walk all day without seeing one black face. That was a strange feeling, indeed. It made Langston feel as if he were truly living in a foreign country, but it wasn't really another country at all — it was just Canada.

Heading out on foot struck Langston as a Canadian pastime. Couples actually went out on walks. Held hands, kissed, walked, kissed some more, kept walking, looked at the trees, which looked starved. In Baltimore, the trees were five times as big, ten times as old, and a hundred times more frequent — but nobody bothered walking under them. Walking was something you did from your car to the house, or from your door to the bus stop, if you didn't have a car.

At the University of Toronto, Langston was no better than an average medical student. He studied hard just to stay in the middle of the pack. He didn't have the smarts of a nuclear physicist, but he did have two things going for him. One — he wasn't obsessed about getting high marks. Learning the material well and getting out with a medical degree would be good enough for him. And two — he had a phenomenal ability to concentrate. He could block out the noise of the bassist playing in the house or the prostitute fighting with her pimp. He could absorb a chapter of anatomy in a crowded café. In the fall of his first term in medical school, he studied right through three parties in the Pembroke Street rooming house. And he could fall asleep in seconds. Any time, any place.

Tenants in the rooming house started losing money, watches, and shoes not long after Langston moved in. People eyed him as he walked up the stairs. He assumed it was because he was black. One day he came home to find that his lock had been jimmied and twenty-five dollars stolen from the shoe box under his bed.

He stepped out of his room and stopped the first person he

crossed — a tenant named Dorothy Perkins. She was carrying a basket of laundry down the stairs. Dorothy was also studying at the university, but had avoided Langston since he had moved in.

"Excuse me, ma'am." She stopped and turned around and waited for him to continue. "Somebody has just stolen twenty-five dollars from my room. My only twenty-five dollars, as a matter of fact. It was here two hours ago. Have you seen anybody who doesn't belong in this house?"

"You, too?"

"What do you mean, me, too?"

"You had money stolen, too? We've all been losing things — money, watches, chains, rings — for the last few weeks."

"The last few weeks! I moved in a few weeks ago."

"Yeah," she said with a grin. "We noticed."

"Wonderful," he said. "Let me tell you something, ma'am."

"Excuse me, but — "

"Please let me finish. I don't steal. I don't need anybody's chains or watches or rings. I don't need their money. I mean, I could use it, but I wouldn't take it. I'm a student, and I don't steal. I do need my twenty-five dollars, however. It was my food money."

"I'm sorry about your twenty-five dollars. I lost forty. But I was trying to tell you something."

"What's that?"

"Ma'am sounds like it's out of the American south. It traditionally suggests an imbalance in power between two people speaking. Generally, the ma'am has the power, and the one speaking to her doesn't. I would appreciate it if — "

"What are you studying, anyway? I heard you were at the university, too."

"Sociology. As I was saying, I would appreciate it if you would refrain from calling me ma'am. It shows a deference that I find socially offensive." Langston felt his cheeks burning. "I'm sorry about your money," she said. "That's tough luck. You may call me Dorothy. Now, if you'll please excuse me." Langston stepped to the side, and Dorothy continued down the stairs with her load of laundry.

The next day, Langston was holding a small, cast-iron frying pan, about to set it down on his hot plate, when he heard a scream. Still holding the pan, he stepped out of his room and saw a door open down the hall.

Dorothy rushed out. "There's a thief in my room."

"Where'd he go?"

"In the bathroom."

Armed with the frying pan, Langston headed toward the bathroom. A young boy dashed out, crashed into Langston, knocked him off balance, tried to make a run for the hall, but turned when Dorothy beat him to it and slammed the door. He ran to the open window and climbed out onto the fire escape.

"Stop or I'll shoot," Langston cried out.

The boy got all the way out. Langston pursued him, frying pan in hand. He struggled out the window and again shouted, "I'll shoot!" The boy skipped to the edge of the platform. As he was about to take the steps down the fire escape, Langston hurled the cast-iron pan. It caught the boy on the shoulder. The boy fell down. The pan tumbled onto the fire escape, clattered down the stairs, slammed into the landing one flight down, and fell out into the air. It landed in the alley one arm's length away from another tenant named Mario. "Jesus Christ," Mario screamed.

"Sorry," Langston shouted.

"You trying to kill me or what?"

"Come on up. I caught a thief."

"You what?"

"He shot me," the boy screamed. "I've been shot. This man shot me."

"Settle down. If I'd shot you, you wouldn't be hollering like that. All I did was slow you down with a frying pan."

Dorothy joined them on the fire escape. "You could have hurt him."

The boy started crying. Langston stepped up to him. White boy, torn jeans, dirty hair, dirty face, only thirteen or so. Not old enough to have hair under his arms.

"What's your name, son?" Langston said.

"Johnny Riley."

Mario arrived, breathless. "Is this the little fucker who took sixty bucks out of my shoes last week?"

"Calm down, Mario," Langston said. "He's just a kid. Get some ice, would you? And Dorothy, could you bring me a wet washcloth?"

Dorothy turned away, went to the bathroom, and brought back the washcloth. Mario got ice from the store next door. Langston wrapped the ice in the washcloth and pressed it against the welt on the boy's shoulder.

"Two weeks in med school and he already thinks he's a doctor," Dorothy mumbled.

"Why's he babying the kid?" Mario said.

Langston let it be known that he wanted a minute alone with the boy. He led the youth to his room.

"Do you know where I come from, Johnny?"

"Africa? You're not a cannibal, are you?"

"Don't be an ass. I'm from the United States. Down there, you can get shot breaking into somebody's home."

"So why didn't you shoot me?"

Langston grinned and placed the washcloth back on Johnny's shoulder. "I didn't need to. I had the frying pan."

Langston struck a deal with the boy. Nobody would call the cops, if Johnny would bring back the money and the goods he had stolen.

Langston opened his door. Mario and Dorothy were there, both smiling. "You folks hear all that?"

"Sure did," Mario said.

"Does it suit you okay?"

"It suits us fine, Mr. Social Worker," Dorothy said.

"I would have beat him up," Mario said, "but I guess that's why I'm a gardener and you're studying to be a doctor."

Johnny went home. Mario followed him, to make sure he came back. He did return, with most of the money and the stolen goods. Langston took Johnny on a walkabout and made him meet everybody he'd stolen from. People seemed to accept getting most of their money back, and Johnny went home.

Langston asked Dorothy if she had heard of Baltimore crab cakes. She hadn't. He said there was a nice place by the waterfront that served them.

"Is that an invitation?" she said.

"It is. I wouldn't like you to miss out on them."

Dorothy smiled and touched his arm. "Well, let's try them, sometime."

The tenants at 117 Pembroke Street took good notice of the new black medical student. They saw his U.S. army trunk delivered to the house a week after he moved in. They noticed that he ate kippers for dinner. They heard he had rented his room at a bargain price. After he nabbed the house thief, tenants began approaching Langston directly. He helped one man write a letter to his parole officer, and guided another to a doctor for treatment of venereal disease.

One evening, while he was reading an anatomy text and whistling "The A Train," Langston heard a knock on his door. He got up to answer it. Before him stood a young woman whose bright red lipstick made her mouth look like a kissing machine. Her skin was as white as skin got, her eyes blue and alive, her hair pinned up in a bun.

"You're Langston, I know," she said. "I'm Stella Tanner. I live downstairs with my husband."

"Well, come on in."

Stella stepped in and glanced at the single bed and the books stacked in plastic fruit crates. "I can't stay. I have to go to work. But do you mind if I ask you something?"

"Go right ahead."

"If I don't like somebody who is a Negro, does that mean I'm prejudiced?"

"That depends on why you don't like him."

"It's a her. And it's because she's a bitch. Always giving me a hard time, never nice to me, never nice to the customers, thinks the world owes her an apology."

"Who is this woman?"

"I'm a waitress at the Mars Café. This woman I'm talking about works there part-time."

"The Mars Café? Where's that?"

"You haven't been to the Mars Café? It's more than a café — it's an institution. It's been in business for decades. Nobody will deny that we've got the best raisin bran muffins you ever tasted. And our breakfasts — "

"How about your coffee? You got good coffee?"

"Not bad. Coffee's coffee. Anybody'll give you coffee. But —"

"Sorry, Stella, but coffee is not coffee. There's good coffee, and there's bad coffee. I've been in Toronto for four weeks and I've only found one place so far — one place! — that serves passable coffee."

Stella put her hands on her hips and smiled. "We were talking about whether I'm prejudiced."

"How am I supposed to know? You know the answer better than anyone else."

"I don't think I am. I just plain don't like that woman. But that doesn't have to mean I'm prejudiced, does it?"

"It doesn't have to," Langston said. "I'm prepared to accept that you're not prejudiced, if that's what you want to hear me say. But just don't prove me wrong."

Stella leaned forward and kissed Langston on the cheek. "You're a doll. My husband told me what you did the other day with that kid who'd been stealing from everybody. I gotta tell you I was very impressed. For a while, my husband and I wondered if it was you who was ripping everybody off."

"So maybe you are prejudiced, after all."

"Very funny. Why don't you come by the café sometime?"

"I will."

"I shouldn't be telling you this, but Dorothy Perkins told me she fancies you." Stella let out a loud laugh. "If I wasn't married, I'd be giving her a run for her money."

Langston found that the best way to keep up with his medical studies was to plan his weeks from start to finish. During the academic year, they all went the same. Classes or library study from eight a.m. to eight p.m., Monday to Friday, with breaks only for his bagged lunch and a stroll outside to clear his head. In the evening, he would walk home, buy food, and make dinner. His meals were always quick and cheap, and never required more than a pot, a plate, a bowl, and cutlery. From nine to midnight, more studying. From midnight to one a.m., he would listen to jazz, go for a walk, write a letter or two, or take a bath. On Saturdays, Langston slept till nine and studied from then until six. On Saturday nights, he partied, chatted with his co-tenants, or went out to see westerns. On Sunday mornings at ten, he'd order the all-you-can-eat breakfast special at the Mars Café, eating three plates of scrambled eggs, sausages, hash browns, and toast for seventy-five cents. Then he'd stroll south to Kensington Market, pick up cheeses, cold meats, kippers, and sardines, spend an hour reading the *New York Times*, and knock back an espresso in an Italian café on College Street. Then he would walk home, drop his food in the tenants' common fridge, eat lunch, and study until eight in the evening. After that, it was free time.

On one such free evening, Langston wandered into the common room of the Pembroke Street house and found Dorothy Perkins trying to explain the differences between the Canadian and the American electoral systems to Mario and to Stella.

"You're telling me that in the United States, you don't even get to vote directly for or against the president?" Mario said. "You gotta vote for people in this electoral college, who then vote for their candidate? What good is that? Why not just vote for the president without anybody standing between him and the voters?"

"Well, our system's just as indirect up here," Dorothy said. "We don't get to vote for a prime minister."

"Sure we do," Mario said.

"No, we don't," Dorothy said. "Let me explain."

"Let's ask Langston," Stella said. "He's gonna be a doctor. He'll know."

"What difference does it make if he's going to be a doctor?" Dorothy said. "Why are you people always putting doctors up on pedestals? Doctors are among the most conservative, reactionary forces in North America."

"Maybe," Stella said. "But they're smart. And we never had one living here before."

"What are you talking about, smart?" Dorothy said. "Why should he know any more about politics than you or me?"

"Don't get overheated," Stella said. "I'm just asking the man what he thinks. He's been standing here with us for five minutes and you haven't let him open his mouth yet."

Dorothy glared at Stella.

"She likes him," Mario said. "Why else would she be running him down all the time?"

"Like him? I can't stand good-looking, cocky, successful men!"

Langston finally got a word in. "Well, thank you, Dorothy. I like you, too. Remember that crab dinner we were talking about some time back?"

"Take your crab and crack it," Dorothy said. She stomped out of the room.

"She's a bit sensitive today," Mario said.

"Must be her period," Stella said.

Dorothy stepped back into the room. "That's an insulting comment."

"What's wrong with saying you're having your period? Are you?"

"Your question is insulting to women. And it's none of your business."

"I can't insult women if I'm one myself. Langston, is there any way that I — a woman — can insult women?"

"What are you asking *him* for?"

"Cool out, chick," Stella said. "We know you like him. And he likes you. This isn't high school, sweetie. You're allowed to like people. We all got hormones."

Dorothy stood speechless beside Langston. She turned to him, and planted her mouth on his. He pulled back, slightly. She clasped his head with her hands and kissed him for at least ten seconds. Mario drummed the table with his fingers.

"Ladies and gentlemen," Stella called out. "In this corner, we have Cool Cat Cane. And in this corner, we have Puckered Perkins. Let the two of them do battle no more."

"Battle?" Langston said. "All I did was ask her out for crab cakes."

"And I accepted," Dorothy said.

"When?" he asked.

"Didn't you hear me?" She kissed him again.

They made plans to see each other on the next weekend.

On every street they walked, people turned their heads. Langston liked to catch them red-handed. He would turn and wave at the very moment another had pivoted to stare.

"You're quite the looker, Miss Perkins. You've been making heads swivel since we left Pembroke Street."

"They're not looking at me, kiddo," Dorothy said. "They're looking at us."

"Well, when they look at us, they're really looking at you. They're thinking, damn, that woman is fine on the eyeballs."

Dorothy placed her arm in his. "Am I fine on your eyeballs?"

"Ma'am," he said, prompting her to poke him in the ribs, "you are fine on my pupils, and easy on my irises, so fine, indeed, that I'm already looking past the crab cakes. Kiddo, I'm going to have you for dessert."

Dorothy coughed in her throat, took her arm out of Langston's, straightened her skirt, and said, "Well, you know what they say about carts and horses. How about if we concentrate on lunch?"

It was the first time Langston had set out to have a good meal in a good Canadian restaurant. It was also the first time he had been accompanied to a restaurant by a white woman. He figured it could go one of three ways. The maître d' could tell them that all the tables were reserved — although Langston had tried to eliminate that possibility by making a reservation by telephone. The maître d' could be cold and uninviting. Or, he could treat them like any other couple. The latter it turned out to be, and Langston made a mental note that he now had two restaurants — this one and the Mars Café — that he could fall back on in need.

They started with the house wine and lobster chowder. They clinked glasses. Langston mentioned that the restaurant was a long step up from Pembroke Street.

"Pembroke has its down sides," Dorothy said, "and it certainly isn't as clean or quiet as I'd like, but it's important to me to support a mixed rooming house."

"Mixed?"

"Mixed race, and mixed sex. You don't find it all that often here. I want to support it."

"So you're making a statement by living there."

"Sure."

"Not me," Langston said. "I met the landlady on a bus and she said she had a vacancy and that's the end of the story."

"But don't you feel socially engaged, living in that house? You may have arrived by fluke, but now that you're there, don't you feel committed to it?"

"Not particularly."

"You'd just as soon live anywhere else?"

"It suits me for now. I like the cheap rent. I like the people. I like you."

"I suppose it's too much to ask a doctor to be progressive."

"You've got a point," Langston said. "Medical training transcends all racial and cultural differences and transforms each and every one of us into a social swine."

"You're making fun of me."

"I was returning the favor. Stop trying to make a political issue of the fact that I'm not wedded to the rooming house. I don't go around getting wedded to things or people every day. Give it a break, why don't you? Laugh a little."

"Wedded to things or people. I like that. I do get worked up pretty easily." Dorothy told him that she had thought of herself as a socialist until recently, when she'd begun hearing more and more rumors about mass arrests and killings by Stalin in the USSR. Apart from her MA studies in sociology and her part-time secretarial job, Dorothy said she worked as a volunteer for the Toronto Labor Committee for Human Rights. It documented and fought cases of discrimination. It was trying to convince the Ontario government to pass human rights legislation. She asked if he was involved in any sort of social activism.

"This feels like a job interview."

"It isn't. We're just chatting. Over a very nice lunch, by the way. So. What are you committed to?"

"Nothing, other than that I'm quite religious."

She straightened. "Really? What religion?"

"I'm an orthodox carnivore."

She broke into a fit of laughter. "You're incorrigible. I love it. It's your humor. It's so — well — human."

"I am. Despite my race."

"That's not what I meant, and you know it."

He touched her arm. "I come from a family that would interest you. My father is a church minister. And my great-grandfather escaped from slavery, settled in Oakville around 1850, and —"

"Oakville? You've got to be kidding. Oakville is lily white."

"It may be now. I wouldn't know. But I was born there. I haven't been back, though, since I left it as a boy, in 1930. But Oakville was by no means entirely white in 1850. First, the Mississagi Indians were in the area. Second, a group of fugitive slaves found work in the town."

"What was your great-grandfather's name, anyway?"

"Langston Cane the First."

"So what are you?"

"The Fourth."

The moment the waiter set crab cakes on the table, Dorothy jumped up and ran to the bathroom. Langston bit into the corner of one crab cake, and then put his knife and fork down and waited. After five minutes, he walked over to the ladies' room door and called out her name. No response. He pulled the door open. Someone was retching inside.

"Dorothy, is that you?" More retching. Langston pulled the door open, poked his head inside, saw nobody, strode in, and found Dorothy kneeling in a stall. He asked if she was okay. She muttered. He put his hands on her shoulders, and she slumped back. Someone came through the entrance. Langston leaned back, stuck his head out of the stall, and began to ask for paper towels, when the woman saw him and screamed. She fled.

Wonderful, he thought. Here come the cops. Here comes the Klan. Here come the forces of good. Here come the headlines: *Negro Arrested in Women's Toilet.*

The maître d' and the woman burst back into the washroom.

"What's going on?" the maître d' said.

"It's all right," Dorothy said. She climbed to her feet, flushed the toilet, wiped her face, and stepped out of the stall. "I was sick. That's all. Sick. Something I just ate made me violently ill, and he came in to help me."

"Who is he?" the woman asked.

"He's my friend."

The woman took a step back.

Langston put his arm gently around Dorothy and guided her to the sink. "Don't worry," he said softly to the woman. "She enjoys being my concubine."

Langston helped Dorothy into a taxi, took her home, and tried to put her right to bed.

"I don't want to go to bed," Dorothy said. "I want to have a shower and brush my teeth and change my clothes."

"Did you eat anything new today?"

"I wasn't going to admit it, but I've never had lobster before."

"Good thing you never got to the crab cakes. Black folks' food is pretty strong stuff."

Dorothy rubbed the back of his hand. "Ha ha." She kissed the backs of each of his fingers. They were long, and slim, and smooth, as if someone had rubbed a fine coat of oil into them.

Langston massaged the corner of her mouth and ran a finger along her lips. "Mind if I join you in the shower?"

"That is absolutely out of the question. But come back when I'm feeling better. Do come back, concubine."

They barely spoke during the next two weeks. Dorothy rushed to work before Langston woke, and Langston studied at the library until late at night. He had several examinations. He thought he had done fairly well, but it turned out that he had scored on the fifty-eighth percentile. He tried not to be disappointed. The fifty-eighth percentile wasn't too bad. Nobody would throw him out of medical school if he stayed ahead of fifty-seven percent of the students. The day after his exams ended, Langston found a note under his door. *I'm going to Windsor this weekend. Want to come along?*

Langston dropped in to see her. Dorothy explained that she and others in the Toronto Labor Committee for Human Rights were trying to push the government to enact anti-discrimination legislation. It was well known that some restaurants in Windsor refused to serve blacks. She wanted to document it.

"Is this your idea of a date?" Langston asked.

"No. But it could turn into one after we're done in Windsor."

"Well, a date in the traditional sense — we watch a Gary Cooper movie, or catch Ella Fitzgerald singing, or Illinois Jacquet playing sax at the Colonial, or go walking in High Park — would be fine with me. But going to Windsor is not."

"Why not?" Dorothy said.

"I don't need the aggravation. Why should I go all the way to Windsor for the privilege of being turned out of some redneck's restaurant? Because that's what you want me for, isn't it? You need a black man. You need a Negro for your experiment."

"Yes, we need a Negro. But it doesn't have to be you. I have other friends. I just thought you'd like to come along."

"I wouldn't enjoy it," Langston said.

"Do you think blacks in Windsor enjoy getting kicked out of restaurants?"

"The whole idea is naive."

"It is *not* naive, goddamn it. I hate that word. My mother used to say everything I did was naive."

"So you get me thrown out of a restaurant. Then what?"

"We go to the newspapers. We inform the minister of labor."

"If I were so desperate to experience segregation, I would have stayed in Baltimore. Down there, the only restaurants I can sit in are black-owned. If I want restaurant food, I have to buy it take-out at the back door. If I want to kiss you in the street, I've got to look over shoulders — yours and mine — first. I was an American Army soldier, kiddo. Men with the brains of squirrels got to be my commanding officers — solely on the basis of pigment. I left that and I'm not going back. I like you, Dorothy. I like you a lot. But I don't need to go to Windsor. I don't need any lessons about segregation."

"Nobody's giving you any damn lessons. We want you to help us deal with a problem. So how about it?"

"*No.*"

"Bit sensitive, are we?" Dorothy said.

"I hate that goddamn word. Just as much as you hate naive."

"That's the first time I've heard you swear. So you do feel some sort of social passion? You are an activist, of a sort."

"Activism, no. Magnetism, yes. I feel an animal magnetism for you, kiddo."

They spent the night together. They rolled and tossed and climbed and thrusted half the night and half the next morning. Dorothy called in sick and Langston missed the only day of classes he would ever miss, and they touched and held and kissed every square inch of each other. They couldn't stay apart. They slept only briefly, and awoke to find themselves making love again. Finally, they showered and walked about downtown and stopped in cafés to drink from the same coffee mug and took a streetcar to High Park and walked around Grenadier Pond and ate dinner at the Mars Café and watched an early movie and fell asleep together in his bed and didn't wake up until dawn.

"I'm gonna be late," Dorothy said.

"I'm behind in my studies," Langston said. "Way behind."

"How can you be way behind when you were on top of things a day ago?"

"I was on top of you a day ago."

"But it was worth it, wasn't it?" she said. "Don't worry. I won't trouble you again until the weekend."

"The weekend? How did you know I had decided to come?"

"I don't know. Something about your animal magnetism."

"I had a good routine going. You went and broke my concentration."

"You'll get it back." Dorothy kissed him on the lips and whispered in his ear. He thought of her every hour that day.

On Sunday, they drove to Windsor with Cleta Morris and Jack Hanson — Dorothy's labor committee friends. Jack was black; Cleta white. Jack and Langston entered Hunter's Grill in downtown Windsor. A sign said Please Seat Yourself. They were left unattended for fifteen minutes. Finally, they hailed a waitress, who started for their table but was stopped by the owner. He was a stout little fellow, mid-fifties, dressed in a tie, a white shirt with a ketchup stain, and black pants. The owner asked what they wanted. They said a menu. He handed over menus reluctantly. They ordered the luncheon special. He said the luncheon special was sold out. Okay, they said, just bring us toast, soup, and coffee.

They waited for half an hour. Sorry, they were then informed, we have run out of soup today. Maybe you should try another establishment. They left.

Ten minutes later, Dorothy and Cleta entered the restaurant and asked for a table for four. Four? the waitress asked. Dorothy said their husbands would be over in a few minutes. Fine, said the waitress, who led them to a table and took orders for two luncheon specials and two orders of soup and toast, with coffee all around.

The waitress brought the food out quickly enough, and then offered to hold the men's food in the kitchen. Dorothy said that wouldn't be necessary. Langston and Jack walked in and sat down and started eating. Other customers began to stare and shake their heads. One woman mumbled to her husband that the four were troublemakers. Two couples put money on the tables and left the restaurant hastily.

The owner approached the table. "I'm going to have to ask you to leave."

"But we've just started," Langston said. "This food is scrumptious."

"Don't worry about paying. Just get out." The owner retrieved a soup bowl while Langston was bringing a spoon to his mouth.

"You want us to leave?" Langston said softly. "You look like a man who could use five dollars. Why on earth would you not want paying customers?"

"I think you know. Get out."

"I just don't think I can move without an explanation."

"We don't serve colored."

"I'm astonished. I had no idea. But that's okay — I want to reassure you that I didn't order colored. Actually, I don't eat colored people. All I had in mind was piping hot tomato soup."

"You're bothering my customers. Get out before I call the police."

"May I ask your name?" Langston said.

"Tony."

"Tony what?"

"Tony's good enough."

"Well, Tony Goodenough, it has been my pleasure to meet you. You make a very nice soup. Colored people like canned soup. We're doing our best to stop digging into crocodiles and the like. Your canned soup would have civilized me substantially. Good day, Mr. Goodenough. I hope you don't mind seeing your nice face in the newspaper."

"Get out."

Langston stood up. Dorothy snapped a photo of Tony.

"No pictures," Tony said.

"Don't worry, we'll make sure it's a nice shot," Langston said. "Take another, Dorothy."

Within an hour, Langston — as a member at large of the Toronto Labor Committee for Human Rights — described the incident in a letter to the *Windsor Star*. Within six hours, similar letters had been dropped off at the office of the Ontario minister of labor and at the *Toronto Times*. The *Windsor Star* didn't touch the story. The Toronto paper ran a small blurb on the back pages. It didn't name the restaurant or use the photo. The Ontario minister of labor mailed Langston a letter insisting that the Ontario government was opposed to racial discrimination, but that it couldn't prevent such an incident.

Dorothy wanted to take him back to another restaurant in Windsor the next week, but Langston refused. "You made your point, Dot. I don't want to spend my Sundays getting kicked out of restaurants. It's a good cause, but — "

"Damn right," she said.

"I have to study."

"That's egotistical."

"If I don't study, I won't pass. But I'll take up the fight once I'm a doctor."

"Once you're a doctor, you'll be a reactionary."

"Don't count on it."

Dorothy left town for two weeks to visit her parents in Winnipeg. When she returned, she didn't look up Langston. Another week went by. Langston slipped a note under her door, inviting her to lunch the next Sunday.

They walked for an hour in High Park, saw Gary Cooper playing in *High Noon*, and returned to Langston's room, where they played a game Dorothy invented and quickly regretted. He spent fifteen minutes scouring two pages in one of her sociology texts — *The Polish Peasant in America* by W. I. Thomas and F. Znaniecki — and then had to put it down and see if he could answer her ten questions about it. One of them was: What is meant by the phrase "the definition of the situation"? Langston answered: "It's how you define a situation that you're in. You come to assume a set of principles underlying a given situation, and if those principles are subsequently violated, you feel upset or displaced, because your definition no longer holds for the situation."

"Not bad, Lang."

"It's easy to be not bad in sociology," Langston teased her. "All you do is use your common sense. But try applying common sense to the world of anatomy. It just won't work. You have to memorize the stuff, bone by bone, tendon by tendon."

They switched roles. Dorothy tried to absorb two pages of *Gray's Anatomy* and answer questions about the human heart. But the ventricles, atria, and chambers flummoxed her. Langston teased her ceaselessly. "I think the definition of this situation is that medicine is harder than sociology. So now you see why I can't keep going to Windsor."

Dorothy pulled him down to the bed and planted her lips on his.

Langston and Dorothy barely saw each other for the next two weeks. Langston had to slip a note under her door again to invite her out. He found it a tiresome way to communicate. It didn't feel right to work so hard for something that he wanted to take for granted. She came by his room that evening.

"Come on in," Langston said.

"No, thanks. You're studying, and I'm tired. Sorry, but as for your little note, I've made other plans for Saturday."

"Other plans?"

"Another guy. I'm seeing a fellow that evening, if you have to know."

"Who?"

"Oh, come on," she said. A smile broke out on her face. "Don't tell me you're jealous. You are! I love it. How boyish!"

"Boyish! I happen to think we have something going on here."

"We have had a few things going on, here and there."

"Here and there? Listen, kid, remember your sociology text? What was it called again?"

"Forgot already, huh? *The Polish Peasant in America.*"

"Yeah," Langston said. "It talked about the definition of the situation. I say, we have a situation here. I define it as me seeing you and you seeing me, and nobody else in the picture. So why don't you call it off with this fellow?"

"We've made plans."

"I'll come along."

"Don't be ridiculous."

"Take me along and introduce me. It doesn't have to be a big thing. Just say, 'I want you to meet Langston Cane. We live in the same house. We sleep together. He saved my life in the ladies' room of a nice restaurant, when I was throwing up lobster chowder. He's crazy about me. Do you mind if he joins us tonight?'"

Dorothy slapped her thigh and doubled over in laughter. "What are you trying to tell me? What, exactly, is the definition of our situation?"

"You want a formal definition? A thesis? A manifesto? I'll try to come up with something. But call that other fellow and call it off."

"You're sweet, kiddo," she said. She kissed him. He kissed her back. But she stopped it there. She wouldn't break her Saturday date, but said that she'd see Langston on Friday if he was free.

Several months passed. Langston studied all day long, but he never let the books cut into his sleep. He and Dorothy worked out a beer hour. Every night, at ten-thirty, they got together to split a beer. More often than not, they slept together. Eventually, they bought a larger mattress and converted her room into a bedroom, and his room into a den and makeshift kitchen. Still, Langston studied mightily. He managed to pull himself up by a few percentage points and score in the sixty-sixth percentile of the students completing their first year of medical school. In his second year, Langston hit sixty-eight percent on the students' bell curve. In his third year, he hit seventy-one percent. He figured that was about as good as he was going to get. In January of his fourth and final year, Langston asked Dorothy to drive him to Oakville.

"Didn't you tell me you were born there?" Dorothy asked.

"That's right."

"So why are we going there today?"

"It's a surprise. Just get up off your rusty dusty and take me out there, would you?"

They got to the town in forty minutes, exited from the Queen Elizabeth Way, and took Trafalgar Road south toward the lake. They parked by George's Square and walked east along Sumner. After crossing Reynolds and passing a few houses, Langston disengaged his arm from Dorothy's and pointed at a green, shuttered house. Up top, around an attic window, it had what looked like a lookout tower — a small, square extension from the house.

"What's that?" Dorothy asked.

"It's called a widow's walk."

"Why?"

"This house used to look out over Lake Ontario. And traditionally, the wife stands up there looking out and waiting for her husband to come home from his days or weeks on a lake schooner."

"How do you know about all this?"

"After my great-grandfather settled in Oakville, the ship captain who helped him escape — a man named Robert Wilson — built this house. With the widow's walk."

"And where'd your great-grandfather go from here?"

"Back to the States, later."

"After slavery ended?"

"Not quite. I'll tell you about it sometime. But that's not the end of it. The house was moved from the lakefront to Sumner, around 1900. My parents bought it around 1925 — and I was born here. We lived in this house until 1930, when we moved back to Baltimore."

"What other amazing things do you have to tell me?"

"I would like to buy this house. My parents have offered to help. But I would need your financial assistance, too."

"Hang on a moment, there, Langston, dear sir. I think we require a definition of the situation. You want me to spend my savings, meager as they are, on your house — "

"Our house. It would be ours."

"Ours, in what way? We need a definition, please."

"As man and wife, if you are prepared to enter into a marital definition with a superficial medical student — soon to become an intern — who will not have serious income for a few years yet."

"Can you put that into plain English?"

"Will you marry me?"

Dorothy slipped her arm through his and tugged him toward the water. "I'll think about it," she said.

"And then what?"

"I will likely say yes."

"In that case, how about if you say it now. Just to ease the mind of a poor, broken down, unsophisticated —"

"Yes, I'll marry you. How is that for an answer? But aren't you supposed to be offering me a ring or something? Oh, never mind, sociologists don't stand on principle. Yes. *Yes*. YES!"

"Ring? Yes, a terrific idea. How about a little engagement ceremony?" Langston whistled between his teeth. A truck pulled up from around the corner. Mario, their co-tenant at Pembroke Street, was behind the wheel. He stepped out of the front seat with a bouquet of roses.

"Look at them all!" Dorothy laughed. "How many roses have you brought?"

"Fifty-four. For this year."

Mario hugged Langston and kissed Dorothy. "The roses were my idea," he told her. "My idea, but he went for it in a big way."

Langston removed a small box from his pocket. "This ring, however, is my idea."

Chapter 7

WHAT WERE THE FIRST THINGS I noticed about Baltimore? I had to turn off Sarah's heater, and roll down a window. The air was humid. I had left the remnants of winter in Toronto and arrived in spring in Baltimore. The air seemed pregnant with things to come. It seemed to be saying, I'm in your face, sucker, so breathe me in before I get too hot. Exiting from Highway 83 South, I saw a boy of twelve or so saunter across Twenty-ninth Street. He kept his back to the car. Didn't even look around. Timed it so that he would be out of my way by a foot or so as I went by. All I saw were the jeans tight around his ass and the brown of his neck and the hair shaved close to his head.

Through my side window, I watched a boy standing outside a store with bars in the window, taking something from the hand of a man and running down the sidewalk. Then something snapped my head up and down and made my teeth crash together. I mashed the brakes. Sarah stalled. I figured I had hit a pothole. I started her up again, and hit another hole in the road. I listened for the clunking sound of a round tire gone flat. Nothing. Sarah was all right. I kept driving.

Apart from potholes, I noticed the absence of vegetation. There were no trees or grass. If my father had come to Toronto complaining about the lack of trees, he sure as hell hadn't come from Twenty-ninth Street just east of Highway 83. Deals were going down in doorways. People were handing bags to each other. Nobody walked in the streets or on the sidewalk. People either stood in doorways, or, if they had to get out, they ran. Cars drove fast. A number passed me. Drivers seemed to know where the potholes were. I came to a red light. I stopped. We tend to do that in Canada. But another car behind me and one lane over surged through the light. Two youths ran up to my car wielding something in their hands. Here we go, I thought. First I failed to avoid a pothole, then I failed to run a red light. They have caught on to the fact that I'm an out-of-towner. One of the boys, who was fifteen or so, stood outside my windshield and smiled. He raised his arm. Here we go. He lowered his arm, and I saw he was carrying a squeegee. He washed my windshield. He cleaned it very well, I will say that for him. The light turned green. The windshield washer's younger helper stood in front of the car. The washer came around to my side and signaled for me to roll down the window.

"That's a dollar, mister."

"Hope you don't mind foreign currency."

"Say what?"

A car blasted us with a horn and flew by on our left.

"Never mind. Here's a dollar. Thanks for the wash." I dropped a Canadian loonie in his hand and saw him turn over the coin and look at it critically. I drove off. In the rearview mirror, I saw the boy shrug and give the loonie to his partner.

I went through another light. The street switched as quickly as a TV channel. Now I had a park on my left, and trees topping red-brick low-rise apartments on my right. I also saw white people. They were walking in the street. One of them stopped to kiss the woman beside him. I turned north on Charles Street into the Homewood campus area of Johns Hopkins University.

I had to pay cash up front to rent a room for one week in a residence owned by the university. At $185 U.S. a week, I didn't want to extend my stay. The apartment overlooked the corner of Thirty-third and St. Paul streets. I heard three ambulances go by in my first hour there. But the space was good enough. It had a bedroom, a bathroom, a furnished kitchen, and a desk. I began my search for housing the next day in the Homewood area. Saw a few For Rent signs. One place was both expensive and filthy. Another flat was answered by a little man, in his early fifties, with a goatee and John Lennon spectacles. He looked me up and down and up and down again and mumbled something half under his breath that was so outrageous I couldn't believe he had said it. What I thought I had heard was "Octoroon, I presume." Where I came from, not very many people knew the word meant someone who was one-eighth black. But Baltimore was obviously not Oakville. He asked me if I was clean and had clean habits. While I tried to ingest the question and figure out what answer to spit back, he offered "reduced rent in exchange for certain nocturnal services, to be specified at your request."

"No, thank you," I said. "Octoroons don't go in for such things." I looked for puzzlement or reaction in his eye. What I saw was a slight lifting of the brow and a grin that pulled his upper lip above a silver canine tooth.

"We must not know the same octoroons," he said, still speaking barely above a whisper, and condensing the word into two syllables, so that it sounded like *octroons*.

I took my apartment search elsewhere. For two days, I

checked the *Baltimore Sun* and tramped up and down Charles Street, St. Paul, North Calvert, and Greenmount, as well as the perpendicular east–west streets from Thirtieth to Thirty-fourth. Little was available. I found nothing that I could afford or would care to live in.

On my third day of searching, I found a crowd of people at the corner of Thirty-second and North Calvert. Each person was shelling out a buck-fifty for a kebab of barbecued meat. A black man who seemed about my age was grilling the meat on a makeshift stand. He sat on a miniature foldaway picnic chair — a backless variety that would have been appropriate for a six-year-old — next to a paper bag full of bread rolls. He shifted his weight continually from the back of his butt to the tips of his toes, as he sat forward. He was lean, and gave off the air of someone who was relaxed, yet ready to run. His eyes were young and abundant — too big for his slender face. He wasn't as young as he first looked — he had star-shaped wrinkles at the corners of his eyes, and his tightly curled hair held silver threads. I watched as he managed eight kebabs over the sizzling coals. He lifted the metal skewer off the grill with his bare fingertips, moving deftly. He opened a roll, clamped it around the kebab, pulled the meat off, and asked the final customer in the crowd: "Special Cameroonian hot sauce for you?"

The young woman, who looked like a first-year Hopkins student, asked her friend: "Is it any good?"

"Absolutely," her friend said. "Get it with the sauce. It's awesome."

"I'll have it with sauce." She took the kebab after the man poured sauce onto it from an opaque plastic bottle. "What kind of sauce did you say it was?"

"Special Cameroonian hot sauce," he said. She still looked

puzzled. "It's a delicacy from the Republic of Cameroon."

"That's like Africa, right?"

"Yes. Very good. Cameroon is in West Africa, bordered by Nigeria, Chad — "

"Okay, enough, my brain is fried, I can't handle a geography lesson right now. But it's really good. Thanks." The young woman and her friend walked away.

"Would you like one, too?" the vendor asked me. "Or two, perhaps. It's getting late. I will give you one for a buck-fifty, or two for two-fifty. Closing down deal."

"Just one, thanks," I said.

"Come on, my friend, take two for two-fifty. I'll tell you what. I'll give you two for two dollars. This will make you happy. When you eat them, it will be truly impossible to be sad."

"Okay, you win, give me two," I said. This seemed to please him. He hummed as he pulled the meat off the kebabs. I ordered his Cameroonian hot sauce.

"You say that very well. You've heard of Cameroon?"

"Yes. I've been to Mali."

"That's wonderful. Students around here, they like my kebabs, but they don't know Cameroon. They don't know where it is, even. Some of them do not even know where the continent of Africa is. And these students, let me tell you. They are very wealthy." He gave a meaningful rub of his thumb and index finger.

The barbecue stand was cheap. Very cheap. It looked like a model you could buy for ten dollars at the hardware store. Beside it was a cardboard sign with *Yoyo's Fine Foods* in black letters.

"Your name is Yoyo?" I asked.

"That's what people call me," he said, "because I bounce back when people try to knock me down. Where are you from, that you know of Cameroon and have been to Mali?"

"I am from Canada."

"Canada? I have been to Canada. I worked ten years ago in Winnipeg. You know Winnipeg? It is the coldest city in North America. But I liked it very much."

"Sure, I know Winnipeg. My mother was born and raised there."

"Well, I lived there, one time, for about a year. I would have liked to go back, but it could not be arranged. There was a woman in that city, a woman I loved. Her name was Hélène Savoie. I would give anything to see her again. I would give anything to be back in Canada."

I bit into the kebabs. The meat was succulent. They were the finest kebabs I had ever tasted. They fell apart in my mouth. "These things are absolutely incredible."

"I can't believe you used to work in Winnipeg," I said.

"Well, I did. Hélène Savoie was a reporter there. So was another friend of mine, Mahatma Grafton. They're both working in Toronto now."

"I've met Mahatma Grafton. Black reporter, right?"

"That's him," Yoyo said. His smile vanished. "Here comes a cop. Give me my two dollars now quick, please."

I handed over two ones.

A white officer — about six four, a belly as far out as a beer barrel, arms the size of some people's legs, night stick in his hand — got out of the cruiser.

Yoyo spoke first. "Hello, Officer, would you like a kebab on the house?"

"You got a vendor's permit?"

"I had one, Officer, but I lost it. Would you care to taste —"

"You can't sell this stuff without a vendor's permit. Meat, huh? You need more than a vendor's permit. You also need a license from the Maryland meat inspection department."

Yoyo turned over a kebab, checking to see that it was perfectly done.

"Have one, Officer. Then do to me what you must. The day is late. My kebabs are so good, they have been known to produce orgasms."

The cop actually grinned. I could not believe that a six-four white cop with a night stick in his right hand was grinning in the presence of a law-breaking African street vendor and a Canadian recently mistaken for an octoroon.

"Smells so good I'd fight back my own grandmother if she tried to take one outa my hand. Okay. Make one up for me. How much they cost?"

"It's on the house, Officer," Yoyo said. He lifted the kebab off the grill, clamped a bun around it, pulled away the skewer, and handed over the snack.

The officer bit into it carefully. He smiled. He glowed. He sighed. He burped. "Gimme another, would you? For my partner. You got something to wrap it in? No? Hell, then I'll just have to eat it." Yoyo surrendered his last kebab. The officer wolfed it down. "I've been barbecuing meat for twenty years and I never got it to taste this good. I'd ask you how to do it, but I got to run. Listen. I catch you selling here again, I'm gonna have to charge you with selling uninspected meat without a city permit. It could land you a big fine. So, don't let me catch you here again. Deal?"

"Yes, absolutely. Thank you very much."

The officer smiled, took a look at me, cocked his thumb back, and said, "Good stuff, isn't it?" and got into his cruiser and drove off.

"I have to split," Yoyo said.

"You know of a place to live around here, by any chance?"

"What are you looking for?"

"A room. With a private toilet, and shared or private cooking facilities. It should be clean and cheap."

"I have just the thing for you. I will be pleased to assist a man whose mother comes from Winnipeg. And if I help you, maybe you can help me get into Canada again."

"I'm afraid I have no influence at the border."

"Well, don't worry. Come along."

"What are you going to do with the barbecue stand?"

Yoyo used pieces of cardboard to pick up the barbecue and hide it in some bushes in a park behind us. "I'll be back to pick it up when it's cold."

"What if someone steals it?"

"In Cameroon, maybe. In my country, people can lift all kinds of hot items. But here, in the United States — never. Americans have no calluses on their fingers. So this, my friend, is too hot to pick up." Yoyo grabbed his rolls and skewers and meat, and signaled for me to follow him. "I won't fail you, my friend."

Chapter 8

YOYO HAD AN ODD WAY OF WALKING. He wasn't a tall man — only five eight or so — and he barely bent his knees as he walked. His hips had no choice but to swing, almost like a woman's, to keep up a fast walking pace, and Yoyo knew only one walking speed — extraordinarily fast.

As we went to meet his landlady, I asked Yoyo, whose real name was Hassane Moustafa Ali, how he had come to settle in Baltimore.

Yoyo said he would tell me, although his story was a secret. "You have African blood, don't you?"

"Yes. As a matter of fact, I was mistaken the other day for an octoroon."

"That means one-eighth black, right?"

"I'm four times more than that," I said, "but who's counting?"

"Left side, right side, left foot, right foot, it's all the same to me," Yoyo said. "You look like a man I can trust."

"Your secret is mine," I said.

Yoyo said he had worked for a Cameroonian daily called *La Voix de Yaoundé* until April of the year before. That month, he was sent on a plum assignment to cover a United Nations conference in New York. While he was there, Cameroonian army officers staged a military coup. Yoyo's newspaper had been government run, and when the government fell, the new regime arrested most of the editorial staff. One of Yoyo's colleagues — also in New York for the conference — applied for political asylum. He was jailed and deported to Cameroon after three months of court arguments. Yoyo chose to go underground.

"So why did you come to Baltimore, of all places?" I asked.

"Baltimore is not so bad," Yoyo said. "It has lots of black people — nearly three-quarters of the people here are black — so I blend in easily. Yet it also has a rich white population, so I can have people to sell kebabs to. Do you know that in half a year of selling kebabs in Baltimore, I have yet to sell to one black person?"

"I don't count? You're counting me as an octoroon after all, aren't you?"

Yoyo laughed. "Other than you, I mean."

"So you're here illegally?"

"Shhh," Yoyo said. "You can't be too careful."

As we walked, Yoyo held forth on his theory that there was an inverse relationship between the risk of mugging and the cost of renting. Proximity to risk had much more to do with lowering the price of a flat than, say, a broken toilet handle, or an uncomfortable bed, or a fridge door that wouldn't close. In the campus neighborhood, risk peaked near Greenmount and Twenty-eighth Street. The safest area was Charles Street, near Thirty-fourth, but Johns Hopkins University owned most of the buildings there and they were too expensive, anyway. St. Paul was slightly cheaper, but had the disadvantage of being an ambulance route.

Yoyo had settled on Adell Street, near Thirty-second Street, which was about dead center on the risk–cost axis. He showed me his flat. He had no kitchen, but had a two-burner hot plate on an old telephone stand. He had no counter or sink for dishwashing. His fridge was three feet high. Yoyo had bought it for eleven dollars from a university student. His bathroom was enormous. It had a large window overlooking a back alley, a long enamel bath with no shower head or shower curtains, a sink full of clean dishes, and a little rack for Yoyo's shaving and toilet items. Yoyo's bedroom had no bed, but a long straw pallet on a rug. Yoyo owned a vacuum cleaner — also purchased at a bargain price from the departing university student — and said he used it daily. When you slept on the floor, he said, you wanted to keep it clean. Indeed, when I looked around, I noticed that the apartment — from its light green walls to its hardwood floor in the small living room–eating area to the bathroom tiles to the bedroom rug to the windows — was immaculate.

Yoyo owned a television with a miniature satellite disk sprouting grasshopper antennae, and showed it to me proudly. Sony Trinitron. One of the best, he said. "I love this television. It helped me improve my English." He also owned a radio, which he had wired to an old car battery. Yoyo attached a clip to one of the battery heads and switched on the radio. An announcer's voice said we were listening to WEAA, Morgan State University Radio. "I pay for my own electricity. Why pay for the radio, when I can hear it for free?" He had found the battery in the alley behind Adell Street. It was cracked, and surely useless in a car, but it had enough juice for the radio.

Yoyo said an American friend had come over to visit once, and expressed horror at the apartment. "He said I was living in abject poverty. Abject — I had to look that word up. It means extreme, or absolute. But this isn't poverty. I eat well, I sleep well, I am healthy, I am not cold at night, I am making some money, I don't pay any taxes — my friend, this is not poverty. You have been to Africa. You know what I am saying."

He had a point. But I didn't see what it had to do with my finding an apartment, and I finally told him so.

"How much do you think this place costs?" Yoyo asked.

"Four hundred a month?"

"Only two hundred. Because there's no kitchen. The absence of kitchens troubles Americans. So I knew I could negotiate a good price when I saw this place had no kitchen. The empty flat upstairs does have a kitchen, although that may be unfortunate for you. But I will talk to the landlady. She likes me because I keep it very clean in here. It's not clean upstairs. But you can clean it. Americans are very funny in that respect, too. It's always better to rent a filthy apartment for a low price and then to clean it up — but they don't like to do that. What's the trouble? All you have to do is get down on your knees and use a little elbow grease. Elbow grease! How do you like that? It's an American idiomatic expression. I found it in my *Webster's*. The departing university student — he now lives in Wisconsin, by the way, which is on the way to Winnipeg and apparently almost as cold — explained the term to me."

Yoyo took me across the street to meet the landlady.

Elvina Peck had her gray and white hair pulled back in a bun. Her eyes were big and unmoving as she examined me, and her skin was almond brown — about halfway between Yoyo's complexion and mine.

Yoyo introduced me as an honorable Canadian traveler, knowledgeable about Africa, with maternal roots in the wonderful city of Winnipeg.

"Yoyo," Elvina said to my friend, "you talk just like your name, don't you? You sure bounce at a person with a mouthful of words. Can't your friend speak for himself?"

I introduced myself, said where I was from, and that I was looking to rent a flat on a monthly basis.

Elvina unfolded her arms. I was surprised to notice the form of her biceps, even though the wrinkled skin hanging from them jiggled slightly as she moved. Despite the fact that it was still only March, she wore a short-sleeved white blouse and bright orange slacks.

"Well, come on in, Mr. Cane. You look like an honorable sort, but I'd like to find out a little more about you."

Elvina turned and walked down a dark hall, her thongs clapping against the hardwood floor. Yoyo and I followed her into the living room. She motioned for us to sit. She took a stool by the window and pried open the blinds to peer down at the street while we did business, which lasted about fifteen minutes. It was one of the strangest interviews I had ever had. She asked the names of my parents, of all things, and what they did. She asked the names and occupations of my grandparents, and grunted in the affirmative when I told her that my grandfather and great-grandfather had ministered at the African Methodist Episcopal Church on Druid Hill Avenue.

"I thought you had colored blood in you. But if you don't mind me saying so, you've just about passed over the edge. Well, I'm not going to ask what you're doing in Baltimore. I don't even want to know. You don't smoke, do you?"

"No."

"Good, because there's no smoking in my house. No dogs or cats?"

"No."

"Good. Don't buy any. Except for purse snatchers and wife beaters and the occasional state governor, dogs and cats are among the most vile creatures on God's green earth. All they do is tear apart my garbage and leave their business in my yard." Elvina cleared her throat. "I suppose a man needs a woman or two, always has and always will, and I am not so out of touch as to stand in the way of your biological functions. But if I see a lot of wildness going on, you're out the next day."

I could have opposed this restriction of my civil liberties, but thought the better of it. I didn't know anybody in Baltimore, anyway.

"How much you willing to pay?" Elvina asked.

"I haven't seen the apartment."

"It's like Yoyo's, but a bit bigger. It has a kitchen with a counter and a sink for doing dishes, and a fridge and a stove and they work. The bathroom works, too. Water runs. New toilet. Tub, but no shower. I'm telling you right now the whole place needs cleaning. How much you willing to pay?"

"Two hundred a month."

"That's what he's paying," she said, looking at Yoyo. "Yours has a kitchen."

"Two twenty-five. I really can't afford any — "

"All right, two-fifty. You give me cash when I give you the keys, and you give me a fifty-dollar deposit in case you break a window."

I went to inspect the flat. Yoyo came along. It was as Elvina had described it. I was able to open the windows, which was a good thing, because the air inside hadn't moved for an eternity. Dust covered the fridge, stove, counters, and walls. Cobwebs rounded the corners of the bedroom. The bathroom tub was stained brown, and the window was too filthy to see through.

"I'm a good cleaner," Yoyo said. "But I have to make my living. This is America. I got you this apartment, and I don't ask for any gratuity. But here is what you can do for me, my friend. Pay me forty-five dollars cash — special rate for friends — and I will clean this apartment for you. I will clean it top to bottom, floors, walls, bathtub, fridge, everything. It will take me three hours, working fast. I am a very good cleaner. You saw my apartment — you know I tell the truth. I have soaps and gloves and brushes and a broom and a vacuum and this incredible American product called Javex and another called Windex — so you don't have to buy anything. Give me another ten dollars and I will help you find someone to sell you secondhand furniture very cheap, but very good, and I will even help you carry it. That I will do because you have visited Africa and because your mother comes from Winnipeg. Forty-five dollars won't kill you, but it will help me very much. What do you say?"

I said yes.

We crossed the street again. I paid Elvina Peck from my wallet. I also paid Yoyo. Elvina gave me the key.

"You shouldn't walk the streets with that kind of money, son. This is Baltimore. This is not Canada."

"I had to pay, and you said cash."

"Don't get logical with me, son. I'm saying you walk these streets with that kind of money, some thug will knock you silly with a crowbar — and that's on a good day."

I thanked her for the advice, shook her hand, and stepped out the door. Yoyo remained inside, asked me to wait, and closed the door most of the way.

"Mrs. Peck," I heard him say, "you remember our agreement."

"What agreement?"

Yoyo sighed audibly. "We have an agreement, an honorable agreement, I hasten to add."

"What agreement?"

"Mrs. Peck, I am a perfect tenant. I keep your place spicky-span."

"It's spic and span. But get to the point."

"You said fifty dollars off my rent if I find you a good tenant."

"I said that? When?"

"You said it last year, when I moved in."

"Well, all right, if I said it, I said it. On the first of next month, if he's still here, and if he's paid me on time, I'll give you fifty dollars off."

"Thank you. You should let me clean your place sometime. I would clean your whole house for just forty-five dollars."

"Are you out of your mind? Men can't clean. I have outlived one son and two husbands and none of them ever cleaned anything except their own teeth."

"Spicky-span, in the great tradition of African cleanliness, I tell you," Yoyo said. "If the men you knew didn't clean, it's because they were Americans, all offense intended."

"*No* offense intended, Yoyo. You say, *no* offense intended."

"Yes, that's right, no offense intended. They were Americans. Americans can put a man on the moon. I saw a show on TV says they can even slide a tiny little microscope into your veins and look inside your body, look at your heart, your knees, whatever. Americans know how to do lots of things, but they don't know how to make coffee, they don't know how to barbecue meat, and they don't know how to clean houses. But I am not an American. I am a Cameroonian. My father knew how to clean, and his father before him. All the men in my family line knew how to clean, and if you just pay me forty-five dollars, you will see that I can make your house spicky-span top to bottom, money-back guaranteed."

"Spic and span, hunh? And if I'm not happy I get my money back?"

"That is the abject truth."

"Who you calling abject? Young man, you talk faster than a cyclone."

"I'm not so young, Mrs. Peck."

"As far as I'm concerned, you're younger than I am by a long sight and will stay that way till long after I'm dead and gone. Let's talk about that cleaning another time. Go help your friend."

Yoyo stepped outside. We walked down the steps together. He asked me when I'd be moving in. I asked him to help me find some furniture the next day. Yoyo said he could help me in the morning. In the afternoon, he'd be selling kebabs. Yoyo asked for my key. He said he would clean my flat late that evening.

I showed up at Yoyo's door at nine o'clock sharp. He opened it before I could knock. I had already forgotten how black the man was. He was as black as coal. He was so black, he was almost blue. He was so black that even his irises and his pupils seemed one color.

"Hello, my friend. Come upstairs. Look at your apartment."

It was transformed. The walls gleamed. The floors were shining, the cobwebs gone, the bathtub stain greatly diminished, the fridge and stovetop and windows glistening. I stomped on the rug and saw no dust rise. Yoyo said he had cleaned my apartment during the night. He didn't like wasting time cleaning during the day. Daytime was for making money on the street.

Yoyo took me along to meet a student who was about to move out of her apartment at Charles and Thirty-first. He negotiated a single mattress and box spring, a lamp, two chairs, a table, and some pots and pans and kitchen utensils, claiming all the time to be the buyer, and asking my opinion about goods that he should or shouldn't purchase. He played up the poor-Cameroonian-refugee role and bought all the stuff for sixty dollars, and got the student — a young woman from Weldon, North Carolina — to throw in two bath towels, two washcloths, and three dishtowels for free.

We carried the stuff by hand. It took us four trips, and Yoyo hurried me the whole time. We completed the buying and moving in less than two hours. Yoyo left me sweating on one of my new chairs.

"I have to go. Time to make money. Stay cool, my friend."

Chapter 9

MILLICENT ESMERELDA CANE was my father's older sister, and I had never met her. As far as I could tell, she and my father had not seen each other in years. My father habitually denied that anything had set them apart. Once, when I was a teenager, he said to me: "Sure I love her. She's my sister. But she's down there and I'm up here, so why make a fuss of it?" I didn't believe him. I already knew that Mill had skipped my parents' wedding, and that she had a thing about blacks staying within the race, and that she had never married — but that was all I knew.

It wasn't hard to find her house. The phone book showed an M. E. Cane on Robertson Avenue. I drove by and saw a woman on the porch gesticulating at a man who was backing away. I parked and walked up the stone path. The man now struggled toward me with a heavy box in his arms. I heard him mutter, "Damn that old bat." The box was open. I saw several volumes of the *American Encyclopedia*.

I walked up to my Aunt Mill. She was, as my father once said, as big as a house. Her forehead was pulpy, she had three chins, and she just got bigger and bigger from there on down. She looked at me over the rims of her half-moon glasses. "He *told* me I could return them at any time, and I'm returning them, so that's just too bad, isn't it? But man! He talked so much I wanted to hit him. On and on and on he went. So what do *you* want?" I said I was her nephew. "I ain't got any white nephews. Not around here. So git off my — Wait!" She pulled the glasses down to the nub of her nose.

"I'm Langston Cane. The Fifth."

"You Cane men pass that name down the line like it was an antique table," Mill chortled.

"I don't know what you have to laugh about, with a name like Millicent Esmerelda."

"Oh my, he's lippy, just like his daddy. I guess I got no choice but to tell you to step on up, Langston Cane the Fifth. You're not in trouble, are you? Drugs? Guns? Police after you?"

"No."

"I shouldn't have asked. Look at you. You walk like a prep school boy. You ought to move your backside when you walk. Roll your butt and straighten your back. Around here, you have to look like a predator."

"I've been walking this way all my life. I'm not going to change now."

"Don't come after me for money, 'cause I ain't got any. So you can just call up your daddy if you —"

I stopped climbing the steps. "I don't need your money or his."

"Hit your funny bone, did I? Well, git on up these steps. And pick up that *Baltimore Sun*. You'll spare me bending down, which is a good thing, 'cause when I sink that low, I've got no way to get back up."

I handed her the newspaper and stepped inside. Mill's house

looked and smelled like a mausoleum. I didn't believe she had ever opened a window or pulled back a curtain. Her shelves, desk, table, even the top of her television were covered with sculptures and mugs splashed with the names of foreign cities. Her living room looked like the inside of a Niagara Falls tourist shop. But the most striking thing was her collection of teddy bears. She had imitation grizzlies, kodiacs, polar bears, and bears brown and black. She had bears of every size and shape. They occupied bookshelves, perched on chairs, and saluted from above the fridge.

"Siddown here, let me get this *Sunday Post* off the chair."

Mill looked for a place to put the newspaper and finally shoved it into the garbage bin. The paper began to rise out of the bin. She battered it back down with the heel of her palm.

"What can I get you?"

"Nothing, thanks. I've eaten."

"Good. 'Cause I don't have much here. I usually order in. I only cook for the people at church. And that's more than I care for. It's beyond me how any woman could spend her life cooking for a husband." Mill edged the glasses back down her nose. She was darker than my father. Her cheekbones jutted out, prominent even on her fleshy face. I could hear her low, regular wheezing. The pouches under her eyes were wrinkled and black, but the eyes themselves were alert. I felt them resting on my face. "I heard you lost a baby, and that things didn't work out with your wife. That's too bad."

I looked at her, suddenly aware of how alone I felt. Barring the trip to Mali, this was the first time in years that I had traveled without Ellen.

"How did you know about that?"

"I hear from Aberdeen from time to time. So how are your parents and brother?"

"They're fine."

"Your father is retired now?"

"Semi-retired. He sees patients in the afternoons, a few days a week. My mother still helps him. Does his books, handles appointments. Sean, as you probably heard, is a lawyer."

"I heard he was doing very well."

"That's true. He's a good man."

"You were supposed to be the bright one, though. I heard about all those scholarships you got."

"That was a long time ago."

"True enough. So what are you doing in this no-good city? Why in the world would you leave Canada? You ought to be up there right now, making up with your wife."

"We're divorced."

"I don't know what you want in Baltimore, but I can't help you. I've been getting along fine by myself for more years than you've been living, and I ain't about to let things get all stirred up now. How about we say good-bye? I might see you-all up in Canada one day — 'cause I'm meaning to get up there. I spent part of my childhood in Oakville, you know." With a great effort, Mill lifted herself up off the couch. She walked with her back bent.

I got up. "Take care of yourself, Mill."

"You look like a baby, you know that? You've got a cute little baby face." As I brushed by her on my way to the door, she slipped something into my shirt pocket. "That's in case you're short."

I picked out the fifty-dollar bill. "I didn't come here for money." She wouldn't take it back. I put it down on a teddy bear. She slapped it up and stuffed it into my pocket as I stepped outside. I slipped it in her mailbox and jogged down her steps.

"Good-bye, son," she called out.

"Bye, Mill."

I walked down the path toward Sarah.

"That your car?" she called out. I nodded my head as I unlocked the door. "Ugly little thing. Is that what people drive in Canada?"

"We've just got this one model."

"Don't mock me, son. I'm not as dumb as I look. Where you staying?"

"Three-oh-eight Adell Street. In Charles Village."

"Good. Down here in West Baltimore, black folks would eat you up."

"There are black folks in Charles Village."

"Not the same kind," she said. "Around here, folks would use you for target practice. Well, if the police lock you up, don't call me for bail." I looked at her evenly. "I don't hold no grudge against you, boy, even if your pappy did marry a white gal. It's just that I don't want to see you, is all."

I drove away. In the rearview mirror, I saw her watching right up until I turned the corner.

Charles Village didn't have a lot of shops and restaurants. In Toronto, a neighborhood teeming with students would have had delis and coffee houses on every block. Not Charles Village. The only place to eat on St. Paul Street was the Homewood Deli. It was gritty, unpretentious, and cheap. It served croissants, but on paper plates. Come to think of it, it didn't sell a lot of croissants. More popular were grits, scrapple, corn biscuits, pastrami, and chipped beef. The Homewood sold regular coffee — none of the funny varieties with South American names and injections of steamed milk.

I got a window table at the Homewood and ordered chipped beef and coffee and got a refill after that. I wrote about the meeting with Mill and gathered up those pages and all the stuff I'd written so far and stuffed them in a big envelope and scribbled down Ellen's address and almost mailed off the whole thing before I changed my mind. I had also written a few drafts of a cover note. The first draft said, *I've been thinking of you, Ellen.* That got torn up. The second one said, *Still love you, kid.* I shredded that, too. The third one, which I finally crumpled and threw out, said, *I still think of you.* I resolved to go on discovering and writing about my family history, but decided that sending it to Ellen would do no good.

I saw Yoyo go out at about eight one night with a bucket of sponges, detergents, rags, and rubber gloves. He crossed the street, rang at Elvina's door, and went in. Later that night, I heard him return to his rooms downstairs, whistling. I pulled a pillow over my head and tried to sleep.

The next morning, we stepped outside at the same time. Yoyo had his barbecuing stand and two folding picnic stools under one arm, and bags holding food, charcoal, and utensils in another. I walked with him to the corner of Thirty-second and North Calvert. Yoyo placed two baking dishes of marinated and skewered meat on a picnic stool. He covered them with ice packs and supermarket bags. I poured coals into his barbecue stand and lit a few starter cubes. Yoyo bought fast-acting charcoal to minimize his set-up time. He never set up in the same location two days in a row. He avoided busy streets, and offered a free kebab to anyone walking into or out of any house next to where he worked. Yoyo set out his special sauces in bowls on the sidewalk. One was labeled *Crocodile sauce — hot!* and the other *Cameroonian magic — mild.* The coals took fifteen minutes to burn and lick with flames, and settle into gray, glowing embers. Yoyo laid four kebabs on the grill. He gave me two dollars, and instructed me to cross the street and wait for someone to approach. Then I was to beat that person to the barbecue stand, order a kebab immediately, and rave about it for as long as anyone would listen. It sounded corny to me, but it worked. Two young men stopped and listened to me and bought a kebab each. Others came behind. Yoyo sold another fifteen kebabs in five minutes. After that came a lull. I said I had to be getting along.

"What do you do during the day?" he asked.

"I look around. Think. Visit the city."

"This is a holiday for you? You are vacationing in Baltimore?"

"Not exactly. I'm not vacationing. I have no job."

"I could help you set up in another part of the city. You buy everything and you sell everything and you just give me a 30 percent cut for the first two weeks. You can make money selling meat. Americans like meat — especially when it's good and cheap and they can eat without having to sit down. For Americans, it's always run run run. Shall I help you set up tomorrow?"

"No, thanks, Yoyo. I'll help you from time to time, but I'm not interested. It's not what I do."

"But you're not doing anything. You have no job."

"I have no job, but I am doing something."

"What?"

I wasn't sure how to explain to Yoyo that I was trying to reconstruct the lives of my ancestors. Three more kebab buyers came along, so I took off.

Chapter 10

Two weeks passed. If I couldn't connect with Mill, I'd never get any serious family research done. I resolved to try again.

I dragged myself out of bed at six-thirty on a Sunday morning. Whose brilliant idea was it to set church services so early? If Sunday was supposed to be a day of rest, why did churchgoers have to get out of bed so early? I shampooed my hair and picked it out and shaved, and wondered if there would be anybody — one solitary soul — in the African Methodist Episcopal Church congregation that morning with a complexion as light as mine.

I had called the church the day before.

"Bethel A.M.E., good morning and praise the Lord," said a young woman on the telephone. I asked about hours of the Sunday services. Seven-thirty, ten, and one in the afternoon, I was told.

"Seven-thirty in the morning?" I asked. "Do you get anybody out that early?"

She giggled. "You're not from around here, are you?"

"You could say that."

"Seven-thirty is our most popular time. Have you been saved?"

"Saved?"

"Has Jesus entered your soul?"

"Not to my knowledge."

"Then you'd better come at seven-thirty."

"Why?" Perhaps the early service had a special section for hopeless sinners.

"The sooner you get down here, the less chance there is that something else happens first."

"Something else?"

"Your heart could give out. A bus could knock you over. Somebody could shoot you. This *is* Baltimore."

"You ought to get a job welcoming tourists. Any other reason?"

"Our security guards watch the cars parked for the seven-thirty service. You can park in safety and locate your automobile after Jesus has saved you."

"And if he doesn't save me this first time around?"

"Your car will still be there, honey. The Lord has time on his hands."

It was a fine, sunny morning. Two cardinals, blood red, perched on a branch over my car. I drove south on St. Paul, then west on Twenty-ninth. I saw a man and a woman running north on Charles Street. No other soul on the street, no other cars in motion, and they didn't see me coming. They stopped at Twenty-ninth and kissed. She ran away from him, and he gave chase.

I saw no other people and no cars in motion until I got to Druid Hill Avenue and saw a stream of cars heading south, which was the way I had to go. Behind just about every wheel was a woman. Every woman was black. Just about every one was old enough to be my mother. And every one wore a church hat. I put aside my city map. These women would guide me to the Lord.

They guided me south on Druid Hill Avenue into the old heart of the black community. The area had thrived in the time of my grandfather, but now it was neglected and withering. It was at least sixty degrees Fahrenheit. In the lanes bisecting Druid Hill, I saw men stretched out against stone walls, sleeping or dead. Half the stores had boards nailed across the windows. The other half had iron grates guarding every possible point of entry. On the sidewalks, I saw pop cans, popsicle sticks, and syringes. On the ledge outside a window above a corner variety store, I saw a small American flag perched inside an apple juice can. Nobody moved. Nobody was in sight. Seven on a Sunday morning, and all that moved were the cars ahead of me, driven by women in church hats.

I saw hats with purple flowers, pink ribbons, yellow lace, blue thread. I saw hair under the influence of gels and sprays. I saw not one bare head. And I saw few men. Most of these cars were big American models, Fords and Buicks with V-8 engines. Their doors were locked and windows sealed. I had the sense that if these suburban interlopers had their druthers, they would enter the inner city in army tanks. I rolled up the windows of my Volkswagen Jetta.

South of Mosher Street, the women started pulling over and parking. Dark men in dark suits drew the women forward with their fingers, helping them park within a foot of each other.

I parked at the corner of Druid Hill and Lafayette. I was glad that my hair was longer than usual, and combed out into an afro, because I didn't want to be seen as a white visitor. I wanted my race clearly marked. I got out of the car.

One of the street ushers closed the door for me. *"Salaam Alaikham,"* he said.

"Wa Alaikham Salaam," I answered, glad to have traveled enough in Africa to have heard the salutation. I knew it was used by the Nation of Islam in America, and wondered why Nation of Islam converts were helping suburban blacks get to an A.M.E. church.

"Visiting from Ontario, are you?" the brother said, noting my license plates.

"Sure am."

"Have a safe visit."

"Thank you."

"Don't linger after the service. It ends at eight-thirty, and this neighborhood wakes up at eight-forty-five."

"Are you going into the service, too?"

"No, sir. I stay out here with my brothers and watch the cars. You could leave your windows down. You could leave your keys in the ignition. Nobody will touch your car."

He was a young kid, no older than eighteen. Tall and skinny, but the suit fit him perfectly.

"Can I ask you a dumb question?" I said.

"No question is dumb."

"Are you a Muslim?"

"No, brother. I'm a member of the A.M.E. youth congregation. My parents been at this church, and their parents before them, since the turn of the century."

"Then why'd you give me a Nation of Islam greeting?"

"That's just the way around here, brother. NOI is cool. And it's not just a Muslim greeting. It's an African greeting. We're all Africans, aren't we? Aren't we, brother?"

"Yes, we are." I grinned at him. "Except for those of us who are, well, half brothers."

He grinned back. "Nobody's counting halves and quarters. If you're one of us, it's that simple. End of conversation."

I turned to look at the A.M.E. church, one block down. "I'd better get going. Don't want to miss the service."

"Well, brother, since you asked me a question, let me ask you one. I saw you coming with that Ontario license plate, and I just *knew* that you wouldn't know what I was saying when I gave you the greeting, but you had to go and prove me wrong. Where'd you learn that stuff?"

"I belong to the Nation of Islam."

He gave out a chortle. "I never saw no Nation of Islam man wearing brown socks with blue trousers. Not outa the house, anyway. And you're from Canada. It's too cold up there for Muslims."

I could have told him I'd traveled a lot in Africa, but he might have thought I was bragging. So I just said, "I've been around."

"You ain't been anywhere like Baltimore. Have a good day now."

I fell in behind two elderly women on the sidewalk. The taller one had the build of a linebacker. She wore high heels, panty hose, and a white hat with one yellow feather pointing skyward, as if to say, "You mess with me, and you'll have to mess with Him." The other woman was six inches shorter and as wiry as a turkey. She jolted forward with robotic, staccato steps. For an instant, I wondered if she was performing a pantomime. Her hat was the color of orange sherbet. It sat on a bald head. I knew this because I saw her take off her hat and whack her companion's sleeve.

"Got 'im," said the short, bald one.

"What you hitting me for, girl?"

"I got 'im, Maggie. A hornet was fixing to sting you."

"Ain't no hornets on this street. Ain't no people, neither."

"We're here, Maggie. We got a congregation of a thousand people."

"We don't live on Druid Hill Avenue. We're like aliens. We land for an hour and then we take off."

"You run that mouth of yours nearly as much as my husband does."

"I love you to pieces, Eleanor, but don't you mention me in the same breath as that no-account, dimwitted numskull."

Eleanor laughed, shaking her arms out. "You know what that man did last night? He called out for me to bring him a beer."

"Hasn't he been doing that for forty-three years?"

Eleanor said, "Yes, but he was sitting in the bath. Here I was, making lunch for after church today, and he calls out for a beer in the bath."

"I'd a poured that beer on his head. You oughta quit givin' that man money for drink."

"Only thing he's good for is eating and drinking."

"You oughta divorce him," Maggie said.

"People don't get divorced at seventy-eight years of age," Eleanor said. "It's too late."

"Then you oughta kill 'im."

"He's barely living now. And I can't kill 'im. He ain't valuable enough to kill. I'll leave that business to the Lord. It's too late for me, Maggie. I'm stuck with that man to the grave."

"Ugh! Anybody ever put me to rest beside my no-good ex-husband, I swear to God, the six o'clock news would be talking about a second Resurrection. I'd climb out of my own grave faster than Jesus. I wouldn't even spend the night."

Eleanor, the short, bald one, slapped her hands together and bent over in laughter. "You oughta watch your mouth, Maggie. That's not Sunday language."

Maggie stopped to adjust her purse. I walked up beside them on the sidewalk, and caught Eleanor looking at me.

"Good morning," I said.

"Praise the Lord," Eleanor said.

"Is that the A.M.E. church?" I asked.

"Sure is," Eleanor said. "You visiting?"

"I sure am."

"Where you from?" This came from Maggie, who snapped her purse shut.

"Canada."

"Canada. My, my. That's a long way off. You have relations here?"

"Just an aunt. I think she's a member of the A.M.E. congregation."

"What's her name?" Maggie asked.

"Millicent Cane. You know her?"

"Millie Cane? Sure we know Millie! You're Millie Cane's nephew?" Maggie edged her glasses down her nose. "Good God Almighty, you don't look like any relation of Millie Cane. You're pushing white, son. Pushing awful hard."

"Leave him be, Maggie," Eleanor said. "Most folks that light would just go ahead and pass. They wouldn't come on back to the A.M.E. church. Leave him be, I say. Welcome, son. Welcome to Baltimore. Is Millie expecting you?"

"No. But I'm sure I'll bump into her."

"I wouldn't count on that," Maggie said. "We got a thousand people comin' out on Sunday mornings. But we'll find her for you. Help me up these steps, son. I got arthritis. Days like this, I get the feeling my bones are made of potato chips."

I extended my right arm, and Maggie took hold of it. Eleanor took my left arm, clawing it like a bird. We ascended eight steps into the church foyer.

Five young men dressed in black suits, clean shaven, hair cut so short it looked almost shaven, too, stood by three piles of newspapers. The *Afro-American*, the *Baltimore Sun*, and the *Washington Post* were each stacked so high they came up past my waist.

"Newspaper?" one of them asked me.

I hesitated. I wanted one, but didn't want to bring it into the church.

"You pay an extra fifty cents here," Eleanor said, "but it goes to the church scholarship fund."

"I'll get one on my way out," I said.

"That's what we all do. But you pay now. That way there's no lineup when you're heading out. You just take one and go."

I paid with a ten-dollar bill for the *Afro-American* and the *Post*. The young vendor pocketed the bill and ignored me. I checked the handwritten signs by the newspaper stacks. They listed the prices as three-fifty for the *Post* and two dollars for the *Afro-American*.

"Don't you owe me change?" I said.

"We don't make change," he said.

"You owe me four-fifty."

"You gave me ten dollars. You asking for it back?"

Maggie stuck her face into the nose of the young vendor. "This man has come all the way from Canada to attend this service. He helped me up the steps, and he's agreed to buy two papers. Now you put that black hand of yours into that cheap linen pocket and dig out some change this minute."

The young man slapped four ones and fifty cents on top of the newspaper stack. I retrieved the change.

"What's the matter with you?" I asked him.

"Ain't there enough white churches where you-all come from?"

Maggie slapped the man. Snapped his head right back. "Shame on you. Shame on you. You got no sense of manners, have you? You're all mouth. You're uncouth. I ever hear you speaking like that again, I'll tie you up like a butterball turkey and roll you down the street."

Eleanor steered me inside. "Uncouth, uncouth, uncouth," she muttered. "Maggie did right to slap that cretin. A little bit of violence never did any harm."

Eleanor sat with me in a pew while Maggie looked for Mill. The sanctuary had room for more than a thousand parishioners. In the back, above the entrance, was a balcony for spillover crowds. The men were dressed in browns, grays, and blacks, but the women were made out like peacocks. I saw orange, yellow, red, purple, white, green, rose, blue. I was undoubtedly the lightest-skinned and the worst-dressed in the church. Some of the women wore long African robes. Eleanor saw me looking at them.

"You ever been to Africa?" she asked me. I told her that I had. "People dress like that over there?" I told her that the ones who could afford to did, at special events. "Well, these women have never been to Africa. They just got it in them to look African. I could never wear one of those robes. To me, it's putting on airs."

We sat silently for a moment. Then Eleanor said, "I bet you was sweetness indeed, when you was born. You hardly weigh a thing. Slim shoulders, practically no backside, little head, I bet you was easy as pie to bring into this world. Your mama was lucky. My first son weighed eleven pounds two ounces and he came so close to killing me that I nearly killed him. Know what he weighs now?" I looked at her with eyebrows raised. "Would you believe three hundred and thirty-three pounds? Sits in a regular kitchen chair, he breaks it. Has to take a bus, he needs two seats. He's the size of two grown men and they still call him Junior. Here comes your aunt, boy! Here comes Millie."

Mill had her hair up in a bun. Her eyebrows were pulled up, too. She came alongside Maggie — and looked just as big and solid. "What you come to the Lord's House for, son? I thought you were a Canadian atheist."

"I wanted to see the church where my grandfather ministered. I wasn't going to bother you, but your friends insisted on finding you."

Maggie broke in. "You came all this way and didn't want to see your own flesh and blood?"

"Oh, he wants to see me all right. But I don't want to see him," Mill said.

"What you saying?" Maggie said. "You've got yourself a perfect nephew. Little washed out, color wise, but that ain't his fault."

Mill slid in beside me. With her eyes, Maggie ordered Eleanor to move over so that she, Maggie, could sit on my other side. When Maggie started chatting with Eleanor, Mill elbowed me. "I told you I don't have any money, son."

"And I told you I don't want it."

"But you want something. So what is it?"

A woman took to the pulpit before I could speak. She began praising the Lord.

"Is she the minister?" I asked.

"She's the warm-up act," Mill said. "She gets to holler and shout, but she doesn't get to call herself preacher, so nobody listens to her."

Next came the choir, which cawed out a horrid version of "Bridge Over Troubled Water."

"Anybody ever tell you that all black people can sing, just send 'em on over here on Sunday morning," Mill said, yawning.

"Tired?"

"I cooked until midnight and was back at it at five this morning."

"For what?"

"Hot lunch after the service."

"For the members of the congregation?"

"And their guests. It's served around nine in the morning, but we call it lunch, since we've all been up since God knows what hour. Lunch is five dollars, if you're interested. But we give it out for free to anyone who shows up at our back door. It's for the homeless. It was your granddaddy's idea." The choir was followed by deacons' statements. Then came the minister. "This man can't hold a candle to your grandfather."

"Why?"

"He has no power. He's into highjinks, like all the modern preachers. He hasn't been speaking for two minutes, and he's already in high gear. He's got no more timing than a bull has with cows. Your granddaddy was quiet and severe, but he gave the congregation something to think about. People these days just want dancing and screaming. They all want to carry on like Pentacostalists."

"You were right when you said that I wanted something from you," I told her.

"You want to know all about your daddy and your granddaddy and so on. But why should I talk to you? I don't like your father. I don't like your mother. And I can't say I like you." Mill held her hand against her mouth to hide a grin. I let her last words stand, to make her live with them.

The service went on for an hour. It felt a marathon. I don't know how anyone managed to sit through it, except by dint of practice or the ability to sleep while sitting with one's head straight. It was broken, occasionally, by the choir, and by the universal obligation to get up and walk by a collection hat as the minister and his acolytes watched the size of the bill that fell from your hand. Then there were prayers, and Bible readings, more prayers, announcements, the sermon — and designated moments for people to swoon in the arms of Jesus.

"Don't believe a word of it," Mill said as one woman after another got up and screamed and had to be revived.

It struck me as a miracle that the entire congregation hadn't fallen asleep. I felt hungry, and itchy, and anxious to talk. Maggie, Eleanor, Mill, and I ended up together at a table in the church cafeteria. I paid for my lunch and for Mill's before she could open her purse. "I don't need anybody paying my way, son," she said. "But I guess I have to give you one family story now, to get you off my back."

"What kind of story?" Eleanor asked.

"I'll tell you one about my father, Langston Cane the Third, who ministered at this church."

Mill said Langston Cane the Third took over the Bethel A.M.E. Church on Druid Hill Avenue in 1930. "We had just moved to Baltimore after seven or so years in Oakville, and my father — your grandfather — didn't like Baltimore one bit. By comparison, it was cramped, crowded, dirty, and uncivil. Although the Bethel A.M.E. Church had a large congregation, it was short of money. It was running a deficit. Yet Cane believed that parishioners were giving generously.

"They called him the Reverend L.C. He wasn't a tall man, but he stood so upright and dignified and walked so much like an African head of state that people thought he was taller. People thought he stood six feet tall, although he was just five ten."

I knew the story. My father had told it to me ten times.

When Reverend L.C. took over the church, he found that money was draining away from it faster than water through a sieve. It had a five-thousand-dollar deficit that was growing larger every month. The membership had taken a beating in the last year; the immensely popular preceding pastor had left and created his own church, taking with him a third of the A.M.E. congregation. The Reverend L.C. had to stanch the hemorrhage of A.M.E. members and win back some who had left. On one hand, he had to take strong actions. But on another, the wrong actions would drive even more members away.

For several consecutive Sundays, the Reverend counted the number of people in his sanctuary. He watched, row after row, to see how many people were dropping money into the bowls. He knew he had six hundred members, and he believed that four hundred and fifty of them were giving, at an average rate of fifty cents each. That would have meant $225 each Sunday. But the collection was consistently turning up no more than $120. The Reverend assigned a volunteer from the Young People's Bible Study group to assist the woman in charge of collections, Rita Dougall. But Rita Dougall always managed to get away from the young man before she sealed the money in an envelope and turned it over to Langston's wife, Rose.

Rita Dougall was a mainstay of the church. She knew every member. Her mother and grandmother had been active members; her father had once been the church secretary. She baked cookies and supplied lemonade for every church function, and had other church members to dinner every Sunday night. If she left the church, she would take seventy-five people with her. For the past five years, she had managed the Sunday collections.

The Reverend calculated that Rita was skimming a hundred

dollars a week off the top. Probably sharing the proceeds with the bishop.

He knew he couldn't confront her without direct proof. He couldn't remove her arbitrarily from the position — she would fight for it, and pull people away from the church if she were forced out. The idea hit Reverend L.C. one Saturday night as he worked on a sermon. He would talk about the importance of volunteer service. He would describe it as the backbone of a community. He would hail some of the most generous volunteers in the history of the Bethel A.M.E. Church, and, as he was approaching the current era, he would say that volunteers were so critical to the functioning of the modern-day church that he planned to host a reception for them soon.

The promise of a celebration sent a hum of excitement through the sanctuary. The next Sunday, to a bigger congregation than had been seen in months, the Reverend L.C. announced that a volunteer awards ceremony would be held by the church — hosted by the Reverend and his wife — in three weeks' time. There would be a free lunch before the ceremony, speeches made, and certificates of recognition handed out.

The Reverend and his wife organized the event. Rose and other volunteers baked for days, setting aside cookies and cakes and pies. The Reverend had certificates typed and framed, consulted with five church seniors to make sure nobody was left out, wrote a paragraph of praise about the good works of each award recipient, and developed the major award for Rita Dougall, the collections maestro.

At the climax of the ceremony, the Reverend made a twenty-minute speech about Rita's good works, presented her with a certificate, a bouquet of flowers, and a formal letter of thanks from the bishop, and awarded her with the new title of director of youth services. Another person — a close ally of the Reverend's — was made collections coordinator. Rita Dougall was edged out of the money by being promoted.

"He was a clever weasel, your granddaddy," Mill said. "Time for me to get on home. Why don't you find your manners and offer to drive me?"

"I didn't know you didn't have a car," I said.

"I have a car. But I don't like driving downtown. Too many fools on the road for me."

"You're fortunate to have a fine young man drive you home," Eleanor said. "I can't get my own husband to drive me to church."

"Never you mind about this so-called fine young man," Mill said. "If he's so fine, what's he doing in Baltimore? Where's his family? Where is he working? Where are his wife and children and pay cheque?"

"Shush," Maggie said. "Don't judge people so harshly, Mill. Especially, don't judge on the Lord's day, in His building."

"I wasn't judging nothing. I was just asking questions."

"Judgmental questions," Maggie said.

"Oh, leave me alone," Mill said, "and stop judging my questions." They all laughed.

"Don't forget to pick up your papers on the way out," Maggie told me.

Mill held on to my arm on the walk to the Jetta. It was still there, with windows and wheels intact. Nobody was guarding it any more. It was one of the few cars still parked on Druid Hill Avenue. Mill told me to turn left on North Street and right on Hilton and left on Alto, and then I'd find my way to her street again — and then she began to snore. She awoke with a start when I turned off the ignition in front of her house.

"Come on in, son, and tell me what it is you want." Mill kicked a *National Geographic* magazine out of her way as she stepped into the hall.

"I want to know about my father. And his father. And the two Langston Canes before them."

"Why?" She indicated for me to sit down. I sat in a sofa that sank a foot on contact.

"I just need to know."

"Why don't you just get on with having a job and starting a family and forget all that stuff?"

"Can't do that."

"You're not one of them, I guess. You're not a real Cane. You've fallen off the treadmill, or never gotten on it. You like to look about you. You're more like a woman. Women like to look about them. Men charge straight ahead."

"I don't know about the man-woman thing. Some men charge ahead, others don't."

"What kind of stories do you want to hear?" Mill asked.

"Stories about my father, and grandfather, and my great- and great-great-grandfathers, and their wives. Stories about you, too."

"I'm not telling you any stories about myself, or about your father. But say I tell you something about the others. What are you going to do with it?"

"Write about it."

"Write what?" Mill asked.

"A novel."

"How are you going to do that? I don't have enough stuff to fill a whole book."

"I'll use my imagination to fill in the holes."

"You'll be using a lot of imagination, in that case. What's the point of filling most of a book with your imagination?"

"That's what writers do. That's what I want to do."

"Well, don't ask me to read it. But if you have your mind set on writing a book, I'm not going to stand in your way. Come with me."

I followed Mill down a dusty hall and into an old bedroom overflowing with boxes, chairs, books, domestic goods. "This box, here," she said, tapping it with her foot, "has stuff on your grandparents. You can look at it if you want. But only this box."

The cardboard box had letters, high school photos, certificates, church documents, and transcripts of oral history interviews that Langston the Third and Rose had given. I opened an old letter. Its corners crumbled. It was dated April 1917. One year before they were married.

"My dear pagan buzzard," it began. "The carnations were beautiful. Thank you! But we can't go on like this. My parents would never consent to my being courted by a Protestant, and I have trouble seeing the viability of it myself. Although, I must add, that you fly a league or two higher than most all of the world's pagan buzzards. There are other fish in the sea. Cast your net accordingly. With sisterly affection, Rose."

A response, also dated April 1917:

> Dear Rose,
>
> How about a photo, so that I might contemplate your sisterly affections, and consider how to convert them into something less austere? All's well at Lincoln. Am keeping first-class grades, although I don't know what I'll do next year, with the war heating up. With a kiss blown your way, Langston.

Chapter 11

LANGSTON CANE THE THIRD was the fourth of nine children of Langston Cane the Second and Lucinda Richards. His father was also an A.M.E. minister, and Langston the Third was born in 1896 in the family's parsonage in Annapolis, Maryland. His meager education in the local segregated school was supplemented for an hour each evening by lessons from his father in spelling, arithmetic, geography, and African American history. That was what his father called it, even at that time. "People will call you all sorts of names, but don't you listen to them. In this house, you're an African American. And don't you forget it. Look at your skin. Look at it. Be proud of that color, son. It marks your African heritage. Your heritage is as rich as the Nile is long." By the time Langston was twelve, the lessons included memorizing the Lord's Prayer in Latin, and learning phrases in Greek and French. Langston senior reinforced the lessons with the back of his hand when his son failed to pay attention. After the lessons came Langston's chores. He washed dishes. He washed the kitchen floor. And he pumped well water, even in the wind and rain. Snow fell only a few times each year, but the wind off Chesapeake Bay was almost enough to knock him down.

In 1908, Langston's father became the minister of the biggest A.M.E. church in Baltimore. He oversaw its move to a new location on Druid Hill Avenue, and found a part-time job for his son at the *Afro-American* newspaper on Saratoga Street. Langston learned about copy editing and typesetting. He ran errands. He lifted stacks of papers from a livery wagon. He was paid seventy-five cents a week, in pennies counted out one by one by the magnanimous publisher, F. Y. Pickard, whom Langston secretly dubbed Fuck You Pickard. Pickard knew everybody in town, received free tickets to every show at the Royal Theater, got free meals from the segregated restaurants, and carried on as if he were Napoleon Bonaparte. He lectured to Langston about clean living. He hectored him about conscientious work habits. He babbled endlessly about discipline and education, of which he had none. One week, Langston neglected to enter Pickard's edits to a sentence about a restaurant that he favored. The copy, as submitted by a college student, described the restaurant as "serving good meals within the colored community." Pickard, who hated the word "colored" and was always trying to find ways around it, had scribbled "superlative repasts for people of our race" on the copy, but Langston forgot to retype the review. As a result, Pickard ranted and raved and docked Langston's pay for the week. Langston was infuriated. He'd been counting on buying a ticket to see Ruby Blake play piano at the Royal that Friday.

The next week, Pickard edited copy about a tenor from D.C. who was coming to sing at the Royal. The article went on about the tenor's accomplishments and performances around the country. But one line mistakenly said "the unknown tenor from Washington, D.C." instead of "the well-known tenor from

Washington, D.C." Pickard failed to catch it. Langston, in a spirit of vengeance, chose to overlook it. Pickard berated Langston when the newspaper came out and the complaints flooded in. Langston replied that he had carried out Pickard's edits to the letter, and how was he to know that Pickard had wanted it to be "well-known" instead of "unknown"? Pickard replied, "For the same reason that, for the second consecutive week, I'm going to make your salary unknown to you."

"You can't do that."

"You'll call me Dr. Pickard if you please."

Langston knew from his father that Pickard's only doctorate was in bullshit. The man hadn't been to college.

"You can't do that, sir."

"And why can't I do that, young man?"

"Because I worked for that money. I worked ten hours last week and you gave me nothing after one small mistake. And I worked ten hours this week and you're giving me nothing after one small mistake. I am an African American, of the same race as Hannibal, who defeated the Romans in the Alps, and if you don't pay me the two weeks I'm due, I will defeat you."

"I don't believe the world has ever seen that much mouth on a twelve-year-old. And just how do you plan to defeat me?"

"I will tell everyone that you refused to pay me. Everyone I know will refuse to read your paper. Every guest that eats at my father's table. Every parishioner who knocks on my parents' door. Every parent of every friend of mine in school. We will boycott your paper. We will mount pickets."

"Take your miserable pay. You ought to be a lawyer."

Langston pocketed the silver dollar and the half dollar — the first time he'd been paid in something other than pennies. "Oh, and Mr. Pickard?"

"It's Dr. Pickard to you!"

"F. Y. Pickard?"

"Did you hear me? It's Dr. Pickard."

"You are no doctor. You didn't even finish school."

"Your insolence is otherworldly! Wait till your father hears how you've spoken."

"You're no doctor at all. My daddy told me. You're a fake, Mr. Pickard, and I quit."

"You're fired."

"I'm afraid I quit first. Good day."

Langston endured four strokes of a paddle to each buttock that evening. Late that night, he heard his parents laughing.

"That boy's got to get his mouth under control," his father said.

"He seems to have gotten the better of Pickard, anyway," Lucinda said. "You may have gone overboard with your stories of proud African warriors."

Langston senior chuckled. "That boy will turn out just fine."

Langston Cane the Third went to Frederick Douglass high school in Baltimore, graduated, and won a scholarship to Lincoln University in Pennsylvania. His own father had studied there, graduated with a bachelor's degree in sacred theology, and gone on to obtain a doctorate in divinity. All the expected things happened to Langston at Lincoln. He got top marks, became manager of the football team and led the freshman debating squad. But two other things happened. The United States prepared to enter World War I, and Langston met Rose Bridges.

They were introduced through a mutual friend, at a social gathering held at the Bridgeses' residence. Residence, indeed,

Langston noticed, stepping onto a covered verandah and into the three-story home. *Residence* has three syllables; *home* has one. The front door had a brass knocker. A chandelier hurled squares of light around the living room. A staircase, wide enough to take two linebackers between the oak banisters, wound up to a second floor. Dr. Edward Bridges, a dentist who was known to have a number of white patients, and Mrs. Hazel Bridges stood at the door. Mrs. Bridges greeted him. She kissed Langston's friend, who was an old family acquaintance and a known Catholic. Langston received an assessing nod and a handshake.

"What did you say your last name was?" Mrs. Bridges asked in a nasal tone. The woman could have passed for white, she was so light-skinned. She clasped one of her wrists with the other hand and studied Langston.

"Cane." Langston met her eyes equally. Green. The woman had green eyes, reddish-brown lipstick, and brown hair combed straight back.

"Where are your people from?"

Africa, just the same as yours, he wanted to say. But he didn't. He had heard, from his friend, that Dr. and Mrs. Bridges had a daughter of incomparable beauty. So he just said, "Baltimore."

"I thought that name was familiar," Mrs. Bridges said. "Your father is of A.M.E. stock, I believe."

"My father is the minister of the Bethel A.M.E. Church in Baltimore, if that's what you mean."

"Well, isn't that a fine thing," she said, forcing a smile. "And I suppose you're at college now. Morgan?"

"Lincoln."

"I'm sure you'll do admirably there. Well, help yourself to something to eat. Get yourself a nice big helping."

Langston looked straight at her green eyes to drive her gaze away. Most people, if they said something insulting, flinched if he looked right at them. But Mrs. Hazel Bridges kept watching him. He held her gaze equably. Then he allowed himself to be led away by his friend.

His father had always said Langston should stand tall, back straight, chin up, in the finest African tradition. No head hanging for a son of Hannibal. The coach of the Lincoln debating team stressed the same point. He didn't actually mention Hannibal, but he knew about the dignified way to hold oneself in public, and drove that message home time and again. So Langston kept his head high and caught sight of Mrs. Bridges' eldest daughter — the one he had heard about. She stood in a corner holding a bottle of Coca-Cola. She had been watching him. Watching him hold off her mother's stare.

Langston allowed his lips to lift, just enough to let her know that he'd seen her looking. He thought she would smile back because he figured that she would enjoy watching a young man stand up to her dominating mother, but she didn't smile. She turned quickly to take the arm of her younger sister.

"What's the name of Dr. Bridges' daughter?" Langston asked his friend.

"Which one?" Ed said.

"The one I'm going to marry."

Ed chortled. "Her name is Rose. And that'll be the day I'm president."

"Introduce me."

"Not so fast. What's wrong? This your first high-society party?"

It was. But Langston wasn't listening. He accepted a fried oyster on a cracker from a maid carrying a platter, and tried to find a way to eat it without putting the whole thing into his mouth. He raised the entire snack with his right hand, shielded his mouth with his left, and put the thing where it was meant to be. Rose was looking at him again. She had a grin all over her face. Langston headed over to meet her.

"Rose Bridges? I've heard of you from my friend, Ed Ryan."

"And what is your name?"

Those first five words made Langston fall in love with her. Rose had the loveliest voice he had ever heard. It barely lifted above a whisper, but it radiated confidence.

"Langston Cane." He reached out with his hand. She shook it. It was a lovely hand. Smooth. Long, piano fingers. Nutty brown. Cool, though. Her hand was cool. It stayed in his just long enough for that thought to register.

"You sound as if you have a sore throat," Langston said. "Can I get you something to drink? Lemon in water, perhaps?"

Her brown eyes held him like an embrace. This was the woman for him. Langston sensed that she knew it, too.

"No, thank you. My throat is fine. I always sound like this."

"Really?" Langston said. He found that he had to lean forward to catch all of her words. "Well, it's a very nice voice, nonetheless. Ed says you're at Howard. How do you like it?"

"Fine, I suppose," she said. "I would have liked to go to Radcliffe. But mother wanted me close to home. Loretta's going, though. Loretta, this is Langston Cane. Langston, my sister, Loretta."

Loretta, who was lighter than Rose, gave Langston a calculating glance. Langston could imagine the questions going through her mind. But Ed came to the rescue. "So, Loretta, what are you going to take at Radcliffe?"

"Pre-med," she said. "I'm going to be a doctor."

A maid with a platter came up again. This time she was serving crab cakes and hot biscuits. Langston shook his head.

"Don't be shy," Rose said, laughing. "I already noticed your difficulty with that oyster." Langston tried not to grin. "Go ahead," Rose said. "I'm having one. You take this one, I'll get another."

Langston took it and eyed her as he bit into it. She eyed him back. She had her mother's poise, that one.

"Lincoln is debating against Howard next Friday," he said. "I'll be on the Lincoln squad. Why don't you come out? We could talk."

"I'd love to, but I've got classes and a volleyball game that day."

He took a step closer, to hear her more easily. "And after your game?"

"Are you always this forward?" she said.

"Never." For a moment, Langston felt tongue-tied.

"I saw my mother interrogating you," Rose said.

"Why do you suppose she seemed so suspicious?"

Rose let out a laugh. It was tinged with nervousness.

"Go ahead," Langston said. "Tell me." She spoke at the same time that laughter rang out from a corner of the room. Langston asked her to repeat herself.

"You're dark, you're poor, and you're not Catholic."

Langston was wearing his best — as well as his only — suit that day. He'd taken meticulous care in dressing. Had shaved perfectly, shined his shoes. "I am by no means poor. And how do you know I'm not Catholic?"

"If your family was wealthy or Catholic, she would have heard of you. She wouldn't have been inquiring. So what did you tell her?"

"I'll tell you if you have a soda with me after that volleyball game."

"Okay. One soda. Around two p.m. in the Howard cafeteria. But tell me who you are."

"Langston Cane the Third."

"The Langston Cane part you already told me. If you're the Third, who is the Second?"

"He's an A.M.E. minister in Baltimore."

Rose's face lit up with delight. "And you told her that?"

"I sure did."

"I've got to go."

"Why?"

"My mother beckons, if you must know. Don't turn to look."

Rose's mother was upon them. "Excuse me, dear, someone wishes to meet you." She steered her daughter to safety. Langston glanced around the room. He didn't see one face as dark as his. Actually, Dr. Bridges was richly complected. But he was permitted. He was a success. And it was his home.

Rose Bridges didn't come to the cafeteria. Langston waited for fifteen minutes. He waited half an hour. He walked around the campus, checked the gymnasium in vain for volleyball players, checked the cafeteria once more, and left Howard University. He had won his debate, in which he had argued in favor of the resolution that "Negroes suffered as much in the Reconstruction Era as they had during slavery." But he felt entirely dissatisfied. Already, he had taken an afternoon away from classes to travel to D.C. for the debate. And instead of taking the long trip back to Pennsylvania in the university bus — which would have been free of charge, and which would have involved a ham sandwich and drink provided by the school — Langston had stayed on to meet Rose. Now, on his own meager savings, he had to locate a place to stay for the night, find something to eat, and then make it all the way back to Lincoln the next day. His father had demanded that he keep a rigorous accounting of his expenditures, and Langston would have trouble justifying this leisure time in Washington.

He considered taking a bus straight back to Pennsylvania, but rejected that idea. He considered knocking on the door of his friend Ed — the fellow who had taken him to the Bridgeses' residence — to sleep on his spare mattress. Things might come to that, but Langston rejected this possibility for the time being.

He started walking. It gave him time to compose his thoughts. He had to create an excuse for popping by Rose's house uninvited. *Hello, Rose, is everything all right? You had me worried, not showing up at Howard. I thought you might have injured yourself at the volleyball game.* No. Too transparent. *Hello, Rose, I waited for you at Howard. I hoped not to leave D.C. without rescheduling a visit for another time.* No. Too direct. *Rose, how are you? . . . Yes, it was for today. But don't worry. Why don't we try again later? I'm in town again in three weeks. Or, if you're not terribly tied up, I'll be in town until Sunday.* No, how would he swing that? Where would he stay? What about his budget?

Forget the rehearsals. He did not want to sound rehearsed. This would have to be a case of spontaneous creation. Of improvisation. As a debater, at times he entered into a competition called "impromptu public speaking." It was usually a one-on-one match, in which he and another contestant were given slips of paper and two minutes to prepare. One slip of paper would say: *You must argue in favor of this statement. . . .* And the other slip would say, *You must argue against this statement. . . .* Dropping by the Bridgeses' residence would be a case of impromptu public speaking. Before he got to Rose, he would have to get by her mother. She would set the tone for their meeting. No — perhaps Langston should take the quick lead. After all, he had the element of surprise. Mrs. Bridges would be shocked by his arrival. How quick was she? How shrewd? How much of a panic would his visit generate? She would assume there was more to Rose and Langston than she had first thought. She would assume that they had seen each other, in at least some circumstance, outside her house. Yes, he told himself, take the lead. When she answers the door, throw her off balance, greet her civilly, reintroduce yourself, ask if you might have a word with Rose. Yes. That was the way. He knew he didn't have to worry about Rose. She would make it easy for him. She wouldn't say a word against him — not in front of her mother. Rose Bridges liked him.

Langston wanted to arrive well in advance of the supper hour, so as not to oblige the Bridgeses to invite him to eat, but he didn't want to work up a sweat by walking too fast. So he walked at a comfortable pace, neither hurried nor leisurely, and covered the distance in just over an hour. He checked his watch when he got to Linden Street — it was four-fifteen. He checked it again, after walking a few blocks under the shade of the lindens — four-twenty. He used the brass knocker, rapping twice. The door opened.

"Dr. Bridges?" Langston said, extending his hand.

Dr. Bridges met him with a casual smile, and shook his hand. "I saw you the other evening. You are —"

"Langston Cane. We didn't actually meet the other night, but —"

"Yes, yes, but I saw you. Rose mentioned you to me. Come to see her, I suppose?"

"Yes." My, my, this couldn't be easier.

"I'm afraid she's out." Damn. "Won't be back before dinner." Double damn. "My wife informed me that you're of the Baltimore Canes."

"Yes, sir, I am."

"Well, say hello to your father, for me."

Triple damn. This would get back to the old man. "You know my father?"

"As a matter of fact, I do." Dr. Bridges was a tall man. Three inches taller than Langston. He leaned over, conspiratorially, and, with a grin on his face, said, "I was raised in an A.M.E. family, too."

Langston's face opened into a natural smile. "Is that a fact?"

"It sure is. What brings you to D.C. again?"

"I lead the Lincoln debating squad, sir, and we were up against Howard this afternoon."

"You beat 'em?"

"We cleaned their clocks, sir."

"I like to hear that. I was a Lincoln man myself. Are you in a hurry? Why don't you come in? All the women are out, right now, and I was just taking care of some paperwork, but I'd much rather catch up on the goings-on at Lincoln and so forth."

"All right, thank you. It would be my pleasure."

"Sit down. Take your blazer off. You've worked up a sweat. Don't tell me you walked all the way from Howard?"

"I had some time on my hands. And I don't mind a little exercise."

"Humph! I don't mind a little exercise, but I don't mind a little drink now and again either. This is the only time to snatch one, when the women — well, when Hazel — is out of the house. How about a shot of brandy?"

If he consented, Mrs. Bridges would smell it on him, probably see his glass the moment she came in. But Mrs. Bridges was going to be an enemy no matter what he did.

"Thank you, I'll have a little, straight up."

Dr. Bridges grinned as he splashed an ounce — no, two ounces — into a wide glass.

"Straight up, as you requested."

Dr. Bridges had been to Lincoln to study sciences, but spoke of it lightheartedly, almost disparagingly — in contrast to the reverent tones of Langston's father. Dr. Bridges, apparently, had taken his degree in dentistry at Harvard. Langston noticed that the man had long, agile, smooth fingers — much like Rose's. Langston's father had always made his own accomplishments sound as if they'd been torn from stone. But this man had a way of minimizing his successes — perhaps because his visitor was a dark young man from an A.M.E. background. Langston wondered if the offhanded treatment was a subtler version of Mrs. Bridges' open dismissal. He vowed to be careful with the brandy, which burned his throat.

In the middle of stories about a stodgy professor of Greek who had terrorized Lincoln students twenty-five years earlier, and of a young white woman who had come to him recently, expecting to find a white dentist, Dr. Bridges asked Langston if he had dinner plans. Langston said he really had to be going.

"Nonsense," Dr. Bridges said, "it's a Friday evening, you've won your debate, you may as well stick around and catch up with Rose, and how well do you know her, by the way?"

Langston put down his glass and said something to the effect that they'd only met recently.

"You can imagine that a fair number of young men ask to take her out."

"She is so vivacious, I can understand that."

"Vivacious. Yes. But you're the only young man who has had the courage to knock on our door. On his own initiative, I mean to say."

"Well, we had been planning a visit earlier today, but it fell through."

"Yes, yes, so you said. Here they are now. All three coming in together. Let's put these things away, shall we?" Dr. Bridges winked, snapped up the two glasses in one hand and the bottle in the other, and disappeared.

Mrs. Bridges was first in the door. She took a step back when she saw Langston rising from a chair. "Oh, you gave me such a fright."

Loretta came in next, saw Langston, and frowned. "Oh, hello. I saw you at the party. It was Cane, wasn't it? Langston Cane, of Baltimore?"

"That's right," Langston said, unsure of whether to walk over and attempt to shake her hand. He decided against it.

Rose finally appeared, with bundles under each arm. Dr. Bridges came out of the kitchen at the same time. "Hello, Daddy," she said. She put down her packages and kissed her father. Then she turned to Langston and offered her hand. "Hello, Langston. Sorry about today. Our tournament ran late, and then I had to meet mother and Loretta."

"That's all right, Rose. Nice to see you again."

Rose turned back toward the front door. "Mother, you met Langston the other night. Langston Cane the Third, I believe it was."

"Hello again, Langston," Mrs. Bridges said. The accent was on *again*. "What brings you here today?"

Dr. Bridges planted a friendly hand on Langston's shoulder. "Young Cane and I were having a chat about Lincoln. I was telling him about my old days there. And he was about to tell me about how things are these days at my old alma mater."

Hazel Bridges cleared her throat. "Rose, would you help me in the kitchen?"

Dr. Bridges stepped in. "Why don't you let her stay out here and chat with Langston? He walked all the way up from Howard to pay her a visit."

Langston flinched. So much for avoiding the poor-boy image.

"Yes, dear." Mrs. Bridges cast a stern look at Langston. "But don't delay. We have much work to do."

"Oh, and darling," Dr. Bridges said to his wife. "I've invited Langston to dinner. And Langston has accepted. Isn't that right, young Cane?"

"Yes, yes, sir, I'd be delighted."

"Wonderful," Mrs. Bridges said, moving quickly to the back of the house. "Wonderful. Come along, Loretta."

Langston waited until mother and sister were out of earshot, and then pounced. He judged that the old man wouldn't mind.

"Rose, would you like to step out for a walk, for a few minutes?"

She smiled easily at her father and said, "That sounds like a lovely idea."

The sky was darkening against the trees. Once they were alone outside, Rose let out a sigh. "Do you know how many questions I'll have to answer?"

"I didn't mean to embarrass you. I just wanted to make sure you were all right. We *had* planned to meet, and you didn't —"

"What did you tell my father?"

"Nothing much. He did most of the talking."

"Didn't he ask you how we met?"

"He did. And I explained that we had only met recently."

"You led him to believe that we've seen each other before?"

"Not entirely. I just evaded the question."

"I don't know why I was so nice to you. I never should have said I'd see you at Howard."

"That's a fine thing. I missed my ride back to Lincoln to see you. I skipped lunch to see you. I have to take a bus back to school out of my own budget. But if you don't wish to see me, all you have to do is say so."

"I don't wish to see you."

"I'm afraid I can't accept that statement."

Rose started to giggle. "All right, let's walk. You got me out of helping make dinner. That's something to thank you for. Let's walk, let's talk. You've got nerve, I can say that for you. Most boys, they see a pretty face, they can't function. They lose their dignity. You've got that. Too much dignity, perhaps, but at least you've got it. Now tell me about yourself, Langston."

They walked for forty-five minutes — long enough that even Dr. Bridges stared as they came back in. Rose's father excused himself and retired to the study. Mrs. Bridges asked Rose to help her with the table. Langston sat by himself in the parlor, relieved not to have to think or prepare his words for a moment.

Dinner was served. Mrs. Bridges called upon her husband to bless the table. Langston bowed his head, and found the blessing thankfully secular. Pope-ism — that's what his father called the Catholic faith. Candles, ornaments, trinkets, rituals. Pope-ism.

Dr. Bridges got the conversation around to war. Langston was glad to discuss something so inoffensive. What role should America play? And, within that role, what was the role of the American Negro? What danger did the Germans offer? How far would they go? Langston was thankful that he'd been devouring newspapers since he'd been paid seventy-five cents a week at the *Afro-American*. He had plenty to say. Plenty to show the Bridgeses of Washington that he could manage talk of war.

Over dessert, Rose stunned her parents and Langston. "Mother and Daddy, Langston is taking the bus back to Lincoln tomorrow morning. Could we put him up in our guest room tonight?"

"That's all right," Langston said. "I have made arrangements for this evening, it is not necessary to —"

"Nonsense," Dr. Bridges said. "We won't leave a Lincoln man out in the cold."

Again and again, on the bus back to school the next day, Langston played the scene in his mind. He was with Rose at the central bus depot.

"I'd like to see you again," he said.

"My parents wouldn't permit it."

"With due respect, you are not indentured to your parents. If you truly have no desire to see me again, just tell me."

She laughed heartily. "And I know just what you'll say." She lowered her voice to mimic him. "'I'm afraid I can't accept that statement.'"

"I'd like a kiss before I get up on this bus."

"Am I required to agree?" She stood close and looked in his eyes.

"One kiss and one date. Friday in three weeks. At the Howard cafeteria."

"I'll shake your hand."

"You have a lovely hand, Rose."

"Are you trying to grow a mustache?"

"I might be. Why not?"

"I'm not fond of facial hair."

"So you'll kiss me, if I don't grow one?"

"Let's talk it over the next time we meet."

"Friday in three weeks?"

"All right. All right."

He took her hand again, and resolved not to ask once more for a kiss. It was beneath a Lincoln man to beg.

Rose leaned forward and kissed him on both cheeks. "I like you, Langston Cane."

He climbed onto the bus. Or he floated. He actually floated up those steps.

Hazel Bridges met Rose on the wide staircase with the stained oak banisters.

"Your father and I would like to have a chat with you, dear."

"Now is as good a time as any." Rose followed her mother to the parlor.

Each sat in a wing chair. Rose wished her own chair's wings would jut out far enough to protect her face from the scrutiny of her parents.

"He's an interesting boy," her mother said.

"Yes, quite."

Rose's father said, "He's an upstanding lad, and I have nothing against him. But I wouldn't like to see your studies compromised."

"I'd like to know how serious his intentions are," her mother said.

"Very." It gave Rose pleasure to see her mother's mouth fall open.

"What, precisely, does that mean?" her father said.

"He likes me. I like him. How can you support the vote for women — how can you pretend that you want me to have an independent mind — and then try to tell me whom to see and not see?"

"The boy holds himself like some African prince!" her mother said. "Some prince! I'll bet he'd never seen running water before he sauntered into our house and filled his stomach."

"Hazel, please," said Rose's father. "This boy's father is no jackboot minister. He holds a doctorate in divinity from Lincoln University."

"We only care about your future," her mother said. "Your father and I will let you transfer to Radcliffe next year, if you promise not to see him again."

"You're trying to bribe me," Rose said.

"We love you, Rose. This is only for your own good."

"You mean it's for your own good. Good night."

Langston had his one suit cleaned and pressed. He was wearing it now. He was the only person in the Howard University cafeteria wearing a suit.

Rose showed up on time, but wouldn't stand near him, or even let him take her hand. "My mother nearly read your letter. She would have opened it, if I hadn't picked up the mail first."

"It was a perfectly innocent expression of my sentiment."

"*I couldn't kiss you, and now I'm so blue.* If my mother had read that, she would have had a conniption." Langston thought it wise to keep his mouth shut. "If you want to write me again, do it care of the Catholic Women's Study Group at Howard. Don't put a return address or a name on the envelope. Get a woman to write on the outside of the envelope, so it won't look suspicious."

"Let's go for a walk," Langston said.

Rose let her hand brush against his as they walked outside the chapel. "Mother wants to send me to Radcliffe next year, just to get me away from you."

"I shaved off the mustache."

"Didn't you hear what I just said?"

"You had my full attention, and you still do."

Rose faced him calmly. She allowed a hint of a smile. Langston placed his fingers on her shoulders, leaned in, and kissed her lightly. She did not part or move her lips, but she did not back away from him.

"You're sweet," she said.

"Men aren't sweet."

"That was a compliment. Don't let it go to your head."

From across the football field, a waiting bus driver sounded his horn. It was time to drive the Lincoln debating team back to Pennsylvania. Rose walked him across the football field.

"Can I see you in three weeks?" Langston said.

"Maybe. I'll send you a note."

"My father got wind of our meeting. Your father let him know."

"What happened?" Rose said.

"My father offered to send me to Harvard if I didn't see you again."

"Aren't you so very funny. But seriously, what happened?"

"He didn't want me to inconvenience or impose upon your parents. But he didn't seem troubled by my interest in you. In fact, it seemed to humor him."

"How liberal of him," Rose said. She blew him a kiss.

Twice more, they met secretly in the spring of 1917. Rose made an effort never to mention Langston's name, but Hazel Bridges knew that something was up. She had discovered that Langston Cane would be moving home for the summer break, and Baltimore was too close for comfort.

One week after Rose's classes ended, Hazel took her on a steamer to a colored people's lodge near Arundel on the Bay.

Hazel stuffed her luggage with crossword puzzles, books, and magazines — anything to distract her daughter. She also arranged for friends with eligible sons to arrive at the same time.

The lodge was run by an old man — Captain Haynes — who had been receiving the Bridgeses and other families for fifteen years. The lodge had six guest rooms, a screened verandah with lounge chairs, and a sitting room with a fireplace that was kept roaring on cool spring nights. Captain Haynes served crab cakes and corn bread at breakfast. He served baked oysters at lunch, and he served soft-shell crab for supper. His cook made pies, strawberry shortcakes, and biscuits. They served lemonade, hot chocolate, milk, and all manner of juices. Wine and brandy were available for discreet purchase and consumption behind closed doors. There was badminton. There were sailboat rides. There was fiddle music and square dancing at night. There were long afternoons to pick soft-shell crabs right off the beach. There were boys from all sorts of colleges, staying with their mothers. Rose danced, ate, walked, sailed, finished a book every third night, and took horse-drawn rides to the local Catholic church, which admitted light-skinned Negroes such as Rose and her mother.

After the month at the lodge, Hazel took Rose and Loretta to New York City to see relatives for two weeks. Then they stayed at another summer resort in Vermont for two weeks. That brought them to the end of July. And Langston, Hazel had learned through her husband, would be at his parents' summer home near Frederick, Maryland, in August.

Langston was unable to reach Rose in the summer, or in September. Finally, he wrote to her at her home:

Dearest Rose:

I miss you terribly. We all know what absence does to the heart. Could we see each other as soon as possible?

They met on campus at Howard, in the second week of October. Langston felt sick to his stomach, he ached to see her so badly. And he felt worse when he saw her walk up to him cautiously. This was not a walk that carried with it a kiss. This was a hello-how-are-you-let's-not-get-involved walk. She said she couldn't see him again. She said the pressure was just too much from home, that it could never work out with such pressure. Her parents were dead set against it, his parents probably were, too, there were too many differences between them, it was best to let it drop.

"Good-bye, Langston. Please don't fight this. You're a good man. Somebody will love you. You'll make somebody very happy."

"I can't even think of being with somebody else," he told her. "We are made for each other, Rose. We belong together."

"Please don't make this difficult, Langston."

"I'm afraid that I simply cannot accept the word good-bye. Not from you. Let me shake your hand. I will see you later."

He wrote to her at Howard. He wrote to her at home. He took the bus to D.C. twice and scoured the Howard University campus. Finally, he managed to have a message delivered to her through Ed Ryan, who had first brought him to the party at the Bridgeses' residence.

Two weeks before Christmas, Rose agreed to see him again.

"You are the most persistent bull terrier that ever walked this planet," she said.

"You're sweet."

"How devious of you to resurrect that word. But I'm not so sure about that mustache."

"It's the price you pay for refusing to see me."

"Shave it off."

"It's not so bad. Come here a minute."

"Well, for just a minute."

Her body just seemed to fit against his. She felt his hardness, right through his trousers. It aroused and terrified her.

She was going to tell him one more time that it couldn't work. But he beat her to the punch.

"Rose, let's sit down. I have something to tell you."

Rose wondered if the man was crazy enough to propose to her. Was he stark raving mad? Surely, he doesn't think she would . . .

"I'm going to enlist in the American Army. I'll likely be sent overseas. So the best thing would be for us not to see each other again. But when I come back, if you're still free . . . "

"*No!* You're just a boy. My boy! You're not going away — not over there!"

"We shouldn't meet again. It's not fair to you. But I do love you. And, as I said, when I come back — "

"Do you know how many boys my mother threw at me this summer?"

"How many?"

"I lost count. But still I dream only of you."

"Don't tell me that the prospect of war has turned you into a romantic."

Rose put her wrists up around Langston's neck. Again, she felt his hardness. This time, she leaned into it. "Kiss me."

"If I don't enlist, they will conscript me. But if I enlist early, I could make officer."

"You're not going to any war."

"Yes, I am, Rose. We shouldn't be doing this. I don't want you hurt. I'd rather die than see you hurt."

"You talk too much. Do you know that? Turn this way. Look at me. Look in my eyes. What's the matter? Scared of me? That's better. Now. Pay close attention to what I have to say." She brought her lips against his.

In June 1917, Langston Cane the Third was one of 1,250 black men accepted into the colored officers' training camp at Fort Des Moines, Iowa. It was considered a great honor to be accepted. Langston took careful note of the articles in the Negro press by Benjamin Curley, general secretary of the Central Committee of Negro College Men. Curley wrote: "There is a terrible responsibility resting upon us. The Government has challenged the Negro race to prove its worth, particularly the worth of its educated leaders. We must succeed and pour into the camp in overwhelming numbers. Let no man slack. Let us not mince matters; the race is on trial. It needs every one of its red-blooded, sober-minded men. Come to camp determined to make good. Up, brother, our race is calling."

Langston had to pay his own way to Iowa, but he was reimbursed at the rate of three and a half cents per mile traveled. He received seventy-five dollars a month in training, and knew that if he succeeded in winning a commission, he'd make at least $145 a month.

Training lasted for four months. It included fitness, training in the science of war, instruction in French and German, and endless drills. Recruits were up at 5:45 a.m. doing sit-ups and push-ups. They ran two miles before breakfast, attended lectures after breakfast, and were put through hell by Colonel C. C. Ballou, his staff, and a group of colored non-commissioned officers from colored regiments of the regular army.

At six o'clock one morning, while he was making his bed, Langston was interrupted by his sergeant.

"Where is Private Barnes?"

"He's temporarily absent, Sergeant," Langston said. "Will return momentarily."

"You haven't answered my question, Private. Where, precisely, is Barnes?"

"In a state of intestinal discharge," Langston said. "Discharges have been frequent and intense since four a.m. Will provide other medical diagnosis if required, Sergeant."

The sergeant burst into laughter. "Thanks for the details, Private. At ease."

Barnes, whose bunk was next to Cane's, hobbled into the barracks. He was looking down, fastening his zipper, when he bumped into the sergeant.

"Sergeant! Didn't see you!"

"It is evident that you didn't see me, Private. You're advised not to speak the obvious, unless it is asked of you."

"Yes!"

"At breakfast, Private, I want you to drink two glasses of juice and two glasses of water and eat nothing, is that understood?"

"Yes."

"And after breakfast, Private, I want you to report to the

infirmary and explain that I have ordered you to stay in bed for the day. Is that clear, Private Barnes?"

"Yes."

"At ease, Private. Fasten your fly. And thank Private Cane for informing me about your frequent and intense discharges."

The men in the barracks burst into laughter. Barnes grinned sheepishly at Cane. The sergeant nodded at Cane. The men in the barracks, who had heard of Langston's background, dubbed him the Reverend Doctor.

Private Langston Cane aced his French tests. Trigonometry was a swindle, no sweat at all. Trig had been harder at Douglass High School in Baltimore. Keeping clean and polished was no difficulty. But Langston was falling behind in drill. The art of ordering soldiers in formation eluded him, and his superiors knew it. They were looking to fail about half the candidates in the camp. Everyone was fighting to make officer. Each soldier knew that emerging from camp with the single stripe of a private on his sleeve would be a major letdown for race and family. With just one stripe, it would be harder to find girls, harder to find jobs after the war, harder to stand tall and do whatever they wanted to do. Almost everyone at Fort Des Moines was college-educated, and everyone was gunning for a commission. From Colonel C. C. Ballou on down, the commanding officers were looking for any excuse — *anything* — to ax candidates from the running.

Langston Cane the Third was on the verge of failing his drill test. The problem was the hollering. He had learned since boyhood that the art of persuasion lay in lowering one's voice. When your message peaked, you decrescendoed. Forced your listeners to sit on the edge of their pews. But war was different. War required hollering. If you wanted fifty men to turn right, you didn't lower your voice. The truck going by would drown you out. But Langston just couldn't get drill right. Couldn't project dignity and holler at the same time. The test had been two days ago, and he had blown it. They had given him fifty men in formation right before him, in an open field. Gave him a sheet of paper, with a penciled diagram. They let him look at it for one minute. He had one minute to memorize it. The field was a square. One short, thick line indicated where the soldiers were waiting in formation. The arrows indicated where Langston was to lead the men. North twenty yards. East twenty-five yards. North again for thirty yards. Turn 180 degrees. South fifteen yards. Turn 45 degrees. On one knee. Weapons out. Fire.

Langston had it clear. He knew exactly what to do. He hollered, hurled invective, articulated every syllable, got everything right up to the point where the men marched north again thirty yards. Got them turned around 180 degrees. He got them south, as required, fifteen yards, didn't forget to turn them side by side. FIRE. Damn. Damn of all damns. There went his career. There went his stripes. He forgot to get the men down on their knees! He tried to recover. Innovated. Improvised. HALT. Return weapons to side. One knee. Weapons out. FIRE. But he saw the examining officer make a notation in his book. Saw that he'd blown it. Saw his future evaporate. The parents of Rose Bridges would be a hard sell, but they'd never let her go to an army private.

A day went by. Private Barnes, his best friend, tried to comfort him. "It was the smallest of errors, man. Don't you worry. They saw you recover. That proved you had brains."

But Langston knew better. He knew he was in trouble. That

night, he went to see Lieutenant Wright. Langston rapped on the door and was ordered in and asked his business.

"You saw my error in the field, sir."

"What about it?"

"I know how gravely it will compromise my chances. And I'm afraid I can't let that happen."

"What does that mean, you can't let it happen?"

"I have excelled in every element of my training, sir, and I know you won't contest that."

"But you didn't excel at drill. Nice maneuver after your mistake, but you committed an error, as you said yourself."

"I'm afraid I cannot accept the blemish on my record, sir."

"In a war situation, you could have had those men killed."

"I want another chance, sir. I want it and I deserve it. Give me another map, sir, and another chance. Make it harder, if you like. Judge me solely on the harder test. But I'm requesting that test. I'm requesting it tomorrow."

"I'll consider your request."

"Thank you, sir."

"Dismissed."

Langston got the word that night. Lieutenant Wright woke him in his bunk. "You'll have your chance, Private. Tomorrow morning, before breakfast. We're waking up the men half an hour early so you can do this, Private. You're going to have some surly soldiers on your hands. Good luck."

"May I have permission to leave the barracks, sir?"

"When?"

"Right away, sir."

"What for?"

"Collect my thoughts, sir."

"Permission granted. It is 23:10 hours. I want you back in

your bed at 00:45. That gives you five minutes to get dressed, ninety minutes to get collected. Good luck."

"Thank you, sir.

Langston throws on a coat to hold off the chill of the September night. He walks out into the drilling field. It won't do. Too close to the barracks. He has some hollering to do. Beyond the field, and beyond the artillery range, half a mile from the barracks, there's a deciduous forest. They've had physical tests in there. He has had to pull himself up ten yards of rope, climb up on an oak branch, take another rope, swing like a madman to another branch, land there, and climb back down to the ground on another rope. And do it all under two minutes. He's had to prove his skills with a compass, locating a package under two feet of earth with nothing more than a sheet of compass directions. He's had all sorts of tests in that forest. There are oak trees, willows, birches, and maples. Tonight, the trees will be his men.

He imagines the map and the instructions. They'll be harder, this time. This time, they'll really try to throw him. Something new. Yes, something new. Drill the men for attire, it will say. Find one man in error. Bawl him out. Total humiliation. Eject him from the group. Then, thirty-five yards north. Twenty east. Ten south. Revolve 45 degrees to the west. Knees. Weapons out. Fire. Reload. Fire again. Weapons back. Up. Twenty north. Weapons out. Fire. Reload. Fire. Reload. Fire.

Langston imagines all those orders. He stands straight, stiff, and marches up to a young oak. His face is five inches from the bark. The tree is barely thicker than a man's neck. Langston grimaces as if he means to strangle it. Here comes the hollering. Hollering so that his spittle hits the bark. "Polish your boots this morning,

Private? . . . You call that polished? . . . Why is the right toe scuffed?
. . . Don't look down while I'm talking to you! . . . Right toe is
scuffed, and what's with this button? . . . This one! . . . Are you a
soldier of the American Army? . . . Do you mean to defend the
lives of American women and children? . . . Do you mean to
defend their lives with a button hanging by a thread? . . ." Snap.
He rips a dry twig off the oak. "Toe scuffed, button off — you're
a disgrace to the American people, Private. . . . Let me hear you say
that: I am a disgrace to the American people. . . . Yes, a disgrace.
Say it again. . . . I am a disgrace to my family . . . to my future wife
. . . to my future children. . . . The whole world will know of my
disgrace in the American Army. . . . Get out, Private. You don't
deserve to be with these men. . . . Get to your barracks this instant,
Private, and I'll deal with you later. OUT! . . . THIS INSTANT!"

Langston finishes disciplining the oak tree. Now he zeros in
on four birches planted side by side. "WHAT ARE YOU MEN
SMILING ABOUT? SOMETHING MAKE YOU PARTICU-
LARLY HAPPY THIS MORNING? NO? GOOD!"

Now, to every maple and willow within the sweep of his arm,
Langston hollers: "March. March. March. March, I said. Halt.
Around, forty-five. March, twenty paces. March, march, march,
halt. Around, forty-five. March, march. Halt. Around, forty-five.
Knees. Weapons out. FIRE. Reload. FIRE."

Langston doesn't use up all the time the lieutenant has allotted
him. For one thing, he doesn't want his voice to be hoarse in the
morning. For another, he has sensed that someone is watching
him in the woods. It must be the lieutenant. Actually, it's two
men. The lieutenant and his sergeant, surely. Langston mustn't
appear underconfident. This is just a routine test. With twenty-
five minutes to spare, Langston finishes his drill, puts the trees at
ease, dismisses them, and jogs back to the barracks.

On October 15, 1917, Langston Cane became one of 639 officers to graduate from the colored officers' training camp. He was among the 204 men to make second lieutenant.

Langston proposed to Rose Bridges on a finely graveled path along the Potomac River. He was wearing his uniform. She found him awfully striking. Years later, she recalled that she would likely have turned him down, had it not been for the uniform. She had the presence of mind to impose certain conditions:

First, he would consent to having their children baptized in a Catholic church, and would never become an A.M.E. minister.

Second, he would respect her desire not to have children or to become pregnant before she finished her current senior year at Howard.

Finally, he agreed to keep the marriage secret to all parties until Rose had determined the appropriate moment to break the news. If the people at Howard University learned that she had married, they would expel her.

Langston accepted, so she accepted. They eloped two weeks later. With Langston on a two-week pass, and Rose executing a flawless alibi, they escaped to Philadelphia and were married by a Baptist minister. In a fine resort paid for by Rose, they spent one long and sleepless weekend together. Rose insisted — absolutely insisted — on coitus interruptus. Langston didn't mind. Rose had accepted him. She had taken his ring (although it would be pocketed when they left the resort). Man and wife. She loved him. That was all that mattered. They returned from the seventy-two-hour honeymoon, holding hands throughout the train ride from Philadelphia to D.C.

"How about if I escort my wife home?" he said.

"I can't let you do that."

"We won't tell them anything."

"I know we won't tell them anything. You've already solemnly and soberly agreed to that, Langston Cane."

"Yes, I have, Mrs. Cane."

"Then just let me get home from the bus station."

"How about if I accompany you to the end of your street, then."

"All right, Mr. Cane. That, you may do."

Rose was to graduate on May 4, 1918. They broke the news to her parents one week earlier. Rose had finished all her studies, passed all her exams. The graduation was just a formality. She had already bought the gown.

Rose left home one evening after supper, wearing a pink dress with white trim. It was tight around the bust and firm around the waist. She had asked her mother to button it up for her, but provided no explanation for her outing, other than that she'd be back shortly, and wanted to see both parents then.

"She looks as if she's off to a prom," Hazel Bridges mumbled.

"Or somebody's wedding," Loretta said.

Rose returned one hour later with Langston. He was in uniform. They hadn't seen him since the overnight stay a year earlier. Loretta and Mrs. Bridges made all the necessary exclamations about the attractiveness of his uniform. Dr. Bridges exhaled deeply.

"Mother, Daddy. Loretta, would you come over here, please?"

"I'm busy."

"Loretta!" Rose said sharply. Her younger sister came to sit with them.

Mrs. Bridges stood and waved her hand at Langston. "If you have the intention of asking —"

Rose cut her off. "Mother, let me speak, please."

Dr. Bridges supported her that far. "Yes, please, Hazel. Sit down. Don't leap to any —"

"Mother, Father, Loretta: Langston and I eloped and married two months ago."

Loretta gasped. Dr. Bridges shook his head in slow amazement. He stood, slowly. "I don't know whether to slap you or to kiss you," he said.

Rose pouted. "Slapping might get you into trouble with my husband."

"Well, I don't exactly condone the means, but I must offer my sincerest —"

"Oh, come here, Daddy."

Father hugged daughter. Son-in-law watched mother-in-law keel over. Faint. Drop dead — or so it seemed — on the floor. She did a professional job of it. Almost hit her head going down.

"Look what you've done to mother," Loretta screamed.

"Oh Loretta," Rose said, "settle down. Where are the smelling salts?"

Langston — on Dr. Bridges' insistence — stayed for dinner. Mrs. Bridges stayed in her room. Loretta stayed away, for the most part. That left Rose, her father, and her husband to spend the evening together. They ate scalloped potatoes and crab cakes. They drank brandy. They had pecan pie and French vanilla ice cream and all took second helpings. But Langston was not invited to spend the night.

Langston got his shipping orders the next month. He was to sail for France in June 1918 as a second lieutenant in the 368th Regiment of the Light Infantry Division of the American Expeditionary Forces.

"Your mother wished me luck," Langston told Rose as he prepared to board a train at Penn Station in Baltimore. "She said I had a handsome uniform. But I know what she is praying."

"Shush, baby."

"She's praying I come back in a box."

"I said shush."

"Don't worry, Rose. The Langston Canes are moving targets. We don't get hit."

"I hit you, Langston. I hit your heart."

"Yes, but I let you in close. No Germans will have that chance. And your mother won't either. Don't let her poison your mind, Rose."

"You sound just like her. *Don't let him poison you against Catholicism, Rose.* Don't worry about me. Just keep your head low."

"Don't worry about my head. I'm going to write you every day."

"Fine. But please keep your helmet on."

"Not every letter will get through, but if I write you every day, you should get at least one a week."

"Watch out for snipers."

"Don't even think of such things."

"Be brave, but don't be stupid, my darling. Go on overseas and shoot some Germans and come back to me just as soon as you can."

"That's the woman I married. My little girl. My Rose. Give me one more kiss."

"I don't want to start feeling sad again. You'd better go. The train is waiting."

"One little kiss. Just one peck on the cheek."

"Oh, all right, you big baby. Here."

Chapter 12

I ALREADY KNEW A LOT OF WHAT I came across in Millicent's box on Langston the Third. But I'd never seen any letters before, and never imagined anyone had kept them.

June 20, 1918

My girl!

Did you get the card I wrote from New York? I've been writing you daily on this rig, but my little stack of letters won't be moving anywhere until we land. We're scheduled to reach England tomorrow, stay put briefly, and then move on to France.

You'll never guess who I'm sailing with. Philip Ryan, brother of Ed Ryan, who led me to that fateful party at your parents' home. You may recall the party I'm speaking of. Philip is a grand fellow. He, too, made second lieutenant. Great to have him around.

Our mood is pretty good. We're constantly on the lookout for subs. We're going to win this war, no doubt about that, but you can't be too careful with the Germans. Sometimes one of the Deutsch subs gets in a lucky shot and sends a thousand love letters to the bottom.

If I don't hear from you regularly, I'll start writing you poetry.

Regards to everyone, most particularly your affectionate mother (smile).

Your boy,

Langston III

July 15, 1918

My boy,

Your letters are few and far between, and then suddenly the postman delivers four on one day! It's enough to make me "knock him upside his head," as the expression goes, but I suppose it isn't *his* fault.

I'm spending July and most of August with your parents, at their summer home near Harpers Ferry. Most charming. In the evenings, after dinner & dishes, your mother and aunts and sisters all sit out on the balcony in their Sunday finest, regardless of the day of the week. The women even put on makeup. There's nothing to do but watch horses, buggies, and the occasional car go by, or look at the cows in the pasture across the road, but sit there they do, all evening, drinking lemonade and iced tea in their very finest. All I brought were a few simple print dresses.

I've never seen so many pies. Apple, peach, cherry, lemon — I hope you don't expect me to cook as well as your mother!

Waiting, as always, to hear from my boy.

Your loving wife,

Rose

August 17, 1918

My girl!

Just today received your letter from my folks' summer home. Don't eat too many of those pies! I want my wife slender and delectable, as always (smile).

Something strange happened the other day. We're in France. I can't tell you where. We're in trenches, and suffice it to say that I've just settled in. Lovely conditions, as you've no doubt noticed from the scraps of miscellany stuck to this paper.

Anyway, here I am, as green as the other recent arrivals, and am on guard duty while the others try to sleep or at least close their eyes.

It's midnight, or later (I've just checked my watch and the last time I looked it was 23:50), and in the fog and the darkness I see a large, bulky form — I swear it's the biggest man I've ever seen — stepping into our trench.

"Halt," I call out. These are our warnings. One "Halt," and if the response isn't immediate and satisfactory, let it rip. I let it rip. I have a .45 automatic clipped to my belt. Six bullets fit into its magazine and a seventh goes into the chamber. I empty all seven bullets into the body, which lumbers, lumbers, just won't stop coming, and finally crashes down into the trench.

It's a donkey. A damn French donkey, loaded with French wine and bread. Donkey blood everywhere. Wine everywhere. Bread crumbs for every rat in the French mountains. The French, over in the next trench, were really irked. My buddies gave me a real ribbing. But I know the deal now. The French use the donkeys all the time to deliver supplies. Someone might have warned me.

Best wishes to my folks, if you're still with them.

Yours, as always,
Langston III

September 15, 1918

My boy!

I hope you're out of that trench by now! But in case you aren't, you need a basic lesson in language and geography. You're in France, I believe. So if any more of those poor mules come your way, try "Arrêtez" before "Halt." Silly man! Didn't you take French at Fort Des Moines?

Your loving wife,
Rose

Sept. 18, 1918

My girl,

We're in a town in the Vosges Mountains.

I was telling you about my buddy, Philip Ryan. He was having some fun the other afternoon. (Something your faithful never does!) Appears he was passing an hour or two with the willing wife of a sheep farmer. Farmer came home. Philip, trousers half on, took a dive out the bathroom window. Gets back to our lodgings, covered in sheep s———.

Hope these missives aren't getting too bold for you. Can't help it.

I think of you every day. Have your snap in my pocket, but it's awfully wrinkled. Send me another, when you can.

Love,
Langston III

October 1, 1918

My girl,

All the men are blue. I'm doing my best to cheer them up, but it's an uphill drive.

Philip Ryan got hit by a German sniper. Shot twice in the leg. We're hoping he makes it. He had to lose the leg, to cut out the gangrene. We lost six fellows in an awful fight the other day. I came out okay. Scratches, nothing more. Miss you terribly. They say we've nearly won this thing. But when you come across the enemy, he still fights.

I've become proficient with a gas mask. Think I'll bring one home in case your mother makes a stink when she sees I made it through this war. I could do with some hot water. Ticks and other bugs have it in for colored boys' hair. I've a mind to shave my head. But you might not like that. Tell you what. I won't shave my head, but I'll grow a mustache on the boat home.

Love you,
Langston III

November 12, 1918

Darling Rose,

Get out my civilian clothes. The war, as you probably learned before me, is over. We are all desperate to come home. I am dying to hold you. But for now all I can do is touch this paper with the knowledge that it will soon pass into your lovely hands.

Your boy,
Langston

November 28, 1918

Rose,

It makes me sick to say this, but I just got word that we're going to be sitting tight for a long time — possibly a month or two — before sailing home. You might as well prepare yourself NOT to see me at Christmas. The American soldiers over here are in a mile-long lineup to sail home, and guess which ones of us are at the back of the line.

Aching for you,
Langston

February 19, 1919

My girl,

I'm coming home, baby! Now you can get out my clothes!

Haven't heard from you in the longest time, but don't bother writing now. We're on our way! This is just a quick one — a mail orderly is picking up letters. I have to tend to my men now.

Hugs,
Langston III

P.S. The colored boys over here can't wait to get home. They think everything will be different, now that they've fought for their country. I'm not so sure. The way I see it, white people in America haven't seen — and won't necessarily care to know — what we have gone through in the trenches. I'd like to see things change, but I'm not holding my breath. What do you think?

March 24, 1919

Dearest Rose,

I'm so blue I can barely write. I'm sick of the entire adventure. We're still bogged down, waiting to sail home. I am okay, just depressed, and longing to be in your arms again. They promised me I'd be home by February, so I'm taking with a grain of salt the promise of another month — that I'll be home by end of April.

Yours,
Langston III

———————

I imagined my grandfather writing from the trenches, trying to keep his letters focused on love. I imagined his decision not to talk about the war itself, and I understood the request he made in one letter not to be told any bad news from back home.

Mill came into the guest room to say that I had spent enough time with those letters. What was I trying to do in there, anyway — memorize family history?

I asked if I could return and she said to come on back sometime. I said I'd better be on my way and she nodded. So I went. Millicent wasn't one for shaking hands or kissing good-bye. But once I'd stepped off her front porch and was heading toward my car, she called out:

"Say hello to your dad for me."

"I haven't spoken to him, lately."

"Tell him thank you for the cheques. I guess I should have thanked him myself."

"What cheques?"

"Your father sends me a hundred a month. Been sending me a hundred a month for fifteen years. Before that, it was fifty dollars. You didn't know that?"

"No, I didn't."

"He doesn't write. Never says nothing. No photo, no letter, not even a Christmas card. Mind you, I don't write either. He doesn't talk to me, and I don't talk to him. But he sends me money, every month. Tell him I said thank you."

"I don't know if I'll be talking to him soon."

"Then *call* 'im, you hear me? Git on the phone and *call* 'im. I showed you round the church even though you're nothing but a pagan buzzard —"

"Where'd you get that expression?"

"From my mother, bless her soul. I was saying, I showed you round the church, got you lunch, let you spy all over my family documents, now get your father on the phone and thank him for me."

"All right, Mill, I'll do that. I'll call him from a pay phone tonight."

"A pay phone? I don't want you standing in the street announcing my family business!" I wondered, exactly, what she was doing standing at the door hollering at me on the street, but I didn't pursue that argument. "Then get yourself back in here and call right now. What's this nonsense, no phone? What you doing, living like a bohemian? What if someone takes sick? What if someone needs to reach you?"

I skipped back into Millicent Cane's house. "You sit here and make that phone call," she said. "I'll see what there is in the fridge. You eat honey ham?"

I dialed my parents' number. I wasn't expecting an ecstatic reception, and I didn't get one.

"Yeh-es." That was my father. I'd been hoping he wouldn't answer, or that he wouldn't be in. He always sounded put-upon when he answered the phone.

"Dad. It's Langston."

"Son, where are you? Are you in trouble?"

"No. No trouble. I'm in Baltimore. I think you know that. But right now, I'm at Mill's."

I could imagine him sitting up in his chair. "Dorothy," he hollered. "Get on the line, would you? Your first son, the one who has my name? He's at Mill's place. Son, I warned you not to bother her. She has nothing to give you. If you need anything, come get it from home."

"I'm not asking for anything. We're just — visiting."

Millicent poked me in the back. "Thank him for the cheques, and get off the line. That's a long-distance call you're making."

"Mill says thank you for the cheques."

"That's none of your business," Dad said.

"I'm just passing on a message. She says —"

"Gimme that phone," Mill said, grabbing it. She shooed me out of the chair so she could sit down. "Lang, how's it going? Good? Well, I was just saying thanks for the cheques. You don't have to keep sending them, you know. But I have been putting them to good use. Got my porch to fix next. I'm thinking of asking your son to help, since he's sitting here eating me out of house and home. He any good with his hands? No? Well, I might ask him anyway. Nice talking to ya. Bye."

Mill hung up the phone. I don't believe she'd waited for my father to say good-bye. Or much of anything else.

"You like mustard?" she asked me. I hate the stuff, but I felt it politic to nod. "Good, because I put it on your sandwich. I didn't put on any mayonnaise. Mayonnaise is a waste of money. And they say it's bad for your heart. But I got Coke. You like Coke? Go get the platter from the kitchen and bring it in here."

Two glasses of Coke — with ice — and two honey ham sandwiches sat waiting on the platter. I brought them into the living room. Mill told me to push the newspapers off the couch and to sit down and eat. She had a dining room table, but it was too covered in junk to sit at.

"I'm not a brainchild, like your father," Mill said. She didn't give me time to protest. "I like plain talk. I like words I understand. So tell me this. When you write up this family history, are you going to put me in it?"

"Yes."

"You'd better get your facts right, then. I might be able to help you."

I sat back in my chair, wondering how I could work with this woman.

"Be sure to get it right about Aberdeen Williams," she said, out of the blue. "Crazy old bat thought he could marry a white woman in 1930! Humph. He learned his lesson good."

"How do you know about that?" I asked. I, too, had heard stories about Aberdeen in Oakville.

"You seem to think that only men are in your family story. But I was there, too. I used to live in Oakville. Get that through your half-nappy head. I was there, I keep telling you, and I won't be left out of this story. Aberdeen used to take care of me when I was a little girl. I intend to get on back up there and hug that man before we both kick off for good."

"He spends a lot of time at my folks' house, wandering around."

"I was just three years old when I first met Aberdeen. He was a teenager. I used to think he was so old. And now I'm four times the age he was then. Why don't you call him and tell him hello for me?"

I called directory assistance and got Aberdeen's number. But nobody answered the phone. Mill seemed disappointed.

The next day, Mill asked me, "Why're you so interested in your grandpappy, anyway?"

"He and Rose seemed to have an incredible relationship."

"I don't think *she* thought it was incredible. Him, neither."

"In what sense?"

"Get back in that room of mine and keep digging. I got me another box or two on them, diaries, letters, all sorts of junk. I was fixing to throw it all out soon. Takes up too much room."

"Don't throw it out. I might need that stuff."

"If you're going to write about them, you'd better put in the part about their long and rocky road."

June 5, 1919. Second Lieutenant Langston Cane, honorably discharged from the 368th Light Infantry Division of the American Expeditionary Forces, bearer of a medal for bravery displayed in risking enemy fire to drag an injured comrade back to the trenches in the Vosges Mountains, sat at the dining table in his parents' summer home near Frederick, Maryland. He was eating a piece of cherry pie. He felt numb. He had no desire to eat, but he ate anyway. His mother hovered around him. His sisters. In a rare display of affection, his father had shaken his hand three times. Rose, who sat across from him, should have thrown her arms around him and refused to let go. She should have sat in his lap at the table, gushing about her undying and absolute love for him. She should have thrown modesty to the winds and dragged him to a bed upstairs. But all she did was bite back her tears and force a smile.

Langston had waited a year for this day. A year, he'd been away. Fort Des Moines, Iowa. Camp Meade, Maryland. New York. On board the ship to England. To Brest. Dijon. La Metz. The Vosges Mountains. Paris. Nice. The Vosges Mountains again. Paris. Lyons. Normandy.

He had lived for her letters. *My darling boy*, she had written. *Just imagine I'm giving you the kisses I'm sending you. My darling boy, my lover, my husband.* All that, and more. And he had waited. Sometimes, he had waited a month for her letters. Once, in the trenches, he'd gone six weeks with no word. He'd spent a week in a makeshift hospital, a week on his back with dysentery, with more pounds lost than he cared to admit. It was hard to believe a body could give up that much fluid. No word from her all that time. Then, when her letters did get through, there was nothing she could possibly say that was sufficiently passionate or adequately distraught. Rose's crisply penned references to family visits and meals eaten seemed to make light of his longing and his discomfort. In the final months of the war, Rose's letters enraged him. He actually tore one of them up. He was dying of weariness of the whole thing, and felt suffocated by his hatred of the American war bureaucracy.

When they stationed him for weeks in Lyons, instead of sending him home after Armistice Day, he was so angry he wanted to shoot someone. He couldn't believe the destruction he found there. Decay. Desperation. There were no French men. He saw women, and children, and old, old men. But no young men. Children ran up to him for money. So did women. A young war widow took him into her bed in Lyons. Langston went into shock when he left her. He was aghast at himself. Over and over, he muttered, "Look what this war has done to me. If only they had sent me right home." Rose cascaded into his thoughts, and he drove her out. When he left the war widow, he put twenty dollars on her table. It wasn't asked for, but it wasn't refused. She asked him to come again. He never did. He checked himself for a month for symptoms. It was the only month in his entire year overseas that he had not wanted to return home. Never again, he told himself. Never again would he do that.

His letter writing dropped off. Finally, back to Paris. He was too dejected, too sick of being away, to enjoy the city. On to Brest. Then Dover. Sick for three days on the trip back across to New York. His trousers were falling down. With his knife point, he dug two extra notches in his belt. Rose had warned him in one of her last letters that she had put on fifteen pounds. He hadn't told her of his wartime dysentery. The bit he'd put back on in Paris after leaving the trenches was lost again over the Atlantic. He weighed himself in the infirmary during his last day of the crossing. One hundred and twenty-five pounds — twenty-five less than what he had weighed a year earlier.

In New York, the discharge process. The war was over. The returning soldiers had been fêted, long ago. There were no crowds waving, no flags flying. He could have sent a telegram from New York, to tell them he was coming. But he didn't. He resented her not being there in New York. She should have been waiting in the New York harbor, screaming, Langston! My darling! Look at you, my man! She should have known when he was coming. Made the necessary inquiries. In his final letter, from Brest, he had mentioned the name of the ship he'd be sailing on. But nobody was waiting for him in New York. And nobody was waiting for him in Baltimore. And he couldn't get a cab home. Life hadn't changed. America hadn't changed. And Rose wasn't there to greet him. Their house was empty. His key still fit the lock. Nice of them, not to change the lock. Empty house. He raged. He kicked his own bed, swept five glasses off a table. It was a Monday. The first Monday in May. They would be at the family home. Hill Crest. Just outside Frederick. It was two hours away, by a milk-run bus. Second Lieutenant Langston Cane sat in the back, brooding. Ready to shoot someone. In uniform still. Unwilling to take off that uniform until he had stood before his family.

The family summer home was two miles from the bus stop in Frederick. Second Lieutenant Cane decided to hoof it. He was a tad feverish, his eyes so tired they burned.

Langston stood at the foot of the dirt driveway up to the summer home, kit bag by his feet. He stood, waiting for Rose to come get him. He heard a scream from the porch. His girl. His baby. His Rose would come running to him now, and hug him, hold him, take him, guide him, kiss him, lead him up to meet his parents. Wrong. It wasn't her. It was his sister. His sister saw him first. Violet was the one screaming, not Rose. Violet ran down the road, grabbed him, hugged him, damn near knocked him over. Mother was behind her. Where was Rose? Where was Rose? Walking slowly down the driveway. Sniffling. Calling out his name, hesitantly, as if she didn't recognize him. Langston? Langston? She walked more quickly toward him, but never ran. Tears. She took his hand. Pecked his cheek. One single and solitary peck on the cheek. *Come on, Langston,* she said, *what are you standing there for? Let's get some food in you. Come on in, Langston.* He dropped her hand and walked up the drive. Rose walked beside him. She didn't take his hand again. Violet carried his bag. Mother was screaming, now, to her husband in the backyard. *Your son is home. Your boy is back.*

Langston noticed the gleaming hardwood floor, saw his father coming, tall and dark and stately with his hand out. Langston felt it coming and could do nothing, absolutely nothing, about it. Dizzy, swirling, round and round, down. Out.

He woke up in bed. Nobody there. No Rose. Waited for her to come. Waited ten minutes. Finally got out of bed and stomped a bit. She arrived right away. He let her know that he didn't care for her kind words, for her solicitations. They were too late.

Where was she when he was in France? In New York? In Baltimore? Where was she when he was at the Frederick bus depot? Langston felt as dry as kindling inside. He saw Rose crying and didn't care.

The next day, eating with the family, Langston mumbled something about feeling bone-tired. "But you never liked clichés, did you, Rose?"

Rose got up and came to stand behind his chair. "A returning soldier is allowed whatever cliché his heart desires," she said.

Langston managed a smile. When he heard her sniffle, he offered his hand up over his shoulder, and she took it.

"You never told us you won a medal, son," his father said.

Langston felt Rose's breast against his neck.

"My boy," she said. "My boy is home."

He fell asleep before dinner, woke up before dark, slept another hour, awoke before midnight. Up and down through the night. Never more than two hours of sleep at a time. Rose never complained. She stayed by his side, in bed. After three days, four days, a week, he finally started to sleep. Still, he hadn't held her man to wife. For another six days, he went to bed after dinner. On the seventh day, he awakened at ten on a Saturday morning. Looked outside and saw Rose hanging clothes on the line. His parents and sisters were in Baltimore. Father would be preparing his sermon. Violet had a job nearby in Harpers Ferry. Rose was here alone. Langston knew that nobody was in the house. He climbed out of bed, tumescent, and bathed. Still tumescent. Wandered downstairs with a towel around his waist. Let the white cloth fall from his chocolate and — as Rose once observed — supremely edible behind, turned his wife around, took her mouth with his, and tried to get her down on the grass. She giggled, laughed, pushed free. *No, sir. That's out of the question. Get your behind up those stairs and I will follow you when I'm through hanging these clothes. Langston! Stop that this minute. Put that towel back on! What if somebody comes by? Go on, get upstairs. I'm coming, I'm coming, I've been waiting a year for you, my darling lieutenant, so don't you worry. I'm coming.*

Langston taught elementary school in Baltimore for a term, but that didn't work out. He sold encyclopedias, but gave that up after two months. He put up with all manner of ridicule from the Bridges family. Loretta was enrolled in medical school. Rose was teaching elementary school, making better money than Langston. This couldn't last. He applied to law school, and was accepted, but didn't have enough savings to study full-time. His parents had no extra cash, and he refused to let Rose ask her parents for money for his education.

Rose hated Baltimore. She didn't like Langston's state of stagnation. And she certainly didn't enjoy living with her in-laws, in their house, with the stampede of visitors and delegations and bishops and deacons from the African Methodist Episcopal Church. Rose was getting lured by her mother. Hazel Bridges offered to pay for Rose to study law or medicine if she left Langston.

Rose became pregnant. Langston spoke with his father one evening, continuing late into the night. His father made some inquiries. They conferred, again confidentially, late into the night. Rose suspected something was up. She was six months pregnant. Langston announced that he had decided to join the A.M.E. Church ministry. His father had found him a position in Independence, Missouri.

———————

He thinks I won't leave him, Rose told herself. Just because I'm pregnant, he thinks I won't go. He's got something else coming. I have options. I have my family. I don't have to put up with this.

"I'm not going, Langston."

"Of course you're going. *We* are going, together. We'll make do."

"You promised," she said.

"Things change. Situations change. I had no idea, before the war, that I'd be this strapped for employment. We can't keep on like this. It's time to settle down. In our own home. Start our own life."

"Yes. But not like that. I won't go. I'm sorry. You go, if you must. I will not."

"You are my wife."

"I waited for you when you were in Europe."

"I wasn't *in Europe*! I was at war. I was in the trenches. I shot men, and I was shot at."

"And you seemed like such a hero to me, at the time. But when you came back, everything changed. You were self-absorbed, you didn't ask me one question about how I was, or what I had gone through, or what it was like to wait for a husband who might never return home. And do you know what, Langston? You still haven't asked me any questions. You haven't given the least indication that you think about me. Now I'm pregnant and you want to march me off to some outpost of A.M.E. illiterates in Missouri. Well, I won't do it, Langston. I won't go."

Langston stood up. He cleared his throat. He placed his hands behind his back, folded them together. Piano, pianissimo, he announced: "You are my wife, Rose Bridges, and I expect you by my side in Independence, Missouri. I'm leaving tomorrow. Our things are packed. I have committed myself to the ministry. You may take a week, if you need it, but I expect you by my side."

Langston told the members of his congregation — 250 people, mostly old, mostly women, mostly illiterate, some born slaves, some sold on a slave block only a hundred yards from the decrepit A.M.E. church — that his wife would arrive shortly. That she was clearing up their affairs in Baltimore. That she was expecting and wanted to visit the doctor one more time before coming to join him.

"I had fifteen children with no doctor," muttered the oldest woman in his congregation. Ma'am Sandra was the only way she identified herself. She was in charge of the churchwomen who cleaned Langston's parsonage. They had swept the floors and painted the walls before his arrival, filled the mattress slips with corn husks, cleaned the soot out of the wood stove, poured lime in the outhouse, stocked his shelves with food.

Langston was paid twenty dollars a month. The parsonage was given free of charge, and the churchwomen promised to supply him with food.

Rose arrived with two trunks. The trunks, and their contents, were likely worth more than the combined wealth of all Langston's congregation. Rose nearly turned around and left within an hour of her arrival. *We are to eat from the hands of these barefooted churchwomen? And you expect me to accept that?* Langston told her that he needed her. He said he understood that this was a mammoth step down from the comforts she had known, but that they would climb back up together.

Rose agreed to stay the night. She stayed on beyond that. She went into labor in the parsonage. There was no doctor. No running water. Just some old churchwoman who declared herself a midwife and said she had brought most of the congregation into this world, and did indeed seem to know when Rose should hang on and when it was time to push. When the baby's head popped out, Langston saw the midwife's hands move like greased lightning toward the silent, squeezed face covered in blood and mucus and vernix. It took him a moment to register that the midwife had just pulled the umbilical cord clear from around the baby's neck. At that moment, the baby's squalling filled the room. They named her Millicent.

Rose's parents were scandalized when they heard of the conditions in which she had given birth. "Leave that heathen husband," her mother wrote. "Vacate that throwback to plantation living. You deserve better. Your child deserves better! Come to Mother this very day!"

Rose and the baby did leave. The members of the congregation gathered around Langston. They propped him up — as he liked to say — on every leaning side. They fed him, cleaned the parsonage, washed his clothes, and refrained from denigrating his wife within earshot. In turn, Langston ministered to them.

He spoke of slavery and emancipation, war and peace, justice and injustice, parents and children. He attended the sick. He quoted the Bible. He did not speak down to them. He was the first learned black man in their midst. He didn't raise the roof when he gave a sermon. He dropped his voice, when it counted. Decrescendo, piano, pianissimo, *bang*. Love your fellow man, he told them. Feed the hungry. Tend to the ailing. Raise your children with love and with books. The people kept Langston Cane from falling apart. And Langston learned to love the people.

Rose returned when Millicent was three months old. She stayed nearly a year, then left. She returned after two months, then left again, insisting that she would not return to that backwater.

Langston conferred with his father, who intervened. This was the last time Langston senior would be able to help his son, for the elder Langston would die a few months later, at age sixty-three. But first, he wrote to the bishop. He helped find a better parsonage for his son. Langston junior met Rose and Millicent at the train station in D.C., and they moved to Denver, Colorado.

Langston thought they would be safe out west. Safe from the Bridgeses. Safe from Rose's departures. He was wrong. Rose couldn't stand the A.M.E. women, who were always interfering, always trying to tell her how to cook her food, paint her walls, fold her laundry, run her home. They'd tell her how to clean her own backside if she let them. She stayed a year and left. Back to D.C. with Millicent. She stayed away for three months. Her mother pleaded with her not to return to Langston. Hazel Bridges had Millicent rebaptized, as a Catholic. Rose attended the Catholic church on Saturday nights and Sunday mornings. She met an old high school acquaintance, now a young dentist in D.C., and saw him several times.

Langston's sister Violet — now living in D.C. — heard of this young man and Rose. Langston exploded in a letter. Rose exploded back. A male friend of Violet's just happened to cross Rose's dentist friend one evening in D.C., and just happened to land a few blows.

Again, Langston wrote to his wife.

My dearest little girl,
    May I still call you that? There was a time when we spoke in such terms, with no hesitation. At war, I swore that when I returned, I'd never spend another minute away from you. Yet

we've been apart more after the war, it seems, than we were during it.

I know I have failed you. I realize that my patience has been short, many times, and that I have been inflexible in fulfilling my ministerial responsibilities. I know, too, that I have not provided for you in a manner consonant with your material needs and expectations.

All that will change, if you allow me another chance. I have obtained word of a possibility of moving to Canada. We used to speak of Canada, when we were lovers before the war. I know I mentioned to you that my grandfather, Langston Cane the First, a fugitive slave, had escaped to Canada. He lived for some years in a town called Oakville, in the province of Ontario. Oakville is still there. It is not far from Toronto, a major city with all the amenities one could ask for. The A.M.E. has an opening for a small ministry in Oakville. I have made all the inquiries.

Please, keep an open mind. Listen to these details with your mind and your heart.

The parsonage will be provided. From the description given, it is two or three times the size of the Denver parsonage. The rate of pay is a hundred Canadian dollars a month — twice the amount I get here. Oakville is a small but clean town. There is a small Negro community. The town is on the shores of Lake Ontario. The winter is harsh. But we can handle cold climate. All that we've come through will make the climate a mere whim, a hurdle of next-to-no-importance.

I would inhabit an igloo, my dearest, if only to have you and Millicent back.

My baby is almost three years old, now, and I barely know her. She certainly acts as if she barely knows me! Let's change

all that. Come back, Rose. Or, tell me that you'll join me in
Oakville, Canada. Promise me that, and I will meet you in
D.C. and make the trip north with you.

Your loving lieutenant,
Langston

They exchanged a few letters. Rose was interested. She had a few
questions. How many bedrooms did the parsonage contain?
Was there indoor plumbing and an indoor bathroom? Was the
parsonage in the village or in some isolated rural area? Langston
was able to answer them sufficiently. There were three
bedrooms. Yes, there was plumbing and a toilet. And although
she hadn't asked, he assured her that the house had electricity. It
was a modern house located on Colbourne Street, in the very
heart of town.

In her next letter, Rose consented to move to Oakville with
Langston and Millicent. They met in D.C. They spent a week
with Langston's mother in Baltimore. Langston refused to set
foot in the Bridgeses' residence, and nobody invited him. But
the day before they departed, Dr. Bridges came to meet
Langston. He said that he, like the others, had been scandalized
to hear about some of the conditions in which Rose had lived.
That he had been so upset by the conditions surrounding the
birth of Millicent that he had vowed, at one point, to join Hazel
in doing everything possible to sever the husband and wife. But
his position had softened, over the years. He understood and
admired Langston's devotion to his work and to his wife.
Langston must have suffered terribly during these absences! God
bless him. Best wishes to them all. Bon voyage, son-in-law.

———————————

They arrived by train in Toronto in 1923. At Union Station, they were met by a minister of the A.M.E. Church in Toronto. He and his wife put up the Canes for two nights. They visited the waterfront. Walked on Yonge Street. Sat, to their amazement, next to white folks in an Italian restaurant. They were assured, however, that not every restaurant and not every hotel would admit black people. You just had to know where to go. And then it was on to Oakville. Rose loved it from the moment she saw the shops on Lakeshore Road. That night, in a parsonage with running water and central heating and electricity and lights and even a basement, Rose took her husband into her arms. They conceived Langston Cane the Fourth on that night.

Chapter 13

TWO DAYS IN MILL'S HOUSE was enough. I had to get out. She had a thing about not opening windows. The larger the opening, the more chance that some street dweller would climb inside, tie her up, and steal her possessions. Unless a visitor was expected, she did not answer the doorbell. "Whoever it is, I don't want them. I'll just wait until they go away."

It wasn't just the closed door and the atrophied windows that I found stifling. Mill did not wash dishes. She let them pile up in the sink, shoved them unwashed under the sink, and cleaned a plate or fork when she couldn't do without one. I wanted to help her, but didn't know where to start. I wouldn't have known where to put dishwater, or where to put clean dishes. There were two fridges in the house. The one in the kitchen had sour yogurt and moldy cheese. When you opened it, the smell leapt out at you like a hyena. The other fridge was in the living room. It was disconnected. I opened the door and found books, *TV Guides*, and old magazines. At first, I silently cursed Mill for never throwing anything out. But then I thanked her. I was lucky she had never junked our family papers.

I drove home, parked on the street, noticed my landlady peering out from behind her shades, and got into my apartment. Someone rapped on my door. The knock came swiftly, three times. Then three times again.

It was Yoyo. "Hey, man, are you all right? You haven't been around."

"I'm fine," I said.

"The landlady was going to clear out your things, but I reasoned with her."

"What are you talking about?"

"Rent was due yesterday."

"I'll pay her when I go out."

"I would pay her right now, if I were you."

"Have you had lunch?"

"No."

"Then let me take you out. How come you're not working, anyway? Isn't this prime time for shish kebabs?"

Yoyo told me it was a long story. I paid Elvina Peck and apologized. Then I drove north on Charles, past Hopkins, past all the huge trees, past Thirty-fourth Street, drove a few miles north, and then headed west along Northern Parkway until I wound down a big hill toward Mount Washington. While I drove, Yoyo explained that the cops had come back to him. Not the same nice white cop as before — the one Yoyo had bribed with two kebabs. This one was black, and on a moral crusade. No selling meat on the sidewalk without a license! He confiscated Yoyo's equipment, took his money as evidence of illegal earnings, and brought him to a police station downtown. Yoyo actually managed to escape. He didn't want to talk about it any more. He'd tell me later, maybe. I reached over and touched Yoyo's hand. "I know a woman who would pay you to clean her house. And she might have some friends." Yoyo brightened at the prospect. He hadn't eaten in twenty-four hours.

I took him to Le Café Chez Washington, which was run by French immigrants. Yoyo was delighted. Immediately, he started talking to a woman serving bread.

I ordered a croissant with goat cheese and cucumber. Yoyo looked faintly disgusted. He took beef soup and *poulet au citron*. He kept on talking, after lunch, with the woman who had served us. I opened up the *Baltimore Sun*. In the international news section, I found a story from Canada.

— Toronto

Members of the militant black group Africa First, who claim to have kidnapped a prominent white Canadian doctor, have refused to publicly table any demands.

Dr. Norville Watson, 77, a Toronto urologist whose conservative views on integration and human rights have been criticized by black leaders, disappeared while walking on Tuesday night. His wife contacted police after he failed to return home at the usual time.

Less than 12 hours later, a group calling itself Africa First — a previously unknown organization — sent a letter to the *Toronto Times*, condemning Watson's "blatantly racist" attitudes and claiming that it "intercepted him for the good of society."

Police stated that they know nothing of the group. Black community leaders say they haven't heard of it either.

"It could be a hoax," said Dr. Langston Cane of Oakville. Cane, who is black and is also a prominent physician, lobbied for years for the rights of blacks, and frequently crossed swords with Watson in the 1950s and 1960s.

I showed the article to Yoyo.

"Toronto would not be a good place for black people right now," he said. He gave out a hearty laugh. "Africa First. I'd be in big trouble. They'd scoop me right up off the streets. *Hey, you! You, Mr. Africa First! Come this way, please.*"

After two days in Mill's mausoleum, the lunch with Yoyo, and the news about Norville Watson, I sat down and wrote about what I had seen and read and done in Baltimore. Later, I started to think again about Ellen, and about how we had come together and broken apart. Every generation had its story, and I was finally ready to tell mine. I started to write again.

Ellen and I had been planning to have a child, but had decided to hang on a little longer, when I finally got approval from the government of Mali to live in a remote village. I had been wanting for a long time to go there to research a novel. We agreed that I should take the trip, that I might not get the chance again, that it would be hard to do, later, with children. But one night, not long after planning the trip, I didn't bother with a condom. I wanted a baby. I wanted it growing right away. What if I didn't come back? What if I died over there? What if I caught malaria and my fever shot so high that I became sterile? I wanted to plant the seed immediately. Just in case.

When the test came back positive, Ellen said she still wanted me to go. "It's only for two months. You'll be back in plenty of time to catch our baby."

I left her at five o'clock on a June morning. It had been hot the night before, hot and humid for days. Toronto was in the midst of a heat wave, with temperatures around a hundred degrees Fahrenheit. We lived in a flat over a fur store so full of cockroaches that they crawled inside the face of our clock radio, and under the hour and minute hands of the clock on our stove. Lots of bugs, but not a molecule of air. You could open every window, but it made no difference. At night, it was hotter inside our place than outside. We had a secondhand air conditioner in the living room window, which looked out over Dovercourt Road. But the machine couldn't push enough cold air down the hall to make a difference in the bedroom. We draped a sheet over the living room entrance and waited out the heat spell in that room. We ate, read, and slept there. And on the eve of my departure for Africa, we lay there, too sad to make love.

"I'll miss you like crazy," she said.

"No, you won't," I said, stroking her lips. "You'll probably spend the whole summer bowling."

That cracked her up. Ellen had never bowled in her life. When she stopped laughing, she said: "We're never going to split up again, okay?"

"I thought you wanted me to go."

"I do. But never again. Not without me."

"Not without you. Or Babo." Babo was our name for the baby.

Ellen took my arm. "Babo says, *Hey, Dad, you started me, so why don't you hang around and watch me sprout?*"

"You tell Babo," I said, "that I'll be back long before Babo is ready to make an appearance."

Ellen hummed when she heard that. She had a way of humming when she ate good food. She hummed as we lay together. She hummed, and she kept her hand curved below her stomach.

Ellen came down to the sidewalk to see me off. She stood in her bathrobe. I couldn't see any bulge yet.

"*Je t'aime*," she said.

I got into the taxi and took a short breath.

"I'll miss you like crazy," she said.

I nodded. It was all I could do. The car started moving. Then it stopped.

"What's wrong?" I asked the driver.

"Your wife."

I looked back. Ellen was waving. I got out.

"I want to hear your voice," she said. "Say something."

"I love you, Ellen."

Ellen and I took our first trip together when we were sixteen. Years later, people couldn't believe that we had met so long ago and had never been apart. Our first trip was a two-week school excursion to Trois-Pistoles, Quebec, in the spring of 1973. We were ostensibly there to learn French, but our real motivation was to get out on our own. People asked whether Ellen and I were going together. We weren't. We just liked being together. We liked other people, too, but we enjoyed them most when we were together.

We were the same height, at the age of sixteen.

"It's nice for talking," Ellen said. "You don't have to look up or down."

"Nice for other things, too," I said.

"Like what?"

"You know."

"Tell me."

"Walking," I said. Ellen leaned into my arm. She had a laugh that rang out like a bell.

One Friday in Trois-Pistoles, Ellen and I hitched a ride to Bic, a village on the St. Lawrence River just upstream from Rimouski. We tried to check into a hotel, but they turned us away for not being married. A bed-and-breakfast house took us, however. Our window, on the second floor, looked out over the wide river. It was cool outside, perhaps fifty-five degrees, and white caps slid on the river. Our room had an antique dresser, a rocking chair, and a miniature Jesus on a cross bleeding over the bed. Ellen lifted the crucifix off the hook and put it in the closet.

"There's just one bed," I said. "Are you sleeping in the bathtub?"

"I'm going to read a book," she said, tumbling back on the mattress. "Why don't you go for a walk?"

"What for?"

"To buy condoms."

"But I don't even know how to —"

"I'll teach you," she said. "I'll be gentle and understanding. But I expect you to catch on quick."

"I was trying to say that I don't know how to say condom in French."

"Don't worry about that. Just tell the pharmacist what you want. Describe them. You know, something like *un produit en caoutchouc, qui s'étire selon le besoin.*"

"Is this the gentle teaching style you promised?" I said. Ellen burst out laughing. She leaned forward and kissed me.

"Do you remember the time we danced together?" she said.

"It was at Christmas."

"I've been wanting you since then."

"Why didn't you tell me?" I asked. "Why didn't you say you wanted to go out with me?"

"I don't want to *go out* with you. I want to sleep with you."

"If we're only sleeping, why bother with condoms?"

"One of us might wake up with an irresistible urge."

"True enough. I always get up to pee at night."

"Why are you being so smart-assed?" Ellen said.

"I've never done this before."

"I'm not exactly an old hand."

"An old hen? I should say not. I think you're beautiful."

Ellen kissed me again. We sat on the bed. I molded my lips to hers. She took my kiss, and matched it, and we got hot, and then she stopped me.

"Close your eyes." I obeyed. "Now stand up." I did. "Point to where you think my left breast would be." I pointed. "Point to my right breast." I pointed. "Point to my navel." I pointed, lower. "Point to my vagina." I swallowed. A tremor went up my thigh. I pointed, as she instructed, and my finger slid into a warm, wet cavity. I opened my eyes. Ellen had slipped down on her knees and opened her mouth. I shook with desire. I got hard in an instant.

"Go get those condoms," she said. "I don't want a baby."

"Never?"

"Not until I'm thirty."

"I can't imagine being that old."

"Go get the condoms. And hurry back."

In the village of Bupti, not long before the message came that my brother had been phoning the Canadian embassy, I had heard Dionne Warwick's "I Say a Little Prayer for You" on a transistor radio at one in the morning. I got up off the straw mattress and stood at the door of my mud hut to catch the last strains of the song. I saw the back of a man disappearing in the night, and I saw six mules, long-faced, silver in the moonlight, looking at me with wide eyes and pointed ears.

The message came the next day by way of a girl who had walked ten miles from the nearest village with a basket of fruit on her head. She appeared as the village men and I were crouched around a bowl of food, tearing meat from a bird that had been bled and plucked and cleaned and cooked in a tomato and peanut sauce that lit a pleasant burn in the throat. It was a burn I had grown accustomed to, a burn that I could manage, a burn that said, You're among these people and becoming part of them. As I watched the girl lift the fruit basket off her head, I bit unsuspectingly into a hot pepper that flared like a match in my mouth. Suddenly, I heard the girl say *toubab*, the word for white man, which was the way Malians described me, although they knew I wasn't really white, or not entirely so. Then I heard her say *toubab ke ka so*, wife of the white man.

The village men, who had been grunting and laughing and urging me to eat, ceased talking in an instant. They dropped their hands and stared at the young girl. I stared, too. Her eyes were as dark as her skin, her knees looked like knots on twigs, her fingers were callused well beyond her thirteen years, and her feet were lined and wrinkled and dusty. The men burst into a cacophony of questions. I understood that the girl had just walked the ten miles from Kinto. Youssouf, the village elder, asked her something. She answered with her eyes lowered. Again I heard *toubab ke ka so*. Everyone looked at me.

"She brings a message," Youssouf said. "She says you must talk to your brother. About your wife."

The girl spoke again. Five men, all crouched with their behinds just off the earth and their elbows near their knees, again shouted questions at her.

Youssouf silenced them. "She says the message came by telephone to Bamako, and then someone called Sikasso, and then someone called the prefect in Segain, who sent a message to the chief of Kinto."

"What was the message, exactly?"

Youssouf asked the question for me. The men groaned at the answer. They looked at me with long faces. No man touched his food.

"She says she doesn't know."

"Where is the nearest phone?" I asked.

"In the prefect's office."

"How far is that?"

"A long walk. You must go to this girl's village. From there you must take a car to the next village."

"How long does the whole trip take?" I knew it was a stupid question. Youssouf and his people didn't use watches. They used the sun, and the moon, and battery-powered flashlights. They used their arms to hoe and mules to take goods to market. They slept on straw mats in huts that stayed cool even in the heat of the day.

Youssouf said someone would take me there tomorrow.

"What about tonight?"

It would be dark soon, Youssouf said. I knew that. I knew it wasn't safe to walk the trails at night. I knew about the potholes, and the scorpions, and that no phone would be available in the middle of the night.

I thanked the girl for coming, which shocked her, because she thought I spoke no Bambara at all. Then I told her *Alla ka e deme,* which was a blessing from Allah.

The girl mumbled *Amina*, in thanks. She lowered her basket, hoping to sell the fruit, but Youssouf sent her out.

Georges pushed his share of meat my way. "Eat. You must walk a long way tomorrow."

But I could not eat. I had gone off on this trip while my wife was pregnant. To make matters much, much worse, just a few nights ago, I had taken a village woman into my bed.

Light drained from the western skies. Branches of the baobab trees, which had been black against the setting sun, began to lose their details, their shape. A breeze rose as the heat slid out of the air. I went to see Djeneba, Youssouf's third wife, who was scraping the pot in which our chicken had been cooked. She used sand and water and the palm of her hand. She rubbed hard, splashed the pot with water, checked for scum, and rubbed again. She worked in a windowless hut that had a cauldron of water over three burning sticks, a vat of cold well water, and other pots on the earth by her feet. The hut brimmed with smoke.

In i su, I said, good evening.

In i su o koro ke toubabuke, she said, good evening, white brother.

Djeneba was seated on the ground, rubbing the pot with the heel of her palm. The soles of her feet were painted the color of dried blood.

"Your brother has sent for you," she said.

"I will talk to him tomorrow."

"May Allah bless you," she said.

"Thank you."

"Bless your parents, your brothers, your children," she said.

"I have no children."

"But your wife. . ."

"Yes," I said, sticking out my belly, rubbing it.

She laughed hard, shaking her whole shoulders, slapping the chicken pot. She had heard me say that my wife was pregnant, and she had joked with me about it, although she would never admit to such a thing about herself. It was considered bad luck to discuss pregnancy. A woman could go up to her eighth month denying that she was carrying another life.

"Bless your wife a thousand times."

"Thank you. Djeneba, I need hot water to wash."

"I know, *toubabuke*. The water is waiting for you."

"Thank you, Djeneba."

"Men don't thank their women here." She said it again, to be sure I understood. "We feed them, and we wash their clothes, and we do the work, but men don't thank us."

"I will be leaving tomorrow."

"We will all remember you," she said.

"Good-bye, Djeneba," I said.

"Don't say good-bye until tomorrow. But tell me, are all Canadians like you?"

I asked what she meant.

"Would they all leave their rich country to come live with us?"

"How do you know my country is rich?" I asked.

She took hold of my wrist, turned it over, released it. "Your bones are thick."

The bucket of hot water was waiting outside the bathing cubicle. I carried it into the walled enclosure, draping a towel outside the hardened mud to signal that the bath was occupied. I removed my clothing, except for my sandals, and squatted on a small mound, from which water would run. Overhead, birds flitted from branch to branch. Water, hot water, gave off steam from the pail. Using a ladle made from a calabash that had been split, gutted, and dried, I splashed warm water onto my face, neck, arms, and body, soaked my soap bar and washcloth, and scrubbed my face and neck. A breeze stirred in the trees, brushed across my face. I rinsed the soap away with more hot water. I washed my arms and legs and genitals and butt and used the remaining water to rinse myself.

I looked over the mud wall. In the compound, children ran after a mule, which they had harassed into a trot. Chickens picked over the bones of their brethren. One of Youssouf's daughters swept the ground where we had eaten earlier, pushing bird bones and mango skins into a pile. Djeneba passed by with a pail of water on her head. Her feet made no sound. She seemed weightless. She held herself erect, chin high, back arched. Her biceps shone in the moonlight. Her breasts knocked about gently as she glided toward the kitchen. Ellen was in trouble. I was in Mali. And I had been unfaithful to her.

I stayed up late drinking tea with Youssouf. He was an old man, seventy-three, he believed, but he watched the world with a child's curiosity. His legs could still go ten miles under the sun, and his hands, long-fingered and knuckle-swollen, were steadier than mine. Earlier in the day, I had watched Youssouf scrape his hunting knife across an iron block, scrape one side and then the other, until he could slice hemp so fast that the split ends jumped back. I watched as he tugged a stiff-legged goat to the killing ground. He rolled it on its side, bound its front legs with one rope and its hind legs with another. The animal quivered. Youssouf spoke to the animal, placing his hand on its neck. The goat settled down. Youssouf drew the knife hard from the goat's ear to its windpipe and kept the goat still as its blood ran out fast.

As Youssouf poured my fourth tea, I said he seemed to have known the animal.

"What animal?"

"The goat."

"Knew the animal?" he repeated, laughing, and slapped his thigh. "We don't know animals here in this country. We eat them, and we like them in our bellies, especially with tomatoes and gumbo." Youssouf drank his last tea, the fourth being the sweetest, sighed, stood up, kicked away a mango peel, and wished me good night.

I walked to the hut I had occupied for two months, a square hut of mud walls with one door, no windows, a corrugated tin roof, and an earthen floor.

Georges, my roommate, sat on his bed of dried bamboo shoots, back to the wall, shining a flashlight on a sore on his leg. He slid a Sony Walkman and earphones toward my bed.

"Should I look at the cut?" I asked.

"Yes, I was hoping you would."

Pus ran from the sore, so I gave him antibiotic cream.

"So, you bastard," I said, so he wouldn't feel he had to commiserate with me, "I see you were running down my Walkman batteries all night."

Georges broke into baritone laughter that verged on the diabolical. "*Salaud*," he cried out, "you have developed the African eye. You see too much now."

He listened to the Walkman at all hours and had been seen carrying it into the toilet. He also had a habit of falling asleep with the thing wrapped around his ears. For now, however, Georges relinquished the Walkman. He took my hand, and told me that we were like brothers, and said that he was traveling to the capital city with me the next day.

It wasn't a question. It was a statement. It meant, I knew, double the cost for bush taxis, and food, and hotels, and whatever else might come after my phone call to Canada. Georges had no money, but he knew that I had enough to take him with me.

"You need a translator. You need a friend."

He had me there.

Georges worked for the national Ministry of Youth and Culture. When Malian government officials had finally agreed — after several refusals — to let me move into a remote village for two months, they sent Georges to serve as my translator and guide, and also, I suspect, to ensure that my behavior did not warrant deportation.

Spying on me would have been an easy task, but Georges spent much of his days drinking tea with the elders, listening to Radio Moscow on his shortwave transistor, and stalking an eighteen-year-old girl who had been taken as the fourth wife of a man three times older. The only time I could be sure to see Georges was at mealtime — particularly when they were killing an animal in my honor. Georges never missed a feast, and he ate everything he could.

"North Americans like to feel guilty," Georges would say as he sank his teeth into meat. "It makes them feel good. But guilt changes nothing. Food — that changes something. I say, when there's food around, eat it! You never know when you'll see it again."

Georges had traveled around the world. Japan. Europe. Canada. Elsewhere in West Africa. He had been sent by his government on learning missions paid for by host countries. He had been to Quebec and had eaten *tarte au sucre* and maple syrup. He wore a kimono at night and had brought an extra and was honored when I consented to wear it. He had a pack of cards featuring naked dancers from Le Moulin Rouge. But he had no money. His government frequently ran out of money and had to suspend salaries to civil servants. Georges had been without pay for two months when we met. "What can you do if your employer has no money? *Les salauds* — they will pay me after they steal from somebody else." He shot off a cannon of laughter that seemed to echo from a cave.

Georges was snoring minutes later. He could sleep anywhere. Once, I had heard him snore in the back of a Peugeot.

I listened to Georges snore for a while. Then I looked out the door and saw two mules staring in at me. They made no move to enter the hut. They remained motionless for so long that I wondered whether I was imagining them. But I wasn't. I got out of bed and took one step, and they turned and ambled away.

We left before sunrise to avoid the heat. Georges strapped my belongings to a mule, but he urged me to walk. "Why sit on an animal that travels as slowly as you? You'll end up hating it."

It took us four hours to walk to the next village, and another five to find a car and arrange to be driven to a town with a phone. As soon as we got there, I called the operator. Within minutes, my brother was telling me about Ellen.

Sean didn't swear. Didn't say that I had been stupid and blind to run off to Africa while my wife was pregnant. He just said that Ellen, twenty weeks pregnant, had contracted food poisoning and lost her baby. It was a boy, Sean said.

I felt a mix of Novocain and adrenaline flood my veins. *When,* I whispered, *when did she lose the baby?* I knew the answer. The answer was predetermined. *She lost the baby on Saturday afternoon,* Sean said. He kept talking. I lost him for a moment.

Saturday was the night that woman had come into my bed. We'd had a long hour of loving, that woman and I. I tried to tell myself that it was a one-nighter, unimportant to my relationship with Ellen. *Langston. Langston. Are you still there?* My brother was shouting into the phone. I told him I was there. He said Ellen was delirious and running a fever and wanted me to come home. I thought about the flight, every Wednesday, from Bamako to Paris. This was a Monday. It would take twenty-four hours to get to Bamako, and it could take days of haggling to get a seat. I told my brother I'd be there in a few days, if I was lucky. Lucky. What a funny word. My brother sighed. *Langston, oh Langston, do what you can.*

Georges stayed with me until the last minute, pushing through crowds for me. He had used my wad of francs to pay off the airport commissar, an airline ticket agent, the ticket agent's manager, and a baggage handler to get me on the flight. When it came time to leave, Georges pressed a cassette into my hands and said listening to it would make me feel better.

The flight was supposed to leave Bamako at nine p.m., but we didn't take off until midnight. I had a window seat. We finally taxied down the runway and pulled up into the air with the motors crescendoing, god-like, as if nothing could stop them from pulling human beings through the heavens. I peered down to think about Georges escorting me to the capital in a seven-hour bush taxi trip from the south of the country. I tried to see the Niger River, but I could see only headlights of cars crossing the long bridge into Bamako, and a fire burning in the city. A woman sat next to me in the airplane, but she averted her eyes. The interior lights dimmed. All around me I saw a morgue of bodies, travelers twisted and cramped, heads knocking and feet splayed in aisles. Everyone slept but the woman beside me, who remained immobile.

I listened to Georges' cassette. The voice of Ami Koita, a Malian griot, scaling and slithering up and down an octave and a half, was accompanied by a balafon. The staccatoed notes fell as lightly as rain. I turned off the cassette. It couldn't stop me from thinking of Ellen, and of our baby. If it had been a girl, I would have tendered the name Aminata, which meant "the peaceful one." But we had a boy, born early, born dead. Ellen told me, later, that she had held him before they took him away and that he had my fat lower lip. She said a nurse had taken a picture. I didn't want to see it.

I waited for my connecting flight at Charles de Gaulle airport. It was six in the morning. The shops were closed. I had a ten-hour stopover. I was so tired that I didn't trust myself. I wanted to talk to nobody, and to go nowhere. Buses left regularly for the Champs Élysées and the Arc de Triomphe, but I couldn't stand the thought of them. I wanted to lie down and close my eyes and not have to live the twenty hours that stood between Paris and home.

The wait was unbearable. My mind was like an infant. As soon as I turned it from trouble, it crawled back for more. Ellen and I had watched baby videos in a prenatal course in Toronto. I turned from the thought, let my eyelids drop, and slid back to the memory of my infidelity on Saturday. I had been with that woman at night. Ellen had lost the baby the same day, in the afternoon. Mali was six hours ahead of Toronto, so Ellen lost that baby at the very moment that I was . . . I tried to drive out the thought.

I made myself imagine a face massage. I imagined the pressure of Ellen's fingers. She used to edge her thumbs along my brows, tug and pull and stroke my ears, push at cheekbones, forehead, hairline, scalp, and even, when my lids were closed, press gently against my eyeballs. Ellen had massaged my face the night she had become pregnant. My eyes had been sealed and fingers limp and arms asleep when she traced my lips with her fingers, parted them, shifted her weight on the bed, and planted her mouth on mine.

I had been standing in a corridor on the lowest level of the Charles de Gaulle airport, shoulder against a wall, dozing for I don't know how long. Ten seconds? A minute? A man in a brown uniform wheeled a washtub down the hall, away from the tourist shops. I walked that way, too. Trays and dishes clanged. The smell of espresso filled the air. It seemed to say to me, and to me only, that there were wars and pollution and lost babies and more, but there was still coffee, good coffee— at least there was that. The worker I'd been watching unlocked a door, rolled his tub into a closet, locked it again, and turned to meet a young woman striding toward him. She wore running shoes and had a cloth in the belt of her work pants. Her brown hair was pulled into a bun. She leaned into him. He pinched her ass, and she gave out a squeal and brought her mouth to his, and they stood there, fused. Their lips came apart and drew together again as they walked, side by side, across the hall. They ended up under a doorway with a sign in green and orange neon lettering that said *L'Arc-en-ciel*. The Rainbow. He ran his hand up the back of her thigh, rubbed her ass, squeezed it. She took his cheeks in her hands and kissed him as if she were devouring perfect fruit. They moved together into the cafeteria. I followed them.

It was full of flight attendants, pilots, floor cleaners, salespeople. They were all talking, laughing, eating, drinking. On tables I saw croissants and coffee. My stomach grumbled. Waiters wheeled trays of cheeses, pastries, fruit, yogurt, baguettes, croissants. I had barely eaten in three days. The floor cleaner and his lover hailed a waiter and paid for croissants and two bowls of café au lait. I took a table. A waiter came by. He clapped his hands and his dark eyes rose and his handlebar mustache lifted with his smile and he said "*Bonjour!*" like an old friend.

I took a croissant with a café au lait. The waiter poured espresso from a big thermos and mixed in steaming milk. I asked for an *allongé*: lots of milk, little coffee. He teased me about the weak coffee. It wouldn't even kick my heart into gear, he warned, *ça ne fera même pas vibrer le coeur*. Nice place, I told him. *Mais bien sûr*, he said, *c'est L'Arc-en-ciel*. He asked if I had never heard of the Arc-en-ciel, the most famous of airport cafeterias, and shook his head in wonderment at my reply, adding before he left that it was the happiest cafeteria on earth.

The waiter must have noticed my head in my hands. He passed by with a pat on the shoulder and left me another *allongé*.

I stayed in the Arc-en-ciel for hours. When the time came to go, the waiter walked me to the door, his arm through mine, as men do in Europe, and as they do in Mali. He took my arm like a friend, and I noticed his mustache again, protruding like a wishbone. It pulled up an inch and he said, *Courage, mon frère, la vie, c'est comme ça,* and I wondered how he knew, and whether the Arc-en-ciel was real, or whether I was hallucinating.

Sean met me in Toronto at Pearson International Airport. I saw him through the glass walls separating travelers from airport visitors. He was wearing a baseball cap. He waved — a mild, controlled wave — and lifted his eyebrows. I thought about how far I was from the shouting and pushing in the Bamako airport.

We shook hands. He wanted to carry my bags. It seemed important to him, so I let him do it. He drove me east along Highway 401. It felt cool outside. I asked my brother about the temperature. It was eighty-two degrees Fahrenheit. Cool, anyway, compared to Mali.

We each asked how the other was, he saying fine, I saying the same, neither of us saying much at all, although he could see, in my eyes, that I hadn't slept for seventy-two hours, and I could see, in his, that he had watched Ellen deliver the stillborn son that I would never know.

We drove into my neighborhood. Kids were throwing a baseball on Montcalm Avenue. We passed a café where Ellen and I had lunched, two days before I'd taken off. Next to our apartment was a variety store. Tom, the owner, had known Ellen was pregnant. He had surely noticed it when the ambulance arrived. He saw me climb out of the car, waved, stayed behind the counter. My brother handed me my bags. We shook hands. "See you soon," he said. I didn't want him to go away, but I nodded in a way that he understood to mean thanks, and I drifted inside, lifting my feet up the long flight of stairs. I found Ellen sitting on the side of the bed, pushing herself up to her feet, lips pursed but trying to smile, eyes — I couldn't bring myself to meet them yet. She wore a night jacket I hadn't seen before, with a print of purple birds. As she stood, the birds took flight. She put her hand down to her belly. She still looked pregnant to me.

Chapter 14

I SPENT A FEW HOURS IN THE LIBRARY of the Maryland Historical Society, looking for information about my relatives. Then, on a whim, I drove over to Pennsylvania Avenue. I wanted to see where the Old Royal Theater had been, what the neighborhood looked like. First I drove along Pennsylvania Avenue. I saw stores boarded over, and syringes on the sidewalk. I saw children dash across the street, and noticed people looking at my Ontario license plates. Every person on Pennsylvania Avenue was black. A woman crossed the street, pushing a shopping cart full of food. I drove by a street with dozens of cherry trees in bloom. Some of the trees were two stories high, and had branches as thick as my legs. There was no other vegetation in sight.

I parked my car in a lot. I locked it, paid, and had barely put my feet on the ground when a man approached me. He was taller than I am, but much older. Maybe not much older. Maybe just much more aged. I'm a thirty-eight that looks twenty-five. He could have been a thirty-eight that looked fifty. Bowlegged gait. Something jangling in his pocket. Keys. Keys jangling in his pocket.

"Hey, there, brother, you look like a good man, I need a dollar, if you will. My kids are hungry."

I slipped him a dollar bill. It seemed like a good investment.

"Thank you, brother."

I walked up Pennsylvania Avenue. There, the Royal had once stood. Fats Waller had once performed there. And Count Basie. And Joe Williams, Ella Fitzgerald, and The Duke. They had all played at the Royal. My father and grandfather had been in there many times. But now there was nothing to see. The Royal had been torn down in 1971. Pennsylvania Avenue had nothing but tawdry shops left, and half of them were locked.

How did I know the sound of gunfire? How did I know to drop to the sidewalk? *Rat tat. Rat tat tat.* Glass exploded above me, men grunted, a child screamed, I heard the squeal of rubber on asphalt, and I saw a car run a red light. The light was plainly red and cars were coming from the other direction and still this car charged through, and for an instant I found that fact the most shocking of all. I tried to get up. Was I okay? Yes. I was all right. No blood. Glass nearby, glass on the sidewalk, glass not two yards from where my head had been, but no glass on me. My clothes were dirty, and there was gum stuck to my knee. I brushed it off. Then I heard screaming. Two voices? Three? No. Just one. High. Low. Up and down an octave. "My baby! My baby!"

I was up now, and running. Twenty yards away, there was a man face down on the sidewalk. There was blood on his shirt. A piece of his head was gone. The red ooze didn't unsettle me. He was dead, and there was nothing to do about it. Next to him, a woman cradled a boy, ten years old or so. Blood on his jacket, near the ribs. Blood in his mouth. Conscious. A whimper, then silence. Another whimper. Hurts, he said. It hurts.

First aid, I thought. First aid. Check for breathing. Apply pressure to the site of bleeding. But do you apply pressure to a bullet hole? Blood from the rib area, but blood from the mouth, too. The blood at the mouth was foamy. That meant a punctured lung.

Call an ambulance, I screamed. Nobody moved. Ten people around this boy, and nobody moved. I ran to a donut store, grabbed the phone, dialed 911. Funny, the man behind the counter didn't try to stop me, didn't ask questions, just let me do it. I ran back to the boy. Put him down, I said. Raise his head. I turned his head to the side, so he wouldn't choke on his own blood. How old are you? Eleven, he whispered. What's your name? Billy. Help is coming, Billy. Hurts, he said. *My booooy. My baaaaby,* the mother screamed. I told the woman to calm down, for the sake of her son. Another woman said, You a doctor? No, I said, but she's upsetting this boy and he's in shock. No matter, Mr. White Man, he's gonna die, we all die around here, what you doin' here watchin' us all die? He's not going to die, I said. Billy, you'll make it. I had Billy's blood on my hands. Billy's foamy blood.

I heard sirens. The crowd evaporated. Everybody was gone but Billy's mother and the other woman and me. *Step back. Step back.* Cop talking to me. Ambulance men right behind him. *Do you know this boy?* Cop, talking to me. No, I said, I was here when he was shot, and I called the ambulance, but I don't know him. *You see the incident?* Not really, I heard gunfire and hit the ground. *You see the vehicle?* Vehicle? *This was a drive-by shooting, you see the vehicle?* I said it was blue, that it ran a red light, and that two men were in it, maybe a third in the back seat. The cop tried talking to the mother. Impossible. The ambulance crew — a man and a woman — already had the boy on a stretcher. They loaded him and his mother into the ambulance and took off. Nobody was bothering with the dead man on the sidewalk, and nobody was watching me. Nobody but some kid, some thug, who couldn't have been more than eighteen, and who slammed me in the face. Must have been his fist. I was down again, hands up against my face, blood on my hands, mine or Billy's. Hands ripped the pocket of my pants, got my wallet, and were gone.

I lay there for a moment. Nobody came. I got up. Not so bad. Just torn pants. Which of this blood was mine, and which was Billy's?

What the hell happened to you? This was a cop speaking.

What does it look like? I was mugged. Where were you?

I can't be everywhere. What the hell you doing in this part of town? Get in the car. Don't bleed on my seat. I'll get you to the hospital. I've got to take the mother. Let's go.

This might not be my own blood.

Just get in the car.

I'd rather drive my own. I don't want to leave it here. It's right there. In that lot.

No. Get in the car. I don't want you taking off. He signaled to another cop. Suddenly, there were four of them. *Give Joe your keys. He'll drive it.* I gave the keys to Joe, and told him where my Jetta was parked. *Okay, move it. Get in the car.*

The boy was in critical condition. His name was Billy Jones. His mother was taken away. Two aunts came in her place. I was sitting in the hospital waiting room, and was pointed out to them. They thanked me. They shook my hands.

"I didn't do much," I said.

"You stayed with Billy. You didn't run. You helped. That's something. You got hurt, yourself."

I had three stitches above the right eye. It was puffy, and was beginning to turn black and blue. I had a headache. I asked for aspirins. The nurse said they didn't give out any medication without a doctor's approval.

One of Billy's aunts offered me an aspirin. "I'm sorry," the nurse cut in, "but we don't allow the exchange of drugs in any form in this hospital."

"She's giving me an aspirin," I said. "Remember? You wouldn't give me any."

"Sorry, but we don't allow drugs passing between people. Not even in the waiting room. But you can step outside and do it there."

"Forget it," I said.

Billy's aunt smiled at me. It was a smile that said, Don't worry, it's not just you, these people *are* crazy.

A cop came along. He thanked me for waiting for him, told me where to find my car, gave back my keys, took my statement. I noticed the aunts listening.

"I'm going to have to file a report about my theft, I suppose," I told him.

"How much you lose?"

"Hundred bucks."

"We don't do reports if that's all it was. You'll manage. I have to go. Thanks again for sticking around. It's a rare thing indeed."

"I think I've seen you before," said the aunt who had tried to give me the aspirin. "Are you black, if I may ask?"

"I suppose I am."

She grinned. "I thought so. I saw you before with Millie Cane at the A.M.E. Church. Weren't you there a few Sundays ago?"

"I was."

"You related?"

"She's my aunt."

"I knew you were one of us. You're about as light as a white man, but I could tell you're one of us. Your hair. Your nose. Your mouth."

The other aunt cut in: "Betty, stop fussing over him."

The first aunt: "Millie's an old friend. The Lord works in mysterious ways."

"Let's hope He saves your nephew," I said.

On the way home, I stopped at a corner store to buy aspirins. The woman at the counter drew in her breath.

"Relax, I'm no mugger," I told her. "I just got mugged. All I want is aspirins. Oh shit. My wallet. They stole my wallet."

She exhaled loudly, then giggled. "Everybody's nervous in this city." She gave me a pack of aspirins. "Take these. You look like you need 'em. I've seen you around. You can pay me the next time you come by. It's $1.79."

I slept through the night. Woke up with my head on fire. Took three aspirins and two glasses of water. There was nothing to eat in the fridge. I stepped out to buy some food and the *Baltimore Sun*. The crime pages named the man who was shot and killed, and said Billy Jones was listed in serious condition. Nobody had been arrested. I ate a little, took off my clothes and went back to bed.

But Yoyo knocked on my door.

"Look at you. You've been in trouble? I was wondering why it was so quiet in here. I thought you were at your aunt's again. But I saw your car. And there's a woman outside. Your aunt."

Shit. I had a towel around my waist. My face looked like hell.

"Tell her to wait while I get dressed."

I went back into the bedroom. My head pounded as I tried to pull on my jeans. The front door opened and slammed. My bedroom door swung open.

"Langston Cane the Fifth! What you mean by getting yourself shot at in the streets of Baltimore and then not even letting me know?"

Millicent Cane eyed me. I pulled on my shirt. "You could have waited until I got dressed."

"I know what a man's chest looks like, you dang fool. What in the name of Jesus were you doing on Pennsylvania Avenue?"

"Looking for the Royal Theater."

"They tore down the Royal twenty-five years ago. What got into your head?"

"I was just walking around the neighborhood."

Yoyo stepped into my bedroom. "The landlady wants to see you."

"Tell her I was mugged and shot and am busy talking with my aunt."

Yoyo disappeared. The front door opened and slammed again. Elvina Peck marched into my bedroom. Hell, it was a regular open house.

"Miz Cane! I didn't know this was your boy."

"Elvina! How're you? You still up at that Baptist church? This ain't my boy. He's my nephew. From Canada. That must explain it. Only a Canadian would get it into his head to go walking on Pennsylvania Avenue. I guess people in Canada still go for walks. Somebody tell this boy that people don't go walkin' in Baltimore. They walk *to* their car, and they walk *from* their car, and that's all the walkin' they do!"

"Look at your banged-up head," Elvina Peck said. "That would-n't have happened if you didn't spend so much time writing. You need a woman to take care of you. To keep you off Pennsylvania Avenue. You ought to stop all that midnight writing — I seen your lights on late, I seen you scratching your head at that kitchen table. You ought to stop all that thinking and find yourself a woman."

"He had himself a woman," Mill said.

"Puh-lease." That was me.

"Well, then, he'll just have to get himself another." That was Elvina.

Mill said she wanted me to come to church on Sunday, and have supper at her home. As a matter of fact, she'd prefer that I stay with her for the remainder of my time in Baltimore.

I accepted the church and supper invitation, but declined the lodgings.

Mill invited Elvina, too. And Yoyo.

"Mill, how are you going to clean up for a big supper like that?"

"I know how to clean a house, young man. I was cleaning house before your pappy was cleaning you."

Yoyo took Mill's arm. She snatched it away. "Watch your hands, mister."

"I can clean your house," he told her.

Mill looked up at the ceiling. "I never known a black man all my life could clean a house."

Elvina said Yoyo could do it. She said Mill would never believe it, but this man could get down on his hands and knees and scrub like the best of them. "He works. This man knows how to work. He did my house."

"He did?"

"Yes, he did," Elvina said. "He did it once, and now he keeps it up."

"How much you charge?" Mill asked Yoyo.

"Forty-five dollars," he said. "Under the table."

"You'd better charge her eighty," I said. "You don't know what you're getting into."

"Hush up," Mill said.

"That's okay," Yoyo said. "Forty-five is fine. I clean it spic and span, lickety-split."

"You talk funny," Mill said. "Where you from?"

"I am an African."

"We are all Africans in this room," Mill said. "Even Langston here is an African, once removed. What I'm asking is, where are you from?"

"The United Republic of Cameroon. In West Africa."

"Don't tell me where it is, dag nab it. I go to church. We have a map of Africa. I seen that country before on the map. But you talk funny. Other Africans don't talk like you."

"French is my first language."

"It is?" Mill told him he ought to try living in Canada.

"I did live in Canada. I lived for a year in the wonderful city of Winnipeg. A long time ago."

"I don't know where *that* is."

"North of Minneapolis. That's what I always tell Americans."

"That must have been halfway to the North Pole. You must have froze your backside out there."

"No, I had a wonderful time. Nice city. Nice women."

"Don't you talk disrespectful in front of church women. Elvina here, she's Baptist. And I'm A.M.E. When you gonna clean my house?"

"How about tomorrow?" Yoyo said.

"How about today?"

That conversation took place at eleven in the morning. They brought me fruit and cupcakes and tea and juice, and then Mill drove away with Yoyo. I was writing at eleven p.m. when Yoyo came back in. He saw my light and came up to visit. I had never seen him look so tired. He said he took one look at the place and tried to raise his price to eighty-five. But Mill refused. They had agreed on a price of forty-five dollars, she said, so forty-five it would be. That was good money, Mill said, and it was like sixty if you were paying tax. Yoyo told her he didn't pay tax. She said that was un-American. He said he was a Cameroonian, living in America, so being un-American wasn't of concern to him. She said, Look, Mr. Cameroonian, just hush up and clean up this house for forty-five dollars.

Yoyo swept and washed and shook out rugs. He tried to throw out old papers, but Mill wouldn't let him. Finally, he prevailed on her to let him put all her bits of paper in one heap in a supermarket box. He cleaned the bathtub, the shower curtain, the toilet. He sent Mill out for extra cleaner, and for Windex. He cleaned the windows and dried them with balled-up newspapers.

She tried to make him stop for dinner, but he refused. He said he never ate when he was working.

"Elvina was right," Mill said. "You do work hard. Keep it up, and I'll give you a little tip."

The kitchen was the last thing he tackled. Mill had one big sink, with two feet of counter space on each side of it. The sink was bulging with dishes. Dirty dishes. Some unwashed for three weeks. Under the sink, in the cupboard, was a foot-high stack of crusty plates and juice-dried mugs.

Yoyo sighed. A woman couldn't live like this. If he lived like this, he'd go out of his mind. This woman needed a man to look after her.

He took a break. In his two years of cleaning houses under the table in Baltimore, Yoyo had never before taken a break before his task was done. He did, this time. He accepted iced tea, and two soda crackers, and a tall drink of water.

He said he would haul every single dirty dish out of the kitchen. It was too small to work in, with all those dishes. He would place them in supermarket boxes just outside the kitchen door. Then he would wash the counters, the table, the cupboards. Then he would put paper down on the cupboards. Then he would take the dishes, box by box, and wash them, and dry them, and put them away as per her instructions.

"However."

"However what?" Mill said.

"You must pay me the eighty-five dollars. This is too much. What I have put into this house would have cleaned four other houses. Really, four times forty-five equals $180 dollars, but all I want is eighty-five."

"A deal's a deal. But I'll give you a tip. And if you do a good job, I'll make it worth your while."

"I am doing a good job, Mrs. Cane."

"Call me Mill. Everyone else does."

"I am doing a good job, Mill."

"Then keep it up. A deal's a deal."

Yoyo attacked the kitchen. He began at seven-thirty in the evening. And he finished at 10:45. He took no more breaks. Mill sat in the kitchen for the last hour, directing him. "That pot goes under there. The plates, up there. I don't like that mug any more, throw it out."

Yoyo finished. He washed his hands and face. He accepted an iced tea. He washed the glass when he was through. Mill said she'd pay for his taxi, and he did not object.

"We said forty-five, and a deal's a deal," Mill said. "So here's forty-five. Now, here's another forty. That's a tip. And here's ten for the taxi. Thank you, son. I haven't seen this kitchen so clean since — well, I don't believe it's ever been this clean. The house was dirty when I bought it, and after that it just rolled on downhill."

"Thank you," he said.

"Come back tomorrow for supper. Come to church, too, if you like. Have you been saved?"

"Saved from what?"

"I guess you haven't. Come on to church, if you have it in your bones to get up that early. And come on over to supper later."

"Thank you, Mill. I can't go to your church, but I will come to supper."

Yoyo, after telling me that story, said he had to go to bed, and that he was going to the market in the morning.

"What market?"

"You've been here all this time and you don't even know about the Saturday market?"

I told him I didn't.

"It's just down the street. It's outdoors. They sell bread, fruit, meat, fish. I have to be there at seven-thirty. It's beautiful in the morning. Come with me."

"Why do you have to be there so early?"

"Just come. You'll see."

Yoyo rapped on my door. It was seven in the morning, Saturday. I washed my face and hands, picked out my hair, threw on some pants, a shirt, and a sweater, and went out into the May morning with my Baltimore tour guide.

We walked east on Thirty-first Street. The sun was sharp and rising above Greenmount Avenue.

The streets were quiet. I saw some cats dart across a back alley. Electrical wires ran above the alleys and the garbage cans. From the alleys, you could peer at the backs of houses. You saw people's linen on clotheslines. You saw toys scattered on lawns, tennis balls, rocking chairs on porches. Yoyo told me it was like Winnipeg. Like a region called Wolseley, in Winnipeg, where alleys were common as well. I told him I'd never been to Winnipeg.

Yoyo said he had read a book called *How to Succeed in America*. It said you should keep your taxes to a minimum, avoid all unnecessary expenses, and keep your money rolling in from as many sources as possible. It said that a person earning a modest twenty thousand dollars a year living in a cheap apartment with no car, no mortgage, no overhead, no kids, and no debts for things like couches and televisions could live better, eat better, pay for more entertainment, and have less stress than a person with three times the income but five times the possessions.

Yoyo told me that the barbecue business had become too risky. He would probably still be in custody if he hadn't managed to get away from the cop at the police station. He had taken a job — under the table — with the French family that ran the Café Chez Washington. They also sold baguettes, croissants, madeleines, choux-à-la-crème, and other French pastries at the Saturday market.

I asked how he had managed to get away from the cop at the police station.

"Tell you later," Yoyo said. "Here we are."

In a rectangular parking lot the size of a football field, men and women were arranging fruits and vegetables and baked goods. Women were setting up pamphlets at a "Freedom of Choice" table. A girl who looked about ten helped a man take crates of crabs off the back of a truck. One vendor prepared to sell meat directly from the back of his truck. Yoyo found the French family at the north end of the lot. He got right to work, stacking up baguettes on a table, shooing bees away from a box of croissants. He winked and tossed me a croissant with a chocolate strip running down the middle. I chewed it, bought a glass of hot apple cider from a stall nearby, sat on the curb, and watched the market unfold. It was so busy by eight that you couldn't move ten steps without bumping into somebody.

Yoyo took a break at eight-thirty. He wandered over to a black man selling used books from a table. A sign by the table said, *We Conduct Business in the African Way*. Yoyo picked up a book about economic self-sufficiency. A recipe, of sorts, for black success in white America.

"How much is this?"

The man said ten dollars.

"This book isn't new. It has a tear on the third page, and coloring on the tenth. I'll give you two dollars."

"Ten or nothing," the man said.

"I thought you did business in the African way," Yoyo said. "Three dollars, and that's my last price."

"Ten," the man said.

"What do you mean when you say you do business in the African way?"

"It means I set my price and I get it and I get exploited by nobody."

"Well, you won't get exploited by me. I'm not going to buy your book. And nobody else is, either."

The vendor grunted.

Yoyo shook his head and led me away. He muttered about how some Americans seemed not to know the art and pleasures of negotiating. "In Cameroon, vendors set their prices high. Everybody knows that. Bargaining is a way to know the vendor. So you say, *Hey, where are you from?* And he says, *Northern Cameroon.* And you say, *My sister lives there. She says it's too hot, she says she likes it down here, where it's cooler, where you don't burn up at night. Bring down your price two hundred francs, in the name of my sister and your family. I'll bring it down one hundred because your sister is in the North.* And he says, *One hundred francs off, for your sister.* . . . . But this way of talking, of getting to know a vendor, people don't know about that here."

Yoyo wandered back toward the French stall. I told him I had to get going, and that I had writing to do. I watched him take his place behind the table, start talking to customers, taking their money, giving change, handing over baguettes and croissants, telling people about the wonders of French breads. A moment later, he dropped to the ground and slid back behind several legs and got behind the bakery truck and — I saw as I backed out into the street — started running. A cop gave chase. "Hey, you! Stop!"

Yoyo raced down Thirty-second Street, turned left into the first alley, and disappeared. I saw the cop give chase. Five minutes later, the cop came back. He was still out of breath. He wandered up to the bakery stand.

"Who is that man? What's his name?"

"A student, I think," said the woman at the stall.

"I want his name, and his address, and his social security number."

"I don't know that. He just came along, said he was a student, and said he'd sell for us for a few hours if we gave him some bread."

"You're not allowed to hire illegal aliens," the cop said. "I could have you charged with harboring aliens."

"Go ahead," the woman said. "Do what you're going to do. I don't care. But I'm telling you, I don't know his name, or his address, or where he lives, or what his number is."

The cop grunted. "Give me five of those croissants, will you? The ones with chocolate in them."

The woman handed them over in a bag. He fumbled for his wallet.

"It's okay," she said.

"Thanks," he mumbled. He turned to go away. Then he turned back.

"Are you, uh, interested in a coffee? Later, like."

"What?"

"Can I buy you a coffee?"

"I'm allergic to caffeine. I'm allergic to police officers. I don't even like Baltimoreans. So go away. Go, go, go."

"Okay, already." The cop walked off with the bag.

The woman beckoned to me. She remembered me from the Café Chez Washington. She had been at the cash register that day. "Tell Yoyo I'm very sorry, but I don't think we can let him come back. Too risky. We had a Russian woman working for us for three years, we never had any trouble. But it's too risky, when you're black, and when you're illegal. We can't afford to have trouble."

I knocked on Yoyo's door. He let me in quickly, and told me the story. When he had been arrested for selling kebabs on the sidewalk, he had been taken to a police station downtown. They made him turn over his wallet — which contained one hundred dollars. He didn't have any identification, and he kept his key — a long-term precaution against theft — in his sock. He gave the officers a false name. They made him sit in a room. They were about to fingerprint him. He asked to go to the toilet. They said no. He said, "I'm sorry, but I have to empty my bowels, and if you don't let me go to the toilet, I'm going to do it right here." So he was told the toilet was down the hall two doors, and that he had two minutes to hightail it back. Two doors down from the toilet, he found an office. Door open. With a window—a window that opened. Yoyo climbed out that window and dropped ten feet down to the street. That hurt! He ran. Turned a corner and ran some more. One more corner, onto Charles Street. Into a crowded restaurant. Out a back door, into an alley, and away. He was safe for now. But he knew he'd never get away again from the police.

I drove to church on Sunday morning. Parked on Druid Hill Avenue again, with the help of a young man in the street — the same one I'd met a few weeks before.

"Mr. Cane," he said as I got out of the car.

"Hello there, how are you, and how did you know my name?"

"Your name, you'll see, is now known to the members of our church. Billy Jones' family comes here. Word has spread about what you did."

"I didn't do much," I said.

"You were there," he said. "You were there and you did what you could, Mr. Cane."

"Call me Langston. And I'll call you . . ."

"Ishmael. Well, you know, Langston, I don't know how people in Ontario take care of themselves, but around here in Baltimore, and more particularly on Pennsylvania Avenue, when somebody cocks back his elbow and is fixing to plow you a good one, you don't just stand there looking like a bull's-eye."

"Well, at least he didn't have a gun."

"He probably did have one. But he didn't use it. I guess he liked you."

"Guess so. And you know what? When he knocked me down and took my money, I appreciated that fact. I appreciated the fact that he liked me."

Mill was waiting for me inside the door with her two friends, Maggie and Eleanor. She had spoken with Billy Jones's mother and said the boy was improving. They had operated on him to remove a bullet. One of his lungs had collapsed, but the other was fine.

Maggie asked if I'd like to buy a paper. I noticed the stacks by the door. Today, a young woman was selling them.

I paid for the *Baltimore Sun* and the *Afro-American*, and looked again at her. Her eyes were waiting. Leveled on me. Those eyes, brown, wide, alive, said, *Hi, I'm paying attention to you. So you pay attention to me.*

"Thanks," I said.

"You're welcome, Mr. Cane," she said.

"It's Langston," I said. "And you're —"

"Annette Morton. I'll see you later."

"Later?"

"At your aunt's, I believe. For supper, this evening."

Mill nudged me as I stood beside her in the pew. "Cute, isn't she?"

"Who?"

"Ah, don't act like a little boy. I'm talking about Annette Morton. Cute, isn't she?"

"How do you know her?"

"I know everybody in this church. Nothing happens without me knowing about it."

That seemed like a good enough reason not to get involved with anybody from the A.M.E. Church.

The service began with the lesser-ups, as Mill called them. The woman who would never be a fully ordained minister, the choir, the deacons, the announcements. And finally, the reverend. He was a short, squat man with a voice that seemed connected to a megaphone.

"Do you know who you are? You may say you're a citizen of Baltimore, or you may name your family. You may say that you make your living driving a bus. Or teaching. Or plumbing. Or that you're at home, feeding children, washing clothes, reading bedtime stories.

"But who are you, really? We don't know the answer, my friends, until a Divine Moment comes along and our Maker throws a few cards on the table. How will you behave, when the ante is raised? Where will your true character lie?

"My friends, we have among us a Canadian visitor. He is not a practicing Christian. But judge him not on paper. Judge him in the flesh. For he was given a test recently. He was sent into streets overcome with deprivation and violence. I speak of Pennsylvania

Avenue, my friends. He was sent there, and he witnessed what we all fear. What makes us all shudder when we turn on the television. He found himself in the middle of a drive-by shooting.

"Did he dive for cover and not come out? No, my friends. He raised himself from the ground when the bullets had barely ceased, and brought comfort to a young boy of this church, a boy known to many of you.

"He held him. He reassured him. He took care of him and waited for the ambulance that he had called. Indeed, he stayed long enough for some soulless thug to strike him down and take his wallet. Still, he stayed. And he stayed for hours in the hospital, to wait for a word on the young boy, and to comfort the boy's family.

"My friends, that boy will live on. His name is Billy Jones. He has sat among us. He is the son of Harriet Jones, one of our most cherished sisters.

"The young man is also among us. His name is Langston Cane. Would you stand, friend?"

Mill poked and prodded me, so I could do nothing other than stand and stand tall.

Mill whispered, "Don't get yourself a fat head, son. He just wanted to thank you."

I got out of church as quickly as I could without offending Mill. I planned to climb back into bed, flip through the Sunday *Sun*, sleep an hour, and then keep writing. I wanted to have a go at my grandparents' stay in Oakville. I had enough information to start putting it together. I would write until five-fifteen, shower and change, and skedaddle over to Mill's for supper.

As I stood at the door, shoving my hand into a pocket for the key, I flicked the lid of my mailbox. I hadn't opened the box lately. Inside, I saw a green envelope.

It was a handwritten envelope. It had my ex-wife's messy handwriting. Hieroglyphics, almost. Sloppiest handwriting I've ever seen from a woman.

I got inside and slammed the door shut and locked it and tore into the green paper. In doing so, I ripped clean through a photo of my father and a story in the *Toronto Times.* It was the local version of the story about the Watson kidnapping and about my father's comments.

"Langston," Ellen's note began. Not *Dear Langston.* Or *Dearest.* Or *Lang,* which would have carried a trace of affection. Just *Langston.*

> Heard you moved to Baltimore. Not sure if you saw this clipping. Good luck. Love, Ellen.

I threw the note down, picked it back up, and read it again. No news of herself. Deliberate, that. A little motherly, that *Good luck.* And then that meaningless *Love, Ellen.* That one word would have made all the difference, had it been placed differently. Had it begun the note, as in *Langston, my love.* But *Love* at the end of a letter most definitely meant nothing. It meant nothing more than *Sincerely* over a politician's signature.

I was in no state to write. I took the *Baltimore Sun,* got back in the car, and drove over to the Café Chez Washington.

I got a big bowl of café au lait and a seat at a window, and I opened the paper. I was not really in the mood to read, but I flipped the pages anyway until I got to the back of the foreign news section.

DOCTOR'S RANSOMERS DEMAND
RELEASE OF BLACK PRISONERS
— Canadian Press, Toronto

A group claiming to have kidnapped a prominent physician in Toronto last week has demanded $100,000 and the release of five black men imprisoned for violent offenses.

In a communiqué sent yesterday to the Toronto media, a previously unknown organization calling itself Africa First demanded that the "white, mainstream police and judicial establishment set free these five innocent and wrongly convicted brothers" in exchange for Norville Watson, a semi-retired, 77-year-old urologist who disappeared last week.

"Dr. Watson is being treated with consideration, and certainly with more dignity than black men in Canadian prisons," said the communiqué, composed of letters clipped from newspapers and glued onto paper.

I skipped over a few paragraphs giving the names and criminal records — ranging from aggravated assault to armed robbery — of the five black men in question. They were scattered in penitentiaries across the country. But I stopped to read the section about my father.

Dr. Langston Cane, a prominent black activist and a long-time antagonist of Dr. Watson's, complained yesterday about being interrogated by police for the third time in as many days about the Watson kidnapping.

"I have been asked questions intimating that I have some connection with this incident, which is absolutely false. If the police wish to charge me with some trumped-up offense, let them proceed."

Cane repeated his argument — one that has provoked some public anger — that the kidnapping may be a hoax.

"It doesn't seem right. I can't think of any — and I say *any* — group in the black community that would stoop to such a thing. I think this may be some sort of practical joke. I'm not saying that police authorities shouldn't be investigating fully. But let's not get carried away. Let's keep our heads."

What was going on up there in Toronto? Who had made off with Norville Watson? What, exactly, did my father think this was, if not a bona fide kidnapping?

It was time for the continuation of the Norville Watson story. I got a refill of café au lait and started writing.

I met Norville Watson when I was ten years old. I had heard about him many times, and had committed all the stories to memory. There had been that time when he had refused my parents rental accommodation. I knew that they had complained to the Ontario minister of labor, to no avail. I knew that the *Toronto Times* had chosen not to run a story about Watson refusing to rent to them, because it had determined that the man was acting within the law. I knew that my parents had gone after Watson again, once the Ontario government introduced the Fair Accommodations Act in 1953. They sent a black couple to try to rent from Watson, who told them the flat was already rented. Then they sent a white couple, who got the flat. The case went to court. My parents lost again. The judge determined that rental properties were excluded from the Act, and he commented in his ruling that it would be a sad day indeed when the state could start telling landlords to whom they had to rent.

I knew all this, and I knew that my father and Watson settled into a sort of uneasy truce over the subsequent years. Watson kept a small Toronto office, but set up a urology practice in Oakville and worked out of the Oakville Trafalgar Memorial Hospital, where my father also had privileges as a family practitioner.

And so it was with some discomfort that I found myself, one day, bleeding profusely in the emergency room of the hospital. My father was attending a medical conference in Stockholm. I had been playing hide-and-seek in a park just a block from the hospital. I had been crawling on the ground when suddenly I felt in my wrist a twinge like a low-grade shock. I looked down and saw a flash of ivory white deep in my forearm. Next came the flood of red. I slammed the spurting wrist against my chest and held it firm with my other hand, not because I understood the need to stanch the blood, but because the whiteness deep in the flesh horrified me. I said nothing. I whimpered, but didn't cry. I walked into the emergency ward dripping all this brilliant red paint behind me, and saw heads snap up all around as my blood splashed to the floor. I started shaking.

The nurse asked to see my wrist, said she wanted to apply some pressure to it. I began to lift the wrist from my soaking shirt, but when I saw the red paint spurting again, I slammed the wrist back against my chest and she couldn't pry it off.

A tall man was walking toward us. So tall, it seemed as if he'd have to stoop through a door frame. His blond hair flapped as he walked. He had an inch-long goatee.

The nurse said to him, "The doctor in emergency is tied up. Can you help, Dr. Watson? This boy has a dangerous cut."

He stooped down and looked me in the eye. "We're going to help you, son. Let me take your hand. It won't hurt." He tried to pry the wrist from my chest. I wouldn't let him "Scared, aren't you?" I nodded. "It's okay. It's just blood. You have lots of it. And if you need any extra, we have some here for you. Turn your head away. There, that's better." It was better. I turned my head so as not to see my arm. I let him take it. He raised it, clamped something soft against it, lifted me up, put me flat, kept my arm raised, wheeled me away. I knew who he was.

We were in a white room. There were a number of people around the bed. "Need his blood type," the doctor said.

"It's A negative," I said.

"Check it anyway," the doctor told somebody. "What's your name, son?"

"Charles," I said. Charles was my middle name. Charles seemed safe.

"Charles who?"

"Just Charles," I said.

"How old are you?"

"Ten."

"Where do you live, Charles?"

I started shaking uncontrollably. A nurse put a blanket on me. Watson ordered something to do with an IV and antibiotics.

"Charlie. Can I call you Charlie?"

I nodded.

"I'm going to clean up that cut. You've got some glass in there. It won't hurt, because I've frozen your arm. Do you like sports?"

"Golf," I said. I don't know why I said that. I didn't want him to guess who I was. Golf seemed about as far as possible from the subject of my family. And I knew he golfed.

"Ever had a hole in one?"

"No."

"What about hockey? You like hockey?"

"Just golf." It occurred to me that, with my light skin, Dr. Watson wouldn't know I was black. He would never guess who I was. I took a deep breath.

"Son, we do need to know who you are. We need to contact your parents."

I nodded. I swallowed. His eyes were blue. Blue as lake water. Blue eyes, and a broad nose. A very broad nose. Aberdeen Williams had once said to me that it was silly to call people black or white, because half the world was at least some of both. I wondered if Norville Watson had a distant black ancestor.

"Don't be afraid," he said. "They won't be angry with you."

I said nothing.

"Okay, son, we're just going to close up your cut now. It won't hurt. You might feel some pressure on your wrist, but it won't hurt."

I nodded. A few minutes went by. My arm felt like a block of wood. The doctor prodded and pushed against it, but all I felt was the weight of his fingers.

"There. All done. Your arm will be as good as new. You have about twenty stitches. We'll snip them out in a few weeks. You have to keep your arm clean, and dry. I have to go soon. By the way, how did you know your blood type?"

"My dad's a doctor."

Big mistake. I knew, as soon as the words were out, that I had given myself away. His lips parted in surprise. His eyes held mine. They looked at my hair and they fell over my face, my nose, my mouth.

"You're Langston Cane's boy!" I started to shiver. He put a hand on my shoulder. "Don't worry, son. You'll be fine. We'll call him right away." I waited for him to strike me. Or rip out the stitches. He spoke to the nurse. "Langston Cane. The residential number is on Sumner Avenue."

"It's 338-2994," I said. "My mom's home. My dad's out of town."

"That's right," Watson said. "He's at that convention in Stockholm, isn't he?" I nodded. "So are you going to be a doctor, too?" Watson asked.

"No. I don't like blood."

"I can see that. But you get used to it. You didn't really lose that much. It looked worse than it really was. You're lucky. That glass came close to an artery."

"Is it true that you don't like black people?"

Watson patted me on the head. "No, son. That's not the case at all. I like all people. We need all people in this world. All people, all countries, all nationalities."

"Is it true you wouldn't let black people stay in your home?"

Dr. Watson exhaled loudly. He chewed the inside of his cheek. I saw thick black hair on the backs of his fingers.

"Your father and I have had some differences, but that doesn't matter in the hospital. I'm a doctor, the same as your father. My job is to treat you as well as I would my own son."

"But would you let black people into your house? To live?"

"Yes. Of course. I have had many black people in my home. Some of my friends are black people, son. Maybe your father and I will be friends, one day. Maybe you and I will be friends, too. All right?"

"All right."

"My work is done here, son, and other people need my help. I have to go now. You take care of yourself. No more scrambling around on your hands and knees in the park."

"Okay. Thanks for taking care of me."

The nurse came to say that my mother would be right over.

Chapter 15

I WAS NOT LOOKING FORWARD to Mill's dinner party. There would be women in church hats. There would be more fried chicken. It was the only thing Mill knew how to make, apart from potato salad. But I wanted to keep looking at Mill's box of information on my grandfather, Langston the Third, and figured I could sneak a peek — or perhaps even borrow some materials — if I attended. So I drove over, like the dutiful nephew, and brought along Yoyo.

Annette Morton opened Mill's door. She was young. Too young. Twenty-seven, tops.

"Hi. Come on in. How are you, Langston?"

"Annette, how're you doing? This is my friend, Yoyo."

She nodded and shook his hand, watched Yoyo get ushered inside by Mill, turned back to me, and took my hand. Her hand was warm, as if it had been in a pocket, and it held mine long enough to be more than a formality. I felt a quick stirring in my groin and tried to check it by telling myself that it would be just my luck to mistake the signals of a born-again Christian. Still, I couldn't help looking at her again. Her eyes were burnt hazel, her lips on the edge of a grin. She smelled of strawberries.

"Are you two gonna eye each other all night or are you gonna join the party?" Mill broke in. "There's people for you to meet, Langston. Annette, check the corn bread, will you?"

I was reintroduced to Eleanor and Maggie, the two women I'd met when first walking to the A.M.E. church. I met Ishmael, who had watched over my car, twice, while I was in church. Ishmael was a high school senior. He had brought along his older brother, Derek, who wanted to talk. Derek wanted to talk awfully bad. It appeared that he'd been wanting to talk for five years, and that I was the first person willing to listen. After several minutes, Annette came up behind me. I turned to acknowledge her, but was dragged back into Derek's rant.

"It's rough here, rough in Baltimore," he said. "How you find it here? I mean, being a black man and all. Well, partially black, I guess you qualify, especially if you identify, if your thoughts, your mind, your culture are one with ours. I mean, man, I've got to assume that, since you've been at Bethel and up on Pennsylvania. I'll assume you've accepted the burden of blackness. So how do you find it here, compared to Canada?"

"It's an interesting city. It's —"

"Interesting is a white word, man. Interesting isn't a word for people of color. It's a word for politicians, man. But I'll cut you some slack, coming from Canada and all. Black people use that word up there?"

"Well," I said, "where I'm from, I haven't run into masses of black people fleeing the word *interesting*. It's not generally seen as a betrayal of one's racial identity."

"Aha! I detect a capacity for irony. A sign of higher intelligence, no doubt. Racial identity, that's a happening concept. I —"

Annette took my arm. "Cool it, Derek. The man hasn't even had something to drink yet, and you want to get into the only thing you know how to talk about."

"Drink, drink. Be my guest. Make off with the lovely Annette, but return, my friend. Place some interesting ice cubes in an interesting mug of Canada Dry ginger ale and come back for some more interesting and elucidating rap."

"Right," I said. Annette had her arm through mine. It felt lovely. She released me in the kitchen. "I had to get you out of there. You have to steer around Derek. If you get drawn into a conversation, you'll never get away."

I considered asking how I should talk so that she wouldn't get away from me, but ditched the idea. Instead, I poured her a soft drink, gallant gent that I am, and poured myself one, and stood by her silently. We watched Derek work on Yoyo.

"Man, I hear you're an African. That must feel deep, Yoyo. You must have a real sense of racial resonance."

Yoyo laughed loudly and pleasantly. "I don't know much about resonance, my friend. I'm tone deaf."

"But you're black, man. Indisputably undiluted."

"Yes, and I have ten toes and ten fingers, too, but I don't spend much time thinking about how perfect they are."

"What did it feel like, to be in a country where everybody is black, I mean, all the people in power are black, and you know who you are, and what your rights are, and where you're headed as a people?"

"Not toward civil war, I hope. We've got 250 ethnic groups in Cameroon. And as for what it feels like to be in a country where everybody is black, I don't think of it that way. First of all, not everybody is black. There are a few whites. There are some in-betweens. There are some Asians. We, the black Cameroonians, feel very united. Many people who are young and educated spend their time figuring out how to leave."

"Leave?"

"Travel. Visit America. Visit Canada. See the world. You want to see what's out there. You feel you haven't lived a full life unless you get out and see the world."

"But man, what is there to see out here? Racism and ruination. Crippled cities, crippled people. The only —"

Mill stopped Derek this time. She put a drumstick in his hand. "Put that mouth of yours to use on some chicken. If you keep talking about racism and ruination, just as sure as Moses came down from the mount, my kitchen broom is gonna come down on your head."

Derek took a bite and asked Yoyo what he did.

"I clean houses, lately. You know anybody who needs house-cleaning?"

"That's bourgeois."

"I'm not bourgeois yet," Yoyo said. "But I'm working on it. Maybe I'll be bourgeois after I've cleaned another two hundred houses."

Mill ordered everybody to sit at the table. Yoyo helped her to carry out the plates. I sat next to Mill. Annette slipped in beside me. She put her hand on my arm, touched my foot with hers. We smiled.

On display were honey ham, baked corn biscuits, fried chicken, potato salad, baked acorn squash with honey and butter, Coke and ginger ale and white wine, potato chips, taco chips, and salted cashews. There was also lemonade. The eight of us sat around the table. Mill said grace.

"For what we are about to receive, all these good things, all these good people, for people like Langston here, who sticks up for little

ones on Pennsylvania Avenue, for people like Yoyo, who has nothing and doesn't yap about it and works his backside off and never
runs his mouth except to ask for more money, which I won't give
him, for people like Maggie and Eleanor and Ishmael and me, who
give so much time to the church, for people like Annette for their
beauty and their brains, but not in that order, for people like
Derek, who have their heart in the right place even if they say the
wrong thing, but mostly for life and for love between people, may
the Lord make us truly thankful, Amen. You can dig in now."

The table fell silent for a few seconds, except for the clinking
of knives and forks and spoons and the dropping of bread and
squash onto plates. We all started eating. Annette's foot pressed
against mine. I turned to look at her. Mill nudged me with her
elbow. "Cute, isn't she?"

I pretended I hadn't heard. Thankfully, we were interrupted by
three sharp raps on the door. I knew those raps. Instantly. Not
too many people think enough of themselves to announce their
arrival that way. He used to do it when I was a child, in my room,
and he had something to say to me. *Rap Rap Rap. Son. May I
have a word with you?* If I didn't answer him pronto, he would
open the door anyway.

Mill, too, recognized the sound.

"You know who that is, don't you?" she said, looking at me.
"I never did like people come visiting without announcing
themselves."

Mill got up, wiped an ant-sized trace of squash from the
corner of her mouth, and walked to the door, mumbling. She slid
the bolts free. Removed the chain. Turned the knob.

"You're just in time for dinner, come on in." Mill returned to
the table. As she sat down, she called over her shoulder, "Turn
those bolts back in place, fix the chain, and pull up a chair."

"What kind of way is that to welcome your brother after forty-odd years?" My father took off his coat, slid open the closet door. "I can't believe this, Mill. There's actually a place to hang a coat. There are actually guests sitting at your table. Have you changed? Some sort of profound organizational metamorphosis?"

"You should have left all them extra syllables up in Canada," Mill said. "No. I ain't changed. It was cleaned up by Yoyo, that's all."

"Cleaned up by Yoyo," my father mimicked. "I won't even hazard a guess as to the meaning of that. A form of Zen meditation, perhaps."

"Yoyo is my name, Dr. Cane," Yoyo said, standing up. "It's a pleasure to meet you. I am a friend of your sister's, and of your son's."

My father allowed his hand to be shaken. He peered at Yoyo's face. "Pleasure to meet you, too. Pleasure to meet somebody sufficiently civilized to stand up and shake a stranger's hand."

"Civilized!" Mill mumbled. "Is dropping in unannounced civilized?"

Eleanor and Maggie gushed over my father, and said how proud the congregation was of me. Mill prevailed upon him to join us at the table.

My father's gaze fell swiftly on my face. My right eye and cheekbone were still swollen and discolored from the rubbing I had taken.

"I can see that he handled himself adroitly on Pennsylvania Avenue," my father said. "I'm not even going to ask what a son of mine was doing on Pennsylvania Avenue in this day and age."

"Handling himself more honorably than his tomcatting father used to do on the same street half a century ago," said Mill, who passed him a plate of ham and potatoes.

"How in the world did you hear about it?" I asked

"From Aberdeen," my father said.

I looked at Mill.

"All I did was tell Aberdeen what happened," Mill said. "If you don't want me talking about you, then don't go getting yourself half killed on Pennsylvania Avenue."

Derek Wedburner, the man of monologues, the master of diatribes, inserted himself in the conversation.

"I can see, Dr. Cane, that you're a man of some distinction. Of a refined vocabulary, undoubtedly the product of a sound education. That must be something of a shock for whites in Canada — to see such an educated African man in their midst."

My father cut him off. "I'm not an African. Yoyo, from the sound of his accent, is likely an African. I'm not an African, any more than you."

"But I am an African," Derek said.

"If you are an African," Yoyo said, "tell me the capital city of Burkina Faso."

"I don't know, but —"

"It's Ouagadougou," Yoyo said, "and if you were African, you would know it."

"This is not a matter of geography," Derek said. "It's a matter of the diaspora. We people of color —"

"*People of color*," my father snorted. "For all its pretension, it sounds to me just the same as *colored people*."

"It's not the same," Derek said. "Not the same at all, if I may beg to differ. *Colored people* comes straight out of our American heritage of slavery and segregation. *People of color* evokes a diaspora, a scattering, a collectivity of people of all races —"

"Except whites," I said. "Except maybe Latin Americans.

And Sicilians in the summer. Or perhaps you should have a new category for them: people nearly of color."

Mill clapped her hands. "I guess that's about what you'd be, Langston," she said "Let me introduce you-all to my nephew of near color."

Derek said, "People of color have some things in common, and should move collectively to —"

"I've never known Indians and blacks and Asians to get together with each other any more than they get together with whites," my father said, "and I don't see how the term *people of color* is going to make them all start loving each other."

I asked Yoyo what he thought. He said he wanted to think about it. Perhaps he would write an opinion piece on the subject for the op-ed page of the *Toronto Times*. He could use the money, anyway.

"So you're a journalist, are you?" Derek asked.

"Well, I was in Cameroon. But I know somebody at the *Toronto Times*. She could help me get it published there, I bet."

"And why did you leave your country? Why have you contributed to the brain drain from Africa?"

"Brain drain," Yoyo said. "That's very funny. My brain would probably have been draining, thanks to a blow from a shovel or a bullet, had I returned to Cameroon. I was a political columnist in a newspaper run by the government. And while I was over here on an assignment, the government was overthrown."

"Forget that political stuff, nobody cares about it anyway," Mill said. "Clean homes. Set yourself up a little company. Keep your prices low. If you keep working as well as you did for me, I could find you ten new customers next week. You could make yourself a pot of money."

"Son," my father said, "I'd like to have a word with you."

"You haven't come all this way to taste my chicken?" Mill said. "Why don't you leave that boy alone? He ain't botherin' no one. If he wants to look through old boxes and write us all up in his story, what's the problem?"

My father stood up and walked over to the window. He pulled back a blind, stared out into the night, and turned back. "I'd rather not discuss this in a community forum."

"These are my dinner guests, Langston. These are the first dinner guests I believe I've had since you abandoned the U.S.A. And I'm not asking them to leave. So why don't you just eat some chicken like ordinary folks do?"

My father surprised me by joining us again at the table and eating most of what Mill gave him.

When we had all finished eating, Mill looked at my father and asked, "You're not mixed up in that kidnapping, are you?"

"No."

"You should stick to doctoring."

"Thanks for your opinion."

"You've grown older, Langston. You've put on weight. Where'd all your hair go?"

"That's unkind, Mill, but I won't reciprocate."

"You always liked to use big words when you were uneasy, Langston. So what do you want with us, then? Why have you come all this way?"

My father looked at me. "I want you to come home, son I don't want you mugged again on the streets of Baltimore. I want you to stop poking around in things that are best left alone. I'll tell you all you need to know."

"Thanks, but no thanks," I said. "I've got a few things to do down here yet. But I'll let you know when I'm ready to come back."

"Son," my father said, "It's been a long day and I'm tired. I'm staying at the Lincoln Hotel on St. Paul Street, which isn't far, I believe, from where you are. Come have breakfast with me tomorrow morning. I have some things to talk about with you."

"Okay," I told him.

"You don't have to stay at no hotel," Mill said. "I got an extra bedroom here. It's clean. Yoyo fixed it up."

"Thanks, Mill, but I've made a hotel reservation." I noticed Annette again, who looked at me, too. My father stayed for an hour, absorbing mild barbs from Mill without reacting, and helping himself to peach pie and ice cream. He left after a decent interval. So did Maggie and Eleanor. I offered to give Annette, Derek, Ishmael, and Yoyo rides home, and managed to drop off the men first.

Making love to someone within a day of meeting her has not happened to me before, and I doubt it will happen again. Annette's front teeth were small and white and had the narrowest of spaces between them and seemed all the more delicious as I ran my tongue over them. But I had been moving quickly all day and I felt embarrassed about smelling bad. Those of us who haven't had sex or had any chance of it for a month or a year or a decade tend to let a few items of intimate hygiene slip. I was in need of a shower and I told her so, and I stayed in there for five or ten minutes, shampooing, cream-rinsing, sudsing until I felt a swoosh of the shower curtain and a nudge — no, two soft nudges against my back — and there was Annette pressing herself against me under the falling water. I had finished washing myself, so I washed her. I started with a bar of soap and a blue facecloth, and I moved it around her forehead, which was broad, and her lips, which were round, and her neck, which was smooth and cool, and everywhere the washcloth and soap had been, my mouth followed. It followed down her neck, along her arms, across her breasts, which sloped down and lifted out and up, perkily, and over her nipples, which were dark, very dark, and standing in salutation. I found her navel, and parts lower, and got to my knees. While she tugged my ears and played with my hair, I washed her and rinsed her and nibbled and sucked. She slid onto all fours and raised her lovely labia at me from behind and I entered her while reaching around to stroke her swollen clitoris and hanging breasts and she turned her mouth to the side and took mine in hers between gasps. That did not go on long, I will admit. Not nearly long enough. I lost my charge within minutes, but she seemed patient, seemed ready to wait. We separated and got out of the bathtub and toweled each other. She stretched me out on her bed and told me to close my eyes. That was the first thing she said. It was one of the only things she said that night. I had nothing to say at all. Wanted to say not a word. She began oiling and massaging and stroking my feet, and ankles, and calves, and — well, I am still amazed to think how many times and in how many ways we loved each other that night.

I found a parking ticket appended to my windshield wiper at four that morning. I didn't care. I unlocked the door. Had I really done those things? Home, Langston. Go home, I told myself. Get yourself three and a half hours of sleep. We know it will be deep. Get yourself up, shower, and get on over to meet your father.

I met my father in his hotel restaurant. "What exactly are you doing down here, son, and how long do you plan to stay?"

My father sat well back in his chair, legs folded, in contrast to the directness of his question. He had already eaten, so I just ordered tea with cream. I have always liked cream in tea. I thought of Annette. *You want anything? Tea? Coffee?* she had asked as I was leaving.

No, I've had everything I could need or want. But a phone number. How about a phone number?

Why don't we just see when and where we meet again? You told me your address. And you know mine. Let's just leave this as simple as it has been.

"If this is to be an interrogation, I don't think I'll take part," I told my father.

"Fair enough," he said. I could see him thinking. You can build homes, build your life, build your career. You can even fertilize the egg that grows into a human being. You can fertilize five or ten of them, and nurture them. But you can't force an infant to eat something he won't eat. You can't force an infant to sleep when he won't sleep. And you can't force a son to grow up in a father's mold.

I stirred my tea. I put sugar in it. I never put sugar in tea, but it occupied my hands. My father was aging. His hair had faded gray, almost white. He had deep grooves under his eyes. He was a brown-skinned man of the indisputable variety. Your unthreatening black professional type.

"How's Mom?" I said.

"Wonderful. As usual. I love that woman, Langston. She's worried about me. This kidnapping stuff has not been easy on us.

For the first two days of the kidnapping, reporters camped outside our house. Every time I came in or went out, they wanted a statement. It has affected her sleep. She's been up a lot at night."

"But she's okay?"

"Yes. And doing better. Things seem to be settling down. No more press around all the time. They really run you ragged." My father cracked his knuckles one by one.

"Mill is quite the woman," I said. "I'm sorry I missed out on her, all those years."

"Well, we've been through a few things. I'm sure you'll find out about them. When you do, be generous, son. Be generous to your elders. You can't possibly know everything, even when you think you do."

"I think I like you more when we're not at home together. In Oakville. At the house, I mean."

"I catch your drift," Dad said.

"Catch my drift? Don't tell me you're going to start talking like Derek."

"You mean the people-of-color guy over at Mill's? No danger of that."

"So what's this kidnapping all about, Dad?"

"I don't know. You've seen the papers. Norville Watson was out walking and never came home. Some group that calls itself Africa First is tabling ridiculous demands. It sent a video of Watson to a news station yesterday. I saw it on TV last night. Watson was shown sitting quietly, apparently unharmed, on a chair in an unmarked room. I'm sure the cops are viewing it carefully. He looked at the camera and said he hadn't been harmed, and seemed about to say that he would not cooperate when the tape was killed. He's one tough monkey."

"You remember the time he sewed me up?"

"He phoned me in Stockholm to tell me about it. His secretary tracked me down and put Watson on the line, and he told me what had happened and that you were fine. He was very professional. I was grateful for that."

"So what kind of hoax do you think is being pulled?"

"I don't think it's a black group that's got him."

"That's a striking thing to say."

"Because if a black group had taken him, they wouldn't be using inflammatory rhetoric. They'd be bending over to make sure everyone knew they were pros, and in control, and wouldn't act rashly. They wouldn't have asked for a measly hundred thousand dollars, because they would have known it would mark them as amateurs. And, being black, they sure as hell would have known that the government would never release black prisoners. So I think somebody else has Watson, and is trying to use the black community as a decoy. And it's working. In the last four days, police have brought in more than fifty blacks for questioning."

"So what do you think this other group wants? Who do you think they are?"

"I haven't a clue."

I finally gave in to my hunger and ordered a croissant and two poached eggs and a tall glass of orange juice.

"Good to see you're eating well, son." My father grinned. "When Aberdeen told me about your little accident, I wanted to come right down and see you."

"Really?"

"Yup. Heard from Ellen lately, by the way?"

"Just a note the other day, basically telling me to get lost. Why?"

"Just wondering. Take care of yourself, son. You could have been hurt on Pennsylvania Avenue. It's worse than when I used to hang out there."

"You knew it well, did you?"

"There was barely a bar I didn't know, or a bed I didn't share."
He smiled. "But that was before I met your mother." He stood
up. He said his plane was leaving in two hours.

"Mill will be sorry you didn't attend church with her."

"Well, I'm not waiting until next Sunday. Anyway, I couldn't
stand it. They would make me stand up. They would treat me like
a long lost son, instead of the miserable atheist that I am. They
would invoke the wondrous names and accomplishments of my
father and grandfather. And they would make me eat chicken.
Which I detest. I can't face all that stuff. I'll leave it to you."

"Thanks for dropping the interrogation, Dad."

"It wouldn't have worked, anyway. See you soon, son. I hope."
He shook my hand and left the restaurant.

A week or so later, while I was with Annette again, and most of
the rest of Baltimore was sleeping, Yoyo sat at his kitchen table
and brought his pen to paper. I know, because he told me about
it. Diversify, diversify, he kept telling himself. He had to keep all
sorts of activities going. He had been selling barbecued meat, but
had to let that go. He had sold croissants at the Saturday market,
but now he had to let that go. He was getting more cleaning
work now — at the dinner party, Maggie and Eleanor had both
asked him to come over next week to clean their homes, and
Yoyo had agreed, but wouldn't give a fixed price until he had seen
their houses. But that was the only thing he had going now.
What if that fell through?

Cleaning was not a sure thing. Yoyo had to diversify. He
would write. Langston Cane was up writing every night and
every morning in his kitchen, and he wasn't even a writer. He

even admitted it. Had never published anything. Had never been paid for his writing, except for a few thousand speeches that an educated twelve-year-old could have written. Yet, nevertheless, he said he was writing. Didn't expect to make any money from it, didn't know if he'd finish it, didn't even know if it was worthy of being called a novel, but he was at it, writing every day. So would Yoyo. But Yoyo had to be focused. He couldn't afford to waste time on hand-wringing, anxiety-laden memoirs that might never be finished or published. No. He had to do something marketable. Something that he could finish in a day, and something that he could sell.

He would write an opinion piece. He had seem them frequently in North America. When he had worked during a year-long journalism apprenticeship a decade ago in St. Boniface, Manitoba, he had noticed them appearing daily in the *Winnipeg Herald*. Yoyo would fire a few off to the *Toronto Times*. Two of his old friends from Winnipeg, Hélène Savoie and Mahatma Grafton, were working there. Hélène could help him publish his piece. He wanted to get in touch with her anyway. He wanted to see that woman again. She could help him negotiate a good fee at the paper. Three hundred dollars would be nice. It was more than one month's rent. It was exhilarating to think that he could make three hundred dollars just by sitting at a table and writing. Yes, Yoyo would start to write. He would take on the major issues of the day. He would sign them *Hassane Moustafa "Yoyo" Ali, Underground in America*. The first one popped out in two hours.

Dear Reader,

I wish to propose an alternative to the terms used to describe people of African heritage.

I will start by focusing my attentions on a linguistic

phenomenon — namely, the term *people of color*.

It is impossible to evaluate the term *people of color* without considering its predecessor, *colored people*. *Colored people* used to be a term sympathetic to people of Any Known Blood, but no longer. It is now reviled.

Some people today prefer the term *people of color*. This choice baffles me. You have a noun, a preposition, and another noun. Normally, such a construction would suggest belonging, such as People of France, or Jesuits of Italy, or Knights of Columbus. But it's an awkward construction. The preposition weighs down the term. Do we say People of Left Hands? It seems to me that *of* is the operative word. What is the difference, for example, between intelligent people and people of intelligence? The difference is in the attitude of the speaker. The user of the latter term wishes to emphasize the value of intelligence. The word suggests that the next word to follow is positive. That's why people say *The Duke of York* instead of *The York Duke*.

If one sets aside historical nuance, little remains to distinguish between *colored people* and *people of color*. The difference resides in the attitude of the speaker. If you use *colored people*, you convey that you don't care that the word offends black people today. If you use *people of color*, you wish to celebrate color. But to this writer, *people of color* rings with self-importance. It is one thing to celebrate one's heritage. But it is quite another to see oneself as the navel of the universe.

I propose that we entirely abandon the words *color* and *colored*.

May I submit the term *people of pigment*?

True, the weighty *of* remains. But the tone of self-importance is neutralized by alliteration. Matching the first
letters of adjacent words is common in children's literature,
and in cartoons. In English, even more than in French,
alliteration has the effect of adding a touch of levity. Porky
Pig. Mister McGoo. People of pigment. Follow me
through, dear readers. To express this idea in terms of an
arithmetic equation, *pomp + levity = equanimity.*

Let's examine other arguments in support of *people of
pigment*. For one thing, the new term constitutes a clear
departure from the word *color*. It is unlikely that any
reasonable person will suggest replacing this expression
with *pigmented people*, which, unlike *colored people*, has no
tradition in our lexicon. For another, *pigment* is a compact
and pithy little word. It is merely two syllables, and easy to
pronounce. In the term *people of pigment*, both nouns start
with the bilabial explosive *p*, a highly enjoyable consonant
for the mouth to deliver — one that gives a person the
sensation of power, or at least control of one's destiny.
Finally, by retaining the word *of* — perhaps the most
underrated preposition in the English language — we
ensure that people enjoy the desirable connotations of
pride and respect. People of pigment, unite under this new
term.

Yoyo mailed the story to Hélène Savoie, who, as I heard later,
fed the story to the op-ed editor — a man named Brian
Coolidge. He tossed it down on his desk on top of a pile of unso-
licited pieces. He said he didn't read handwritten copy. Hélène
took it back, typed it on her computer, printed it, and gave it
back to Brian.

"You're the most persistent —"

"Just read it," Hélène said. "This guy has a quirky take on things. You might like it."

Brian pushed his reading glasses up the bridge of his long nose. He chuckled in the second sentence. He laughed midway through the fourth. He roared with laughter three more times and, at the end, declared the piece the best satire he'd seen in a year.

"He didn't intend it as satire," Hélène told Brian.

"Do you think it's funny?" he asked her.

"Yes."

"So do I. So will half the city. I'm using it on Friday."

By Wednesday of the next week, the *Times* had received eighteen letters to the editor praising Yoyo's piece. One letter-writer complained that Yoyo's piece was a vitriolic attack on the sensitivities of people of color. But that writer drew fire from four other scribes in the following days. Brian asked Hélène to send Yoyo a note with the cheque. Could she please ask if he had any more articles kicking around?

Chapter 16

I STOPPED BY ANNETTE'S PLACE twice over the next few days, but did not find her home. Or, at least, she did not come to the door. The second time, I could see from the street that there was a light on in her apartment. Maybe she'd had enough of me. Perhaps she had another man up there. The two years of celibacy had been tough. Staring ahead at another long road of abstinence promised to be even tougher. I tried not to think about Annette or Ellen. I dove into writing again. I was ready to resume the story of my grandfather, Langston Cane the Third.

In April 1923, two sharp blasts from the Marlatt and Armstrong tannery awakened the Cane family at six-thirty on their first morning in the new Oakville residence.

Actually, they awakened young Mill, who was a light sleeper, and her mother Rose, who wondered who had cause to blow on a whistle at such a pagan hour. Langston Cane the Third slept through the whistle, and the ruckus Millicent raised over the cold enamel toilet seat, and the voice Rose used to settle her daughter down.

"Don't irk me, daughter, I'm not in a mood to be irked. Sit on that toilet before I heat up your behind with the back of my hand."

Langston slept through the sound of the milkman ringing his bell as he led his horse-drawn cart of farm milk. He slept through the clatter of hooves and the tinny horn blasts of Studebakers and McLaughlin-Buicks driving on Colborne Street. He slept through the second tannery whistle at nine, and he was still sleeping when Rose came to rouse him at nine-thirty.

"Wake up and eat your last grits and scrapple. I walked over to the dry goods store. The owner has never even heard of grits. Or scrapple."

"We'll have to try another store," Langston sighed.

"He said he knew every store in town and that I'd never find grits or scrapple. Up here, he said, Grits are Liberal politicians. Some people dislike them, he said, but nobody has gotten around to eating them."

"Sounds like a jovial fellow," Langston said.

"He was. Spoke with an accent. British, kind of. But not quite."

"How about if you and I practice our British accents in bed?"

"Millicent is awake, I'll have you know," Rose said. "Why don't you get dressed and make yourself useful?"

"I was hoping you found me useful last night."

Rose snorted. "We don't want to get overrun with babies."

"We're far from overrun," Langston said.

"We're heading that way, I tell you. I'm with child."

Langston jumped up and hugged Rose. "Since when are you pregnant?"

"Since about twelve hours ago."

"You can't be pregnant. You couldn't know it yet."

But she was. And she did.

After breakfast, Langston heard a timid rap at the door. He

opened it, and a gust of cold air blew in. He shivered and said hello to a young black man who looked about sixteen or so. He was built like a twig, and as black as the night. He had friendly eyes, big teeth, and a voice like a bird. "Hello, Reverend Cane. I'm Aberdeen Williams."

"Step right in, Aberdeen Williams. It's cold out there."

Aberdeen stepped in, removed his hat, offered his hand, and smiled. "No, not really. You'll get used to it. I hope I'm not troubling you."

"Not at all, sir, not at all," Langston said. He liked what he saw: a young man with bright, attentive eyes. A man of a caring and Christian disposition — something Langston would later declare that he could determine at a distance of twenty paces, solely by examining a man's carriage.

"Nobody calls me sir, Reverend. Aberdeen will do. Or Ab." Aberdeen had a high voice. He also had a slight stammer that receded in the thick of conversation. He was no taller than five seven.

"Aberdeen is a fine name," Langston said. "I've always been partial to names with three syllables. Wish I had one myself."

"It comes from Scotland, Reverend."

"You're the oddest-looking Scotsman I've ever met."

Aberdeen laughed. "My grandfather insisted on the name. He had heard all about the hills and the beauty of Aberdeen, in Scotland, and he insisted that my mother name me that way."

"Be thankful they didn't call you Edinburgh."

"The A.M.E. folks are going to like you, Reverend. I can see that."

Rose approached the door. "Ask the gentleman to take off his coat."

"I'm no gentleman, ma'am. I'm just Aberdeen. Pleased to meet you."

Rose smiled at him. "Call me Rose. And come have tea with us."

Mill, nearly three at the time, wandered into the kitchen where they sat. Langston beckoned to her. "Come sit on my lap, child. Meet our new friend."

"No," Mill said.

Langston frowned. Since the family had reunited, he hadn't had any luck getting his daughter to sit on his knee or hug him or play with him.

"Mother's daughter," Rose explained to Aberdeen.

Aberdeen and the two adults sat down. Mill climbed up on Aberdeen's lap and let her head fall back against his chest. Aberdeen grinned, embarrassed.

"Looks like you've found an admirer," Rose said.

"Hi, Mill, I'm Aberdeen."

"Hi, Have-a-Bean. I'm Mill."

Aberdeen let it drop that he'd been the A.M.E. Church sexton when the last minister had been present, and that he hoped to have the honor of continuing with that work. Langston said he was sure they could come to an arrangement. Rose excused herself, saying she had some work to do. Mill stayed put. "Mill, don't you want to come with me?"

"No," Mill said. "I want to stay here, with Have-a-Bean."

"Actually, cutie-pie," Langston said, "Daddy has to step outside now. He wants to ask Aberdeen about a broken gate."

"Oh, all right." Mill climbed down and ran out of the kitchen.

Langston put on a thick gray sweater and stepped outside. Aberdeen wore only a light spring jacket.

"You'll freeze out here," Langston said.

"No such thing," Aberdeen said. "It's nice out today. Look.

The ice has cracked on that puddle over there."

"Where I come from, ice would be a crime in the month of April," Langston said. He didn't have to show Aberdeen the broken latch on the gate. Aberdeen walked right up to it and toyed with the hood. He asked for a screwdriver and wrench. Langston brought them outside.

"See how it's bent here, on top?" Aberdeen said. "It looks as if somebody flattened it with a rock. That stops the metal tongue from entering the mouth of the latch. I'll see if I can straighten it out. If not, I'll get a new one." Aberdeen screwed the latch more tightly into place, then twisted it up. "It's not pretty, but it ought to work now. Try it."

Langston slid the gate shut. The latch fell down easily over the metal tongue.

"There you go," Aberdeen said.

"You've just become the A.M.E. sexton and handyman," Langston said. "What do you charge, by the way?"

"I don't charge for that," Aberdeen said. "I'm not one for being a deacon, or for public speaking. But I can fix anything."

"Well, that's good. Because I can't fix anything. My father couldn't, either."

"I hear tell your grandfather was quite something with his hands."

"How do you know about my grandfather?"

"He was a Langston Cane, too, wasn't he?"

"How on earth did you know that? From my reckoning, he would have been here in the 1850s."

"My people have been here for a long time. My grandfather also came here as a fugitive slave. Your grandfather, or so the story goes, was quite the rat catcher. From what I hear, he could catch any rat he went after."

"I can see we have a lot to talk about."

"We do, Reverend. We do."

On his third day in Oakville, Langston discovered Neall's ice-cream parlor. A bell rang as he entered the shop. He stood before an ice-cream counter, behind which a curtain was drawn. He heard something from behind the curtain. At first, it sounded like running water. He listened again. It was ice. Ice being stirred, crushed, broken, stirred some more.

"Just a minute," someone called from the back. One of the roundest women he had ever seen stepped through the curtain. "Yes, sir," she said.

Langston wasn't wearing his collar. He checked with his fingers, to be sure. Indeed, he wasn't. And he wasn't known to the people in this town. He was a stranger, a black stranger, and they still called him sir. Langston decided then and there that he liked Oakville.

"I'd like a small amount of ice cream," he said.

"All we've got is butterscotch ripple for the time being."

"A pint of that, please," he said.

She handed him a container. "Packed this morning," she said. "Do you have somewhere good and cold to keep it?"

"I'm going to dispense with it in short order. I have two helpers."

She laughed. "They'll love you for it."

"They'd better," he said, smiling.

Mill was napping when Langston got home. He nudged her shoulder.

She stirred, and complained. "*Ehhhh.*"

"Mill, I have ice cream here."

"*Ehhhh.*"

Langston got a spoon, dug out a fleck, and placed it on her lips. She brushed it off with her arm and turned from him. "Go away, Daddy."

He felt anger flash across his forehead. He was tempted to shake her and have harsh words with her. She had barely spoken with him since the family had reunited. But he stopped himself. Better to leave her alone, wait for her to come to him. Langston carried the ice cream back to the kitchen. They had no ice yet, and he didn't want to eat it alone.

"Rose?" he called out. No answer. "Rose," he called out louder. Still no answer. He heard sounds from the bedroom. Conversation. Laughter. He strolled that way. Aberdeen was in their bedroom, on top of a stepladder, attaching a shade to a naked bulb. Rose leaned against the wall, heaving with laughter as Aberdeen told a story about how hard it was to find colored people's food in Oakville.

"And then," he said, "I said to the man in the store, 'Well, if you don't have scrapple, what do you have?' and he said, 'Just regular food, mister. Regular food for regular people.'"

During their first week in Oakville, the Canes found all sorts of salesmen knocking on their doors. Men selling ice, flowers, bread, milk, and fruit all came by. The baker's man moved his bread in the back of a new McLaughlin-Buick, but the others brought their goods on horse-drawn carts. Mill would have nothing to do with any of them, except the ice man. She thought he was selling ice cream, so she followed Rose and Langston out the front door. Langston patted the horse's head.

"Since when do you know about horses?" Rose asked him.

"Since the war," he said. "There were horses in every French village. Want to pat the horse, Mill?"

"No. I want to pat it with Mommy!"

The ice man, who was about sixty, with blue eyes, a gray-white beard, and forearms shaped like bowling pins, chiseled off three brick-shaped chunks. "You folks must be from the States," he said.

"Why do you say that?" Rose asked.

He hammered a chisel so that the ice cracked down the middle. "Because you look in people's eyes. People in these parts won't look a stranger in the eye. Unless they're missionaries or want your money." The ice man chipped a bit of ice, shaped like a thin wedge of cheddar, brushed off the flecks of sawdust, and handed it toward Mill. "Sugar, would you like a sliver of ice?"

Mill stomped her foot. "I don't like sugar and I don't like slivers."

Langston told his daughter to say thank you. Mill refused. "Say it, Mill, or you're going inside."

"He wants to give me a sliver. I don't WANT to say thank you," Mill said.

"Hey, I'm off," the ice man said.

"How much do we owe you?" Rose asked.

"Free ice to first-time customers."

"Thank you," Langston said. He instructed his daughter to say the same. She looked at her shoes. Langston tried to lead her inside. She pulled her hand free. He reached for it again, and she hit it. He lifted her up and carried her, kicking, into the house. Rose heard the slap from outside. She heard Langston order the girl to her room. And she heard the petulant footsteps tap along the oak floor.

"She's so angry, she won't even cry in front of you," Rose told Langston.

"I won't have her walking over us, or ignoring our instructions."

"I don't like it either, but you're going to have to win your daughter's affections and respect."

"I don't know how."

"Relax," Rose said. "Be yourself. Treat her the same way you treat adults. Leave the disciplining to me. If you keep hitting her, she'll never talk to you."

"I don't know what her problem is."

"It's not just her problem. It's your problem, too. You haven't had the chance to get used to each other. You haven't spent enough time together." Rose rubbed her man's back. "Give it time, Lang. Time is all it needs."

Four days later, Aberdeen and his sister Renata — a young woman twice his size — knocked on the door. Rose, who had just put on makeup and a dress with a print of red poppies, shook their hands and invited them in. The woman introduced herself as Mrs. Williams. She nudged Aberdeen as Rose led the way to the kitchen table.

"You two sweet on each other or something?" she whispered.

Rose heard the question and turned. "I'll tell you what, Mrs. Williams. I'll speak respectfully in your house, and you'll do the same in mine."

Renata Williams stared at Rose. Rose stared right back. She took a moment to measure the big-boned woman. She was in her twenties, and dark, like Aberdeen. All two hundred and twenty pounds of her.

"Don't mind her, Rose," Aberdeen said. "She didn't mean anything by it. You know, sisterly teasing, that's all."

"You two are siblings?" Rose asked.

"What'd you call us?" Renata said, her tone arching.

"Brother and sister," Rose said.

"That's not what I heard her say," Renata muttered to Aberdeen. "She said *sib* something."

"Siblings means brother and sister. But drop it. Let it go. Let's start over. Would you like some biscuits and tea?"

"Her cooking any good?" Renata asked her brother. "She don't look like her cooking is any good. No meat on her at all."

"The biscuits are from the bakery. We're still settling in here and I haven't had time to do any baking. Tell you what, Renata," Rose said.

"It's Mrs. Williams to you."

"Where I come from, people leave their surnames at the door."

"This isn't where you come from. To you, it will be Mrs. Williams, please and thank you."

"Then it will be Mrs. Cane to you. And as I was saying, you can eat a biscuit civilly and close that mouth of yours, or you can remove yourself from my house this moment." Rose slapped a biscuit down on the table. No napkin. No plate. No knife. No butter.

"This parsonage belongs to the African Methodist Episcopal Church. And I'm the head of the Ladies Church Auxiliary. I fixed this house up for you. Cleaned the walls. Washed the floors. Even cleaned the bathroom. This is our church's house, Mrs. Cane. You're just living in it."

Rose was holding a fork when she heard that. She wanted to stab it into the woman's arm. She was tempted to take the brewing pot of tea and dump it on the woman's lap.

Langston, who had been at the dry goods store, came up behind Rose and patted her bottom gently, in a way that Aberdeen and the woman next to him couldn't see.

Rose spun around. "Don't touch me," she hissed, and left the room.

"I wouldn't let any woman talk to me like that," the woman said.

"She isn't any woman," he said. "She's my wife."

"Well, I wouldn't put up with it," the woman said.

Langston forced a smile and introduced himself.

"I know who you are, Reverend. I'm sister Rennie. Renata Williams. President of the Ladies Church Auxiliary." She nibbled on her biscuit. Langston brought her a plate, a knife, and butter. He did the same for Aberdeen. He poured them tea, and listened to Rennie Williams ask why he hadn't invited the congregation over. Wasn't he going to meet with his parishioners before Sunday? What time would service be?

He asked her what she thought he should do. She liked that. She liked that very much. Already, Langston thought, as her answers whizzed over his head, he'd have to get this woman tied up in committees and report writing. He'd make her put so many reports together that she wouldn't have time to get in his way. He drifted back to the essence of her hectoring. She said the members of the congregation wanted to meet him before Sunday.

"Come on over," Langston said.

"Are you serving food?" she asked.

"There will be food," Langston said.

"Expect forty people," she said.

"Bring them for dinner. We'll hold it on Friday night. We'll have a pot luck. That means everybody brings a dish or a plate of food, and something to drink. The Reverend and his wife and child are exempted from this work, by virtue of this being their first week in Oakville, of their having a million things to organize in time for the first service, and of their having no money." That worked. She laughed. Langston could see that he'd have to keep this woman busy, and laughing. Aberdeen chuckled a little, too.

"Lang." Rose called him from the other room. He stepped out to see her. "I'm sorry I was rude to you. Tell you about it later.

But if you're inviting forty people, make sure they bring their own dishes, too."

Langston returned to the kitchen and told Aberdeen and his sister not to forget the plates, bowls, cutlery, and so forth. "Dishes for forty, please. You organize it, Rennie. I'm leaving it in your capable hands. Let's say Friday at the supper hour. Friday at six."

Rennie shook Langston's hand. "The people will like you, Reverend."

Langston walked with them to the door. "Pleasure meeting you, Rennie. Aberdeen — come again." The brother and sister stepped out. Langston turned back into the house, and Rose came up to him.

"I'm so glad you came at that moment," Rose said. "If you hadn't, I might have taken out your .45 automatic and plugged that woman. She is as coarse as a bear."

"But be careful," Lang said. "I was out walking yesterday, trying to find out the Negro section of town. I ended up near the lake. I can tell you that our people don't live in that area. The houses are opulent down there. I was walking by one when I saw that woman. I couldn't help but notice her, being big and black and in such a rich area. She was entering the side door of a big home. So she works for rich people. Let's not forget that she has the power to put us in a poor light in the eyes of white people."

"You mean I don't get to shoot her after all?" Rose said. "Pity."

The day of the party, to get out of the house, Langston asked Aberdeen to take him on a walking tour of Oakville.

"Where do the colored people live in town?" Langston asked.

"We don't really live anywhere," Ab said.

"You've got to live somewhere."

"We're just sort of here and there. Not in just one place."

"Where do you live, Ab?"

"Here and there."

Langston resolved not to press for details. He had noticed that Aberdeen wore the same clothes every day. In the street, a little brown boy caught up with them. "Reverend Cane? Mrs. Cane said you'd be walking on Colborne. Mary Coombs has a sick son. She says he's dying."

"I know where they live," Aberdeen said. "I'll take you there."

The first thing Langston noted about Hope Street was the mud. Colborne was paved. And on the nicer streets in town, the earth was packed down hard. Not here. There were no car tracks, and hardly any horse cart tracks. There were sheds, shacks, and cottages, half of which looked as if they'd been bent out of shape by a hurricane. Children in the street — most of whom were white — had runny noses and torn clothes.

A woman ran outside to meet them. Aberdeen introduced her as Mary Coombs.

"My boy, Reverend, my boy is dying. He's not been too good lately either, stealing and lying and carrying on, and I want him prayed for before he meets his maker, oh Lord, oh Jesus, what am I to do, *don't let my baby die!*"

Langston put his arm around her shoulder. "There's nobody going to be doing any untimely dying today. Take a breath, Mary. Good. Slow down. Breathe in. Take me to your son."

The one-room shack had no running water, or electricity, or wooden floors. Langston felt the bumpy earth under thin rugs. It was damp in the room. The wood stove gave off no heat. Langston touched it. Cold. A boy, thirteen or so, lay on a mattress. A brown overcoat covered him.

"What's your name, son?"

"Ken."

Langston touched his forehead. The boy was burning up. "Can you stand up?"

"No."

"How long have you been sick?" Langston asked.

"Five days."

"When was the last time you had something to drink?"

"He can't drink nothing, Reverend," his mother said. "Can't keep it down. Reverend, did you bring a Bible?"

Langston turned to the woman. "Mary, your boy needs help. Medical help. Go get two strong friends." She didn't move.

"Am I gonna die?" the boy asked.

"No," Langston said. "You're going to live. That's an order. You're going to live."

The boy sighed. "I got the runs again. I got to go."

"Where's the toilet?"

"Outside," Ab murmured.

Langston carried the boy to the outhouse. He managed to get Ken's pants down and put him on the seat. Langston backed out, heard what sounded like water running on and on and on, and then a loud thud. The boy had fallen backward. Unconscious. Langston lifted him out of there, pulled up his pants, and carried him back to the shack. "Where's the hospital?"

"We don't go there," Aberdeen said.

"Is there a doctor who works with colored folks?"

"He moved away."

"Let's carry him to Colborne Street. Someone there can help us get him to the hospital."

"We can't go there, Reverend," Mary Coombs said. "It's useless. Just pray for my boy. Pray for him."

Langston cleared his throat, and assumed his army officer voice. "Mary, there are times for praying, and there are times for doing. This is a doing time. You called for my help, woman, and I'm going to give it. I will personally see to it that your boy receives medical care. Is that clear enough?"

"Yes, Reverend."

"I'm going to take your boy to a doctor. Do you want to come?"

"No, Reverend. Not now. I'm not feeling up to it."

"I'll send for you once we have someone looking after your son."

Langston carried Ken south on Kerr to Colborne Street. Then he turned the boy over to Aberdeen. "Hold him upright till I find us a ride."

Langston tried to wave down a man driving a horse and buggy. The driver called down that he was in an wretched hurry, and clipped by.

"Try Hillmer's," Aberdeen said. "They'll stop for you."

"What's Hillmer's?"

"That motorized livery service coming along."

Langston stood out in the road and hailed the bus, which had a hood, lamp lights, tires out front, and a boxlike contraption for the driver and passengers. The driver sounded a shrill horn. Langston stood his ground and kept waving. The brakes squealed. The driver, who had a woolen cap pulled over his head, leveled clear blue eyes down at Langston.

"What's the big idea stopping me in the middle of the road?"

"Sorry, mister. I've got a sick child. We need to get him to the hospital." Langston climbed the three steps before the driver had time to say no. The bus was empty. "Come on, Aberdeen. Bring that boy up here."

Aberdeen had trouble making it up the steps with the boy slung over his shoulder, so Langston skipped back down to help him. He grabbed Ken under the arms and Aberdeen held him under the knees. They lifted him up into the bus.

"You're lucky I have nobody in this bus," the driver said.

"This boy needs medical attention. If you can take us to the hospital, I'll make it up to you."

"All right, all right, sit down, let's not block the road any longer."

Langston seated the boy next to the window, and sat next to him to keep him from keeling over. They turned north on Dundas Street and were at the hospital in minutes.

"What do we owe you?" Langston asked the driver.

"Forget it," the driver said. "Just get that boy to the doctor." The driver let the bus idle and helped Langston carry Ken down.

"Thank you," Langston said. "You're a good man."

"Don't mention it," the driver said. "And don't take any guff from the nurse inside."

As Langston and Aberdeen carried the boy inside, a nurse accosted them. "Whoa — whoa. Wait! Where do you think you're going?"

"This boy is sick. He needs to see a doctor."

"The doctors are busy. Do you have an appointment?"

"No."

She told him he'd have to make an appointment. He said he was there to make one — immediately. She said that would be impossible. Langston saw the futility in arguing with her and decided to go over her head.

The hospital door opened. An old woman with a cane walked in. She was as white as a starched shirt.

The nurse turned to her. "What is it, dear?"

"Swollen legs again."

"Just sit down over there, and we'll see what we can do," the nurse said.

Langston signaled to Aberdeen to take the seat next to the woman. Then, in an inspired moment, he laid the boy down on the floor. Langston took off his jacket, rolled it up, and placed it under Ken's head.

Another woman appeared a few minutes later. She wore a white overcoat, and white shoes. She was about fifty, and had lake-blue eyes and gray hair pulled back in a bun. She conferred for a moment with the nurse and approached Langston.

"Hello, sir. What is your name?"

Langston identified himself, explained that he was an ordained church minister, and that he had been asked by a distraught mother to help this boy. He asked if they could see a doctor.

"I am the doctor on call, Reverend Cane," she said. "Dr. Evans is the name."

Langston didn't miss a beat. "Wonderful. Where should we take this boy?"

"In here."

They carried Ken into an examining room. She asked the men to strip him down, put him in a clean green gown, and have him lie down on the table.

The doctor returned a minute later, and began prodding, touching, asking questions. The boy was delirious, drifting in and out of consciousness.

"Where does he live?"

"Hope Street," Aberdeen said.

"Where does he get his drinking water?"

"From the creek, from wherever," Aberdeen said.

"Has he had diarrhea?"

"Yes. A great deal, according to his mother."

"He's dehydrated," Dr. Evans said. "He's got some kind of

intestinal bug. We've got to build his body fluids back up. His pulse is weak. His blood pressure is low. You can die from diarrhea, you know. Children, especially, are susceptible. But I think we can turn him around quickly enough."

The doctor told a nurse to give the boy a tepid bath right away. She also told her to prepare a glucose and saline solution. She wanted him to drink a cup every half hour. Dr. Evans helped the nurse get the boy into a bath, and then she returned to Langston.

"I'll have a church collection taken up to cover the medical costs," he said.

"Don't bother, Reverend. I can waive fees, when it's warranted, and circumstances appear to warrant it now."

Langston smiled at the woman. He had found an ally. Perhaps this woman could deliver Rose's baby. "What's your name?" he said.

"I told you. Dr. Evans."

"Your first name."

"Wendy. Dr. Wendy Evans."

"We are holding a party this evening for our church congregation. Drop by, if you like. We live in the parsonage next to the African Methodist Episcopal Church on Colborne Road."

Langston and the doctor shook hands.

"Ab," Langston said, "why don't you stick around the hospital for a bit? But be sure to bring Mary Coombs to the party tonight."

Aberdeen Williams stopped in at the Oakville bakery late that afternoon. It was run by Adam Cullen, an old schoolmate.

"Adam, do you have anything broken around here?"

"We got a toilet that won't work. Why?"

"Let me fix it for you."

"Sorry, Ab, but I don't have the money for that."

"You don't have to pay me."

"Then what do you want?"

"Give me ten pastries, for a party. Now show me that toilet."

Aberdeen climbed up on a chair to reach the tank, which was up on a shelf near the ceiling. In less than five minutes, he had fixed the tank. It had a round ball that was supposed to fall with the water line and, when it hit a certain point, trigger a flow of water back into the tank. But its arm had snapped. Ab replaced the broken section with wire.

"These here odorless toilets are more trouble than they're worth," Adam said. He had been watching Aberdeen. "You ever heard of someone having to fix an outhouse?"

For his work, Aberdeen received ten chocolate cream puffs. When he got to the party, he noticed that the parsonage had been split into two camps. The living room area, near the front, was run by his sister. Rennie had punch and iced tea out there. She poured refreshments for each guest and introduced all of them to the Reverend, who in turn introduced guests to his wife and daughter. The kitchen, on the other hand, was under Rose's control. In between introductions at the door, she set up plates and cutlery and arranged the food on tables joined together.

Fifty people had arrived by seven-thirty. Every person brought food. There was potato salad and macaroni salad. There were sweet potatoes and fried chicken drumsticks. There were meat pies, meatballs, and glazed ribs. There was corn bread, Italian bread, and French bread. There was apple crumble, apple pie, and apple butter. People stood eating and laughing on the porch, the balcony, the front yard, and the sidewalk. Drivers slowed down to look. The people of Oakville had never seen Negroes partying. The food flowed on and on. The men were dressed in suits and ties, the women in dresses, fine gloves and hats, polished shoes, and shining buttons.

Rose gave Aberdeen one of Langston's jackets. Aberdeen put it on gratefully. He wondered if Rose was with child. She was as slender as a woman could be, and her cheeks were angular and smooth. Even her fingers were long and slim. Her eyes were dancing acorns, alive as a child's. Her skin was the color of well-creamed coffee. That was why his sister hated Rose so much, he knew. The woman was too fair for her own good. Rennie, who had spent years washing the floors of the wealthy, would naturally hate a black woman who looked almost white and would probably be beautiful until she died.

The Reverend thanked the guests for coming to his house — and for bringing their own food. They laughed, so he played that out a little more. Told them that they were going to have to take the leftovers back home with them or buy Rose a bigger ice box. That was very clever, Ab thought. He lets everyone know that they will survive on church members' donations, but he doesn't say it outright.

Aberdeen thought Rose and Langston formed the most striking couple he'd seen in years. Langston was not a tall man. Only about four inches taller than his wife. Five ten, and not an inch more. But upright. Proud. Strong.

"We heard about you having a hard time getting help in the hospital," someone called out to Langston.

"Yes, but we did get help. We *did* get in the door, and we *did* see a doctor, and young Ken Coombs is now recovering there, as I understand it. Isn't that right, Mrs. Coombs?"

"I thank you for that. You worked a miracle, Reverend," she said. "That hospital don't take colored folks."

"It did today."

"But it won't tomorrow."

"We'll work on that when the time comes," said Reverend Cane. "In the meantime, if your child has severe diarrhea, give him plenty of water with a small amount of sugar and salt mixed in. That's what the doctor told me today."

"A prayer," Mrs. Coombs said. "Say a prayer for my boy."

Fifty heads bowed in the living room. The men and women stood shoulder to shoulder. Langston asked the Heavenly Father to take care of the weak, and the ailing — Ken Coombs and all others — and restore to them the strength due all human beings. "We are here to help each other. Why else do we live? What else could be more noble and more gratifying than to extend a hand to one who needs it?" He followed that up with the Lord's Prayer, and reassured everybody that he was not going to deliver a sermon to fifty people standing on their feet. "Bless you all."

They ate and ate. Aberdeen wrapped up some tuna casserole, four chicken thighs, a platter of home fries, a bowl of kidney bean salad, and three servings of bread pudding, and gave it all to Rose. "Put this in your ice box. It will be tomorrow's dinner."

"Only if you'll join us. Langston and I want to talk with you."

"Can't say no to that," Ab said. He spent the rest of the evening playing with Mill. She climbed on his leg. She liked to put her feet on his feet and make him walk her along the ground. She liked to climb up on his back. She made him lie down, and then she lay on his back and told him to try to roll her off. "Have-a-Bean," she called out as she played with him.

Langston came up to watch the two playing. "She sure loves that man."

Rose squeezed his hand. "And I sure love this man."

Two months later, Rose wrote to her parents. She told them

about her pregnancy, about Mill, whose relations with Langston were improving, and about Aberdeen Williams, who was a jack-of-all-trades, church sexton, and babysitter all rolled into one. It turned out that Aberdeen had no place to live. He moved from one person's house to another, and had been unable to find employment after losing his job at the local Marlatt and Armstrong tannery, which had dismissed a quarter of its workers a year earlier. The Canes had a spare room, and they received enough food from the members of the congregation to provide for an extra man. In exchange for room and board, Ab fixed up the parsonage, worked as church sexton, made many meals, ran errands, and took care of Mill.

"But the most fascinating development," Rose wrote, "has been to witness the transformation of your son-in-law into a local leader. The congregation has grown in size from eighty-five to two hundred. Langston has jumped right into the community. He has taken a number of sick or elderly Negroes to the hospital. Already, some colored folks are going to the hospital on their own account — something none of them did before.

"Our only real conflict is about money. I hate living in some-one else's lodgings. Oakville's Negro community considers this parsonage to be its home. We are merely the tenants and are to be eternally thankful for this house, which is one quarter the size of your home. I don't know where we'll put the little one when he comes along. Langston says we'll find a way. I'm sure we will. I do love the man. You'd love him, too, Mother — if only he were a few shades less Negro, Catholic rather than Methodist, and of wealthier stock. By your own reckoning, Mother, these are his gravest defects, yet they are all accidents of birth. So please stop trying to get me to leave him. We are together as man and wife, and we shall remain so until the end.

"Your loving daughter, Rose."

Four months after their arrival in Oakville, Langston found a part-time job working in the ice sheds along Sixteen Mile Creek. Four days a week, from nine until two, he helped load blocks of ice onto the horse-drawn carts. After his first week on the job, he complained about his stiff back, sore knees, and aching wrists.

"Ice is hard on a man," he groaned. "It's cool in the mouth, lovely in punch, essential to every kitchen. But if you work with it, ice becomes ugly and ungiving. It is nothing but cold, hardened, soulless water. It will yield only to chisel and hammer. I could take out my .45 automatic and fire into a block of ice, and it would barely do any damage. And heavy — Lord Almighty, ice is the heaviest thing going. A fifty-pound block of ice has got to be the most ungodly object in the world."

Rose said she hated to see Langston wearing himself out in the ice sheds, and that she was fed up with living in the A.M.E. parsonage. She said she had decided to accept her parents' offer of ten thousand dollars to buy a house in Oakville. She planned to get a nice home on a treed street somewhere east of Sixteen Mile Creek. It would have windows that you could open and shut without the help of a crowbar. And she wanted an electric, ice-free refrigerator. And she was going to buy the house and the fridge before the baby arrived.

"Go ahead, love," Langston said. "You were going to do it, anyway."

"True, but it's nice to have your consent."

"Now I must ask your consent for something," he said.

"What's that?"

"I plan to enter studies for a master's in theology at the University of Toronto in the fall. I've been working in that ice shed to raise tuition fees."

"Quit that silly job. Your tuition fees can come out of the house money."

Aberdeen Williams had never been happier. Rose, who was four months pregnant, was starting to feel uncomfortable. Ab was now called upon four or five times a week to make supper. When Rose cooked, she made sauces, pie shells, and meringues. Aberdeen, on the other hand, made feasts out of leftovers. He made wet hash once a week by frying diced potatoes, tomatoes, onions, and day-old meat loaf. He used tomatoes that gardeners gave him in exchange for fixing broken hinges. The tomatoes had enough juice in them to keep the hash simmering and wet. Aberdeen also made tea biscuits and corn bread. He didn't use measuring cups or spoons but dumped flour, baking powder, cornmeal, brown sugar, and cream straight into the mixing bowl. The bread always turned out well. Ab taught young Mill to cut with a knife, pour cream from the jug, and light the oven.

People called on Ab to put in new sinks, lay floors, shingle roofs, install shelves. They rarely paid him, but he didn't mind. They gave him food, free rides in horse carts and cars, extra clothing, and ice cream. In the summer, he brought home quarts of strawberries every week from people desperate to give him something — anything but money — for his services.

A young, unmarried white woman by the name of Evelyn Morris asked Ab to get her garden in order. She lived with her mother in a small house on Florence Street, and she wanted the entire backyard converted into a vegetable garden. Ab spoke often of Evelyn to Rose. Evelyn had asked for a huge garden to be put in. He helped her install stakes for the green beans and tomatoes.

"Is Evelyn attractive?" Rose asked.

"Not like you."

"I didn't ask if she's like me, silly. Do you like her?"

"She's white, Rose."

"I know that, you silly man."

"I guess I like her. She makes the time go by."

"Why don't you invite her over for dinner?"

"I'll think about it."

"I wouldn't get bogged down in a lot of thinking, Ab. Men aren't too good at that. Just do it."

"The Reverend is a thinker."

"It's his job to be a thinker. But when he was courting me, he didn't stop to think. He just dove straight into trouble."

Ab gave a long, slow laugh. "Good thing he did."

In August, after Ab had been away from the house for several days, Rose caught up with him, and she asked where he had been.

"In rehearsals for the minstrel show. It raises money for charities. They need some Negroes because of all the Negro parts in the show. Some of the white people get dressed up as Negroes, you know, shoe polish and all that, but they like to have a few real ones, too. It's a lot of fun. We do it every year. Last year, we raised $130."

Langston joined them. "A minstrel show in Oakville?"

"We do one every year," Ab said.

"And you're taking part?" Langston asked.

"Want to join us?"

"I don't care for minstrel shows."

"You'd like this one," Ab said. "Last year one man laughed so hard he fell off his chair and broke his arm."

"What made him laugh so hard?"

"Some part in which a gardener — this is a white man, dressed up as colored — can't find his trowel. He can't find it because he has planted it."

"Would it have been funny if a colored gardener had dressed up as white, looking for his trowel?"

Ab chuckled. "I don't think so. It was funny because this colored man couldn't find it, and thought the trowel had human qualities, and had walked away from him. He was trying to talk to it, shout at it, telling it to come back. A white man, he wouldn't do that."

"But a black man would?"

"I see where you're coming from," Ab said. "You want me to say that a colored man wouldn't really have done that either. And that's true. But still, this scene cracked everybody up. You sort of had to be there."

Ab continued attending his rehearsals. Occasionally, he teased Langston about it. "Sure you don't want to come along now, Reverend?"

A week later, Langston engineered a minister's swap. He would deliver a sermon at Knox Presbyterian Church, and the Presbyterian minister would speak at the A.M.E. Church.

Langston did not believe in fire-from-the-pulpit, revivalist sermons. He believed in the quiet exposition of irrefutable logic. He believed in appealing to the minds of his congregation, rather than reaching them through the lowest common denominator of gospel music and pulpit thumping. His was not a church in which people fainted dead away in the arms of Jesus. His was a style of sober, rational thought — but packaged in rhythm, cadence, and current references to keep his congregation awake. Jesus, he knew, entered not the hearts of sleeping men.

Knox Presbyterian Church was packed on the day of Langston's guest sermon. The title of his sermon was advertised as "Modern Appliances, Ancient Souls."

Langston began by observing how rapidly life was changing in the 1920s. "We have cars, and buses, and radios," he said.

"We have the advent of electric refrigerators, electric hair curlers, electric toasters, and electric ovens. Ladies and gentlemen, our entire homes are going electric. As a matter of fact, my wife has informed me that our own marriage will be short-circuited unless we have an electric refrigerator by the end of this month."

Langston waited for the laughter to subside.

"No need to get into further details about this electricity business. Curling tongs, shaving gadgets, and on it goes. Someday, someone will surely find a way to electrify my toothbrush."

More laughter.

"If Jesus were here today, he'd say, 'Step back, ladies and gentlemen. Step back from your material preoccupation and ask yourselves what is key to the human experience.'

"We need not look far for answers, my friends. We need look no further than the Bible. Love thy neighbor. Sound familiar? Not thy neighbor's wife" — again, Langston waited for the laughter to die down — "which is an entirely different thing, but thy neighbor."

Langston looked around at the people in the pews.

"As you know, your neighbors include the brown-skinned brothers and sisters of Oakville.

"People — all people — have innate dignity. They are much more than, as Darwin tells us, the last in a long line of apes. Yes, I say, man has soul, intelligence, and dignity. So, the question must be asked: At what price do we erode that dignity?"

Move it along, Rev'rend, someone cried from the back. *You're picking up steam, so move right along.*

Half of the congregation turned to see who had interrupted the guest minister. They saw the face of Renata Williams.

Langston had pleaded with the members of his congregation to stay at their own church out of respect for the Presbyterian minister, but fifteen or so Negroes had ignored the request and slipped into the back of the Presbyterian church.

"Don't you mind, folks," Langston said. "That sister of mine wasn't intending any disrespect. That's our way, in the Negro churches. We invite response from the pews."

I say, move it along, Rev'rend.

"I'm moving, sister, but I just can't run as fast as you."

Langston waited for the laughter to die down.

"Let me ask a question, my friends. Suppose someone wanted to make a mockery of your child in a school play. How would you react to that?"

I'd bust it up, Rennie shouted from the back.

"Exactly. You wouldn't let it happen. You wouldn't want any child of yours to be the subject of gratuitous indignities. But some of you will be helping to perpetuate such an indignity right here in Oakville."

Not a person moved. The only sound Langston heard was that of a pencil scratching across paper.

"I understand that, in two weeks, members of the Oakville community — white and colored people — will put on a black-face minstrel show in the Gregory Theater. I understand that it's a fund-raising event for charity. That it's a showcase of singing and acting talent in our town — including the singing of our own Negro community.

"I understand all that. But I want you to understand something. It violates the dignity of the Negro people."

Tell it, Rev'rend. Tell it like it is.

"We were brought over in slave ships. But we survived and we are here today. We have our families, and our churches, and we want, essentially, what all human beings seek. Food. Shelter. Comfort. Love. A sense of things higher.

"Having survived slavery, and Reconstruction, and lynching, some Negroes don't care to see themselves mocked in a minstrel show.

"Depicting Negroes as blackfaced clowns tripping over themselves in ignorance is an indignity to us. It has no place in a town that lent a helping hand to fugitive slaves just two generations ago. God gave us dignity, and we must not squander it. Let us pray."

It turned out that a local reporter had been in church when Langston gave his guest sermon. The story ran the next day on the front page of the *Oakville Standard*, under the headline *Negro Minister Denounces Minstrel Charity Show*.

All week, Langston fielded visits — most of them angry — from the charity organizers, the mayor, the high school principal, and the editor of the *Standard*. The editor seemed angrier when he left than when he arrived. The next issue of the *Standard* condemned Langston as "an American interloper with no understanding of the people of Oakville." The *Standard* demanded an apology. Langston refused. Someone threw a rock through the parsonage window. Langston refused to budge. The controversy brought colored people together. They agreed — with Aberdeen Williams now leading the charge — to withdraw from the production. Organizers killed the minstrel show two days before the event, but the debate raged on for weeks. One editorial sarcastically called for a ban on all public humor.

After the minstrel show was canceled, Aberdeen told Langston that he was ashamed he'd taken part in the show previously.

"Don't be ashamed," Langston said. "You've done the right thing now."

Aberdeen went to the Oakville library. He borrowed a book called *Ancient African Kingdoms*, and read about Kankan Musa, the emperor of Mali. He read about the vast routes for the transport and trade of salt and gold. Musa, apparently, had been able to muster an army of two hundred thousand men. He had traveled as far as Mecca.

Next, Aberdeen borrowed a book about Egypt. When he finished it, he asked Langston: "Did you know that black Africans built the pyramids? Nobody told me that in school. I never even thought of Egypt as being in Africa."

Ab read every book he could find in the Oakville library about the history of Africa. Then he started reading about the West Indies. He read about the slave trade. He read about Christopher Columbus. He came to Langston again.

"Did you know that Columbus intentionally gave the blankets of his sick shipmates to South American Indians, to wipe them out?"

Langston shook his head and admitted that he had never heard that.

When Ab had exhausted thirty books in the Oakville library, he started having books ordered in from out of town. Langston grew weary of his questions. He told Aberdeen to take a course in history at the University of Toronto.

"I could never do that," Ab said.

"You can do it. All you do at university is read books and listen to people talk, and then write about what you've been reading and hearing. You'd like it. And it's not as hard as you think."

"I don't think I could do that, Reverend."

While Langston mobilized the Negro community, handled complaints about the minstrel show cancellation, commenced studies at the University of Toronto, and continued writing and delivering weekly sermons, Rose started looking for a house. She walked every street in town. She headed west on Colborne and north on Kerr, just to be sure there was nothing up there she wanted. There wasn't. Oakville's poorest families lived there. Many were without electricity and running water.

Rose walked east on Colborne, south along Navy, and east on King, but the houses close to Lake Ontario were too ostentatious. The Turner empire, as Rose called the mansion where Renata Williams worked, had sprawling gardens, a tennis court, a goldfish pond, a pagoda, and a barn. It was almost indecent. Rose didn't need that much. And she had to be sensitive to her husband. He'd lose credibility if he moved into a mansion. Rose didn't want a house right by the lake, anyway. Too many people went by. Walking, talking, riding, driving. At any rate, the houses closest to the water had rat problems. She'd read about it in the *Standard*. A rat story had shared the front page with the minstrel show business, several days earlier. That decided the matter. The Cane family would not live by the water.

It took Rose only a day of walking and scouting to decide on a neighborhood: north of Colborne and east of Reynolds. It was quiet. It was modest. There were one or two colored families around. It was on the north edge of town, but only a five-minute walk from the center of things.

She picked a house on Sumner Avenue, between Reynolds and Allan. It was a two-story wood house with yellow trim. It looked modest from the street. In the yard, a spruce tree had grown taller than the house. A large window fronted the living room. Simple, square pillars supported a verandah. That was good. Langston loved porches, but he'd never go for rounded pillars. Too evocative of plantation history. The unassuming front would win over Langston. But the spectacular rear satisfied Rose. The current owners had doubled the size of the house by expanding backward. On the second floor, there were three bedrooms near the front of the house and a large new master bedroom at the back. On the ground floor, the addition contained a room with a huge fireplace. The house had two bathrooms with running water and odorless toilets. There was a study on the ground floor. Rose would ask Ab to knock out the wall between the kitchen and the dining room. She believed a big kitchen brought people together to talk, and she wanted a family with lots of talking. Rose took her husband's arm as they stepped in the front door.

"Nice tree out front," he said. "I like spruce trees. Nice porch, too. We'll need two chairs."

"What do you mean, we'll need two chairs? You haven't looked inside yet. How do you know you'll like it?"

"I can tell."

Rose showed him every room in the house. And in every room, Langston said "Fine." He spent an extra moment in the study. It seemed like a good place to do work. Reading. Writing. Thinking. This would be a house where great work could be done.

"Buy it," he said. "Ab will be moving with us, I expect."

"Of course," Rose said. "I knew you'd want that. He'll have the first bedroom at the top of the stairs. Overlooking Sumner. Mill will be in the next bedroom. The baby will be on the other side. And we're in the back, overlooking the yard."

"Terrific."

Rose bought the house in September 1923 for seven thousand dollars. She set aside the remaining three thousand dollars from her mother's gift for furniture, a car, and Langston's tuition and book costs.

Ab managed the move. All the people who owed him for gardening, cabinet making, and repair work were called upon to help. They packed boxes, loaded some on horse wagons and others in the vaults of cars, hauled them from the A.M.E. parsonage to the new home on Sumner Avenue, and unpacked them according to Rose's instructions.

Having paid for the house, Hazel Bridges invited herself up to help Rose prepare for childbirth. Langston enjoyed the new house, but he didn't think it was worth having a mother-in-law around for two months. Ab stayed away from the house a great deal. He was around to cook and clean and help take care of Mill, but he slept elsewhere. He stayed out of Hazel's hair.

Langston dreaded his weekly trips to the University of Toronto. He telephoned — a phone had been installed in the new home, along with an electric refrigerator — from the university three times a day to check whether anything was stirring in the womb department.

Rose and Langston planned in some detail how they would handle things during and after the delivery. Langston would suspend all obligations. If the baby was born on or near a Sunday, he'd bring in a backup minister. Ab would look after Mill. Langston would have nothing to do but be with Rose.

"I don't want you anywhere but with me. During, right after, and for days after that. I want you with me, husband. And I want you with the baby. I want you two bonded, from the start. I don't want any of the troubles you've had with Mill. You're going to diaper, hold, and cuddle him."

"How about if I hold and cuddle you?"

"I won't say no to that."

Rose's waters broke at two o'clock in the morning on the first of December — three weeks before her due date.

"Thank God it's not a Sunday," Langston said. "Sunday I would have had to preach. And thank God it's not a Tuesday. Tuesday I would have had to go to university. And thank God it's not a Monday. Shoot. It *is* a Monday. I'll have to cancel an appointment."

"Shut up, dear pagan buzzard, and get me a towel. Hurry. What a mess."

"What should I do?"

"Get me a towel."

"Here. Here's my shirt. Now what?"

"I don't want your shirt, silly. Calm down, Langston. Look at me. Good. Calm down. Get me a towel and get mother to ring the doctor. Then walk over to Mr. Pearson's door. He's offered to drive me to the hospital, any time of day, come hell or high water. Now's his chance."

"But it's two in the morning. Shouldn't we wait till dawn?"

Rose opened her husband's dresser drawer. She picked up his .45 automatic. She pointed it at him. "Move it, buster, before I shoot."

"That's not funny. Put that away. That's not for joking."

Rose laughed and put the gun away. Then she gasped. "Hurry. This is going to be a fast labor. I can tell."

"You sure you want to be here for this?" Dr. Wendy Evans asked Langston. He figured watching the delivery couldn't be as bad as waiting outside with Hazel. So he nodded, yes.

"Breathe, Rose," the doctor said.

Langston breathed with her. *Huh, huh, huh, huh.* They got her over that contraction. And another. And another.

"I want to push," Rose said.

Dr. Evans examined her. Pushed her hand, starting with two fingers held close together, right up into that big black hole that resembled nothing Langston had ever seen before. Rose moaned long and hard, an animal, other-worldly moan of pain, when the doctor's wrist disappeared in there.

Rose would be ready soon, Dr. Evans said. She just had to ride through a few more contractions. Those contractions lasted an hour and a half. Langston peeked out into the waiting room. Mill was asleep on Hazel's lap. That was good. That meant Hazel couldn't get up and try to barge in.

Two hours after Rose got into the delivery room, Dr. Evans let her push.

"When you push, don't let go," she said. "Hold your breath and push and don't stop until I tell you, okay? It's going to hurt, but you're going to push right through it."

Rose looked at Langston and tried to grin. "What are you looking so pale for, you weak-kneed pagan buzzard? I'm the one having the baby. If you faint on me, I'm bringing mother in here."

"I've been in the trenches of France, dear, so I can handle a delivery once every few years."

Rose groaned. Her back arched. She clenched Langston's hand and pushed, pushed, pushed, pushed. "*Ow*. That hurts. That burns. Me oh my, that burns. Water. Nurse. Doctor. I want water. *Ow*. Not again."

"Deep breath, Rose, deep breath and push. All right. Okay. I can see the head. I can see hair. Push."

More screaming. More hollering. All sorts of yellow and red muck coming out of that big black hole. Langston wondered if lovemaking would ever be the same.

On the fourth push, a head popped out. Covered with filmy water, black hair plastered to its scalp. Soundless. Not a noise. Was it a boy? A girl? Was it alive? Wendy Evans leaned in and ordered Rose to push again, and took hold of the baby's head, holding it beneath the jaws, and pulled while Rose pushed. She pulled and Rose pushed and the rest of the little one rode out in a wave of blood and water and white gunk and meconium. The baby had a penis and swollen balls.

"It's a boy," Langston shouted.

Rose likely would have told her husband he was mad to want to call their son Langston Cane the Fourth. *How long could this go on?* is what she probably would have said. *Aren't you folks getting tired of that name?* But she was angry at her mother, who tried to boss everybody around the house. She scared Ab away, acted like an army general around Mill, and induced Langston to take every opportunity to get out of the house. So Rose agreed to the name to spite her mother, who preferred Joseph.

The baby seemed to like his grandmother. He spent a lot of time in her arms. Langston allowed Hazel that time with her grandson since she'd booked a train trip home in one week.

When the departure day came, Langston offered to escort Rose's mother to Union Station. It would be easy for him, since he had to go to school that day anyway. No, thank you, she said. She preferred to travel alone. So Langston took the eight a.m. train to Toronto, and Hazel left one hour later.

Baby Langston, as Mill called him, was passed from hand to hand at the baptismal party. He was darker than his mother, but not as black as his father. He was a fairly big baby, at seven pounds, fifteen ounces, and he was gaining weight fast. His legs looked like little tree trunks. He had a double chin and chipmunk cheeks. His fat little lower lip came to a point, like a beak, in the middle, just like his father's. And eyes. What eyes. Whatever there was to see, Baby Langston devoured it. When he lay in bed between his parents, which his father frowned upon but Rose allowed from time to time, he would move his head back and forth, back and forth, inspecting his parents in turn. And he lived by a simple rule. If you put him down, he cried. If you picked him up, he stopped. Consequently, he spent a lot of time in a lot of people's arms. Mill's. Ab's. Rose's. Langston's.

Aberdeen began bringing Evelyn over for dinner. Evelyn was a trifle jumpy, Rose noted, but quite cute, and fond of Ab. She was slender, but with a healthy bosom, and had a smooth, clear complexion. She had a lively way of speaking when she relaxed, and liked to laugh. She knew how to listen, and to respond to conversation, and she seemed interested in Ab's obsession about African and South American histories. Lately, Ab had started suggesting things that Rose found preposterous. She said nothing, because she didn't wish to discourage Ab, who was devouring books with undying thirst. Ab actually suggested that Negroes from the West Coast of Africa — Cape Verde, Rose heard him say — had been the first to discover America. They had beaten Columbus by more than two thousand years. Rose heard Ab say that mud bricks, adobe houses, certain specialized musical instruments and feather work — all originating in West Africa — had been found in certain pre-Columbian South American Indian cultures.

Rose wondered if opposing the minstrel show had been a big mistake. It had derailed Ab's preoccupation with fixing broken things, and had flung him into the waters of pseudo history.

"What is this?" Eric Small, the minister at Knox Presbyterian Church, handed the letter to Langston. Rose, holding Baby Langston, stood with her husband on the porch.

"I don't know, what is it?" Langston asked, opening the letter. "Who's it from?"

"Aberdeen Williams."

"What's it say?"

"Just read it."

It was addressed to Eric Small. Copies had been sent to four other church ministers, the mayor, and the head of the Oakville library.

Dear Sirs,

Given evidence that people of African origin sailed from the West Coast of Africa in intricate and powerful papyrus or reed boats and traversed the Atlantic Ocean in a westward direction, and given that predominating winds and currents would have assisted greatly in a trans-Atlantic crossing, and given that the most westerly coast of Africa is only 1,900 miles from Brazil as the crow flies, and given similarities too numerous to mention between South American and African artifacts, let it be acknowledged that the Negro Peoples were the first to discover America. After the Indians, that is.

The point is, that Negroes beat Columbus by more than two thousand years.

Be it respectfully proposed that our schools and governments and churches recognize the early Negro Adventurers on an equal footing with Columbus.

Yours truly,

Aberdeen Williams, Oakville

P.S. I can provide numerous books and articles to back this up.

"Has this man completely lost it?" Eric Small asked.

"The ideas *are* interesting," Langston said.

Rose stared at her husband. "Not you, too?"

"I'm not saying I believe it. But I'm not ruling it out."

"I can't believe this," Small said.

"Is your grip on history so unerring that you can dismiss a theory without investigating it?"

"You've got to be kidding," Small said.

"No. But do you want to know how to get Aberdeen Williams off your back? He's a little smitten. If you ignore him, he'll just keep writing letters. What you want to do is defuse him. Send him a letter, thank him for his observations, and say that you'll give them due consideration."

"Due consideration," Small said. "Nice euphemism for the garbage bin."

"Well, say what you want. But thank him for his letter. That ought to satisfy him. Tell the mayor to do the same thing."

The next spring, Ab asked Langston if he had time for a long chat. They walked along the waterfront, passed the ice-cream store, and got a cone each. They asked for single-dip cones, but received double-decker scoops with chocolate sauce on top. Payment was refused — Ab had done some work recently in the back of the store. They started walking in town, but people kept stopping them to talk. Finally, they walked west on Colborne, crossed the bridge, continued on to Kerr, and headed south to the water reservoir. There was a walking path around it, about a third of a mile in circumference. It was abandoned. It was a beautiful evening. There were no bugs out yet. It was early May, and no people were in sight. They walked around and around the path.

Langston had feared, initially, that Ab wanted to talk about his obsession with the Negro discovery of America. But he didn't.

"When we met," Ab said, "remember how I surprised you by saying that I knew your grandfather had lived in Oakville?"

"I do."

Ab said his own father had been born in Oakville, and that his grandfather — like Langston's grandfather — had come to Oakville as a fugitive slave. What is more, they had been brought across the lake by the same schooner captain, a man named Robert Wilson.

Ab spoke of how his own grandfather had earned his living, and of how Langston Cane had earned his living — and a very good living at that — as a rat catcher and a stone hooker. He lifted shale off the bottom of Lake Ontario and sold it to people who wanted to lay foundations with admirable, solid, flat, inexpensive rock.

Ab said he had heard these and other stories directly from his grandfather, who had lived till 1915.

Langston asked why Langston Cane the First had left Oakville.

"This is what I wanted to talk to you about," Ab said. "You have opened my eyes to world history. You've helped me see the history of the Negro peoples of the world. I feel I must tell you something of your own family history. If you didn't get it from me, you wouldn't get it from anyone."

"What do you have to tell me?"

"My grandfather, aside from being a blacksmith, was the A.M.E. Church sexton. He kept certain documents. He told me about them, but he kept them, too. When he died, I went through his materials, and I kept some of his papers. Among them were some A.M.E. Church documents concerning your grandfather." Ab handed a package to Langston. "The set of papers in the broad envelope second from the top is the one that will be of greatest interest to you. It is the only one concerning your grandfather. The others are A.M.E. Church papers, but unrelated to his trial."

"Trial?"

"Take them. Read them."

Langston spent two hours in his study, with the door shut. Rose asked to see him, and he asked her to wait. Mill asked him to put her to bed, and he told her he'd look in on her later.

At ten o'clock that evening, Langston called Ab into his study.

"These are very damaging papers," he said.

Ab said nothing.

"They could do great harm to my family."

Ab remained silent.

"I'm not one for destroying historical documents, although I'm tempted," Langston said. "So I am speaking now as reverend to sexton. And I will ask you, sexton, to seal these pages, and to put them in a place where they will neither be damaged nor found — preferably a safety deposit vault at the bank. I will sign across the seal."

And sign he did. He wrote, "These Documents Are to Remain Sealed for at Least Fifty Years. Dated May 7, 1924. Signed, Langston Cane, African Methodist Episcopal Minister, Oakville."

"I will ask you to speak of this to no one," Langston told Ab. "Nor shall I speak to anyone of this. Not even to my wife."

Ab shook the Reverend's hand. "I will take care to do what you said. And I am pleased that you have chosen not to destroy history."

Langston winced, and bade the man good night.

Rose swamped Ab with work to get his mind off that African nonsense. She had him build cupboards, put in a new garden, prune the pear trees, and install shelving in Mill's room. Neighbors noticed Ab's work and started buying his services. For the first time in his life, Ab starting making money. He dropped the books for a spell, and earned good money — always leaving time to care for Mill and little Langston — for the better part of three years.

Rose Cane would never forget the month of October 1929. It was the month that the stock markets crashed, and that her bank savings evaporated. It was also the month that her voice gave out on her. At first, she thought she had a cold. A sore throat that would go away. But her voice became increasingly scratchy, with no sign of improvement.

After the stock markets crashed, the people of Oakville lined up to get their money out of the banks. But there was no getting any money out. Aberdeen Williams was among those in line. Miraculously, he had hidden all his savings in the Canes' basement. So it was safe. But the sealed A.M.E. papers on Langston Cane the First were in a safety deposit box, and Ab wanted them back in case the bank closed permanently.

The bank manager spent hours talking to people in the line, sending them home one by one. People waited anyway. They waited to talk, to be consoled, and to be turned away. When Ab's turn finally came, the manager looked at him suspiciously.

"You have a safety deposit box with us?"

"Here's the key," Ab said. "It's box number 139. Can I get my papers?"

"Come this way."

Aberdeen hid the papers with his substantial wad of savings in the Canes' basement.

Three months later, Ab walked over to Evelyn's home late one evening and knocked on the door. This violated a cardinal rule. He was not to do anything that would tip off Evelyn's mother to the fact that they were still seeing each other. She had thought the relationship was over, and had warned her daughter that she would call the Ku Klux Klan if Evelyn started seeing Aberdeen again.

"My daughter is in bed. What is wrong with you, knocking on the door at this hour?"

"May I see her?"

"No, you may not."

Evelyn came up behind her mother. She put on her coat, slipped on her boots, put on her mitts and earmuffs, and stormed out into the night without a word to either her mother or Aberdeen.

Ab had to run to catch her.

"I told you not to knock on our door," she said. "Do you realize what trouble you may have caused?"

"Come down to the lake with me."

"Why?"

"There's a full moon tonight. I have something to give to you."

Aberdeen proposed to Evelyn that night.

"Ab, I never thought you'd do it. Mother will cause trouble, though."

Ab tried to kiss her. She pushed him away. "Someone might see us."

"They're going to see us, Ev. People are going to have to get used to it. We're going to be man and wife. Out in the open. Married. Right?"

"Right." She let him kiss her.

Aberdeen and Evelyn asked Langston if he would marry them.

"Are you sure you want to do this?" Langston asked.

Evelyn nodded. In Langston's view, nodding didn't signal a strong commitment. Ab said that he did, indeed, want to go ahead with it.

"What does your mother say?" Langston asked Evelyn.

"I haven't told her yet. But she has already said that she would call the Ku Klux Klan if I saw Ab again. She thinks I broke off with him a year ago."

"The Klan?" Rose said. "In Oakville?"

"She has said more than once that she might call them."

"She'll settle down after we're married," Ab said.

"Even if she does," Rose said, "the whole thing won't be easy." She coughed. She put her hand up to her throat.

Ab asked if she had been to a doctor yet to have her throat examined.

"Why should I?" Rose said. "All the doctor will say is that I have a sore throat, which I already know. But we're not talking about me. We're talking about you two. And I'm saying, you have no idea how hard it will be for you, as a couple. Even here in Canada."

"If people can't handle it, we'll just make new friends," Evelyn said. "Or we'll stick with colored folks."

Ab laughed nervously. "I know some colored folks who won't be too happy, either."

Langston told Evelyn to talk to her mother. "Invite her to your wedding. Let her decide if she wants to attend. And yes, my friends, I'll marry you."

"Do you mind if I spend the night?" Evelyn said. "I'll tell my mother in the morning."

Rose stared at the woman. "No. It's not all right. You're not married yet, and we have children in this house. If you're serious about this, you should go talk to your mother tonight."

"All right. I'm sorry."

Ab offered to walk Evelyn home. The two stepped outside. Rose watched them through the study window. Aberdeen wrapped his arms around her and put his lips into hers. She crushed her body against his and roamed all over his shoulders and back with her hands. Rose looked on, astonished, excited, and disgusted. She didn't think much of Evelyn. Rose would urge Aberdeen to set a wedding date way down the road, and she would hope that he would break it off before the big day.

In bed that night, Rose curled up against Langston. He moaned in pleasure. Rose rubbed his neck, his back. She rubbed his butt. She ran her hands down to the back of his calves, and up again. She reached around the side of his face and planted a kiss on his lips.

"Did all that wedding talk heat you up?" Langston said.

"That will be for you to judge," she said.

He rolled over onto his back. She straddled him. While he fondled her, she guided him inside her. He let out a long, slow breath. She gave out an odd sound. A sound he'd never heard from her before. She sounded as if she was gagging. She fell forward. He fell out of her. She covered her mouth and ran to the bathroom.

Rose was sick all night. She was sick all morning. Her fever hit 103. Langston asked Ab to look after the kids, and he drove her to the hospital. A colored nurse admitted Rose. Oakville had come a long way, Langston thought, since he'd brought Ken Coombs to the hospital years earlier. The nurse put in a call to Wendy Evans.

They took Rose's blood. They X-rayed her chest. They bathed her to bring down the fever. Rose stayed in the hospital overnight. The next day, Langston met with the doctor.

"We'd like to run some more tests," Wendy Evans said.

"Why?"

"Let's talk when I have some clear lab results."

"Out with it, Wendy," Langston said.

"The fever and the vomiting were probably due to the flu. Nothing serious at all. But I'm worried about Rose's throat. She's got a high white blood cell count. It could be cancer. I want to keep her here overnight, and then have her examined at the Toronto General Hospital."

Langston's arms dropped by his side. He couldn't say a word.

Ab offered to look after the kids.

"You're a good man," Langston told him. "You're probably the only handyman in Oakville who knows how to make meals and take care of children. I may be away for a couple of days."

"Don't worry about how long you're away. Reverend, you're walking around in circles. Sit down. I say, sit down, Reverend. There. Better. Sit right there and drink this milk slowly. I'm going upstairs to pack your bags."

Ab ached with desire to see Rose before she left for the hospital in Toronto. To touch her cheek, to stroke her hand. *I have always loved you, Rose,* he thought. *Always have, always will. You're the best woman I've ever met. No disrespect toward my intended, but you're number one.* Ab fought off the urge to ask for a moment alone with Rose. He wanted to take her hand and hold it and listen to her scold him for being so silly. He wanted to tell her something outrageous, perhaps that Africans had not only discovered America, but had been the true founders of Rome as well, just to hear her cluck in disapproval. But Ab didn't ask to see Rose. The Reverend needed time alone with her. They came first. Man and wife. Ab would die for either of them. He would die to keep them together.

Langston rode with his wife in the back of the ambulance.

"Get better soon, Rose. If you don't, the Good Lord may dispatch your mother back to Oakville."

Rose's brown eyes danced, but she couldn't laugh. It hurt too much. She asked Langston not to tell any jokes. Laughing hurt her too much. She said she felt the pain most acutely in her throat.

Surgeons removed a minor growth from Rose's left vocal cord. She underwent three days of needles and X-rays. Langston spent some nights in her room, sleeping in a chair beside her bed. He spent other nights at home. He took the children to see her on the weekend. He made a day of it, took them to the zoo, bought them hamburgers and ice-cream cones, and took them back home — on the train. And then he left them and took the train right back into the city.

Langston met with a team of doctors a week after Rose had been admitted. They told him that the vocal cord growth was malignant. Rose had throat cancer.

"To be honest with you," the sarcoma expert said, "it does not look good. Dr. Evans told me to be straightforward with you, so I will. You should start making plans. Your wife will be lucky if she lives another six months."

Langston hadn't even caught the sarcoma expert's name. He stared at the man. He had been a minister for ten years, but he'd never found it so hard to say something meaningful. He remembered meeting Rose on the Howard University campus. He remembered the first time they kissed. He remembered the first time they fell onto a bed, pressed together. The words came to him one by one as he spoke.

"I'm afraid I just can't accept that answer." Langston blinked three times. Saliva bubbled at his lips. Mucus dripped from his nose. He turned. Wendy Evans put her arm around him, and began to lead him from the room. He stopped her. He blew his nose. He turned to the other doctors. "I must step outside to compose myself. But you should know that I reject your prognosis. My wife will live. We will dig to the very bottom of this disease and beat it. You can tell her she has cancer. I, in fact, will tell her momentarily. But don't say a word again about how long Rose has to live. She has her life, still, and it's not over yet. Not by a long shot. Gentlemen. Wendy." Langston left the room.

Langston had completed a master's in theology at the University of Toronto several months earlier — as a part-time student, it had taken him close to seven years — but now it seemed all for naught. The congregation was dwindling. Jobs were so scarce that hoboes were knocking on his door for food. Langston never refused any man food. If there was nothing else in the kitchen, Langston would prepare a peanut butter sandwich for a man at the door.

Langston sent a telegram to Rose's parents. He let them know about the cancer, and about the treatment. At his insistence, Rose had been diagnosed by another team of throat and cancer specialists at the Mount Sinai Hospital. The initial diagnosis was confirmed. But this team of doctors suggested a treatment called radical X-ray therapy. Essentially, it would involve a month of regular X-ray treatments to burn the cancer out of her throat. The doctors warned that it would be exhausting and painful, and that it would scar her throat. They warned her that there was no guarantee that the treatment would work. But they felt it was the best they could do, and they wanted to begin immediately. Rose and Langston agreed.

In the letter to her parents, Langston said that Rose was in "the best medical hands in Toronto." Rose's parents would be welcome to visit. Hazel wired a message back the next morning. Dr. Bridges was ill, but Hazel would come up the next day.

From her hospital bed, Rose had asked Langston how Evelyn's mother had reacted to the news of the engagement. Langston's mouth dropped open. "You forgot to ask, you silly ass," Rose said. "Bring me news tomorrow." She rubbed the back of his hand. "Husband, are you eating well?"

Ab took the train to Toronto to visit Rose. He told her that Evelyn's mother had pulled out all the stops. She had cried. She had raged. She had claimed it would be the most unhappy day of her life. She had threatened to kill herself if her daughter went ahead with it.

"No mention of the Klan?" Rose asked.

"No mention of that," Ab said. "I'm just hoping she makes good on her promise to kill herself."

"Aberdeen Williams," Rose croaked, slapping his hand. Her hand remained on his. He left it there. She fell asleep. He kissed her and left.

Hazel arrived a week before the first X-ray treatment. She and Langston got along civilly. Hazel had aged, it seemed. When

Langston picked her up at Union Station, she said: "No mother can tolerate the notion that her child could die first." She sobbed on Langston's shoulder.

He put his arm around her. "She's not going to die, Hazel. She's got a will of iron. Like someone I know." Hazel brushed her tears away and, for the first time, kissed her son-in-law.

Hazel, at first, chose to stay in a hotel in Toronto. She wanted to be near her daughter. She wanted to be there morning, afternoon, and night. But after two days of that, Rose prevailed on her to go to Oakville. "Go see your grandchildren. Go see Langston. He needs your help." Privately, Rose told Langston that she was sick of having her mother at her bedside. Cancer or no cancer, Rose could only take the woman in moderate doses. Hazel came to Oakville. There were no sparks. Mill allowed Hazel to read to her. Langston junior climbed all over her. One evening, he suckered her into reading him five books before turning out the light.

"He's only supposed to get one book," Langston said gently from the door.

"It won't kill him," Hazel shot back. "The worst thing it'll do is make him want to read and write half his life, like someone else I know in this house."

Hazel and Langston compared notes on the Depression. At her home on Linden Street in D.C., people were also knocking on the door, asking for food.

"And what do you do?" Langston asked.

"What anybody but a pagan buzzard would do," she said. "I give him a sandwich. One day last week, I made eight sandwiches."

"So that's where Rose got that expression."

"Pagan buzzard?"

"Yeah. She's been calling me that since we married."

Hazel gave out a laugh. "That's how I used to refer to you,

when I was trying to talk that wife of yours out of marrying you. Good thing for you she has such a thick head."

Hazel visited Rose two days before the first X-ray treatment, and explained that she would be back on February 2 for the big day.

The X-ray treatment was to take place at four on Saturday afternoon. Langston made all the necessary arrangements. He canceled the Sunday service, which he didn't want to have to think about. Ab reassured him that he would take care of everything. Feed the kids, play with them, get them off to school if Langston decided to spend a couple of days in Toronto. By the way, he hoped Langston didn't object, but Evelyn was getting an awful lot of heat from her mother, it was terrible, it was beyond description. Could she spend a few days with Ab in the Canes' house, until things cooled down? Sure, Langston said.

The plan was for Langston and Hazel to take the two o'clock train to Toronto. Hazel had wanted to leave earlier in the morning. In fact, she had wanted to leave the night before. But Langston had convinced her that Rose would be better rested and more relaxed if she didn't see their two faces peering at her constantly for hours and hours before the operation.

Mill and Langston junior attended a birthday party that morning. It was a costume party. All the kids were to dress up as clowns. Ab helped them put on pajamas and hats and silly necklaces, and trundled them off to the party. Langston was thankful to have them out of his hands. But he did go to pick them up at noon. He wanted to talk to them as they walked back home.

Langston junior, at the age of six, already knew more about cars than his father. But he had never before seen four cars coming his way with hooded men on the running boards.

"Look, Daddy. Lookit all those men on those Model Ts. Wow, Daddy."

Mill clapped her hands. "Oh, Daddy, is this a surprise party? Did you plan a surprise party for us? Look, Daddy. White ghost costumes! Torches! Fire! I love fire! Neat!"

Langston's arms reached out in front of his children and pulled them, in one quick breast-stroke movement, hard against his ribs.

"Ow, Daddy! That hurts!"

"Hush!"

Five cars. Down a block, at Allan Street. Heading west on Sumner. West toward them. The cars were moving slowly. They made no sound. Two or three men were perched on each running board, holding torches. They made no sound, either. Covered in those devilish hoods. White hoods. Eyes like slits. Five cars, and twenty men, in all.

Langston's first thought was his gun. In his dresser drawer. He was on the corner of Sumner and Reynolds. His house was three doors away. Too far. Too far, with his children exposed. He imagined Rose screaming at him. *My babies! Get my babies away from there!* He pushed them between two houses. They splashed across soggy grass. "Daddy, my shoes," Mill cried out. "Where are we going?"

"Shhh," Langston said. He picked up his kids and dropped them over a fence. He climbed up and over and down and made them run again. They dashed between two more houses and turned left on Randall. No sign of the Klansmen. They crossed the street and ran another fifty yards. Langston looked back, ahead, to the sides. No Klansmen in sight. He ran up to the house of Presbyterian Church minister Eric Small. The door was unlocked. Thank God. He slammed it behind them. "Eric," he called.

Roberta, his wife, ran down the stairs. "Eric's out, Langston. What's wrong?"

"The Klan!"

"The what?"

"The Klan."

"Langston, honestly, what are you talking about?"

"The Ku Klux Klan. At my house."

"The Klan? In Oakville? You're kidding!"

"After I leave, lock your door. Hide my kids in your basement. Call the police."

"The police, Langston, is Bob Phillips. That's the only police we have. And he's out. Bob is with my husband in Burlington. Church business."

"Stay with my children."

"Don't go out there," Roberta said.

"I have to. My mother-in-law is in my house. So is Aberdeen Williams. So is Evelyn."

"Don't go out there, Langston. I forbid you."

"Take good care of my kids, and don't let them out." He ran outside.

She called after him. "You have a family, Langston. Don't be a hero."

He turned back to her. "Call neighbors. Call someone in Burlington. Someone, anyone. Get them to help you track down the police chief."

Langston stole between houses, over fences. He cut east, slightly, and crept into his backyard. He could see nothing by the west side of his house. He lay in the cold, wet grass. On the east side, he saw the five cars stopped in the street. He saw the hooded men. He tried the back door. Locked. Shit. He kicked in the pane, reached his hand in, cut his arm, turned the knob, opened the door. He saw a shadow move in the kitchen. He walked that way. The kitchen was in the middle of the house. Visible neither from the front, nor from the back. He heard breathing. "Hazel, it's me. Langston." She stepped out to face him. She was holding his gun. She pointed it at him. "Hazel, put that gun down. Hazel. Put it down." She was shaking. He strode up to her, brushed the gun to her side, and then lifted it from her hand.

"You cut your arm," she said. "Did they do that?"

"No. I did that. Breaking through the back door."

"What is the Klan doing here? You never told me they were in Canada."

"They never told me they were coming."

"Where are the children?"

"They're safe. They're with friends of mine."

"White friends?"

"Yes."

"That's good."

Langston crept to his study and looked out the window. All five cars had stopped on the street. The men in white hoods stood in a semi-circle, facing the house. Three men were carrying a wooden cross onto the lawn. Another man brought a stepladder from the back of a car. He opened and climbed up the ladder and used a ham-sized mallet to bash the cross into the grass. It stood. It wobbled. He bashed it down some more. It was a good eight feet high.

It had been mild and wet for a week. If regular winter weather had been upon them, Langston mused, these men would never have been able to hammer the cross into the earth. And they wouldn't have been as comfortable in a wicked January wind.

"Where's Ab?"

"I sent him and the girl downstairs. Told them not to come up."

The stairs to the basement were located behind the kitchen. Out of sight from the street. Langston climbed down there. "Ab? Evelyn? It's me. Langston."

Aberdeen Williams held an ax in his hand.

"That won't do you much good, Ab, there's twenty of them outside."

"My mother sent them," Evelyn said.

"Stay down here," Langston said. "Don't move and don't make a sound."

"What are you going to do?" Ab asked.

"Tell them you're not here."

"They won't believe you," Evelyn said.

"Hide in the corner. And hang on to that ax."

Langston telephoned the police station. No answer. The mayor wasn't home, either. He called Ab's sister. Renata worked for the Turner family, and he reached her there.

"Why's the Klan pickin' on little bitty Oakville?" she asked.

Langston told her to bring Bob Turner. They needed a white businessman to talk some sense into these folks.

Renata said she'd bring him right over. "How's Rose? she asked.

"Rose?"

"Wasn't she going to have her operation today?"

Langston dropped the receiver. He had forgotten about the X-ray treatment. He picked up the phone. "Renata, I wouldn't come if I were you. Just send Turner."

"I'm comin' over, Reverend. You been taking care of my soul for seven years. Now I'm gonna take care of you. Gonna git me a gun and send those men to the fires of Hell."

"For God's sake, don't bring any weapons. These men are looking for provocation."

"They already got plenty of provocation. They got that fool brother of mine sleeping with white trash. Stand back, Reverend. I'm coming over."

Langston hung up the phone and turned to his mother-in-law. "We've got to get to Rose," he said.

"She will have to wait," Hazel said.

"Her treatment is in three hours."

"One thing at a time. We'll get there soon as we can."

"I could get you to safety, if you'd like to go now," Langston said.

"I'm not stepping out of this house with the KKK there. Those men are looking for colored blood. They're looking for any known blood they can find."

Langston saw them light the cross. It had been soaked in gasoline, and it caught like kindling. He scribbled down three telephone numbers. This is the mayor's residence, he told Hazel. This is the police station. This is the baker's number. They're all good men. Good white men. Call them. Keep trying.

Langston dressed before going outside. He dressed for a sermon. He put on his collar. He checked to make sure that his .45 automatic had a bullet in the chamber and all six in the magazine. The pistol went under his belt.

He stepped outside once the burning cross had settled into quiet flames.

"I am Reverend Langston Cane. What do you want?"

The tallest hooded man — the one who had pounded down the cross — said, "Clear out of here, Reverend. Stick around and you'll burn down with the house."

"What do you want?"

"We want the nigger Aberdeen."

"He's not here."

"Bring him out or we'll burn the house down with you and him in it."

"I'm telling you he's not here."

"We're going to burn a second cross on your lawn. Time enough for you to think about bringing out Aberdeen."

Renata Williams, all two hundred and twenty pounds of her, came puffing along the sidewalk. Bob Turner, a man of seventy years, trailed behind her. He slowed down as he eyed the crowd; she sped up.

The ringleader climbed up on his stepladder. He lifted his ham-sized mallet. He pounded the second cross once. He pounded it twice. He raised the mallet to pound again, and found himself rattling and shaking and tumbling to the ground.

"What do you think you're doing, you wooden-headed fool?" Renata Williams fell on the man as he tried to get up. Two Klansmen tried to pull her away. They couldn't budge her. One grabbed her arm and twisted it. She punched him in the nose. A third punched her in the nose with a thud that Langston heard. She fell to the ground. The man who punched her drew back his boot. "Kick me, you dog. You'd do it, wouldn't you? Kick a woman. Go ahead. Do it."

An audible click made the man turn around. "Touch her again," Langston said, "and I'll shoot you through the head. I was a second lieutenant in the American Army and I'm still a good shot. I'll put a bullet through your forehead if you touch her again."

Renata Williams climbed to her feet. It took her thirty seconds. No one moved. "Thank you, Reverend."

"Stand back or we'll kill you and your sweetheart," the tall leader said.

Renata walked up to Langston. She was holding her face in her hand. "He broke my nose, Reverend. That coward broke my nose."

"What do you fellows want?" This time it was Bob Turner. He'd walked right up to the Klansmen.

"We want Aberdeen Williams," the tall one said.

"He's not here," Langston said.

"The girl's in there, and he's in there, too," the tall one said. "Her own mother told us they were in there."

"How about if we bring the girl out?" Turner said. "Would that satisfy you? Fellows, there's no point hurting anybody here."

"We ain't got all day," another Klansman shouted. He threw a rock at the door. It missed. He threw another. It hit the door. He threw a third, and it shattered a pane of glass in the living room window. Others started throwing rocks. Every pane was shattered.

"Hey, you," Renata shouted. "You, the young one, who threw that first rock. I know you. I know your voice."

"You don't know nothing," he said, and threw another rock.

"I know your voice. You're John Mitchell. I delivered you. I diapered you. I know your family. I'm gonna tell your momma you're here. You oughta be ashamed, consorting with these hoodlums. What got in your head, boy?"

"You don't know me," the rock thrower said. His voice caught in his throat.

"John Mitchell, I'm gonna lift that hood right off your head. I'm gonna lift it off for all the world to see."

"You stay right there, woman, or we'll hit you so hard you won't wake up," the ringleader said.

Renata Williams started walking toward the man she'd identified. The ringleader stopped her. She bounced him with her chest. He hit her with a blow to the cheek. She tried to grab his hood. He cocked his arm back. A gun went off. The ringleader froze. Then he turned. Langston was pointing his revolver straight up. "The next one's right into you, mister."

Renata kept walking. Langston called her back. She ignored him and kept walking toward the young man she'd identified. He was fifteen paces from her. Ten. Five. He turned and ran. He ran to Reynolds Street, turned south, and disappeared.

"Who else do I recognize around here?" she called out. "Anybody else I've diapered? You all ought to be ashamed of yourselves. You. What's your name?"

The Klansman stepped back. "Let's burn it down, fellows, and clear out of here."

The men advanced toward the house with burning torches. One threw a torch on the porch. Langston ran up to it, and managed to kick it onto the grass. "I shoot the next person who throws fire this way."

"*Aiiieee*," Renata shouted. She jumped the ringleader, bounced him right over, ripped through the cloth until she found a face. She sat on the man. Sat right down on him and smacked him.

"Gentlemen! Gentlemen!"

Bob Phillips, Oakville's police chief, stepped out of his car.

The mayor and the Presbyterian Church minister got out, too. They were all holding guns.

"I am the chief of police of the town of Oakville. I've sworn these two men in as deputies. Reverend Cane, do you agree to be my deputy?"

"Yes, I do."

"Good. He's sworn in, too. You fellows got here four officers of the law, and if any harm comes to them, or to anybody else around here, you're in hot water. You're already in hot water, but it's going to get hotter if you start acting foolish. You. The Negro woman. Get off that man! Stop slapping him about or I'm gonna have to charge you, too."

Renata got up slowly. "My nose is broken."

"We'll deal with that later," the police chief said. "You hooded men. Put down them torches. I say put 'em down and stomp on 'em. Stomp 'em right out. And take off those God-awful masks." Langston studied each white face as it was unmasked. He didn't see anyone he knew. Renata, however, recognized three of them, and cussed at them until Langston touched her arm.

The police chief kicked over the burning cross. "I never seen such a bunch of plain fools in all my life. What's the matter with you men? You got no respect? You're gonna make a laughing-stock out of Oakville. People are gonna talk about us across the country. *Oakville? Oakville. Isn't that the town where the Ku Klux Klan burned a cross?* Ain't you men got a drop a sense in your heads?"

"One of them already ran off," Renata said. "He was John Mitchell, of the Mitchell family on Dunn Street. I knowed his voice. I oughta know. I changed that boy's diapers."

"We'll deal with him later," the chief said. "You fellows line up, hands behind your backs."

"Come on, now," the ringleader said. "You're not taking us in, are you? Do you know what's going on inside that house? A colored man is in there, shacked up with a white woman."

"So I hear. So I hear. Bring her out, Reverend."

Langston entered his house. He came out moments later, with Ab, Evelyn, and Hazel.

"You better get yourself home, woman," the police chief said to Evelyn. "Where's your self-respect? Go on home and face your mother."

"What about him?" a Klansman said, pointing to Aberdeen. "What about him?"

"This is his home," Langston said, "and he's broken no law."

"We're gonna get you," the Klansmen called out to Aberdeen. "We're gonna get you, nigger. And if it's not us, it's gonna be our friends. We're gonna hunt you out and we're gonna —"

"You're gonna get charged with uttering threats," Phillips said. "So shut your mouth before I shut it for you."

The police chief ordered the men into a single line. "You're gonna walk to the police station, and if any of you try to run, I'm gonna shoot off your legs," he said.

"What about our vehicles?"

"Impounded, as of now," the chief said. "Used in the commission of an offense."

"What offense?"

"Arson. Assault. Mischief. Using a mask unlawfully. Give me some time, and I'll think up some more. Get hiking, fellows. We've got paperwork to do.

"Git yourself cleaned up, Langston. Someone will be back to pick you up. I'm told you gotta get into Toronto to see your wife. One of my deputies will get you to the train in fifteen minutes. Someone else will watch over your house, clean up for you. Don't worry about a thing. You've got enough on your mind. We'll take care of things for you. You're good folks, Reverend Cane. This should not have happened to you. And I happen to know that ninety-nine people outa a hundred in Oakville would agree with me."

Langston nodded. He thanked the police chief and stepped inside, after Ab, Hazel, and Renata.

"Your hand is still bleeding," Hazel said. "You'll need stitching."

"We'll take care of it at the hospital."

Renata spoke up. "Aberdeen Williams, you're still my little brother, and I oughta whip your behind, consorting like that with white trash. Look what you done. Look what trouble you brought on the Reverend."

Aberdeen said nothing. His head was down. He would look at no one and his shoulders were shaking. "Leave him alone, Renata," Langston said. "He's done no wrong. Get yourself together, Ab. Go see the kids. I left them with the Smalls, on Randall Street. Stay there with them. I wouldn't come back to this house for a day or two. Don't let any suspicious-looking person see you enter the Smalls' house."

Ab began to shake uncontrollably.

"For God's sake, brother," Renata said. "I got a broken nose. What are you so worked up about?"

"Renata," Langston said, "I love you. You did great things out there, and I thank you. But you're not helping now. So please go home."

"Yes, Reverend. Regards to Rose, Reverend. Tell her she's going be all right. Tell her I broke my nose protecting her property. That'll make her day, Reverend. Good-bye, Mrs. Bridges. You look like your daughter, you know that? You're even fairer, though. You're so fair you're almost one of them. But don't mind me. Pleasure meeting you. You got a daughter with a will of steel. I didn't like her at first, but I respect her now. I respect a will of steel."

At the hospital, they were two hours behind schedule. When they were finally ready to conduct the first treatment, Langston had still not arrived. "Let's go ahead and do it," Rose said. "If my husband's not here, it's for a good reason."

They bombarded Rose with radium X-rays. They had warned her that it would burn her throat. It would leave her with the sensation of a throat on fire. It would leave her with a permanent burn scar. But if it worked, it would save her life. I don't care about the scar, Rose had said. Just do what you have to do.

It was over by the time Langston and Hazel got to the hospital. Rose was asleep in the recovery room. Langston had time to get eleven stitches put into his hand. He didn't mind the stitches. It helped pass the time. He wanted desperately to look into the eyes of his wife. All he asked for was for Rose Bridges Cane to open her eyes.

Langston fell asleep in the waiting room. Hazel finally nudged him.

"She's up. She wants to see you."

"You saw her already?"

"She's fine, Lang. She's fine. Go on in there."

Rose was told she would spend a month in the hospital. She would have many more treatments. Tests were run. Langston went back and forth between Oakville and Toronto. He knew every bend in the train tracks. Hazel stayed home with the kids.

A party of fifteen volunteers cleaned up the Canes' home and filled the kitchen with food. Aberdeen Williams fixed the broken windows within twenty-four hours of the incident. The next morning, he kissed the children, left them with Hazel, and walked out the door. He didn't come back.

Evelyn Morris duly went home. Her mother wasn't there. Evelyn cleaned out a drawer, took a suitcase, stole twenty-five dollars from her mother's purse, and left town. She didn't come back either.

Rose recovered. She had a square scar that covered most of her throat, from just under her chin to an inch beneath her Adam's apple. The scar was a mass of bumpy red flesh. Strangers could not meet Rose without staring at her scar. It stayed with her for the rest of her life. She was also left with a hoarse, rasping voice. She didn't care. It was a small price to pay for living.

Most blacks left Oakville during the Depression. The A.M.E. congregation died down to twenty members. A bishop summoned Langston to Toronto and told him that the church would have to be shut down.

Langston, Rose, Mill, and Langston junior moved to Baltimore, where Langston was offered a position at the Bethel A.M.E. Church on Druid Hill Avenue. A.M.E. bishops considered it a terrific promotion. It was based in part on Langston's stance against the KKK, which was reported in papers across Canada and picked up by the press in D.C. and Baltimore. It wasn't a promotion at all, as far as Langston Cane and his family were concerned. Life was much better in Oakville.

"Down here, the KKK wouldn't even give you time to open your mouth," Hazel warned them. "In Oakville, we met their nice northern cousins. But in the States, they'd swing you from a branch and there'd be no talking before or after. As for Aberdeen and that white woman, someone would have put a stop to that nonsense the moment it started."

Mill left Oakville heartbroken at her separation from Aberdeen. She was convinced that she had lost her best friend because he had been seeing a white woman, and nobody could change her mind. In Baltimore, Mill and Langston junior entered a segregated school. The family squeezed into a home a third of the size of the Oakville residence, which Langston and Rose decided to board up and keep, for the time being. There was no point in selling it for peanuts. Maybe they'd get back there one day. Maybe Aberdeen could use it. Rose left the key and a note with Renata — in case her brother came back.

W. A. Phillips, the KKK ringleader, was jailed for a month and fined three hundred dollars. It turned out he was a dentist from Hamilton. The others were each fined fifty dollars. Most couldn't pay the fine. They were given the option of spending two weeks in jail.

Aberdeen Williams and his intended made their way to the Six Nations Indian reserve in Brantford, Ontario. Ab had read all about the Six Nations people. He knew, from his reading, that Six Nations chief Joseph Brant had fought alongside Negroes and the British to drive the Americans back across the Niagara River in the War of 1812. He knew that Brant had allowed fugitive slaves to settle on his land and marry his women. He knew that African and Indian peoples had a long history together. He was convinced, in his mind, that African sailors in reed boats had brought traces of their culture to South American Indian communities, and that, if he could find any refuge at all, he would find it among the Indian people.

Aberdeen Williams and Evelyn Morris were married on the Six Nations reserve by an Indian elder. They spent six months there. Ab fixed things. He put things together. He impressed people with his skillful hands. He didn't impress them too much with his theories about the African discovery of America. "How could you have discovered America?" Wilson Longboat, his first friend there, said. "We were here first. If you discovered America, then what were we supposed to be?"

Evelyn Morris ran off with an Indian. Aberdeen expected as much. He was relieved to be rid of her, although he wouldn't have been the one to break the marriage up. She couldn't hold a candle to Rose Cane. Never did, and never would.

Aberdeen Williams returned to Oakville. He was devastated to learn that the Canes had moved. He lived in their house for a month, fixed everything he could think of to fix. But finally he boarded the house back up and left it. He couldn't stand living there without the Canes. He moved in with his sister. They shared a basement room in the huge residence of the Turner family. Renata cooked, and Ab fixed things. There were all sorts of things to fix. He had free room and board. He had a stash of money that nobody knew about. But he was profoundly miserable. A year passed. Another six months went by. He received letters from the Canes, from time to time, but he was too disconsolate to reply. Finally, in the fall of 1932, he mailed them a cryptic note. Didn't tell them where he'd disappeared to, and said only that Evelyn and he "were no longer." He said the economy was terrible, but that he still had a bunch of money saved up from all that work Rose had engineered for him. He scratched a postscript. "P.S. I'm enrolled in history at the University of Toronto."

Chapter 17

I ASKED MILL HOW OFTEN she had been in touch with Aberdeen after her family left Oakville and moved to Baltimore.

"He came down to visit us a few years later. And he came once again nearly thirty years later, with you and your parents, when you were a baby. I didn't see you or your parents, but Ab came to visit me. And he writes me every year."

"But you haven't seen him in three decades?"

"He came down again when Dad died, and when Mom died a year later. I told a lie when I said I had never seen you before. I saw you and your folks in the church at the funerals. I didn't speak to you, but I saw you. You look just the way you did then."

"And Ab?"

"He stayed behind a few days, each time. He stood by me. I don't think I would have made it through those times, if Ab hadn't been there."

I spent another few days digging through the boxes in Mill's guest room. I found sermons, programs from theology conferences in Europe and all over the States. One box contained correspondence between Rose's physician in Baltimore and the

Toronto doctors who had treated her for cancer. There was a letter from the Israeli government, inviting my grandfather to speak at conferences in Tel Aviv and Jerusalem. There was even a handwritten note from Harry Truman in 1950, inviting Langston to lunch at the White House. Tucked in among pages and envelopes of all sizes and colors was a letter never intended for my eyes. It was written from Mill to her father in 1947.

> Dear Daddy,
>
> I am sorry for all the trouble. Are you ashamed of me? The Bible says Jesus was good to Mary Magdalen. I am glad to know that. I trust you will be kind to me, despite all. The arsenic and bismuth treatments are over. The doctor says it shouldn't come back. I have left that way of life.
>
> Your loving daughter,
Mill

I put the letter back where I found it, and didn't say a word about it to Mill.

The phone woke me up. It rang so loudly, it seemed to have a personality. I finally picked it up.

"Is your head still on that pillow? It's seven-thirty in the morning."

"Mill. How're ya doing?"

"Good. I have something important to ask you. Come over for lunch. Okay? Bye."

I wondered if Mill had come across the letter I had seen. If she knew it was in the box. If she sensed that I had seen it.

The phone rang again.

"Mill?"

"Sorry, dear. This is your mother."

My mother doesn't make small talk on the telephone. My father, yes. It would be in character for him to call to say that I was wasting my time and ought to hightail it back to Oakville and find a job and settle down. He'd phone to tell me I didn't know a thing about black folks and ought to watch out because one of them was liable to manipulate me like a washing machine and pick my pocket in the spin cycle. But my mother would never call on a whim.

"What's up, Mom?" I slipped into my underwear. I could hear her breathing. On went my jeans.

"It's your father."

I pulled on my socks. "What about him?"

"He has disappeared," she said. I scanned the room for my wallet and keys. "I think he's been kidnapped." Mom said he'd gone for his usual six-thirty a.m. walk. He had a busy schedule that day. He had an important appointment in Toronto at eight-thirty. Mom had called the police. They'd tried to tell her to call back if he hadn't returned in another hour. She'd told them who her husband was, and they'd said they'd be right over. "Can you come home?"

My father has placed so many demands on me — get a doctorate, get a job, hold on to your wife, have children — that I have subconsciously arranged to fail at every one of them. My mother has never asked me for anything. I told her I'd take the next flight home. Luck was with me. A Toronto-bound flight was leaving the Baltimore-Washington Airport at nine a.m., and there was still room on it. I made it just in time, and I was in Oakville by eleven-fifteen.

A cop let me in the door. My father was still missing. My

mother stepped up to hug me. When I haven't seen her for a while, I'm always surprised at how short she is. Mom had put on navy slacks, a pink turtleneck, and a blazer. She believed men didn't respect women in dresses. If she was going to be dealing with cops all day, she didn't want to appear feminine.

We sat in my father's study. "You're looking good," she said. "Rested. You look much better than when I last saw you."

"The last time you saw me, I'd just been fired."

A police officer interrupted us to say that some old man had just opened the front door and walked right in. Did we know this old nut or should he be thrown out? My mother asked if he was black. Yes. She said it was Aberdeen Williams, and to leave him alone.

Aberdeen came into the room. He had a slow, careful shuffle.

"Dorothy," he said. "Langston! Good to see you. Glad you could come back. I think Dr. Cane is going to be fine. Don't you worry, Dorothy."

My mother smiled faintly, kissed Aberdeen, and went upstairs to nap. The phone rang. It was Mill. She blasted me for standing her up for lunch. I told her my father had been abducted. She railed on about how I'd promised to eat with her and she'd ordered in Kentucky Fried Chicken and it got stone cold and she phoned me and got no answer, so drove over figuring I was asleep and pounded on the door until Yoyo came around and said he'd seen me take off like a shot in an airport limousine. So what in hell's half acre was I doing back up in Canada and why hadn't I brought her along and hadn't it entered my brain that maybe she would like to come up with me, like to see Oakville again, maybe even like to be there when someone kidnapped her own flesh and blood?

"Is that Mill?" Aberdeen said, prodding me in the ribs.

"Someone wants to talk to you," I told Mill, and gave the phone to Ab.

"That you, Mill? This is Ab, here. Aberdeen Williams."

I could hear Mill's voice shouting through the receiver. Ab held the receiver six inches from his ear.

"Lord Almighty, Aberdeen Williams! How are you? Fine? Good. How old you-all, now? Eighty-eight! I better get up there before you-all back out the door. Tell that nephew of mine to come on back down here and bring me up to see you in Oakville. He took off without telling me a thing."

"It's been a long time, Mill. Why don't you come up here for a visit?"

"When I come up, it'll be for more than a visit."

"Don't run up your phone bill, Mill."

"Right, I'll be seeing ya. Bye." Mill hung up.

"She hasn't changed at all," Ab said. "She's got the same mouth she had when she was six years old."

A reporter knocked on the door. I stood up.

"Don't talk to him," the cop said. "Media coverage would just mess things up."

"I'll take care of it," I said. My father had always said not to run from the media. If you run, they chase.

I found Mahatma Grafton at the door. He started to introduce himself, then stopped and said, "Hey, we've met before."

I nodded. I wondered if he would bring up the business of my getting the Ontario minister of wellness fired. But he didn't.

"I know this is a difficult moment," he said, "but could you say who you think is behind all this? I mean, first Norville Watson, and now your father. What is going on?"

I said this wasn't a good time for the family to speak publicly.

"I understand," he said. "Thanks anyway, and good luck. We

all hope you get your father back safely." We shook hands. I noticed he had the *Toronto Times* rolled under his arm. I saw the word *Cane* in a headline. I asked him if I could have the paper.

"Sure," he said. "It's the afternoon edition."

I saw the news of my father's disappearance in the bold headline. That was the line story, on page 1. Under the fold, I saw a special from Baltimore by Hassane Moustafa "Yoyo" Ali. I pointed to the article.

"I understand that Yoyo is a mutual friend," I said. "I live in Baltimore. We stay in the same house."

"I knew him ten years ago in Winnipeg. He's from Cameroon, right? Speaks French?"

I nodded.

"Take my card," Mahatma said. "Give me a shout, when things get resolved. I hope everything works out for your family. You going back to Baltimore?"

"I plan to."

"Then please give my card to Yoyo. Tell him I'm thinking of him. By the way, a lot of people think you showed a lot of guts, the way you brought that minister down."

I smiled. We shook hands again. I watched Mahatma walk away. He had a car parked on the street. Funny name, Mahatma Grafton. Just about as onerous as Langston Cane the Fifth.

Aberdeen Williams was in the kitchen, rinsing lettuce. "I'm making a light snack," he said. "For you and your mother and your brother, when he comes. I doubt any of you are eating properly. How about salmon on lettuce, with green peppers and carrots?"

I told him it sounded fine. He said he would like to make

more, but the fridge was empty. He promised to have some fruit and vegetables delivered from Longo's Fruit Market.

"I didn't know they delivered," I said.

"They don't. But I've got a friend who owes me a favor. I fixed his toilet last year. He'll bring the food over."

We were introduced to Inspector Robert Hay of the police holdup squad. He would be directing police activities in Oakville. He was a middle-aged man, with a mild paunch and a handlebar mustache. He kept fingering the mustache. Hay asked about the relationship between my father and Norville Watson.

I told him about the rental confrontations. I told him that Watson had successfully opposed an attempt by my father to establish a group home in Oakville for black teenagers who'd broken the law. And I told him that when my father had set up practice in Oakville, he'd had to fight to win the confidence of patients and nurses who had heard, through the grapevine, that he was inexperienced and unreliable. Good at civil rights agitation, one patient of Dad's had been told by Watson, but not so effective in the doctor's office.

It took my father years to build up a decent practice in Oakville. He would never have been able to buy the house had it not been for money from my father's parents, Rose and Langston the Third. They were very excited by the idea that their son and daughter-in-law would purchase the old Cane house, which was sold out of the family in the 1940s. By the early 1960s, my father had built up a unique group of patients. More than one hundred black families in Toronto had chosen my father as their doctor. They didn't care that he was in Oakville. The commute didn't deter them. He opened up his house to them. Many dropped by for coffee with my mother. A number stayed on for lunch or dinner. Some even spent the night. The playroom was made available to their kids. Aberdeen Williams frequently walked the kids to a waterfront playground. There was a steady flow of blacks in and out of our house for the better half of the 1960s.

When Dad finally got privileges at the Oakville Trafalgar Memorial Hospital, he and Watson tried to avoid each other. By 1970, Dad lost most of his Toronto patients. With a wider choice of doctors to their liking in the city, patients were less willing to commute to Oakville. Dad's white practice picked up. He took care of most of the Portuguese families living near Kerr Street. A few dozen families living near our house came to my father because they liked the idea of having a family doctor who lived minutes away. They liked the idea of being able to run over in the middle of the night if they needed to. And Dad was always open to being roused in the middle of the night. He liked it. It made him feel useful. He liked to tell me in the morning that he had been called out at two a.m. to deliver a baby.

By 1975 — the year I finished high school and left home — my father wasn't talking any more about Norville Watson. Their feud was on ice. Out of tradition, they still avoided each other. But the hostility seemed to have diminished. Dad referred some urology cases to Watson. They conferred on the phone occasionally.

"What about more recently?" the police inspector wanted to know.

"Nothing," I said. "Dad tried to see Watson a couple of months ago, but he wasn't in his Toronto office at the time."

"Why did your father want to see him?"

"I think he was tired of thinking of the man as his enemy."

"Is there anyone or any group you can think of that would want to abduct both Watson and your father?"

"No."

Inspector Hay asked where my father went walking in the morning.

My mother answered. "Sometimes he heads down to the lake, and goes west along the water. Other times he heads up Reynolds, along Macdonald, down Balsam, and back home along the Lakeshore. Other times he winds through just about every street in old Oakville."

"His favorite walk is along King Street," Ab said. We all turned to look at him. "I've done it with him a hundred times. He likes to go along Dunn and stop at King Street to look at the old Turner house."

"The old what house?" Hay asked.

"The house the Turners used to live in. My sister used to be their cook. This was back in the twenties and early thirties. Before you were born."

Hay sighed. "But you have no clue where he went this morning?"

"No."

"None of your neighbors saw him out walking?" Hay said.

"What makes you think he's in Oakville?" my mother asked.

"We don't. We think he's been abducted and taken somewhere else."

"He's in Oakville," Ab said.

"On what basis do you say that?" Hay asked.

"Instinct," Ab said.

I flipped through the *Toronto Times*. The headline said *Second Doctor Missing in Days*. The story was mostly old news. It rehashed the business of the Watson abduction.

The cops went out. My mother sighed and put her feet up. Ab brought in the salad. The newspapers said police were interviewing leaders of every black advocacy organization they could find.

"Let's go for a walk," Ab said.

"You still go walking?" I asked.

"Every day. How else you think I've lived so long?"

"Wild sex?"

Ab grinned. "Haven't had much of that for a month or two."

Ab led me west on Reynolds Street and across George's Square. We stopped for a drink in the water fountain. We had gone about three hundred yards, and it took close to ten minutes. Never mind. He was walking. We were outside. We came up Trafalgar, east on Randall, and walked to his home.

He took me inside. His small home was perfectly organized. The kitchen was spotless. Books leaned neatly in one direction on his shelves. "There's something I want to show you," he said.

He took me to his room. He had a small, single bed raised high above the floor on a cedar box that he'd built himself. He'd built drawers in the box. Ab pulled out one of them. He removed a plastic bag, opened it, and pulled out some dried yellow papers.

"Open them carefully," Ab said. "These pages have been sealed. They are 136 years old."

"What are they?"

"Your father liked to talk about Langston Cane the First. The one who came up here on the Underground Railroad. Remember?"

"Sure I remember, Ab. I've been digging around. I'm trying to write about this stuff."

"I heard. That's why I'm showing this to you."

Ab broke the wax seal on an envelope signed *Langston Cane, African Methodist Episcopal Minister, Oakville.* "Your grandfather asked me to respect this seal for fifty years."

"When was that?"

"Almost seventy years ago."

"How come you never showed it to my dad?"

"Your father is a good man, and I love him. But he's a man who does things. Likes to keep busy. You don't give something like this to a man with no time on his hands."

"You could have shown this to me a long time ago."

"You weren't ready."

I took the materials to Ab's kitchen table. He had made it from cherry wood. It was dark, smooth, and lustrous. I opened up the pages. There were two documents.

African Methodist Episcopal Church, Oakville,

August 1, 1859.

    Accused: Langston Cane

    Residence: Oakville

    Occupation: Rat Catcher and Stone Hooker

    Accusation: Bigamy

    Plea: Not entered

    Hearing Date: Set for August 15, 1859.

    N.B. Mr. Cane has been made aware by Rev. Caldwell of the said charge. He has been informed that he is to stand trial in the church. And that, if convicted, he could be excommunicated. Mr. Cane refused to speak of accusation. Displayed anxiety. Lowered his eyes, rubbed his hands ceaselessly.

    Particulars: Langston Cane of Oakville is said to be married to two women. Mr. Cane is known by members of this congregation to have married Matilda Tylor in Oakville on October 11, 1852, in the Oakville A.M.E. Church. Three sons are issued from this union, all named Langston Cane. Mrs. Cane and the three like-named sons live with the accused.

A certain Jean Simms of Hamilton alleges that she, too, is married to said Langston Cane. She claims that he has been supporting her for a year. She claims they lived apart because Mr. Cane said he had to undertake constant business travel. No children issued from their union. Jean Simms was unable to produce a marriage certificate.

A Mr. J. Yardley, a neighbor to Jean Simms, traveled to Oakville to discuss the purchase of lake stones, and recognized the accused from his frequent trips to the home of the said Simms. Mr. Yardley made investigations as to Langston Cane's activities in Oakville, and determined that the accused was married to Matilda Tylor.

The Mayor G. K. Chisholm was out of town, and Chief Constable George J. Sumner was traveling to Kingston, so Mr. Yardley brought details of his discovery to A.M.E. Minister Caldwell.

Signed,
J. Worstell, A. Adams, B. Beck
Deacons of the A.M.E. Church

The second document was dated August 15, 1859. It was called Trial in Absentia of Langston Cane. It gave the same information as the first document, but added:

Given that Mr. Cane has fled Oakville, and that his whereabouts cannot be ascertained, these proceedings have been stayed out of respect for Mrs. Cane (in Oakville) and her three sons.

A collection has been raised for the assistance of Mrs. Cane (Oakville). Mrs. Cane has been forewarned, in the most humane terms possible, that, should the said Langston Cane return, he should face expulsion from the A.M.E. congregation and possible arrest by Chief Constable G. J. Sumner.

Signed,

J. Worstell, A. Adams, B. Beck

Church Deacons

Aberdeen Williams gave me more details. His grandfather had been a friend of Langston Cane, the accused bigamist. They had come together to Oakville on a schooner operated by Robert Wilson in 1850.

There were no photos of my great-great-grandfather, Langston Cane the First. No sketches. He was of medium height, Ab had heard, and "as darkly complected as they get." He had a chest like a barrel. As a fugitive slave, he had apparently spent some nights hiding in damp, coffin-like conditions near Canandaigua in upper New York State.

Ab's grandfather, Paul Williams, worked for years as an apprentice to a blacksmith. Langston Cane quickly established himself as a rat catcher in Oakville. Many of the houses and grain storage facilities near the Oakville harbor had rat problems, and Cane was said to be ingenious in his use of traps and ferrets. When the rat catching was slow, Cane worked as a stone hooker. Shale lay in great abundance on the floor of Lake Ontario. The long, flat stones were perfect for house foundations and walkways. The shale was attractive, but cheap. Stone hooking was hard work. Hooking lake-bed stones in shallow water and dragging them close to the surface was no great feat. But breaking the water surface and lifting the rocks up onto a scow could break a man's back. It was risky business. The scows were frequently overloaded, and prone to tipping in storms. Schooner captains scoffed at stone hookers, and thought of them as buffoons on the lake. But they had courage — no one could take that from them.

Langston Cane was not a church-going man. He took ale, when it was offered, and had a sweet tooth, especially for fruit. Aberdeen had heard that my great-great-grandfather was a womanizer. He married Matilda Tylor. She had come to Oakville as a fugitive and found work as a cook on Captain Wilson's schooner.

Ab said Langston Cane the First was involved in a secret meeting before he fled Oakville. Ab's grandfather knew about it because he, too, had attended the meeting, which included John Brown and Captain Wilson. Early the next morning, Cane was seen riding in a horse and buggy with a furtive, silent, long-bearded white man with unflinching blue eyes. Ab's grandfather said this was the famous John Brown. Aberdeen couldn't substantiate talk that Cane had died in Brown's raid on Harpers Ferry. His grandfather argued to the death that Langston may have done his wife wrong, but that he was a good man. On the morning that Cane skipped town, he left Matilda a pile of gold coins sufficient to sustain her for two years.

"So what happened to Matilda?" I asked.

Ab knew only that she had returned with her sons to Maryland seven years later, when the Civil War ended.

The next morning, there were more cops milling about my parents' house. My mother got a sympathetic call from Norville Watson's wife. My mother wished her well, too, and got off the phone. My mother hated telephones.

Ab came over with Belgian croissants. Ten of them, still warm, in a paper bag. He fixed coffee, which only he and the cops drank, sliced oranges, unveiled a chunk of three-year-old Gouda cheese from Prince Edward Island, and laid out the food for us.

Robert Hay, the holdup squad inspector, whispered: "Who *is* this guy, wandering in and out of your home, bringing food, cooking, looking as if he's four hundred years old?"

"Ask him," said my brother, who had arrived during the night. "He's a form of intelligent human life."

"Go ahead, ask him," I teased the cop. "He may understand English."

"Okay," Hay said. "Who *are* you, mister?"

"I'm the one who told you yesterday that Langston Cane is still in Oakville. Are you listening to me yet?"

"Not this again," Hay said.

"I hope you folks are knocking on doors," I said.

"Give me a break. There are a hundred thousand people in this town. You want us to knock on every door?" Hay turned back to face Aberdeen. "What makes you so sure Cane is in Oakville?"

"Because Watson is here, too," Ab said. "Like Dr. Cane said, you're barking up the wrong tree, looking for black militants."

Hay left us and came back an hour later with an announcement. "Africa First has claimed responsibility for your father's abduction. They say he has 'proved cowardly in the face of demands for black Equality.' They are still insisting on money and the release of prisoners. But they leave no way for us to reach them."

Ab said he was going out for a walk.

"Don't talk to any media," Hay told him. "Don't talk to anyone. This is confidential. Is that clear?"

Ab turned around slowly. "I changed Langston Cane's diapers," he said quietly. "I had his interests in mind before you were born, and I'll be thinking about him long after this case is solved." He left the house.

"He's the best-looking old man I ever saw," Hay said.

I stood up to join Aberdeen outside. Hay opened his mouth to tell me something, and then thought the better of it and remained quiet.

I drove Ab in my mother's car down to King and Trafalgar. We got out to walk along King to Dunn. A warm breeze blew off the lake. Ab wanted to look at the old houses again. He knew every home on the block. At one point or another, he'd been called to fix something in every one of them. He and Renata had worked in the old Turner home on the corner. When he was a boy, Ab said, he sold quarts of strawberries from door to door on this street. First he picked them for one cent per quart. Then he was allowed to keep another three cents for every sale he made. Ab sold so many strawberries in Oakville that he could close his eyes and tell you the color of every door on King Street.

"You ever lay your head down in a strawberry patch?" Ab asked.

"No."

"You should. You don't want to die without having done that. It's a light, sweet smell. You put your head down on the straw and have the impression there are strawberries right in your nose. I have only had one woman in my lifetime, Langston. Her name was Evelyn Morris. And the first time we lay side by side was in a strawberry field. I've been thankful for strawberries ever since. I only knew her for a few years, son. And she wasn't really the woman for me. I guess that's why it never worked out. But I've always been thankful for strawberries. And I've always remembered the softness of her skin. I can still feel it now, on the tips of my fingers."

Aberdeen pointed to a sprawling house with a widow's walk on the second floor. "That's where the Turners used to live."

I told Ab that I had read in one of my grandfather's diaries at Mill's house that Bob Turner tried to help defuse the Ku Klux Klan incident.

"You got that right, boy. Over there, that pink door, behind the poplar tree? The Smiths used to live there. He owned the bakery. I was in and out of that bakery all the time. And the next house? Blue door? The mayor used to live there He was a lawyer, too. The mayor had a fondness for Negro gals. I guess I should say 'black,' shouldn't I? They change the word on us every generation, and I can't keep up any more. Anyway. I never understood how the mayor could carry on with a Negro gal and have nobody up in arms about it, even though the whole town was in the know. Yet there I was, planning to marry Evelyn, and the whole world started shaking. Even your grandmother Rose didn't want to see us tie that knot. Rose. I loved that woman, Langston. I have to tell you, I did love her."

I nodded. We walked some more. Ab couldn't stop talking.

"Hey. That green door. Wait a minute. I don't recognize that car in the driveway. Langston, you ever seen that blue Volvo before? Course not, you spend about as much time in Oakville as I do in California. Stop walking, son. I want to look at that blue Volvo again. You know who used to live here? Dr. Jonathan Philippe Winston. He let everybody know that Philippe was with one *l* and had two *p*'s, like the French. He was real hoity-toity. That was a term my sister, Rennie, always used. She used to say Rose was real hoity-toity. I can't walk fast, but I still got my eyes. Is that a footprint in the garden? Around here, people don't step in gardens. I don't know who lives here any more. Must be renters. They had a For Rent sign up, not long ago. Lemme see that footprint. Here. Just let me get up here on these driveway stones a little more. Langston, somebody stepped on this iris. An iris is a precious flower. And someone has stepped on it. I'm gonna go knock on that door."

"And say what, Ab? 'By the way, have you abducted anybody lately?'"

"The windows are all shut," Ab said. "The drapes are closed."

I sighed.

"Where's your curiosity?" Ab said. "You don't wake up and get it at ninety, you know. Curiosity is like a garden, my boy. Needs cultivating. Indulge an old man. Get behind that car. Get down out of sight. I'm gonna knock on that door."

It took Aberdeen Williams the better part of a minute to walk up the stone driveway, negotiate the six steep steps to the door, and knock. He knocked. He rang. He knocked again. I peered up over the car and saw the door open. There was a chain on it.

Aberdeen Williams started talking to a face past the chain. People in Oakville didn't talk through chains in the middle of the day. I got down lower — too low to see through the windows of the car. Just in case. There was no movement in the street. No cars. No pedestrians.

I heard Aberdeen's voice, although I couldn't make out exactly what he was saying, something about the garden, something about gardening.

I heard a cough. I heard a shout. The cough was Aberdeen's, but the shout wasn't. The shout was my father's. It came from inside the house. The chain rattled, the door opened, the door slammed, and I heard nothing more.

I didn't move for a minute. The driveway pebbles dug into my knees. If I got up and ran, someone would see me. Someone was surely posted at that window, watching to see if anyone had noticed the tussle. I waited five minutes. I waited ten. Nobody would keep watch for ten minutes after the event. Would they? They'd watch for two, or three, or five, and they'd back away. They'd have things to talk about. Things to argue about. People were coming. Not from the house. From the sidewalk, on the other side of the Volvo. Talking. I waited for them to pass the Volvo. I got up quickly and joined two middle-aged women who were power-walking, arms pumping, breathing audibly.

"Excuse me. Somebody's been kidnapped in there. I need to get to a phone. Do you live around here?"

"Let's go, Betty," one said to the other. "Please, mister, just leave us alone." They crossed the street. I ran down the street to the car, drove straight home, and got all the cops in a complete panic. I hadn't even taken note of the house number or the license plate number of the Volvo. Hay started asking me a hundred questions. I babbled a few answers and then said, "Just get the hell over there. I'll talk to you on the way."

Sean walked into the room. He had no idea what was going on. "Lang, you got a call. It's Mill, from Baltimore."

"Whoever the hell Mill is, she can call back later," Hay said. "We're out of here. Come on. Move it." Hay made a call from his cell phone. He set up the scene. Cruisers were to pull along the streets perpendicular to King.

"Ab was pulled into a house midway between Dunn and Trafalgar," I told Hay.

Into his cell phone, Hay said other cruisers were to go onto Front Street, which was parallel, and to the south, and still others onto the streets to the north. They were all to get in place. *Go go go now.* No sirens.

We drove down to King and Trafalgar. Hay told an officer to drive by the house. She came back with the license plate number of the Volvo and the house number, and said the blinds were still shut. A uniformed officer knocked on the doors nearest 398 King, into which Aberdeen had disappeared. Neighbors were asked to leave their houses by their back doors. Tactical police and sharpshooters were brought into position. Inspector Hay and his assistants took over a house a few doors down from 398 King. They set up in the living room by the window overlooking the street. I joined them.

Hay dialed the number for the house at 398. The phone rang once. It rang twice.

"Hello."

"This is Inspector Robert Hay, Special Abductions Unit, Canadian Intelligence Bureau. We have a hundred and fifty police officers surrounding your house. Let me speak to the person in charge, please." Hay clicked on the speakerphone button.

"One minute," he was told.

"Hello," someone else said.

Hay repeated his intro. "We'd like you to come out of the house with your hands up."

"No way."

"I'd like to speak to one of your captives. How about Dr. Cane?"

"He's not here."

"How about the old man? Aberdeen Williams."

"Just a minute."

"Hello." That was Ab's voice.

"Aberdeen, this is Inspector Hay. We met at the Canes' house. Are you all right?"

"Very well, thanks."

"Are Cane and Watson with you?"

We heard Ab ask, "Can I answer that?" Someone took the phone from him.

"You spoke to him. We want the money. We want you to let us out. In our vehicle. We take Watson. You get the others."

"What is your name, sir?"

"You think I'm going to tell you that?"

"Are you a soldier, sir?"

"No more questions. You've got an hour to throw us the money. A hundred thousand. Small bills."

"I'm gonna have to talk to my people about that, sir. I'll call you back."

"What's your phone number?"

"I can't give that out," Hay said, and hung up. "I did that to shake them up. They're amateurs. I'll make them wait for the next call. They won't like that." Hay looked me in the eye. "That guy I was talking to. Do you think he's black?"

"I don't see how it matters," I said.

"Every bit of intelligence matters when you're dealing with kidnappers."

That made sense to me. I told him I didn't think the kidnapper was black.

"Why not?" he asked.

"Instinct," I answered. "Ear and instinct."

An hour or two went by. I left to reassure my mother that everything was under control. While I was at home, Mill phoned again. I asked Sean to tell her I was out. I walked back to the scene. Police had barricaded the street. I got back to the house facing 398 King at the same time as the linguistic expert. He told Hay the voice on the phone was of a young man in his twenties. He was in no position to speculate on the race of the young man. You just can't tell, he said.

Hay dialed the number again.

"Took you an hour and a half," the voice said. "What's going on?"

"Let's get to know each other a little," Hay said. "What did you say your name was again?"

"I didn't."

"Just your first name, then."

"Glen."

"So, Glen, how old are you?"

"Why?"

"Just asking. You sound like my son. About the same age, I mean."

"That's nice. Where's the money?"

"My boss vetoed that one. He told me no way. Not a chance. He said I was out of luck if I wanted money for you guys. He said you had to release one hostage before I could do any serious negotiating with you."

"Just a minute." We waited, briefly. Glen returned to the line. "You can have the old man. We're letting him out. Hold your fire."

Aberdeen walked out of the house. We saw him nod, and he appeared to say thank you to his captors. It took him a minute to make his way down the steps. A cop helped him down and tried to get him to hurry to the sidewalk. But Ab couldn't move quickly enough. The officer picked him up and carried him to our headquarters.

Ab was led into the house. When Hay started to fire away with questions, Aberdeen fainted. "Jesus Christ," Hay said. "Elevate his feet. Check his breathing." I was beside Ab. I had already checked his breathing. His chest was rising and falling. I felt his pulse.

A wet cloth was applied to Ab's face. I held his hand. It was cool. Just bones, and skin. It was weightless. I noticed his nails. They were clean, and clipped, and as pink and transparent as mine.

Ab came to. He was groggy, and of little help to the cops. He couldn't recall how many men were in the house. He hadn't seen my father or Watson. He did say that the man who had released him was young.

"Black?" Hay asked.

Ab fainted again.

"Enough questions," I said. "Get him to a hospital."

An ambulance was waiting around the corner. Ab was carried out within a minute. I called home to tell Sean that Ab had been taken to the hospital, but that he hadn't been visibly injured.

Hay waved me off the phone. He called Glen again. "Do you guys need anything to eat? Hamburgers? Fries? It's on us."

"Food would be good," Glen said.

"How many burgers you need?"

"Five. Hey! Tricky. Very tricky."

Hay gave the thumbs-up sign to his fellow cops. "I'm not tricking anybody. I just need to know how many burgers you want. You like fries?"

"Yeah. And drinks."

"What about Cane and Watson? Aren't they eating?"

"I'm not being tricked again."

"Glen, we know those two are in there with you. I'm just asking if it's okay to send them burgers, too."

"Yes, goddamn it, the five burgers will do. Hold the mustard on one of them. I can't stand the stuff. And hurry up, would you? We're starving."

Hay gave another thumbs up to his partners. And so it went. The food arrived. My father was dispatched to lift it off the doorstep. He stared out at the street, waved, I am sure, in case my mother was able to see this on television — two camera crews were back at the police barriers — and stepped back inside. I hoped he would make a run for it. Later, he said he would never have run out on Watson.

I went home again to see my mother. She wasn't watching it on TV. She was drinking mint tea and barely moving. Sean was with her. I hugged her and went back to the police headquarters.

Robert Hay and Glen, the abductor, had more telephone conversations. A few hours went by. Hay promised them Chinese food for dinner. And then he made them wait endlessly for it. It was dusk outside. It was eight p.m. Hay held on to the food. He called Glen.

"Send over that Chinese food, I saw it delivered," Glen said.

"Release those men, and I'll send you the food."

"Why should we do that?"

"It's late," Hay said. "It will be night soon. You want to stay up all night with cops surrounding your house?"

"We are getting pretty sick of it."

"We'll send you in the Chinese food if you let those men out."

"Just a minute." Glen returned to the phone in a minute. "You sure know how to wear a guy down. Here they come. We were never going to *do* anything to them. We didn't even *want* Cane or that old guy. Both of them sort of stumbled onto the scene and we had no choice but to grab 'em."

My father opened the door. He let Norville Watson out first. The man had a shaggy head of white hair. My father walked down the steps with Watson. A cop hustled them over to our house.

"Are they armed?" Hay asked them right off.

"Pistols and the like," Watson said.

"Hello, son," my father said, smiling. "Glad you came home. Officer, they each have a revolver."

"Each?"

"There are three of them. In their twenties, I would say."

"White?"

"They wore masks and gloves. We couldn't see their skin."

"Your son says he thinks Glen is white."

"He's right," Dad said.

"How can you tell?" Watson asked.

"Instinct," my father said. "Instinct, and a knowledge of speech cadence."

Hay grinned. He called up Glen. He talked them into walking out of the house. Hands up. Sorry. No Chinese food. But they'd get a square meal in jail. Inspector Hay would personally guarantee them that.

Chapter 18

THE *TORONTO TIMES* RAN THE STORY on page 1.

DOCTORS FREED UNHURT

NEO-NAZIS CHARGED WITH ABDUCTION

— Mahatma Grafton, Oakville

The sensational abductions of the physicians Norville Watson and Langston Cane — one a white, right-wing urologist and the other a black civil rights activist — escalated with a third hostage-taking yesterday, but ended hours later when all three were released unharmed from a fashionable house in downtown Oakville.

Three white men were arrested outside the house. Charged with kidnapping, forcible confinement, uttering threats, and various weapons offenses are Glen Houghton, 25, of Pickering; Peter Ash, 23, of Oakville; and Brian Cheltham, 21, of Burlington. Police say all three are members of the Salvation Front, a Toronto-based neo-Nazi hate group that denies the Holocaust and advocates the deportation of blacks and Asians.

The abduction of Watson seven days ago sparked wide-spread concern when a group calling itself Africa First claimed it was holding the urologist and demanded, in exchange for his release, $1 million and the release of a number of black federal penitentiary inmates.

During the first days of the Watson kidnapping, Africa First claimed "it was time for African peoples of the world to unite against white oppressors" and that "capitalists and governments must be forced by law to hire blacks and racial minorities first."

Police interviewed hundreds of blacks in efforts to track down the kidnappers. However, it now appears that Africa First was a front set up by neo-Nazis aiming to discredit black militants and to foment public hostility toward racial minorities.

Cane, who complained from the first days of Watson's disappearance that police investigators were focusing unfairly on black suspects, said in an interview yesterday that he was abducted at 6:30 a.m. yesterday while walking in downtown Oakville.

"I was walking by a house I've passed a hundred times before, and I noticed a strange car in the driveway. I also noticed that flowers had been trampled in the garden. I saw a piece of litter that looked like a medical prescription stuck in a bush near the front door. I went to pick it up, and it turned out to be a blank prescription form bearing Dr. Watson's letterhead. An armed, masked man burst from the door. I managed to stomp on a few more flowers before I was forced inside. Unfortunately, I had no blank prescription forms to scatter to the winds."

Cane said the primary motive of his kidnappers was to

turn the public against racial minorities and controversial measures such as employment equity.

"They were kids, rank amateurs," said Canadian Intelligence Bureau Inspector Robert Hay, who conducted negotiations by telephone with the abductors during an eight-hour standoff in one of the wealthiest neighborhoods in Canada.

Hay said three men claiming to be university students rented the house at 398 King Street a month ago. After Watson was abducted last week, Africa First released its first set of demands. Police stalled while they hunted for the kidnappers.

Police were finally led to the house by Cane's son, also named Langston. In a bizarre coincidence, Cane's son was walking with Aberdeen Williams, an 88-year-old family friend, on King Street yesterday when Williams noticed the same trampled flowers that had attracted Cane's attention. Williams knocked on the door at 398 King while Cane's son hid behind a car. The abductors opened the door and forced Williams inside. Cane's son immediately alerted the police.

"They were right under our noses," Hay said. "That was the only clever thing they did. We never suspected that what appeared to be a group of militant black extremists would be in downtown Oakville. They would have been too visible."

I would have kept reading, but my father interrupted me.

"Hey, son, why don't you put down that paper and have breakfast with me?"

I fixed him fried eggs, sausages, brown toast, orange juice, and coffee. My father has always enjoyed watching people fix things for him. He deserved the pleasure this time around.

He had a singular ability to talk and to eat, but not to appear to be doing both at the same time. At one point he held egg and toast on the tines of his fork, amid his description of his day in the company of Norville Watson. I wondered how he'd ever get around to that food, but the next thing I knew the food was gone and my father's mouth empty. He must have eaten and swallowed when I blinked.

"They had the two of us in a room. I actually slept in a double bed with Norville Watson. Do you know how much room that man takes on a bed? He's six four. His ankles stick out the end. He didn't sleep. But I did. He told me I snored. I told him it served him right for turning me down on that apartment on Palmerston Boulevard. I asked him why the hell he did that to a struggling student, anyway. And he said, 'Let it drop, Cane, would you? I made a mistake. But you pushed me, and when I was a young man, I didn't like people pushing me. But that was a lifetime ago. That was 1951. This is 1995. That's forty-four years, Cane. In less than forty-four years, nations have gone to war and made up and gone to war and made up again. So when are you going to let it drop?' And do you know what I told him, son? I told him that as of now, it was dropped.

"We talked about our children. Did you know that one of his sons is severely disabled? Lives in a group home. His wife has rheumatoid arthritis. I told him my mother had suffered from arthritis in her final years. We talked about our captors. They wore masks the whole time they were with us. You know what they gave us to eat? Canned ravioli. Canned peas. Canned peaches. Neo-Nazis can't cook worth shit. Norville Watson was constipated up to his ears. Kept asking our captors for fiber. They didn't have a clue what he was talking about.

"Did I think I was going to die? We're all going to die, son. I wouldn't want to die just yet. I want to see more of you, for example. I want to be around to help your mother. But I've led a long life. I've had a good life. I've done the things I wanted to do. I wasn't all that worried about it. I didn't think they were going to hurt us.

"Watson and I agreed that they were white. I asked them why they were wearing masks. 'Cause we don't want to be identified later,' the leader said. He acknowledged his name was Glen. I had the feeling it was his real name. He was a simple kid. Doing a stupid thing, but a simple kid.

"I said to him, 'But you're white. Is it that you don't want me to see you're white, since you been writing all that Africa First stuff for the papers to eat up?'

"'What makes you so sure we're white?' Glen said. So I said, 'The way you talk. The way you walk. The way you act. Tell me one thing about black people, if you want me to believe you're black. Tell me one interesting thing about black history. Did you know that black people were the first non-Natives to discover America? They got here two thousand years before Columbus.'

"'Bullshit,' Glen said. So I said, 'You'd never say that if you were black. You would say, Tell me about that nutty theory, anyway. That's what you would have said.'

"Norville Watson cut in to say, 'Anybody with a drop of instruction about the history of the world knows it's preposterous to suggest that black people discovered America.'

"'I'm with the doctor,' Glen said.

"'I'm a doctor, too,' I said.

"'He's a specialist. You're no specialist. I'm with the specialist.'

"'Next time I deliver a baby or resuscitate someone who has stopped breathing, I'll apologize for being a GP. Speaking about emergency care, let me tell you a story. This specialist here. This here white guy? Once, he just about saved my son's life. My son came into the hospital bleeding all over the floor and this white doctor patched him up. So what do you have against black people, Glen? Why are you putting out all that nonsense under the name of Africa First? It just gets folks riled up about black people.'

"'Exactly,' Glen said. 'I can see one person helping another, if they're bleeding, or whatever. But things have gone too far. The minorities are taking over. White people can't even get jobs. They can't get into med schools. We're being crowded out in our own country.'

"'I'm not after your job. My son isn't after your job. We're all after the same jobs.'

"'That's bullshit, mister. Minorities and Jews are running the economy.'

"Watson nudged me. He was trying to tell me to back off. 'I understand what you're saying,' Watson said. 'You want to have jobs. You want a future. You want an education. Those are good things to want.' That Watson was a clever old fox. He knew just what to say. Probably because he still buys into some of that shit. Doesn't matter. He's a good man, in his own way. He's got some upside-down views of the world, but —"

I cut my father off. "If you think he's still a racist, why do you suddenly like the man you spent half your lifetime hating?"

"I didn't hate him. I opposed him. Hate takes something out of you. When you start hating people, you start hating yourself."

"Why would you even want to talk with a guy like that?"

"Nobody wants to take a grudge into the grave. It doesn't feel right. You find yourself thinking you'd like to be able to do something heroic for the very person you fought the hardest."

We walked out onto the back porch and sat in the sun and drank lemonade at seven in the morning.

"Son, I want to talk to you about something important. This trip to Baltimore. You're doing it to hurt me."

"Hurt you?"

"You're trying to dig up painful things from my past."

"It's not got anything to do with hurting you. It's to know my past. I have to know. My life can't go on until I know these things. It's your fault, in a way. You planted all those stories in me. I have to get to the end of them."

"I don't care what research you do with the others. My father, or grandfather, or great-grandfather. But don't dig around in Mill's background, or mine."

"Why?"

"I'd rather be the one to tell you about myself."

"Are you about to tell me one of the stories I never heard?"

"No. No story. I'm going to tell you straight. This hurts too much to turn into a story. When I was in college, in the States, after the war, I did some stupid things. I committed a petty theft. I stole sixty dollars from a cash box belonging to my fraternity at Lincoln University. And I cheated on an exam. I did them on the same day, and I got caught at both. Actually, I was lucky they were the only things I got caught at. On long weekends here and there, I'd been doing a bit of tomcatting and other things on the seamy side of Baltimore. Anyway, I was expelled. It was fortunate for me that my father had clout. He had been to Lincoln. And his father, too. They had both become prominent A.M.E. ministers. My father persuaded the Lincoln people to keep the whole thing off my records. I was being expelled, but on the books it would appear as if I had merely dropped out."

"Is that it? Are you saying the major secret all these years is that you cheated on an exam and stole sixty dollars when you were twenty years old?"

"Twenty-two."

"I can't believe that's it."

"You don't understand the politics of shame. Shame in one's family, and in one's community. I came from a family of people with great accomplishments, son, and —"

"I know something of that, Dad."

"I guess you do."

"So that's it. You have been unhappy about me digging around in Baltimore, just because of that story? Sorry, but I can't believe it. There's more." He smiled. I knew I was right. "Your story doesn't explain why you've gone all these years saying nothing to Mill."

"All right, son. I'll tell you one last story. It has to do with me. But also with Mill. You'll understand, when it's over, why I didn't — don't — want you digging around too deeply in Baltimore. I haven't gotten along with Mill, haven't talked to her, but she's still my sister, and I'm still bound to protect her. You have to promise not to tell Mill that you know this."

"I already know that Mill was a prostitute."

"I can't believe she told you."

"She didn't. I found it out by going through some boxes."

"You mustn't tell her that you know. You mustn't embarrass her with this."

"You don't have to tell me that."

"She hated reading when she was a child, hated schools — especially the segregated school in Baltimore we attended. She dropped out of high school, moved out of the house at too young an age, obviously couldn't support herself, and the next thing you know, she'd become a prostitute. She got out of it, eventually, not long after the war."

"So what's the story?"

"Here it comes. The story takes place in the States, during World War II, around 1945."

Private Langston Cane the Fourth lifted the handbag up the steps into the last car of the train. He had never imagined a bag could weigh so much. It could have been filled with stones. It looked like a bag that lawyers carried out of court: tan leather, strong and supple, its solid, rectangular base a foot long and six inches wide, its sides bulging out like the hull of a ship and drawn back together under two thick handles. A tongue-like leather strap closed the bag. From near the top of one side, the strap had been stretched over the mouth with some force and been made to clip into the other side.

Langston took a seat at the back of the car, where he could see all the passengers and any conductors or military police coming in. He put the bag on its side and tried to slide it under the seat in front of him. It wouldn't fit. He could have put it up on the rack over his head, but he wanted it close at hand, so he spread his army boots and stood the bag between them.

"Don't open the bag," the sergeant had said, just before Langston had boarded the train. Langston had nodded, and the sergeant stood back on the platform, motionless, looking as thick and uncompromising as a tree stump.

The car jolted into motion, stopped, and pulled ahead slowly. Langston listened to the noisy clacking over tracks merge into a steady tremor as the train reached its running speed.

He waited for the conductor to come by to check his ticket. He wiped the sweat off his forehead. He'd been tricked by his own sergeant, and it served him right. Langston had wanted this pass too badly. Never want anything so badly that someone else can exploit you, his father had told him. But that was exactly what he had done. And what was more natural than wanting to see his sister? He was stationed at Camp Lee, Virginia, just a couple of hours by train from Baltimore, where Mill had caught the dose who knew how many times by now. This time, her pimp had beaten her up so badly that her right retina had been detached. She had written Langston, asking for brotherly comforting and spare cash. *Don't tell our old man. I've put him through enough already.* Stationed this close, Langston had to see her. He could be shipped overseas any time.

The sergeant had given Langston instructions, all oral, not one word written down. *So, you got a sister in Baltimore? Whaddya know? I got one, too. I'll be giving you a small package for her.* The sergeant had made him walk off the base, walk three miles in the sun. Then he'd met him on the road, picked him up off the shoulder, and driven him to the train station. That should have made him realize what was going on. But Langston, foolishly, had seen it in another light. He had seen it in the same light as the other games of the sergeant, who was always making his men do unexpected things and preaching about how men at war had to predict the unpredictable. The sergeant was low-class. Uneducated. He hated university boys like Langston, and would hate them till he died. For a scuff mark on a boot, he had once made Langston dig a three-foot hole under the noon-day sun, toss in a penny, fill up the hole, dig it out again, find the penny, and fill up the hole again. Midway through the job, he had given Langston half a cup of water. The sergeant strove to make life more miserable for his company — men of his own race — than could any white officer.

Up until the last minute, Langston had believed that the sergeant had made him walk off the base simply to make life hard for him. To make him work for his three-day pass. How stupid to have been so blind. It hadn't crossed his mind that the sergeant, who seemed to enjoy being hated by every man in the company, was lying to him. *I'll be giving you a small package.* Perfume or chocolates, Langston had imagined, although he now knew that was ridiculous. The sergeant was the last man on earth to give a sister a sentimental gift. But he had said *a package*, not *a bag*. And he hadn't said a bag as heavy as a bucket of stones. He had driven Langston to a rural train station north of Petersburg and had stayed with him in the waiting room, not talking, not looking at him, not even sitting with him, just standing ten feet away and looking out the window. And then, out on the platform, just before the train departed, instead of opening the handbag to pull out a package for his sister, the sergeant had turned over the whole thing.

"Off you go," the sergeant had said, nodding firmly, which, Langston knew, was his way of letting it be known that Pearl Harbor would pale by comparison, that the tentacles of hell would show no mercy, if Langston let anything happen to the bag. The sergeant had walked away to look off the edge of the platform. Langston, hesitating, had seen there was nothing out there but parched grass under sunlight so withering that it made the creosote stink on the railway ties. Langston realized that he should have refused on the train platform. There still had been time. *Sorry, Sergeant, I can't carry this bag for you.* Damn. Langston should have been thinking.

Langston looked out the train window. At the edge of a cornfield, he saw a mongrel digging a hole. The one thing about the army, he had written to his sister, was that they told you exactly what you had to do. All that remained was to follow orders, and you were laughing. Langston now understood how wrong he had been. You could peel whole vats of potatoes without nicking yourself and clean latrines without throwing up and manage to stay alert for guard duty and strip and rebuild your .45 automatic while the sergeant eyed his ticking stopwatch — and still, even if you did it all perfectly, you weren't really going anywhere at all. All you were doing was keeping out of trouble. There still remained ample opportunity to be boxed in and ruined by a colored sergeant who didn't like you because — well, because he didn't like you.

The train rolled north through Virginia. Still no sign of a conductor. Langston stood up and left his bag on the floor and walked to the toilet at the end of his car. Locked. He pulled open another door and walked into the next car. Its toilet, at the far end, was so putrid that it almost drove him away. Coming out of that toilet, Langston bumped into the conductor, who was punching holes in passengers' tickets. He was a gray-haired, square-jawed, well-built man who looked as if he had once played football. He straightened up as Langston mumbled an apology.

"Where you going, boy?"

"I am not a boy. I am a soldier."

The conductor looked at the single inverted V on Langston's sleeve. "Jesus Christ. Now I've heard it all. A private putting on airs. A nigger private who's probably cleaned more latrines than guns."

"If you've completed your personal speculations, I'll just go on my —"

"Where's your ticket, Private?" Langston pulled it from his shirt pocket. The conductor took it. "This ticket says car thirteen. You're in car twelve."

"I'm going back there now."

"I could have you thrown off the train. You're not allowed to leave your car."

"As I said, I'm going back there now. I just had to use the —"

"I hope you're on authorized leave, Private, and that you have the papers to show it. Military police often ride this train. Why don't you go on back and sit down?" The conductor punched a hole in the ticket and handed it back.

The encounter made Langston worry about the bag. He shouldn't have left it. To find a toilet, he had already violated the sergeant's edict. *Don't take your eyes off the bag.* But it was heavy, this handbag. Thirty pounds, maybe more. There was no way Langston was going to attract attention by lugging that bag down the aisle and into some can where there wouldn't be a clean place to put it anyway. It was unfortunate that Langston had had to leave the bag, and even more unfortunate that he'd run into the conductor, who would now probably tell a military police officer, if he saw one on the train, that he ought to check out a mouthy nigger in car thirteen. The military man, if he came Langston's way, would ask what was in the bag. That was his job, after all. He had to make sure soldiers weren't AWOL, and that they weren't carrying contraband.

What would Langston say to that? That he didn't know? Inconceivable. That he was ordered not to look? That he would be pleased to open it up for the military police officer? Absolutely not. Just yesterday, the sergeant had said, "Never expose yourself to the enemy."

"The enemy?" Langston had asked.

"The enemy! Don't you know your enemy, Cane?"

"Sergeant?"

"I'm your enemy! I'm your enemy and don't you forget it. My ambition in life is to trip you up. To make your life so intolerable that you just give up and die. Who else is your enemy, Private?"

"The Japs, Sergeant?"

"Yeah, but you may never see them. Everybody is your enemy. I am. They are. Every private in my company is your enemy. Every one of them would kick the gold fillings outa your mouth if nobody was standing watch over your corpse. Do you understand that, Private?"

"Yes, Sergeant."

"You understand?"

"Yes, Sergeant."

"I said, do you understand?"

"YES, SERGEANT!"

That was the conversation they'd had, all because Langston had knocked on the sergeant's door. Who in hell knocked on their enemy's door, the sergeant had said. After the enemy speech, variations of which Langston had heard daily in the four months that he had been at Camp Lee, the sergeant had taken the unlit cigar stump from his mouth and folded his forearms. They were bulging and muscled and covered with black hairs as wiry and taut as coiled springs.

"What do you want, Private?"

"I come from a good family, Sergeant. My father was a second lieutenant in World War I. He trained in a colored officers' training camp in Iowa and served with distinction in France."

"That's America, Private. You come from a good family, I come from a bad one. But I still get to boss you around. I can still make you do pretty near anything I want. Now get to the point."

"I'd like to have a weekend pass to visit my sister in Baltimore."

"Private, don't you know I don't give my men passes?"

"I have heard that, Sergeant, but . . ."

"No buts. Dismissed."

"May I write you a letter about it?"

"Why?"

"To submit my request formally, so that you may consider it again?"

"Private, if I get some pain-in-the-ass letter that I have to explain to Lieutenant Gudarsky, I will assume that you have time to spare. And I will find ways to occupy you. Is that clear?"

"Yes, Sergeant."

"Dismissed, again, Private."

"Thank you, Sergeant."

"Don't thank me. You hate me. I hate you. Don't take it personally. I hate all privates and powerless human beings."

"All right. I won't thank you. If you prefer, I'll hate you. After all, in the big picture, you don't have a whole lot of power either."

"You were doing just fine until you said that, Private. So watch your lip. Before you go, tell me again why you want this pass."

"To visit my sister in Baltimore."

"What part of the city does she live in?"

Langston could have told the truth: in a clapboard house one block down from a bar on Thames Street, so close to the boats and the bargemen in Fell's Point that he worried each day about her living on the edge of such a quick and willing grave. But, to the sergeant, he just said, "Downtown."

When news had leaked out of Mill's first brush with syphilis, their father had rushed over to help. He had paid for her injections of arsenic and bismuth, as well as two months in back rent, and had prayed for her and implored her to move back home. Mill had promised to straighten out, but she had refused to leave Fell's Point. She had got another dose. Their father had sent money, but nobody knew what became of it. He had driven to Fell's Point one more time, intending to force her into his car. But she had wailed and cursed when he'd started packing her things, and in had come a pimp with one hand in a pocket and had told him to lay off. Their father had asked her if that was what she wanted. Did she want a man who, for money, would usher her to the dead? Did she not prefer her own flesh and blood? Could she not see that she was breaking her mother's heart? She had told him to get the hell out, and he had never gone back.

"What does she do?" the sergeant had asked.

"She's a school teacher," Langston had lied.

"Good enough. You want to go to Baltimore? You want a three-day pass? You want to see your sister and your ailing mother and your dying grandpappy and all the rest of your glorious kin?"

Langston had nodded.

The sergeant had said that Langston could go, no problem, if he made a little delivery first. A little present needed transporting to the sergeant's own sister, on Druid Hill Avenue. Sure, Langston had said. Sure, I don't mind at all.

Langston had heard the edict just one time. That was the sergeant's way. When he had something crucial to say, something that might mean the difference between imprisonment or freedom, punishment or reprieve, he only said it once.

"Don't open the bag, Private. Don't even think about it."

Langston settled back into his seat. The leather bag was as he had left it, on the floor between his boots.

He believed he knew what was in the bag. Nothing else could weigh so much. The sergeant had taken Langston for a perfect sap, a man who wouldn't dare to defy instructions about exactly when and where to deliver the bag.

What were the alternatives? To leave the bag in the train toilet? Somebody would find it, report it, and Langston could be linked to it. Throw it out the window? Somebody would notice. And, at any rate, if the bag wasn't delivered, Langston knew the sergeant would hear about it. So what was he to do? Wait for the military police to come by and ask him to open the bag? That would be the first knot in an endless rope of trouble. Who would take his word? The sergeant would deny owning the bag, and would deny having driven Langston to the train station. After all, he had made Langston walk off the base and meet him on the road three miles from the gates.

The train stopped in Washington, D.C., long enough to let off and take on passengers, and then it began rolling north again. Baltimore's Penn Station was only forty minutes away. If he could just coast for that time, with no military officer in sight or on board, he would be home free. He would get off the train, take a taxi, deliver the bag to the sergeant's sister, or whoever the hell she really was, and then see his own sister. Later, he could get some liquor and some crab cakes and listen to Ella and Duke on the radio. If only he could get that far.

A porter came along the aisle, selling snacks from a cart. He was Langston's age, give or take a couple of years, and about as black as a black man could get, except for some pink, scarred flesh the size of a quarter high up on his left cheekbone and, above that, a cloudy eye that held a wisp of dribbling smoke. The porter flashed a V at Langston, sold a Coke and a bag of peanuts to the minister across the aisle, and then turned back to Langston.

"Soft drink, mister? Nuts?" Langston took one of each, paid, and tipped the man a dime. "If you like," the porter whispered, "I can pour you a little something in that Coke."

"What kind of little something?"

"Jamaican rum. The best. In a flask, right here," he said, tapping his vest.

"No, but thanks anyway."

"Don't mention it. I wouldn't have said anything, but since you're on leave, I thought you might be looking for a little shot of happiness."

Langston said nothing.

"I lost my eye in Fort Sill, Oklahoma," the porter said. "A man in my platoon knew less than my grandma about grenades. Pulled the pin and just tossed the sucker, instead of throwing it. Mushmouth, we called him, although his real name was Winston Everett. Killed himself and woulda killed me if I'd been standing any closer. All I got was a lick of metal in the eye, an honorable discharge, a pension of thirty-eight dollars a month, and a recommendation for this job."

Langston noticed the porter looking at the bag. "I'm sorry about your eye. Colored people got it bad, in this war. We got it real bad."

"That's the truth," the porter said. "Say, let me put that bag up on the rack." The porter bent over and grabbed the bag.

"No, let me —"

"That's what they pay me for." The porter hoisted the bag before Langston could stop him. "What you got in here, soldier? Hooch?"

Langston forced a polite smile. He saw the minister looking at them. "I've got books," he said. "A stack of books."

"Uh-huh," the porter said, grinning. "Books, you say. Doesn't feel like books to me. Damn, this thing is heavy." He leaned a little closer. "Hey, man, I won't tell anybody. I'm your brother." He popped the bag on the rack overhead. Langston turned his face slightly from the porter's rancid breath. "You know, Private, you're a smart or a lucky man to be traveling in the North. If you had been heading south, once you hit Tennessee, they would have Jim Crowed you. Put you in a cattle car. A cattle car, I'm telling you."

The minister across the aisle reached out and tapped the porter's back. "Hey, son," he said, as quietly as he could, "were you just talking about a little flask?"

In one fluid series of movements, the porter withdrew the curved flask with his right hand and unscrewed it with his left and poured unstintingly into the minister's cup and screwed the cap on and slipped it back inside his vest.

"Will fifty cents do?" the minister said.

"Fifty cents will be just fine," the porter said, taking two thick coins and dropping them into his vest pocket. The same pocket, Langston noticed, that his tip had fallen into.

"I'm on my way. You want that bag down from the rack, soldier, just let me know."

As the porter turned to walk away, Langston studied the ridge of fat on the back of the man's neck, and his jacket, which was the color of running blood. The porter walked past a few old men, some women and children, and a few soldiers, colored every shade from high yellow to ebony.

A woman got up and walked down the aisle. Her skirt stopped at the back of her knees. Langston watched the working of her brown calves. He swallowed. He remembered, with revulsion, one of the last things the sergeant had said in the waiting room. *When you're through visiting my sister and yours, Private, I authorize you to find yourself a good clean whore — it won't do you any harm. Not any harm at all.*

Langston stood up and retrieved the bag and sat down with the weight on his lap. He opened it. Not wide enough to see inside, not wide enough to risk the chance of anybody else seeing inside or even seeing him paying too much attention to the bag.

Just wide enough to put his left hand into the dark hole and to feel the cold metal barrel of a .45 automatic. And, beside it, the cylinder of a revolver. And, probing under it with his fingertips, Langston touched the tips of two magazines for bullets, and the ribs of a grenade. He drew in his breath and shut the bag.

He sat for five minutes, thinking. He grew conscious that the minister was looking at him. Finally, thinking of his own father, Langston turned to face the man.

"Do you know Jesus?" the minister said.

"No."

"Will you take a Bible?" The minister held out a Bible in soft cover.

"May I keep it?"

"Yes."

"Actually, may I have another? For my sister?"

"I have only two with me, but if you will use them, I will gladly share them with you."

"Thank you," Langston said, taking the second. He reopened the bag and laid the Bibles end to end, on top of the guns. He laid them flat and forced them down enough so he could close the bag with the strap. A door yawned. Langston heard two loud and unworried voices, male voices that didn't mind at all if everybody listened, coming in from car twelve. They were talking about baseball.

"Soldiers, have your papers ready," a voice called out.

Langston didn't have to look. He knew one voice belonged to the conductor. What an obsequious lackey, calling out for the military police officer, hoping something would happen, something to tell his friends later. A soldier found AWOL or in some other violation of the rules.

"Military officer on board. Soldiers, have your papers ready."

Langston knew better than to lift his head and look. They would see him looking, catch his eyes in that fleeting and vulnerable instant before he let his chin drop.

Langston heard them stop the first soldier.

"Your papers, please," said the military officer. He sounded like a Harvard man. Like the kind of student Langston had met in inter-university debating competitions before his induction. They might have sat across from one another. White boys from Harvard on one side, black boys from Lincoln on the other. "Thank you," said the officer. Now his voice drew nearer. He talked again with the conductor about the Baltimore Orioles. Something about how Baltimore needed a major league ball club and ought to get one after the war. The Orioles were playing the Newark Bears that night in Oriole Park. The conductor was going to the game. A baseball game, Langston thought. A baseball game! How liberating, how far from war and soldiering and military cops and lawyers' bags would be a good seat with a bag of popcorn and a cold can of beer at an Orioles game in the unrelenting heat of the August evening. Just as good would be the same cold beer at a home game of the colored Elite Giants. "EEE-light, DEE-light," the fans would cheer after every broken fastball and stolen base. For baseball, Langston would willingly stand up and clap. He would never do it for the American Army, which considered black soldiers good enough to die, but not to eat with and bunk with whites. But for baseball, and for the home-run hit, sounding like a pistol shot and making the ball arc up up up in complete defiance of gravity — yes, absolutely yes, Langston would stand up for that.

"Papers, please." Now they were about three seats ahead of him. "Thank you." The two men moved closer. Langston heard the conductor blow his nose twice, pause for a moment, then blow it again.

The military police officer stood in the aisle next to Langston. The conductor came up beside him. Langston looked up in measured diplomacy. He saw the military man, a corporal, who was ten or so years older. Star-like wrinkles at the corners of his eyes. Brown hair studded with gray slivers. The face of a man who might let a few things by. Out of the corner of his eye, Langston noticed the minister watching him.

"Your papers, please," said the MP.

Langston handed them over.

"Thank you."

That was easy. The military man was about to move on.

"Say," the conductor said. "You're not supposed to have your bag on the floor. You're blocking the way to the other seat. Put it up on the rack, boy." Langston said nothing. The conductor sniggered. "Private, I mean." To the MP, he said, "He's the one I was telling you about."

Langston did not drop his gaze or turn his head. He allowed the military man to look at him steadily. The country dog strategy, he reminded himself. Look at it straight, reveal nothing, lock your fear in your feet, keep it there.

"Sure," Langston said. His voice tripped on the word, making it sound like *su-uhre*, as if he hadn't awakened fully, or had something to hide.

Langston stood and bent over and grabbed the bag in two places, down low and higher up, and did his best to lift the weight slowly, casually, as if it weighed nothing, nothing at all.

The military man had moved on, but the conductor stood to watch. "That thing looks heavy. What you got in there?"

Langston ignored the conductor and lifted it steadily. He had it at shoulder height now and stood in the aisle, prepared to heft it up onto the rack.

"Private, what's in the bag?" This was the military police officer, turning around and looking at him again.

Langston pushed the bag onto the rack, making it look easy. Perhaps, he thought, being smooth and effortless would diminish the truth of the conductor's words. Langston turned fully around to acknowledge the corporal and, in doing so, caught the upward gaze of the seated minister. His own father was the only church minister Langston knew who spent Sunday evenings playing poker.

"Bibles," Langston said.

Langston didn't stare at the MP. He let the man stare at him. He opened his eyes and looked gently in the direction of authority, allowing his pupils and irises to be devoured on inspection.

Langston made his voice sound humble, but confident, alert but not over-educated, certainly not college-educated. "I have a small stack of secondhand Bibles, donated by the army. My sister volunteers at the Mount Vernon Baptist Church in Baltimore, Corporal. When the army heard of it, they offered these Bibles."

The officer looked at Langston, then up at the bag, then back at Langston.

"Let me see."

Langston brought the bag down and placed it on the seat. He opened it quickly, wide enough to make the black Bible covers visible.

"Very well. Good day."

"Thank you, Corporal."

"And Private?"

"Yes, Corporal."

"I take it you're leading a Christian life?"

"Yes, Corporal."

"You're a model for your community."

"Thank you, Corporal."

The military police officer turned and walked back out the car. Langston saw the minister nod and smile and sip his Coke.

Langston smiled back, confident that the man would say nothing, and ask nothing. He wondered what the sergeant's sister, or whoever she was, would do with the grenades and the guns. Probably store them some place safe for the sergeant. So what would the sergeant do with them? Sell them for profit after the war? Hide a gun in every drawer? Make people like Langston's sister go to bed with men at Fell's Point?

Langston disembarked at Penn Station on Charles Street in Baltimore. He stood in the shade of the station overhang, with the bag on the ground by his boot, waiting a few minutes for the white passengers to get into taxis, hoping he could get one after they took all that they needed. The minister who had given him the Bibles came up next to him.

"Son, you can't get a taxi at the station. Where you going?"

"To see my sister in Fell's Point."

"I'll show you where you can get a cab on St. Paul Street." Langston thanked the minister, and walked a block with him. As they separated, the man pressed a dollar and a business card into Langston's hand and said: "Get a good meal, be rid of your troubles, and drop by my church if you can."

Langston thanked him again, and took a cab to Fell's Point. He got out on Broadway Avenue and walked south toward the wharf. He had been there once before to take his sister to see the Elite Giants. That was before she got in trouble. Or before anybody knew about it, anyway. He remembered the neighborhood. He remembered the Kicking Horse tavern. Mill's flat was only a block away. Italian and Polish women were selling tomatoes and sausages from sidewalk stands. In the glare of the afternoon sun, it didn't look like a street where his sister could catch syphilis or get her retina detached for refusing to sleep with a white trick. Langston walked out on a pier. He passed three fishing boats. At the far end, Langston got down on one knee, opened the sergeant's bag, removed the minister's Bibles, strapped the bag shut, and stood up. He placed one foot on the edge of the pier, looked over his shoulder as if to follow the flight of three gulls inland, opened his palm, and let the sergeant's bag drop into Chesapeake Bay.

I brought my father another coffee. The sun was growing hot on our back porch.

"So tell me, Dad, did you break contact with Mill because she was a prostitute?"

"No. Not entirely. She certainly kept her distance from the family when she was one. But later, we didn't talk because she was angry I had married white and I was angry that she was making an issue of it. We sort of dug our heels in and never let up."

"And one other thing, Dad. How did the army sergeant deal with you when you got back to the base from your leave?"

"He didn't do anything. He barked a lot. Gave me a lot of grief with extra duties. But there was nothing he could say. Luckily for me, I was transferred out of that camp a month or two later." My father looked me in the eye and smiled. "That's enough about me. Let's talk about you, now. What are you doing in Baltimore? What are you really trying to accomplish?"

I took a breath. "I'm trying to write our family story. It's turning into a novel. It's hard for me to admit that I'm trying to write one, because I've failed at everything I've taken on, and I couldn't bear to fail at this, too."

He placed his hand on my knee. "You're not going to fail, son. You're a Cane. Just get back to Baltimore and find out what you need to know and write that book."

Aberdeen Williams was released after two days in the hospital. I went to see him. He gave me some good advice about how to dig up more on Langston Cane the First. He said Robert Wilson, the schooner captain, probably kept diaries. Probably kept business records. He said I should try to find them.

I spent two more weeks in Oakville. Time enough for three more calls from Mill, asking when I was coming back. Time enough to hear from Yoyo, who called from a pay phone to ensure that I was returning to Baltimore. Time enough to take a knock on the door from the reporter Mahatma Grafton. He wanted to know if I could ask my father if he would agree to discuss the police reaction to the Watson kidnapping. I helped set it up for him. My father agreed. Mahatma Grafton got a big front-page story out of it. He called to thank me. I told him I might call on him one day to return the favor. Mahatma reminded me to give his card to Yoyo. I promised that I would. He said, as well, that he would mail me a small envelope to take back to Yoyo. I was welcome to open it, he said. It would contain some money and a letter from Hélène Savoie, one of Mahatma's colleagues at the *Toronto Times*. I said that would be fine with me.

I spent most of my time in Oakville hunting down details on Langston Cane the First. I spent a week at the Oakville library. It had a box of materials on Robert Wilson. I went through every page of it. Nothing of interest to me. Then I went to the Oakville Historical Society. They had sixteen boxes of documents about people who had lived and died long ago in the town. I spent three days going through the boxes, and found nothing. As I was preparing to leave, an assistant told me that there were three more boxes in the basement. I tore into three new boxes marked *Capt. Wilson.* I had to weed through trinkets, newspaper clippings, and programs from local dances. In the second box, I found a diary. I read the first twenty pages. I could make out almost all of the long, looping handwriting. Wilson had brought seventeen fugitive slaves across Lake Ontario, up until 1858. He had wanted to bring over more, but feared capture. He was acquainted with the American Fugitive Slave Act of 1850, which allowed Southern slave owners to recapture fugitives in the Northern free states. He feared that American authorities would impound his boat, and perhaps jail him, if he were found out.

Wilson kept records of financial assistance provided to the fugitives. He noted that, "To a man, they have all been profoundly grateful for services rendered. Most have remained in Oakville, for there is much work here in the shipyards, and they can count on my assistance. All have attempted to remunerate me, after finding work."

I read on. There was a lot of family business, shipping records, and so forth. Exports of oak staves had dropped considerably because, as Wilson wrote, "Oakville is devouring its oak trees in a mad rush for American capital." I pushed ahead to 1859. The year of John Brown's raid on Harpers Ferry. I knew that Langston had skipped town in August, and that Brown had raided the Harpers Ferry arsenal in October. I started scanning Wilson's diary entries for the month of June. Nothing. July. Nothing. But I hit gold in August. I found new information about the history of the United States and Canada.

August 5, 1859

I must rig up my schooner. Several shipments to be made. Will be extremely busy. A strange man asked to see me. He was tall and gaunt and had hollowed cheeks and a long beard. He looked to be in need of a square meal. He declined to give his name. I told him that I had urgent business to tend to. He gripped my hand — and he had a vice-like grip.

He said, "Sir, I am aware of your assistance to the Negro fugitives. I have great admiration for your work. We must talk in utmost confidence. Could you bring the most trusted Negroes to the meeting?"

He came to my residence at nine p.m. We retired to my study. Paul Williams and Langston Cane were waiting there. Two fine Negroes. Two of the finest I've helped across the lake. I closed the door. The Negroes and I sat. The guest paced the room like a cat.

"My name is John Brown," he said. "I am a servant of God. My life is devoted to the destruction of slavery, one of the greatest evils in my country."

The Negroes fidgeted. They were uncomfortable. Paul Williams cleared his throat and would not look at this John Brown, but Langston Cane cast his eyes frequently on the man.

"I am gathering men of vision and daring, including some of my own sons. We are preparing to attack slavery and its perpetrators. We will attack a strategic location in Virginia, in a land of verdant hills, near the Shenandoah and Potomac rivers. Surrounding the area is a large slave population that will revolt at a moment's notice. My men and I will attack when the time is right, and take to the

Appalachian Hills. Dozens, if not hundreds, of Negroes, slaves, and freemen, will join us on the day of the revolt. We will have pikes for those who do not know rifles. We will retreat to the hills, and move south, liberating plantations, amassing quickly an army of Negroes and God-fearing white Christians. We will overtake and crush slavery."

Paul Williams expelled an enormous breath and stumbled to the door. He had trouble opening it, his hands were shaking so. Brown looked at him, waited until Williams was gone, and continued.

"Gentlemen, I need assistance. From you, Captain Wilson, I must request financial help. But any aid that you provide must be considered a gift. It will not be within my means to repay any loan. We need provisions, sir. Weapons, horses, carts, any number of things. And you, Mr. Cane."

I wondered if the Negro Cane would also run from the room. But he didn't run. He licked his lip once, and pulled on his ear, but he looked John Brown in the eye.

"What is your occupation, sir?"

"I am a rat catcher and a stone hooker, sir."

"I beg your pardon?"

"I catch rats. And I hook stones — slabs of shale — from the lake bottom, and I sell them for house foundations and pathways."

"Very well," Mr. Brown said. "What do you say? I must not tarry."

The Negro Cane held his words. I stood and cleared my throat.

"I sympathize with your goal of ending slavery. But I think you've got a bolt loose. You can't overtake the United

States government. They'll hunt you down, and they'll hang you. Langston, don't get involved in this nonsense. If you join this man, you'll never see your family again. You will die young."

Mr. Brown spoke out. "He may die, sir. That may be true. But is he afraid of that? I am not afraid of death. We all die, Mr. Wilson. The question, sir, is *how* we die. Dining in great comfort, or fighting to save our fellow man? He is right, Cane. You could die on this mission. But what a glorious death it would be. Your death would help change the course of history.

I stood up. "No death is glorious. Death is death. Follow this devil, and blood will run. Innocents will die. Is that glorious, Langston? With respect, Mr. Brown, you are a lunatic. Get out now, please."

Brown nodded. "Only a very few have the will to pursue this matter to the limit. I bear you no ill will. You have done good work helping the fugitive Negroes, sir. And you, Cane? Are you with me?"

"I'll think about it," Cane said.

"You have little time for reflection. I have some equipment being repaired, and a new horse to purchase, but I will leave town when my work is done. God bless both of you."

Brown and Cane disappeared into the darkness. There were no stars, that night, and no moon either. Clouds hung low in the sky. It thundered past midnight, but it did not rain.

I flipped ahead to the next diary entry about Langston Cane or John Brown.

August 11, 1859

Langston Cane is in serious trouble. I overestimated him. The Negro Church—a modest little affair that takes itself quite seriously—has called him up on bigamy charges. Langston has fled town. He left an envelope on my doorstep, with coins in it, and his name scrawled on a piece of paper. "For the selfless assistance, thanking you heartily." The writing astonished me. Over and over I read, "selfless assistance, thanking you heartily." A turn of phrase requiring no slight degree of writing sophistication. At any rate, Cane has fled town. I hope that he has not, in his desperation, taken up with John Brown.

I was convinced that my great-great-grandfather had pulled out of Oakville with John Brown. But I still had no idea what had happened to him at Harpers Ferry, or if he had even gotten that far. It was time to return to Baltimore.

Chapter 19

I WASN'T EXPECTING MILL to meet me at the Baltimore–Washington Airport. But meet me she did.

"I've got more boxes for you to look at," she said.

I explained that I needed to rest. I said I had been exhausted by a kidnapping, a sort of prodigal non-return, the discovery of an exam-cheating father, an accused great-great-grandfather, and all sorts of other things.

"What sorts of things?" Mill said.

"Various ones. I'm too tired to get into it right now."

"No, you ain't. Why aren't you looking me in the eye, boy?"

I feigned ignorance.

"You're looking at me funny. Have you been talking to your father?"

I asked if she had any food at her home. Perhaps I would stop by her place and have a bite, if she wished, before going to my flat to sleep.

"I haven't been to university, but I know what a subject is. A subject is what I'm trying to talk about, and you're trying to change it on me. Look me in the eye, boy."

Mill had a large, dark face, with shades of gray under her eyes. Stars radiated out from the corners of her eyes. Bags, too. It was an old, dark, leathery face, with the lines of age gouged diagonally down her cheeks, and across her forehead, and at the corners of her mouth. She wore no lipstick. Her lips were cracked. She licked them.

"I knew it," she said. "I knew it the minute you looked at me, fox-like. He told you about me, didn't he? Didn't he? Don't lie to me."

I told her about finding the letter, and about talking with my father. We arrived at her house. Her stare relaxed. "Come on, git out of the car. I ain't bringing you no meal in here."

We went inside. It was immaculate. She said Yoyo had cleaned up her house the day before. Mill had ordered Kentucky Fried Chicken. She said she was too tired to bake. The chicken was waiting for us, on the table, in the bucket.

"Look at me, son."

I looked at her again. I wondered if the whole family research project was a bad idea. I had forced my way into Mill's life and learned the one thing that she wanted to keep secret.

"Tell me what I used to be," she said.

"A prostitute." I avoided her eyes.

She was smiling. She blinked, and held something back. But she was smiling. "I don't mind you knowing, Langston. That was fifty years ago. You weren't even born. I'm not responsible for things I did half a century ago. So stop looking at me like that. It was more than half a lifetime ago."

I asked why she and my father had gone so long without talking.

"Because he married a white woman, son. I had nothing against your mother. I've never even met her. But she's white. Aberdeen Williams took to a white woman, and the next thing I knew, we lost him and we had to leave Oakville. When we left, I felt as if I was leaving my real father. I loved that man, Langston, I loved him like you couldn't understand. And the way I saw it, I lost him because of a white woman.

"I got into some trouble when I developed into a woman. I saw white pimps running colored prostitutes as if they were cattle. And I saw black men taking off with white women. I could not forgive my brother for leaving me all alone and going on up to Canada and living there with a white woman. It upset the marrow of my bones, Langston. I could not go to his wedding. I could not meet that white woman. I hated her. And I hated him. Because I hated myself. But that's all over now. Your father did what he had to. Even Aberdeen did what he had to. He shouldn't have been messing around with that little old white girl in 1930, but I don't hold that against him now. Aberdeen took what he could from life, and Evelyn Morris was all there was. There weren't a lot of choices for black men back then. There were even fewer choices for black women. Back then, there were only a few hundred colored folks in Oakville. That didn't leave you a whole mess of playing room, when you got down to looking for someone to make babies with.

I told Mill that she should visit my parents, and Aberdeen, too.

"That's what I wanted to do, you cussed fool." She hit me with her hat. "You-all took off on that airplane. You could have taken me with you. Not on an airplane, mind you. I don't go up in those things."

"You don't?"

"The only time you'll catch me up in the air is when I'm flying to meet my maker. You're going to have to drive me to Canada, Langston. On the ground. Fifty miles an hour is as fast as my old body will travel."

I bit into the chicken. I asked if it came from the bucket she had ordered for me two weeks earlier. She swatted me again with her hat.

"Finish up this family business and take me to Canada," Mill said.

"I've got a few things to do still."

"Get at 'em, son. I got some boxes I never told you about."

I said I had to be going home to bed. She drove me. I got out at the door. She put her hand on my arm.

"Son, when I was an itty-bitty girl in Oakville, I used to think Aberdeen Williams was old. I thought Mommy and Daddy were old. Yet here I am, twice as old as they were then. I'm at the end of my life, Langston, and I want to go home. I want to go back to Oakville. If you don't take me there soon, I'm gonna drum on your head with a frying pan."

As far as Yoyo was concerned, cleaning houses was hard work. Lugging meat and charcoal and Cameroonian hot sauce and a barbecue stand around the streets of Charles Village was hard work. Jumping out of a jailhouse window and escaping through the streets of Baltimore was hard work.

But writing was a piece of cake. All you had to do was let your mind float and follow it with your fingers. You could get published in the *Toronto Times*, even if you were an illegal refugee in the United States. You could find the woman you had once hoped to marry, track her down at the *Toronto Times*, and start writing love letters to her while she helped you get published. Writing was a good business in America. It could change your life.

Yoyo had his fourth article published in the *Toronto Times*. A note came from Hélène Savoie, who passed on a request from a senior editor—could Yoyo write a regular humor column for the *Times*?

Humor? How odd. Yoyo didn't write humor. This Canadian editor had to be a little strange. But who cared? He published Yoyo's stuff. He paid him three hundred dollars an article. It was the easiest money Yoyo had ever made. Three hundred dollars for sitting down for two hours to write one article was an awful lot better than seventy-five dollars for five hours of housecleaning. Yoyo's most recent article had been entitled "Columbus Discovered What?" It started like this:

Most Americans think an Italian by the name of Christopher Columbus discovered America.

If Christopher Columbus was the first to see America, the Amerindian peoples must all have been blind.

But this article isn't about the Amerindians. Of interest to this author, since Americans seem so bent on naming the one who discovered America, is to examine who else might lay claim to the discovery.

Three cheers for the Norsemen. These Scandinavian sailors landed on the east coast of North America more than six hundred years before Columbus. But they weren't the first.

It's time to raise the flag in honor of the Africans.

Have planeloads of tourists not witnessed the Negroid features of the stone heads — over two thousand years old

— uncovered in Mexico in 1939 by the renowned geologist Matthew Stirling?

Who do we assume carved those stone heads, dear readers?

Let's drop Columbus from the textbooks, and insert the sailors of papyrus boats from the west coast of Africa . . .

Yoyo reread the clipping of his article. Hélène had attached a short note that said: "Here's your latest missive, in published form. They think you're a riot up here. Keep in touch, H.S."

Yoyo told me about it, and said he had started writing back to Hélène. He longed for his old lover, and he told it to her straight. He wanted her in his bed. Actually, he wanted to be in her bed. In Canada.

"If you are already spoken for," he wrote, "let me know. I wish not to embarrass you. But if your pulse beats as strongly as mine, let us meet again in Canada. Show me the jewels of the world's second largest nation. Show me Banff National Park, where there is a lake, I have read, the color of emerald. Take me to the Niagara Falls, source of unrelenting hydroelectric power and magnet to the deranged, who seal themselves inside barrels and plunge from absurd heights. Take me, dear Hélène, to Oakville — historic refuge for the fugitive slaves of America."

Yoyo was waiting at the door when Mill dropped me off at my flat.

"You went away, my friend, without consulting me," he said. I told him I'd been through a kidnapping and that I needed sleep. "Fine, get your sleep, my friend. I must leave to clean a house. But don't travel north again without advising me. I would like to join you."

"Let's talk about it after I wake up." I tried to close the door, but Yoyo slipped inside. "I want to see my friend, Hélène Savoie, in Canada. I want to marry her. I mustn't say that to her, of course. I have already learned the hard way that speaking too directly about such things can capsize a love affair."

"Speaking of Hélène, she mailed me something to pass along to you," I said. I dug through my bags. My need to sleep seemed to be fading. Yoyo's energy was stirring me. I found Hélène's envelope and handed it over, along with Mahatma Grafton's business card. Yoyo tore open the envelope.

"She says, 'If you can come up for a few days, I'd love to see you. Don't be offended by the cash. It's to help you get up here.' Take me to Canada, Langston. Take me with you."

I don't know how long it took me to become aware of the knocking. *Tap tap tap. Tap tap tap. Tap tap tap.* On the front door. I rolled out of bed, pulled on a pair of jeans, and walked out of my bedroom.

I saw Annette through the window, and had the same thought I'd had when we'd met weeks earlier: she was too good-looking and too young for me. Her face was thin, and angular. Her color was like the smooth side of an acorn. I saw the darker freckles on her cheekbones. Her lips parted into a smile as I opened the door. Yellow dress, with red poppies, hemmed at mid-thigh. Sandals.

"Mill told me you were back," she said. Her voice ran like water, with a hint of laughter in it. Her tongue brushed over those teeth, spaced slightly, and lovely in their imperfection. I couldn't imagine a man not wanting to hold her. I took in a breath.

"You look terrific," I said.

"You were sleeping, weren't you?"

I opened the door wider. Wide enough for her to squeeze through, but not without touching me. "Entry will cost you."

She planted a quick one on my lips. "A woman is watching from across the street."

I waved to Elvina Peck, and realized that my rent was overdue. It was August 4. And I'd been away for two weeks.

"Elvina, how you doing?" I called across the street.

"Just fine."

"I'll get you that rent money today."

"Fine. Take good care of your visitor."

I waved and closed the door.

"You don't have any food in here," Annette said.

"I was away."

"And you didn't warn me that you were leaving."

"I wasn't sure you were interested."

"Wasn't our last time together an expression of interest?"

"Do you mind if I kiss you before answering that question?"

"Kiss me all you like. I like it when you touch me. But remember to tell me the next time. I might like to know if you're going someplace."

I woke up to the smell of potatoes and onions frying.

"I bought you some food," Annette said. There was a baguette on the counter. And a bottle of red wine. I checked the fridge. She'd bought oranges and a cantaloupe. Milk. Juice. Cheese. "I got ground coffee, too," she said. "Want to make some? I'd love a good coffee."

"Sure. Just a minute." I dressed and crossed the street — it was early evening, now — and knocked on Elvina's door and borrowed her coffee-maker.

"You don't keep much around here, do you?" Annette said.

"I didn't know how long I'd be staying in Baltimore. Tell me about yourself, Annette Morton."

She grinned. "You mean now that we've had sex three times, we should get properly introduced?"

"Sure."

"There's not much to say. I've got a BA in English from Morgan College. I grew up in Baltimore and am still here and work at the Enoch Pratt Library. I haven't been shot or turned into anyone's prostitute or been beaten up on Pennsylvania Avenue, and I do have steady employment, so you can surmise that I'm a survivor, for a black Baltimorean."

"How old are you?"

"You seem to need to know, so I don't think I'll say."

"I'm more worked up over my age than yours."

"I'm not worked up over it, so why should you be? Don't judge me because of my age."

"I wasn't judging you, I was judging us."

"Then don't judge *us* according to my age."

"How long have you been involved in the church?"

"This feels like an interview. It's not at all like what happens when we touch. Let's just eat and go out for the evening."

I had been planning to spend a few hours digging through Mill's boxes. I wanted to pin down some more information on Langston Cane the Second. But it could wait for a night. "Sure, let's make it an evening."

Annette cracked some eggs, whisked them, and poured them into the potato and onion mixture. I sliced the baguette and made the coffee. I ran across the street again to borrow a chair from Elvina.

A breeze ran through the kitchen. The sounds of boys playing in the street wafted in through the windows. We could hear crickets, and a couple laughing on the sidewalk below, and an ice-cream vendor ringing his bell. He called out: "Fudgsicles icicles popsicles creamsicles and ice cream, come get your taste of winter in the summer, come cool your mouth for just one dollar fifty." We got up in the middle of our meal and went down into the street to meet this ice-cream vendor. He was about sixty. He wore a baseball cap. He was as black as the night.

"You two lovebirds enjoy yourselves. You only live once. Ain't nobody gonna bring you back 'cause you messed up your life first time around. So, enjoy your loving, and your ice cream, too."

I was going to give him a five and let him keep the change. But he stopped me. "No money. Not tonight. You can buy from me another night, if I'm around and if you want to. But tonight, it's on Old Bill. It's good luck to give ice cream to lovers."

"What makes you so sure we're lovers?" Annette said.

"Young lady, you about the prettiest thing this side of Jupiter. It's evening, now, and getting dark out here. If this man ain't your lover, something's wrong with him."

Annette leaned over and kissed me on the cheek. She said, "He is my lover, and he's a good man, and there's nothing wrong with him that can't be fixed with a little more loving."

We went back inside, and stuck Old Bill's desserts in the freezer. When we finished our meal, we strolled out into the night with the ice-cream cones. We walked south on St. Paul Street until we finished eating them, and then took a taxi downtown and spent half the night listening to jazz at Louie's Bookstore Café on Charles Street.

I left Annette's place in the morning. I asked if she would like to get together soon. She said not to rush things.

Should I call her, then?

No. She would call me. I was thankful that I still had a lot of family sleuthing to do. I needed something to keep me from being overwhelmed with desire for Annette.

I spent four days reading family history documents at Mill's place, and came across a church pamphlet published at the time of the death of Langston Cane the Second. Born in Oakville in 1858, he had traveled with his mother and brothers to Baltimore around 1866. The mother died, and the brothers disappeared, and Langston was taken under the wing of a Quaker by the name of Nathan Shoemaker. He was raised by Shoemaker until he attended Storer College in Harpers Ferry. He went on to Lincoln University, married Lucinda Richards, and became a minister at the Bethel A.M.E. Church in Baltimore.

I read the document twice, fingering the dry paper.

Mill came up from behind me. "Find anything new?"

I mentioned that this was the first time I had seen the name of the Quaker who had adopted Langston the Second. Mill offered to take me to the A.M.E. Church library.

"How come you're suddenly cooperating?" I asked.

"I been letting you eat, drink, sleep, and read all day and half the night in my house for two months, and you call this suddenly cooperating?"

"But you're taking the initiative now. You're actually proposing a course of action."

"Well, the sooner you quit chasing your tail, the sooner you can take me up to Canada to see that brother of mine and meet that mother of yours."

"And see Aberdeen?"

Mill smiled and sat back. "And see Aberdeen."

Baltimore settled into a heat wave. The temperature rose to 110 degrees. The humidity made it feel like 122. Rain kept threatening, but never delivered. A number of old people died in their homes. Thousands of chickens perished on Maryland farms. Restaurants raised the price of meals with chicken.

I spent most days sifting through family photographs and records at Mill's place, which had air conditioning. Annette dropped by one Saturday afternoon, and asked if I could help her. She was going to visit some church elders in their homes. I tagged along and tried to make myself useful. Most of the old folks just wanted someone to talk to. I kept looking at Annette. She had braided her hair and applied red lipstick. She wore loose cotton pants that invited me to try to glimpse her long, brown legs.

"Is he your husband?" one woman asked, while I washed dishes.

"No. He's my friend."

"Is he black?"

"Sure is."

"Bit faded, I'd say. I hear him doing dishes out there. He seems like a good man. Good men are hard to find. I married a willy lump lump. That husband of mine had gristle in his brains and stones in his heart. But your man seems decent. Why don't you marry him?"

"Mrs. Winters, people don't just up and marry like that any more. It's more complicated. It takes time. People have to get to know each other."

"Well, then, git to know him."

Mrs. Winters got up and poked my shoulder. "Young man, do you like this woman?"

"She's a fine person," I said.

"I can tell by the way you talk respectful that you come from a good family. You don't have another woman, do you?"

"No."

"And you never been married?"

"Actually, I have."

"You look too young to be divorced."

"Sometimes these things happen, no matter how hard you try."

"I married a fool," she said, "and I never divorced him. I just waited till he died. I figured he'd kick off early and give me a good long time on my own, and he did just that, thank the Lord."

Annette laughed. She made sure Mrs. Winters didn't need anything else, and then let her know that we had to go. She meant to make three more home visits that day.

Yoyo had been saving money. He was cleaning two houses a day, six days a week. He would have worked Sundays, too, but Mill's church friends wouldn't let him. During the heat wave, Yoyo packed sandwiches and fruit and carrots and celery and ate in the women's homes, after his work was done. Some suggested that he stick around for an hour or two afterward, until the heat subsided. Yoyo generally agreed, if they would leave him alone to do some reading and writing. He could write anywhere, now that he had purchased a portable computer with sixteen megabytes of internal memory, a three-hundred megabyte hard drive, its own software, fax/modem, and printer. Writing had never been easier. The computer purchase left Yoyo with three thousand dollars cash, plus the two hundred dollars that Hélène had sent him for the trip. Yoyo planned to return the two hundred dollars to Hélène. He appreciated the gift. But he felt Hélène would respect him more if he paid his own way.

The letter came without a return address, as if the sender were over confident that the missive would indeed land in my mailbox, or, alternatively, as if she didn't really care. The note itself was hardly better. It was chatty without saying anything of substance, and ended with: "Will be in touch. Ellen."

In other words, "Don't call me, I'll call you." I tried to put the letter out of my mind. The old relationship was holding me back. Perhaps the best thing that could happen to me would be to never see or hear from Ellen again. I ripped up the letter and threw it out.

I spent four hours with Mill in the A.M.E. Church library. We found some old photos of Langston Cane the Second. He was a tall, dark man. Round, full face. Minister's tunic tight around his neck. A level, unflinching stare. A look of confidence, and of serenity. A man with no doubt about his mission in life. There was a photo from the country home where the Cane family summered in northern Maryland. Langston Cane the Second stood there in his black minister's garment, holding his son — my grandfather — close to his side. My great-grandfather, in that photo, looked like a stern sonofabitch. *Fool with me and I'll pop your head off.*

I found something exciting in the church library — a personal memoir that my great-grandfather had written. It was entitled "Langston Cane: A brief, personal recollection, for the purposes of historical clarity. NOT for publication." It was six handwritten pages. I devoured that memoir, and spent the next three days at the Maryland Historical Society, going over records of mid-nineteenth century Quakers in Baltimore. I found the papers of various Shoemakers, including Nathan Shoemaker, who was born in 1826. That would put him at about the right age to adopt my great-grandfather in 1866. I paid a genealogist to help me. She discovered that Shoemaker had kept a diary, and she found it in the Hall of Records in Annapolis. I drove there with Mill, and we hit gold. Shoemaker had written several pages about my great-grandfather.

I told Mill that I wanted to go to Harpers Ferry. She wanted to come along, too. I told her I would need to spend several nights there. Good, Mill said, because that would leave us time to check out the records at Storer College, where my great-grandfather had studied.

"Is it still open?"

"It shut down long ago, but the records may still be there."

"Why do you say that?"

"That's what colored people do, son. They shut down a building and leave all the papers alone, instead of throwing them out. That way, if some fool like you wants to come along once every hundred years and waste three good days digging through it, he's welcome to do so." Mill said we should stay at the Hilltop Hotel in Harpers Ferry. "It has a view of the Shenandoah and the Potomac rivers. It used to be a summer resort for colored folks."

"So you know about this place?" I asked.

Mill smacked me with a magazine. "I have every right to know a thing or two and not have some overeducated, pampered, love-struck, mixed up, half-black child from Oakville underestimating me."

"All right, Mill. You win." I called the hotel and booked two rooms.

When Yoyo heard about the trip, he asked to come along. Annette sounded interested, too. I urged her to join us.

Mill said her car couldn't be trusted in the Blue Ridge Mountains, so the four of us traveled in my Jetta. Yoyo took along his new computer. It had taken him only a few days to get the hang of it, to have a phone installed, and to learn how to use the modem. He had already figured out how to surf the Internet, and how to send his newspaper articles by electronic mail to Hélène Savoie at the *Toronto Times*. On the drive south, Yoyo was already talking about sending another story to the *Times*.

We parked at the Hilltop Hotel and walked to the edge of the property to admire the plunging valley. It dove down to the Potomac River and, on the other side, back up the hills of Maryland. Down river, the Potomac merged with the Shenandoah. Harpers Ferry was nestled into the V where the two rivers met. Trees covered the valley. A breeze lifted up to reach us. Annette was standing beside me. Our shoulders touched. We turned to look at the creaky, wooden two-story Hilltop with the long verandah in front.

Inside, Mill thrust a credit card across the counter.

"I'm staying here with my children," she said. "We reserved two rooms. For three nights. Under the name of Millicent Cane."

The clerk looked at her. The clerk looked at us. There was Yoyo, who was as dark as dark got, and a good deal darker than Mill. There was Annette, who was of a medium complexion, and then there was me — Zebra Incorporated.

"Mrs. Cane, your rooms are ready. Here are the keys. Do you need help with your bags?"

"No. We don't have many bags."

"Are there jacks in the bedrooms?" Yoyo asked.

"No, but if you need to hook up a computer, you can do it in our boardroom," the clerk said.

"Stupendous," Yoyo said.

The clerk gave Mill two keys.

Mill charged out of the stairwell and said, "Come on, Annette, our room is down this way. You men are over to the right."

We had lunch in the hotel dining room. Our window overlooked the Potomac River. Yoyo had a number of questions about the menu. Grits. Hog maws. Corn fritters. Creamed beef. Mill answered the first four questions, and then told him to hush up and order.

After lunch, I said I wanted to get to Storer College right away. Mill said she'd come with me. Yoyo preferred to do some writing. Annette planned to take a walk.

"Why don't you come with Langston and me?" Mill asked her.

"I want to be on my own for a few hours," Annette said.

"Woman of your looks ain't likely to be left alone," Mill mumbled.

I walked out with Annette to admire the valley again.

"Your aunt drives me crazy. Why didn't you tell her we'd take a separate room?"

"I wasn't sure you'd want to do that."

"Of course I do. Why are you so afraid of standing up to your aunt?"

"I'm not afraid of her."

"All you do is kowtow to her. She's got family information and you want it, so you suck up to her."

"I indulge her, but I hardly think I suck up to her. I like her."

"She's aggressive and bossy."

"She's a fascinating person, and I'm fond of her."

"Well, have a terrific time with her this afternoon."

"Why are you being so bitchy all of the sudden?"

"It's not worth a fight. Not worth our first fight, anyway," she said. And she smiled. "I just don't think I can last three nights with your aunt."

"I'll talk to her about it."

"You don't need her permission. We get another room, stay in it, and pay for it. It's that simple."

Mill walked up to us. "There you are. Let's go, Langston. Sure you don't want to come, Annette?"

"No, thank you, Mill. Lang, I'll take care of what we were just discussing."

"Fine. Catch you later."

I turned. Annette said my name. I looked back. She stepped up and kissed me twice on the mouth. Mill acted as if she saw nothing. We drove to Storer College.

The college had closed decades earlier. The facilities, located on several acres of green, sloping grounds, had been converted into government buildings. We knocked on doors until we found a janitor.

I told him we were looking for Storer College records.

"The college closed years ago," the janitor said. He was a short, lean man, close to retirement.

"I know that, but —"

Mill placed her hand on my arm. "What's your name, anyway?"

"Ron."

"Ron what?"

"Ron Alleyne."

"You part of the Alleyne family used to go, twenty or thirty years back, to the Bethel A.M.E. in Baltimore?"

"I might be. Who's asking?"

"I'm Millicent Cane. I been going to that church since I was a girl. My pappy — and this boy's grandpappy — used to be the minister there. I knew of a William Alleyne, used to go there, used to know my father well."

"William Alleyne was my father."

"Ain't that something? I bet we could find lots of other people in common." My aunt slipped the man a twenty-dollar bill. Alleyne told us to follow him inside. He led us to an old classroom.

"You've been working here a while, haven't you?" Mill said.

"Since before the college closed down. Pity it closed. Did a good job educating our people. Did you get yourself to school, son?" the man asked.

I told him that I did.

"He had too much schooling, you ask me," Mill said. "But he does know how to think. When he starts thinking, watch out. You need a rocket ship to keep up with him." Alleyne chuckled. Mill went on. "He's writing a book. It's so complicated it would make your head spin. And he needs some information about his great-grandfather—my grandfather—who studied at this here college. We figure that information could be in your records."

"I don't think I could help with that."

"My nephew here came all the way from Canada."

"You don't say. I always wanted to see Canada. I'm sorry, but those records are in a locked room. You need permission from the college administrator."

"Where's he?"

"Dead and gone," Alleyne said.

"My nephew here drives a funny Canadian car called a Jetta. It's a diesel. I'm telling you, the motor sounds like a bomb going off. And he drove down here all that way." Mill slipped the man another twenty. "There's no more where that came from," she said.

Alleyne took us down a dusty hall, and into what used to be the Storer College library. The books were gone, but the shelves remained. And on the shelves, and on some tables, and on about half the floor, lay boxes. Boxes of Storer College records. There were about forty of them.

"We'll need Annette and Yoyo to help us dig through all this," I mumbled.

"Hush, boy," Mill said. "Mr. Alleyne, we appreciate this. We do. Now we're going to need some time. We're gonna need to be in here today, tomorrow, and maybe the next day."

"I don't know if that is possible," he said.

Mill stood, suddenly. She was a good two hundred and fifty pounds, and five ten or so. In other words, she was four inches taller and about a hundred pounds more imposing than Alleyne. "Now listen here. I just parted with forty dollars, and if you start greasing me for more I'll tell anybody who'll listen you were taking bribes, and I'll keep saying it till you get fired and you lose your pension. We been polite to you, but don't push us. We're good people, Mr. Alleyne. We ain't gonna take nothing, or ruin nothing, or hurt nothing. We're just looking for some information about our family. I'm gonna ask once more politely and I'm not going to ask again. Will you let us sit here quietly for the rest of the afternoon and let us back in at nine on the dot tomorrow morning?"

Alleyne nodded. "Don't tell nobody I let you-all in here."

We spent the rest of the afternoon opening boxes with Mill's pocket knife and filtering through the contents. We found report cards, disciplinary proceedings, yearbooks, and news clippings — but all from the twentieth century. We'd been through ten boxes by the time four-thirty came along.

On the drive back to the hotel, I said that Annette and I were going to take a separate room. I expected an outburst.

"You're a grown man, and Annette is a grown woman," she said.

"I'll move Annette's bag when we get back."

"She's probably already moved it. That young woman knows her mind. Langston. Listen up. Do you realize that girl has designs on you?"

"I'm not sure what designs she has. She hasn't said anything."

"She's not that dumb. But she has designs on you. I never went to university, but I know applied heat when I see it."

"What are you trying to say?"

"She likes you. So you should act honorably. Don't take advantage of her."

"I'm not taking advantage of anybody. I enjoy her company. I like being with her."

"You're thirty-eight years old and you oughta know by now that you can't just enjoy a woman and then walk out of her life."

"I know that, Mill."

"As soon as you've finished all this family research nonsense, I want you to stop thinking so much and go out and do something with your life."

I wanted to say that she sounded like my father, but I held my tongue.

———————

Yoyo didn't show up for dinner. Mill ate quickly and got up from the table. "It's been a long day. I'm not used to all this gallivanting around. We got a long day tomorrow. See you at breakfast at eight."

"Good night, Mill," Annette said.

"Good night, Mill," I said.

We were heading outside when we bumped into Yoyo. He had been writing, and unable to make it to dinner. He showed us the story he was about to file to the *Toronto Times*.

> Imagine that you were living 136 years ago. Remember that although slavery had been abolished for nearly 30 years in Canada, it was still thriving in the American South.
>
> Put yourself in Canada West in 1859. Let's say you are working in a farming community. And let's say that, one day, a tall, gaunt, devoutly Christian man named John Brown enters your home and tells you that he intends to put together a band of 20 men to attack a United States weapons arsenal and armory in Harpers Ferry, Virginia. After overtaking Harpers Ferry, Brown plans to free local slaves and escape to the hills of Virginia. He says he will attract untold thousands of slaves, who will join him in guerrilla warfare on the institution of slavery. Together, they will form a new provisional government of the United States, which, among other things, will enshrine the principle of equality for all human beings.
>
> Would you help John Brown with money or shelter? Would you join his raiders? Or would you declare him a madman and alert the nearest authorities?

It is easy to say that Brown was doomed to fail. But it is just as easy to reply that only violence could overthrow slavery.

Brown put together a troupe of 21 recruits, including at least two Canadians: a black man named Osborn Anderson, and a white man named Stewart Taylor. There is a possibility that a third Canadian, Langston Cane of Oakville, Ontario, took part in the raid. That possibility is currently being investigated by Cane's great-great-grandson, who carries the same name. But I digress.

The men attacked on a rainy night in October, 1859. The battle lasted for 36 hours. Most of the raiders never escaped from Harpers Ferry once they stormed the town. They killed five people — the first of whom was a black baggage master at the train station — and wounded nine others. Ten of the raiders, including two of Brown's own sons, were killed right then or fatally wounded. Seven, including Brown, were captured, tried, and hanged. Five escaped.

In the short run, the raid was a catastrophe. In the long run, the raid — and the sensational news coverage that it and Brown's trial sparked — drove the United States closer to the Civil War that ended slavery.

On his way to the rope, the 59-year-old man said: "I, John Brown, am now quite certain that the crimes of this guilty land will never be purged away, but with blood."

What would you have done, had he knocked on your door?

I told Yoyo the article looked fine, but that I didn't want him referring to Langston Cane the First, or to me. "This is the story of my family. I've brought you into it in confidence, and I'm asking you to respect that. I'll tell it publicly when I'm ready."

"All right," Yoyo said. "I'll take it out. But will you let me write about it, if you determine that your great-great-grandfather did take part in the raid?"

"Let's talk about it later. We're going out for a walk. Want to come?"

"No, I have to change this story, and then send it to Toronto."

Ron Alleyne had swept and dusted the library and opened the windows. Mill gave him five dollars "for a hot lunch." Annette and Yoyo had come along to help out, and we all had bagged lunches prepared by the hotel.

The last five boxes in the Storer College library contained papers from the 1800s.

Mill and I figured that Langston Cane the Second had graduated from Storer around 1880. We found class records for that year, but nothing on my great-grandfather. We looked at 1881. Nothing. Back to 1879. Bingo. There he was. Photo. Tall, dark, nothing if not serious. Tightly curled hair. The records included a copy of his valedictory speech. His academic records. A personal statement required as part of his application to the college. A written undertaking by his guardian, Nathan Shoemaker, to pay tuition and room and board fees.

We got out of Storer College in time for lunch, so we picnicked in the Harpers Ferry National Park. I dropped Mill off at the hotel. She wanted to nap. Yoyo headed out for a walk. Annette and I spent an hour or so looking around the Harpers Ferry museum. I had a word with the archivist working there. I explained that I was looking for information about my great-great-grandfather who, although not in the history books, may have played a role in John Brown's raid. The archivist said he'd see what he could find under the name of Cane. Was there a number at which I could be reached? I gave him my name and the hotel's number, dropped Annette off at the hotel, and went to a quiet café. I let the waitress know that I'd be staying for several hours, and I settled down to write my great-grandfather's story.

Chapter 20

LANGSTON CANE THE SECOND remembered it as the longest trip he'd taken in his life. It had seemed endless. Later, he wrote in a journal that he and his mother and brothers had crossed Lake Ontario in a steam ship, waited in Buffalo for ten hours, taken a horse-drawn cart east to Rochester, waited six hours there, and taken a series of trains that eventually led to Baltimore.

They traveled in the summer, so as not to suffer from the cold. Instead, they suffered from the heat. One of Langston's brothers took along a puppy, but it died while they were in Pittsburgh, waiting in the sun for a train.

Matilda Cane had not been well during the trip. She coughed every hour when the trip began. Two days later, as they pulled into the Penn Station in Baltimore, she was gagging and spitting blood.

In the dust and the heat and the stench of foul fruit and sewers, the woman and her three young sons walked out onto Charles Street.

A man aimed his team of horses at them. Matilda flung her youngest Langston back. This was our Langston. His brothers, also named Langston, were called Senior and Junior. But the little one, aged eight, and already a better reader than his older brothers, was simply called Langston.

Matilda steered her brood to the closest black church, and found a woman who gave them temporary shelter near the Chesapeake Bay dockyards. Shelter meant sleeping on the dirt floor of a cabin where the air was even worse than the rank and fetid stench of the street.

Langston noticed the noise. The commotion. The stink. The heat. But, more than anything else, he gaped at the masses of Negroes. He'd never seen so many black people in his life. In Oakville, colored people were few and spread out. Here, they squeezed into neighborhoods festering with screams and smoke and excrement.

Langston listened to his mother talk to the woman who had taken them in. He heard Matilda explain that she had run out of work in Canada and had come south, now that the war was over, in search of something better.

"Gal, you outa your head?" the other said. "This place is better than nowhere. You oughta git on back up north."

"I can't," Matilda said. "My health is failing."

"The problem with Baltimore is there's too many culluds. There's gettin' to be so many of us that the white peoples are starting to hate us."

Matilda took her boys along for a visit to the Freedmen's Bureau. She had heard that the U.S. government had set it up to protect the rights of the newly freed. After waiting in line, she was asked to state her complaint. She said she didn't have any, but just was in need of work. Langston saw that the man speaking to Matilda wore a U.S. army uniform. He had a mustache, and he had a gun.

"I'm sorry," he said, "but we don't offer employment here. We help people who've been done wrong, and want to put it right."

"I haven't been done wrong, but —"

"Well, watch out, then. Watch those boys. Keep 'em out of the hands of the snatchers."

"The snatchers?"

"Where you been, woman? I'm talking about unscrupulous men who come along and snatch colored children and take them off to become apprentices."

Apprentices. Langston knew that word. He'd seen boys working as apprentices in Oakville. Apprentices to shipbuilders, carpenters, blacksmiths.

Matilda and the boys were turned away. They tried to pass the day walking, but were chased off one street, and away from a water fountain. Matilda, who had money enough to last them a few months, found a market where colored people were buying and selling. She bought four rolls, four apples, and four chunks of cheese. Eat slowly, she told the boys. Chew every bite good and long. It's got to last all day.

The next day, Matilda took the boys back to the Freedmen's Bureau. Thankfully, a different soldier was on duty. She spun out the conversation with him as long as she could. All the while, following advice she'd been given, Matilda kept her eye out for a white man with a kind face. *Find yourself a white man to hire you to clean his house. But stand back when you first try to talk. You talk to the wrong one, he's likely to make a fist and hit you to Kingdom Come.*

There were pencils and paper in the Freedmen's Bureau. For noting complaints, presumably. Langston took to scribbling while his mother talked. *Hello. I'm Langston. I'm eight. Can my mother clean your house? She's an excellent cleaner.* This he wrote on a piece of paper. He gave it to one man who walked into the bureau. The man crumpled the paper and threw it down. Langston waited a moment for the man to move on, then ran over and picked it up and unfolded it and handed it to another man. The man tried to kick him, but Langston danced out of his way. Three more times, he tried to pass the paper along. Once it was ripped in half, once dropped to the floor, and once stuffed in the pocket of a man who didn't look at it. Langston saw his mother engaged in a long conversation with a man in the building. The man reached around and put his hand on Matilda's backside. She slapped the hand away, and he grabbed her hand and slapped her. She kneed him in the groin. Langston watched in horror as the man drew in a long, raspy breath. A soldier urged Matilda to leave immediately, and told the aggressor that he deserved the blow. Matilda gathered up Langston and the others and hurried them out the door. She spat on the road. Langston noticed her saliva was specked with blood. He looked up and saw a tall white man in fine clothes get off his horse-drawn cart.

Langston stepped right up to him. He came up to the man's chest. He looked up at sky blue eyes, and hair brushed to the side. He saw thin, sloping cheeks and a long, square chin. It was a gentle face.

"Mister, can I hold your horse for you, if you're going to tarry?"

"If you can take care of a horse as well as you can talk, we're in business," the man said.

Langston's mother looked at the man. He looked at her. She smiled and raised her hand, as if to say, what can you do with a boy like that? He said he wouldn't be but a minute, and hurried into the Freedmen's Bureau. He was not one but ten minutes. Langston stood waiting and holding the reins of the fine black horse. His mother and brothers stood next to him, waiting.

The man returned. "That was a gentlemanly act. What may I do for you? How about a dime?"

"No, thank you, but could you read this, instead?" Langston asked, handing over a piece of paper.

"Did you write this, lad?"

"Yes, I did. I've been to school. With my brothers. We all can write."

"And where have you learned to write so well, at such a young age?"

"In Canada."

"Aren't you full of surprises. Are you the lad's mother?" Matilda nodded. "And you are experienced in housecleaning?"

"Most experienced, sir. I spent the last three years cleaning the home of Captain Robert Wilson, in Oakville."

"And where is that?"

"In Canada West. On Lake Ontario. Near Toronto."

"You people surprise me with every sentence," the man said. "Do you know who I am?"

"No, sir."

"Nathan Shoemaker. Does that name mean anything to you?"

"We just arrived from Canada yesterday."

"Consider yourself hired. Meet me here tomorrow morning at nine. My wife will keep you awfully busy cleaning, so you'll have to make arrangements to have someone watch over your boys. But keep them somewhere safe. Many have disappeared. Keep well. Until tomorrow!"

Matilda Cane cleaned the man's house for three weeks. Through the church, she found a family that would let them rent a tiny room in their tin and wood shack. There was nothing to sleep on but some old blankets that Nathan Shoemaker had given her to take away. They slept there, and they ate what they could. Cornmeal, and bits of fried bacon, and chunks of bread. Water from public fountains, when nobody was looking, or close enough to give them trouble. The boys were told to spend their days in the church, reading. They stayed in the church and read for a few minutes after their mother's departure. But then the janitor would boot them out. They didn't tell their mother they spent their days on the streets. Why worry her?

Matilda walked to the Shoemaker home and back every day. It took her an hour, each day, and she started work at nine. Each day, she coughed more. And spat more blood. One day, she woke feverish. She was so hot that Langston, who slept beside her, dreamed that his leg was touching a boiling pot. Matilda couldn't go to work. She couldn't get up. For three days, she was sick. She told her boys to go see Nathan Shoemaker if something happened to her. She told Langston that he was the smartest boy she'd ever met, already reading like an adult. She wiped his nose and gave him Shoemaker's address and made him memorize it. On the fourth day, she got up slowly, dressed with great discomfort, and hobbled with the boys to the Freedmen's Bureau. Langston noticed a man following them for the last blocks to the bureau. His mother got to see a soldier fairly quickly. She said she was afraid she was dying. She said she was afraid of what would happen to her boys. She was advised to put them in someone else's custody. Otherwise, she was told, who knew what could happen in the event of her demise. She was advised to see a doctor. She smiled limply. All a doctor's going to tell me is what I already know, she whispered.

Langston saw the man follow them out of the Freedmen's Bureau. He noticed him follow them home. He noticed him for several days running, in the streets nearby, while his mother got more and more sick. She died on a Wednesday morning with her eyes open. Langston and his brothers left her eyes open, thinking that if the phantom man, as they'd dubbed him, came in, he'd think she was still alive. They were alone in the shack. It was raining. Water was getting in through the tin on the roof, and dripping on the floor. They couldn't decide what to do. Langston wanted to go ask Shoemaker for help. His brothers agreed to go with him. They stepped out into the alley. Three men jumped out at them. Phantom man and two others. A horse and cart were just down the lane. Phantom man held Langston. He had white cheeks, stubble, and stinking breath. Langston wriggled free and kicked the man with all his might, right between the legs. And he ran. And ran. And ran. Swearing, and crying, and wailing, and more crying, and the sound of horses moving behind him. Down a side street, up another lane, right through somebody's house, through the front door and through the cabbage-smelling stove area out the back, and onto another street. He knew better than to go back to where his mother lay, dead. He had read the newspaper accounts. Children were being stolen away and made to work. The papers said it was like slavery all over again. Where were his brothers? He had lost them. Where had they been taken? He never found out.

A white woman answered the door. He asked for Mr. Shoemaker. He was told that Mr. Shoemaker wasn't in. He expected to be sent out into the streets, but he was asked if he was accompanied by a parent, and answered, "My mother is dead." He was told to come right in. Langston waited all day for Nathan Shoemaker. He wouldn't talk or eat until the man came home.

Shoemaker took him immediately to the place where Langston had been living.

"My God, the stench," said a man, apparently a brother to Mr. Shoemaker, as they slowed down in the lane.

"It's not their fault," Nathan Shoemaker said. "They've been squeezed in here like animals. What else could you expect?"

The one-room shack had been torn inside out. The belongings had been rifled through, torn apart, scattered against the walls. The money, which had been in a sock under the pallet, was gone. Matilda Cane lay there. Eyes still open. Nathan Shoemaker closed the lids and stood and put his arm around the boy.

Nathan Shoemaker was a Quaker. He was the grandson of a Shoemaker who had been a vocal abolitionist and friend of the Negroes. Shoemaker, the grandson, lived off his interest in a number of mines in western Maryland. He kept a regular diary, and made a few entries about the colored boy he had adopted.

Jan. 15, 1867

It has been five months, now, that Langston Cane has been with us. The Negro lad has little joy in his heart, but he is quiet and industrious and excels at school. I have entered him in a good Negro school at the corner of Calvert and Saratoga. It is run by the Baltimore Association for the Moral and Educational Improvement of the Colored People. I have arranged to have one of our servants take the lad in a buggy to the school. He is also picked up after school. This provokes a good deal of teasing from his peers, but I think it wise, considering the fate of his brothers, whom I have been unable to locate. I suspect they were taken out of the state.

I have informed the lad that I will never replace his father, and that he must eventually take his place among the colored people. I am but his keeper, providing security and shelter. Even in matters spiritual, I have preferred not to introduce him to the Quaker faith, but to escort him weekly to a Baptist church, where he can be among his people.

I do not own this child. I am merely steering him, until he can take the helm.

March 11, 1875

Within a year or two, the Cane lad will be ready to assert his independence. He will attend college, and then university if inclined, and then he will return to his people.

He is respectful to me, and well loved by my daughters, who pamper him. He likes to eat, I can say that for him. I have seen the boy eat six scrambled eggs at a sitting. But he is sixteen and growing strong, and I thank God I am fortunate enough to give him a home.

I have been tutoring him privately in Latin and Greek. The boy can recite extensive sections of *The Iliad* by memory. He is more mentally agile than any lad I have met. I am soon to arrange French tutoring for him. If he is to walk with distinction among his people, he will need much learning.

Langston leads Sunday school classes for children at his church, and consistently earns the number one academic ranking at his school. I couldn't ask for more of him. He is a good boy. He will serve his people well. And he will serve God well.

June 15, 1879

Today, I attended Cane's graduation ceremony at Storer College. It was a special day, especially given that Langston spoke as the class valedictorian. People filled the four-hundred-seat auditorium and the aisles. Most had come to hear a speech by the famous Frederick Douglass. In the weeks prior to the event, posters advertising the address by Douglass were posted widely, even in Baltimore.

I have kept a brochure outlining the day's program. And I was reading it, in the company of the young Cane, where he was quietly composing himself, when Frederick Douglass himself entered our dressing room. I stood and introduced ourselves.

"Pleasure to meet both of you," Douglass said. "I have people to meet before I speak, so you will forgive me for rushing to the point, but I must ask the question that first came to my mind when I saw your name on the program."

Langston looked up at the man. "Please do," he said.

"You won't hold an indiscretion against me?" Douglass said.

"Men of your attainment are readily forgiven indiscretion," Langston said.

"You flatter me. And you clearly know to dance with the English language, which is a fine thing indeed. Alas, here comes my indiscretion. Your name rings a bell. Langston Cane. Were you born in Canada, son?"

"I was."

"Did your daddy join up with John Brown?"

"Before she died, my mother mentioned that possibility to me. But I don't know if it's true. I was just a year old at the time of the raid."

"Well, young Cane, if you had any doubts before, you may dash them now. I knew your daddy. He was traveling with John Brown just two months before the raid. We spent the night together in Chambersburg, Pennsylvania. Brown and I had a lot of talking to do. Your father had a fine sense of humor. Some might have called him flippant, although I found him refreshing. True, he was not entirely serious. He had a huge appetite. He was a good man. I'm sorry he died, son. I'm very sorry about that."

"You believe he participated in the raid?"

"I met him, son. He was on his way with Brown to their secret farm in Maryland, just a few miles north of here."

"I have read a detailed book about Harpers Ferry, but I did not see my father's name mentioned."

"You have to realize that the event was bathed in chaos. It electrified the nation. People panicked. The specter of mass insurrection was raised. Not every name was recorded. Many people were killed, many more than recorded. I mean no disrespect, but some bodies were thrown in unmarked graves."

"After his arrest, wouldn't John Brown have named my father?"

"John Brown was not a man to betray his followers."

"Are you sure, Mr. Douglass, that my father died?"

"Many men died in that raid, son. Many more than were written up in the papers. White men and black men. If you never heard from your daddy again, it's safe to assume that he died in the raid."

Young Cane said thank you, and lowered his head. I stood, and put my hand on Langston's shoulder, and explained that this was a most trying moment for the lad, given that he had a valedictorian speech to deliver.

"Buck up, son," Douglass said. "You'll be fine. You'll do well. Look me up one day." Douglass walked to the door and turned. "Whatever you do, son — don't you go on up to Canada, now. We need you right here in the United States."

Douglass chuckled and left the room. He spoke to the assembly soon after. I have captured the essence of his remarks.

There have been critics of John Brown, and they have been vociferous. They have proclaimed him a lunatic, an ideologue, a madman, and a military idiot. They have underlined the lives lost in the raid, and the lack of tangible results.

Twenty years ago, millions of your brothers and sisters still toiled in the sun, shackled and dehumanized, their freedom stolen, their spirits crushed. Let me remind you that their sweat and their blood produced a huge portion of the agricultural output of this land. They were whipped and mutilated so that white people could smoke pipes and wear cotton clothing and eat bread. Today, twenty years later, you — their children — have completed an education at this fine college. If you think that John Brown's work was of no tangible benefit, think again, my friends. Cast your minds back over the last twenty years.

John Brown, a madman? Mad, no. Obsessed, yes. But how could one not be obsessed, to overthrow a system that ruled with whip and chain? Obsessed, yes. A zealot, yes. And I say three cheers for that. John Brown's zeal in the cause of my race was far greater than mine — it was the burning sun to my taper light. My friends, much has been made of my accomplishments in life. But my accomplishments, next to John Brown's, have proven meager in the extreme. I could live for the slave, but he could die for them.

During a pause in the graduation ceremonies, I visited young Cane again in his dressing room, where he was attending to his suit. I saw him combing his hair, and I noticed his hand trembling. This surprised me, for although he was no match for Douglass, Cane was a skilled and confident orator. But he would not meet my eyes. I lifted his chin.

"Mr. Shoemaker," Cane said, "a man has just been to see me. He has just slipped away."

"What man? Who is he? Has he done you wrong?"

"He asked me if I was Langston Cane, son of Matilda and Langston, born in Oakville, Canada, in 1858, in a home on Church Street. No person in this world, save yourself, knows both the name of my mother and the place and date of my birth. He said he is my father. He asked if I could recognize him. I said I did not, for my father had left home when I was an infant. He was a dark-skinned man, darker even than I. He looked old, and weak. Silver hair. His voice had no power, although he spoke with eloquence. He was most evidently literate. He asked if I could forgive him, and told me not to judge him, for there were things I could never know. He gave me a document. This one, here. He said he wrote it. He said it would explain some things. He said that I should preserve it, and share it with those who might want to preserve his record of things past. He said he was profoundly satisfied to see that I had done well. That it lifted an awful weight from his soul. He said he had seen posters advertising that Frederick Douglass would be speaking, and had read, as well, that I would be valedictorian. He said he was sure that I was the same Langston Cane that had issued from him."

"What else did he say?"

"He asked of my mother. He asked of my brothers. He wept, for a moment, when I told him of their fate."

"What was his appearance?"

"Shabby. Old clothes. Of poor means, although he had a pocket watch."

"This is an elaborate hoax," I told the young Cane. "People will go to amazing lengths to pull the wool over your eyes. Did he ask for money?"

"No. He gave me these ten gold coins, and he said he wished he could give me more, but that he had little more to give, and that I was plainly on the road to success in life. He said he would listen to my delivery, from the audience, but that afterward, he would be gone. I should not see him again, he said, for he had no right to be a lodestone around my neck. He put his hand on my shoulder, and he left. He had difficulty straightening his left leg. He had a limp."

"Shall I find him? Shall I have him detained? He is an impostor. How outrageous to disturb your peace at this critical moment!"

"Let him go. He was a strange man, but he meant me no harm. He had love in his voice. I shall find my peace. Give me a moment, Mr. Shoemaker. I shall speak, and I shall not disappoint you. I should never have come this far, had it not been for your assistance."

I left the room. Cane recovered in time to deliver his speech. He spoke of the need for friendship between people of all races, and illustrated his point by describing the relationship between John Brown and Frederick Douglass. He spoke of the need to rise above racial hatred, and of the need for colored people to take their full place in America. Cane received a rousing ovation. He and I didn't speak again of the stranger. He will do well to forget the intrusion. One must not allow fools and impostors to derail one's mission in life.

Chapter 21

ANNETTE FOUND ME IN THE CAFÉ, amid teacups, a dessert plate, the remaining crumbs of a hamburger, and papers scattered over the table. She touched my arm and sat down. She smiled, which was generous, since she'd had nothing to do on this trip but watch me work and help me out at Storer College. She started to speak, and it must have been apparent that I wasn't listening. I was watching her mouth, reddened with lipstick. I was imagining her mouth against mine. Could I love this woman? What about Ellen? No. It was time to forget Ellen.

"Earth to Langston Cane, Version Five. Earth to Cane, Version Five."

"Sorry, Annette."

"That fellow at the Harpers Ferry museum called. He has something for you. But the museum closes in fifteen minutes. Want to run over there?"

"Yeah. Let's go. How'd you get down here?"

"Took a taxi, so as not to lose time."

I stood and kissed her.

The Harpers Ferry museum archivist was named Alan Perry. He told Annette and me that it was generally accepted that John Brown had twenty-one men with him on his 1859 raid. However, there was some academic debate about whether Brown may have had a few more men. At least one of his raiders had stayed in Harpers Ferry in rented premises. Others might have stayed elsewhere. Still others may have stayed at the farm Brown rented outside town, only to back out at the last minute. Therefore, Perry said, it was hard to be categorical about how many people took part in John Brown's raid. Possibly, the raiders had included Langston Cane, of Canada. Because there was no independent verification of his claim, scholars have tended to leave him out.

What claim? I asked.

Perry said that several years ago, museum authorities had come across a brief, handwritten memoir. In it, the author — Langston Cane — claimed to have taken part in the raid — to a degree. Harpers Ferry hero this man was not. Perry handed me a photocopy of the memoir.

I asked how it had come to the museum. He gave me a copy of a letter to the West Virginia Historical Society, from the Reverend Langston Cane — my great-grandfather — of the Bethel A.M.E. Church in Baltimore, dated 1919.

> Dear Sirs,
>
> As I am getting on in life, I am passing along a document that I received in Harpers Ferry in 1879, from a man who claimed to be my father and who claimed to have the same name as myself.

This man somehow knew that I had been born twenty-one years earlier in Oakville, Ontario, Canada. He even knew the name of the street where I had lived, and the name of my mother. He claimed to be the man who had deserted his family in 1858 — the year of my birth.

My mother, deceased some fifty-three years ago, told me that my father, Langston Cane senior, had left our home to take part in John Brown's raid on Harpers Ferry.

I have no idea whether the man who came to see me was indeed my father, or had done the things he claimed to have done in this report. I read his narrative and found parts of it blasphemous and immoral. I had no desire to share it with my family or to investigate further. Nonetheless, I must state that elements of his alleged flight from slavery and of his life in Oakville — most particularly the business of rat-catching — coincide with stories passed on to me by my mother. Some of these stories I have passed on to my own children.

On the day that he approached me, I was about to deliver my valedictory speech at Storer College, and I was too absorbed by my prospects in life to give his story serious consideration. These days, however, I am nearing the end of a lifetime of work, and I tend to believe his claims. But I don't know for sure. At any rate, all my life, I have kept the matter from my own family, and have simply said that my father was rumored to have died a hero's death at Harpers Ferry.

Not wishing to play God with history, however, I am forwarding the document. I leave questions of its veracity to your judgment.

Yours sincerely,
Reverend Langston Cane
Bethel A.M.E. Church, Druid Hill Avenue, Baltimore

The museum was about to close, Alan Perry told me gently.

"Have you read much about John Brown's raid?" I asked.

"Ten or so books and some scholarly articles."

"Have you ever seen Langston Cane's name mentioned in the context of the raid?"

"Other than in the document I've just given you, no. But that doesn't mean he wasn't there. Just remember — amateur genealogists always like to discover royal blood in the family line. They're never happy about royal screw-ups. This document does not necessarily reflect positively on the narrator, who, if he is to be believed, was your great-great-grandfather. Don't take it personally. You're not responsible for what someone wrote and did 140 years ago."

I thanked Alan Perry. As we went out, Annette told me to give her a lift to the hotel. "I know you want to pore over that stuff, so go ahead. But I don't feel like keeping a bed warm for you. If you're too tied up to spend this evening with me, camp out in Yoyo's room tonight."

"All right," I told her. I dropped her off. And I went straight to another quiet, decently lit, not-too-crowded restaurant, holding a memoir written by my great-great-grandfather in 1877.

Three days later my mind was still teeming with the unforgettable people and events of Langston Cane the First's remarkable story.

Chapter 22

I WAS BORN IN VIRGINIA IN 1828. I will not say that I was born a slave, for I do not care for the word. I was born free, but a tobacco plantation owner named Jenkins stole my freedom. My mother and I and others in our situation worked for him, and for Thompson, his overseer. Thompson was an ignorant mass of a man, quick with his foot to your backside, and just as quick with the whip.

My father was sold south when I was a baby. My mother was sold to a plantation ten miles away when I was five. It took two men to drag her away. From time to time, in the summer, at night, when the moon was full and the sky clear, my mother would come to where I lay on the floor and wake me up. She always said she had been walking half the night and couldn't stay long. She would cry, and hold me, and cry some more. I would stay still, or tell her to stop weeping. It causes me great shame to say that, on the third visit, I told my mother I hated her. She came twice more. But then she didn't come again. Months later, someone told me she had been sold south. I said I didn't care.

I worked in the fields by the age of six. I had been kicked a few times, but whipped only once. The whipping consisted of one light lash, and I was warned it was only a trifle. I took the warning to heart, because that one light lash lit my back on fire.

When I was eight or nine, I was leading a horse to the master's house when I heard the master ask the overseer if there wasn't a boy on the plantation who could be trained to catch rats. They were overrunning his barn and getting into his grain bins and leaving droppings all over the place. The next morning I walked up to the master, swinging two brown rats by the tail.

"Massa, wha' I do wid dese?" I knew how to speak better than that, but that's how I spoke around the master.

"You kill them, boy?"

"Sho' nuff. Put out corn biscuit, massa, an' I jes' wait an' wait an' wait until they come out one after de ubber."

"How'd you catch 'em?"

"Plugged 'em wid stones, Massa."

I became the master's official rat catcher. It didn't quite elevate me to the status of house nigger, but I got to hang around the barn and snoop in the house. The master didn't have that many rats in his house. But I planted five or ten dead ones there, to underline the value of my services. I caught them by sitting long hours in the night, hidden from the bait, with good pitching stones at the ready. I'd sit for hours and hours and hours in the master's house, and soon people stopped asking me what I was doing. They knew I was sitting for rats. I learned to read, that way. One of the master's sons showed me letters and words, that year, and I picked them up quick enough. I didn't get to sit all the time. When the master or the overseer, who often dropped in to talk, saw that I was idle, they made me run chores in the house. They made me bring them drinks in the evening from the kitchen. The master liked coffee in the evening. The overseer had developed a taste for hot cocoa. He liked it brought to him steaming hot. And then he would let it sit and sit and sit until it cooled. He would down it fast in long, continuous gulps. He knocked me on the head with a broom, once, when I didn't serve it to him sweet enough.

I learned to steal from the kitchen, which made me popular with the three old women I lived with. The four of us slept on the dirt floor of a one-room shack. Their men were all sold off or dead, and my mother was gone, so they took care of me and kept me out of trouble.

One evening, as I was sitting on a stump outside the shack, I heard a commotion about the master's house. Hilda, the most beautiful woman I had ever seen, ran from the big house. The master chased after her. "I won't, I won't, I won't," she shouted. She ran our way. She didn't live with us. She stayed in a well-roofed cabin with windows and a porch. The master had put her there. But she was running toward our shacks. Got right close to us before the master grabbed her by the arm and threw her down.

"Never," she cried out.

He reached down to hit her.

I was being taken care of, that year, by a woman named Bessie. She had wide hips, and sagging breasts, and bags under her eyes, and she seemed ancient to me, but I doubt, now, that she was over thirty. Bessie mumbled: "That Jenkins no different from any master I seen. He just grunt and heave once or twice, and it's over an' done with. Then he order you out his fancy home and don't even want to look at you till the rutting mood strikes again. That young gal is carrying on like this some big surprise. She knew what was good for her, she'd just play dead and let him git it over with."

"Git what over with?" I asked.

"You'll know soon enough."

Hilda worked in the master's house. She was an African queen. She didn't walk — she floated. Her long, muscled legs were as smooth as river rocks. Her back was long and slender, and her breasts lifted straight out and up, and this I knew, for I had spied on her washing. Most of the boys I knew had spied on her washing. Men, too, spied on her. She wouldn't let any of them near her, for she was sweet on a boy down the road. I had admired Hilda's face many times. I don't believe there is such a thing as God, for I have seen too much to believe that He would condone the things Man has done to Man. But if I were looking for a reason to try to prove his existence, I would point to Hilda's face. Her cheekbones stood sculpted like ripe plums. Her lips were full and quick to smile. She had a laugh that ran across the air, a high, pelting burst of life that made you stand up in the fields. I used to love to watch her wipe the sweat off her forehead and flick the beads off her hand as she walked through the yard. She had shaved her head, she said, so that no man could take her by the hair. Her round scalp shone in the sun, and although it's hard to think of a bald head as attractive, I stared at it endlessly when her kerchief was off.

"What they gonna do to her?" I asked Bessie.

The overseer, Thompson, had joined the master. They tied her hands to a pole, and they made her kneel. They ripped the dress off her back. I remember her brown breasts bobbing as she cried out.

"Git inside," Bessie said.

"I won't," I said, and I didn't.

It was a cowhide whip, long and tapered, and as it snapped, it cut through her flesh like a knife on a peach. The red juice ran out of her, and it ran profusely. I stood, feet nailed to the ground, mouth open. As they whipped, the men grunted. *Huh. Huh.*

Huh. Huh. I burned with shame for not stopping them. The adults who watched without lifting a hand disgusted me. Hilda gave out a wail not unlike the sound of cats in the night.

Jenkins grew tired of whipping, so he passed the whip to Thompson, who hit her on and on and on. Her wail grew weaker, until it was almost inaudible. But something still came out of her mouth each time she was struck.

"That's fifty, Marster," Wild Bill cried out from among us. He was a grizzled old man who was still alive only because he didn't have the good sense to give up and die.

"Shut up, or you'll be next," Thompson shouted after him. Wild Bill walked away. Disappeared behind the cabins. The whipping resumed.

On the master and overseer went, dripping sweat and passing the whip. I wanted them to finish with her.

"Don't let nobody ever do that to you," Bessie told me. "Go crazy, act mad. Fight every step of the way. They may kill you right off. But if they don't, they'll leave you alone soon enough and find someone easier to whip."

Wild Bill let out a shout. He hobbled down from the master's porch with a shotgun. Every grown Negro in the yard ran back. Way back. Wild Bill was so old he was half out of his mind. He was liable to shoot one of us by mistake. He took five steps toward the overseer, whose turn it was at the whip. He took another five steps. The overseer stopped.

"Put it down, you old coon," Jenkins said.

The overseer said, "He don't know how to use that thing. Just shoot him down. Take out your pistol and shoot him down."

"Arms up," Wild Bill said. His hair was white. His legs were wobbly. He looked insane, dressed only in his underwear. Skin hung off his knees.

"I said, shoot him down," Thompson told Jenkins.

Wild Bill said, "Put down that whip. You messed up that girl bad enough. You oughta be ashamed. Hang your head in the face of God. All this, because that girl wouldn't warm your bed. Ain't you men got wives? What's wrong with — "

Jenkins reached for his pistol. Wild Bill blasted the gun at Thompson.

"He shot me. Damn it, he shot me in the arm." The overseer staggered forward. He fell down. "Somebody call the doctor. I been shot, I tell you, shot."

"Jesus H. Christ, you shot him," Jenkins said. Wild Bill swung his gun at the master. But Jenkins shot first, and shot him dead.

Thompson, the overseer, was led into the house.

We carried Hilda back into a shack. She didn't come out for three weeks. I couldn't look her in the eye again.

The overseer survived. He stopped me, one time, as I brought in his hot cocoa. "What you looking at, boy?"

"Nuthin', sah."

"Good. Then beat it. Ain't no rats in this house tonight."

I beat it. But I did avenge Hilda. It took a few months, but I avenged her. A man came by the house one time, when I happened to be scouting for rats, or pretending to. He sold the mistress some poison — strychnine, he called it — which he said was good for rat killing. The mistress gave it to the cook, who put it in the kitchen, where I found it when I needed it. It took me a lot of experimenting to get it right. I made sure nobody knew what I was up to. In the barn, I mixed some strychnine with rat bait. The rats wouldn't touch it. I mixed in some sugar. That worked. A rat ate the bait, tried to run off, but tipped over before it got out of sight. I set my sights on the biggest pig in the barn, and, one day, I ran to the master and announced that his prize sow had up and died.

I kept serving that overseer hot cocoa. The man started to like me. Called me the smartest nigger on the plantation. Said not to get too smart, or someone would bring me down a peg. He took over the plantation when the master and his mistress had to leave for a week. He took his cocoa as usual, in a huge mug, steaming hot, which he let cool and then drank fast. I served him regular, four nights in a row. On the fifth evening, I hit him with twice the sow's dose. He downed that cocoa and stood up and fell like a tree. I cleaned up his mug and put away the cocoa and told the world that I found him like that when I came into the house. Everyone thought his heart had given out on him. I'm sure it did. Bessie was the only one who knew what I done. I didn't tell her, and didn't admit a thing, but she knew. "You fixed 'im, didn't you?" she whispered one night, while I lay next to her on the pallet on the floor.

I was sold a few years later. A man from Maryland came through, looking, he said, for a boy young enough not to give him trouble, but smart enough to learn about horses. I was presented as one who knew horses, and all barn animals, and was an expert rat catcher. I was stripped, prodded, judged acceptable, and purchased.

Adam Smart ran a livery business in Petersville, in western Maryland. He had scarcely brought me onto his property before announcing that he'd sell me as far south as south could go, if he caught me learning to read or cavorting with free niggers, of which, he said, there were a damn sight too many in northern Maryland. He also said he'd whip my back and butt till the blood ran out of them if he caught me stealing, or fornicating, or drinking whiskey. I thanked him, in my mind, for tipping me off about the good things in life, and made a vow to taste them all.

The man had an Adam's apple that snaked up and down his throat. His blond, dry hair flapped on his head in the wind. He was as thin as a rake, although his hands were ham-sized and powerful. I once saw him grab a stray dog in his garden, hold its leg in a vice grip with one hand, and punch the animal in the muzzle. He also punched horses, and table tops, and me, a few times, until I remembered Bessie's words never to let anyone whip me, and I held him off with a garden hoe. He left me alone after that. But he worked me hard, and all he gave me was a peck of cornmeal and a pound of bacon each week. Since I was the only Negro he had, it was hard to steal from him and get away with it.

I killed rats for him. Sometimes, he rented me out to local farmers, and I killed their rats, too. I became adept at baiting, trapping, and poisoning. I even got myself a ferret. I preferred the jill — the female — because it handled more easily, was smaller and could therefore chase rats from smaller places, and was no less vicious than the male. In Maryland, and in Oakville after I escaped, and in later years roaming around the United States after the Harpers Ferry business, I mostly killed the brown rat. I don't know why it is called brown. It's actually gray. It has a blunt nose, small, furry ears, and a short, thick tail, and leaves droppings with pointed ends.

In Maryland, I also became handy with horses. I learned all the routes around town. I learned which way was north. Passing through Petersville and talking quick to Negroes — free and captive — I learned that to the north, in a land called Canaan, all men were free.

Adam Smart had no wife and no children. I was his only captive. When I was about sixteen, Ruth, a free Negro and a cook, came to live with us. Her husband was a slave who had been sold to Arundel County. She rarely got to see him. The last time she traveled down there to be near him, someone had almost dragged her into slavery. Ruth escaped, and got work not long after that cooking and cleaning and gardening and organizing for Adam Smart.

Ruth and I shared a shack on Adam Smart's property. She managed to steal a handful of candles, on a visit into town. That woman's hands were quicker than greased lightning. She removed a Bible from the master's home, knowing it to be a second copy, and knowing he wouldn't miss it. And at night, on an old mattress that Adam Smart didn't want any more, with a candle lit in the dark, Ruth began to help me read better. Ruth had a long scar down her right cheek, which, she said, had happened in town years ago when a white man with a broken bottle cut her for no reason. In the near dark, I learned to love Ruth's voice, which was firm and gentle and melodious among people she trusted. In the near dark, I learned to read. I read the Bible, cover to cover. I read it all, and I must say, I didn't believe a word of it. That didn't matter. I was reading. Ruth began stealing books, whatever books she could get her hands on, from the master's house. She'd steal them and I'd read them and she'd put them back before he noticed. Ruth said she had taught a few Negroes to read over the years, but never before had she found one who ate up words the way I did. She also taught me to write. And she taught me that until the day I was free and gone — and if I were a man at all, she expected me to get free and get gone within five or ten years — I was not to admit to any white man, woman, or child that I knew how to read.

In the near dark, I learned every inflection in Ruth's voice. In the near dark, I learned to read to her. In the complete dark, my hands slipped over Ruth's scar, and all the places where a woman likes touching. She taught me every loving position she knew, and then we invented some others.

We lived like that until I was twenty-two, when Adam Smart was thrown from a horse and struck his head on a shovel and went into a coma and died. I can't say I regretted the man's death. But his brother came onto his estate, and started talking about selling me off. He didn't need Ruth, and he got rid of her. She came to see me at night. She didn't come for the loving. She came to tell me my time had come. We had talked about this many times. We wrote out a carefully worded pass.

> Please allow this nigger, Langston Cane, who is my property,
> to pass unhindered. He takes care of my livery business, and is
> off to purchase new equipment on my behalf.
>
> John Smart
> Petersville, Maryland

I waited until the next day, when I knew that John Smart had an appointment with a lawyer about his brother's estate. Ruth then wrote a fake letter to John Smart.

> Dear Mr. Smart,
> I hope you will excuse me for borrowing your nigger, Langston. Your brother let me take him from time to time, and I will be happy to pay you for his work, as I always paid your brother. I have some things that need delivering, and so

the nigger has also come away with your horse. Will pay, too, for the use of the horse. I should have the horse and the nigger back by dark. If not, please come see me.

Sincerely,

Richard Symons

I have always thought this was a stroke of genius on Ruth's part. Richard Symons farmed pigs sixteen miles south of Petersville. If John Smart wanted to check out the story, he would have to travel opposite to the way I was heading.

I took the best halter and the best horse, and fed her and watered her well. I took half of the money hidden in Adam Smart's home, and gave the other half to Ruth. I was banking on the notion that John Smart didn't know that his brother kept a collection of coins and bills in a leather pouch high on a ledge in the cold cellar. I ate four eggs and half a loaf of bread. I drank two cups of milk. I crammed apples, walnuts, bread, and dried strips of beef into a saddle bag. I also packed a carrying bag and, on a whim, two rat traps. Indeed, since my flight from slavery, I've hardly been anywhere without a rat trap in a pocket or fold of my raiment. In leaving, I took a few of Adam Smart's clothes. I wore some of them as I climbed onto Smart's prize mare. She knew me well, that mare. And I knew her well. I knew how hard I could run her, and I knew how long I could run her, and I knew how much rest she would need before she could get up and go again.

I hugged Ruth, then stood back to look at her face. A single tear welled up and streaked down to her jaw. She kissed me and put her finger on my lips, then turned around and walked into the barn. I swung up on Nell and began riding north.

I rode in broad daylight and at a casual speed, all day long. At the end of the afternoon, I paid to have Nell fed and watered in a small town. I stood by her in the shade, and chewed on a few slices of the dried beef. Bless Ruth's soul. I would never have known you could dry out beef and keep it like that, had it not been for her. I had a cup of water. Only one man in town asked me what I was doing with such a fine horse, and who I belonged to. I hung my head, mumbled that massa had written out a pass for me, showed the paper, and was left alone.

I gave Nell two hours of rest. When the sun sank low in the sky, we rode out of town. We rode slowly at first, and cantered when it grew dark. We proceeded as quickly as I could judge safe, given the roads and the darkness. We had a full moon. I thought of my mother, stealing through the night to see me. I thought of Ruth, straddling me with her head thrown back and breasts heaving. I thought of Hilda, whipped senseless, and of Wild Bill, shot dead after saving her.

I rode Nell through most of the night, stopping to water her when I found streams and to feed her when I spotted hay. I wrote myself a new pass in the moonlight. This one was from a fictional master, who was sending me ahead to run an errand for him. I tied up Nell and slept for an hour in the night, while she rested. On the third day, I stopped in another town. Three men asked me to produce papers. I massa'd them this and massa'd them that, and managed to have papers from a town ten or so miles back. But as I was arranging a feeding for Nell, I saw more people looking at me. And I caught a notice of my name and a description of the horse on a piece of paper on a signpost. We headed slowly out of town and galloped when out of sight. I ran the poor mare hard until I came to a Negro working outside a barn.

"I'd like to sell you this horse. She's tired, but she's fine."

"Don't want no horse."

"I'll give you a good price."

"Is that horse stolen? If I buy a stolen horse, it's still stolen. And when it's found, I'll be the one they start whipping."

"If you give me a meal and a place to hide, you can have the horse."

"I don't want it, sold or given. I don't want you either. You and your horse both look like trouble. Get on out of here."

I rode Nell a mile up the road. I watered her at a stream. I led her deep into the woods and tied her up to a tree. Then I removed a shoulder bag that carried paper and pencils, what little food I had left, my money, a change of clothes and shoes, and my rat traps. I thanked the stars for small miracles. Adam Smart and I had the same size feet, and the man had two good pairs of shoes.

I hated to kill the horse. But I couldn't have her wandering out onto the road without a rider. She'd give me away for sure. I found a branch that was heavy enough to kill, but light enough to swing hard. I smashed her between her eyes with all the muscle I had. Nell crumpled and rolled over. It hurt me to do it. But she died a good deal more quickly than some Negroes I have known.

It was the right season to steal back my freedom. Corn grew in the fields. At night, I would steal a few cobs, and light a fire in the woods, and throw the cobs right into it, and run off to hide as far away as I could, while still keeping an eye on the fire. If nobody came before the fire burned out, I would return to eat the cobs. They'd be cooked enough by then.

One night, I stole a young pig, led it into the woods, killed it right off and sliced off its ears and cooked and ate them and kept on moving.

A Quaker in Pennsylvania hid me for two days, and warned

me that people had been looking for a runaway with a horse. He fed me, gave me a good bed, and drew me a map. He told me that forty miles north, a Quaker man in a white farmhouse with a big red barn would give me shelter.

I got there, and I stayed three days. I was coughing and sick from sleeping in wet grass. I got half my strength back, and made it all the way to the hills of northern New York State when I ran into trouble just south of Canandaigua.

A church minister was passing in a horse and wagon, and he looked kindly, so I asked him for directions. He said he'd take me close to the town of Naples, and then show me the way. But he didn't stop out of town. He took me right into the middle of it. I asked where he was going, and he said, Stay right there. I jumped out and ran. He shouted out at me.

I ran as I've never run before. Up one street, down another, across a yard, over a fence, and inside someone's door. A tall man with blue eyes and a great beard stood there staring at me.

"Good God, my man, what are you doing? If anyone has seen you, you will have destroyed our work."

"You are a . . . you are a . . . ."

"I am a Quaker. And you are a fool. Get down in that crawl space. Hurry."

I hid on the Quaker's property for a week. Much of that time, I was sequestered outside the house, near the barn, in a hidden crawl space the size of a coffin. People thought they had seen me run to that house. It was inspected three times by a local sheriff. The Quaker had no choice but to hide me underground. I coughed terribly. I had dust and dirt in my mouth, my eyes, my ears, my rectum. I was filthy everywhere. After a week, when suspicions had faded, the Quaker took me back into his home. He took care of me for two weeks. He wrote out maps, and directions, and told me that I was not far from the northern border. When I got to the town of Rochester, I was to go to 20 Lake Street after nightfall. This man's brother lived there. He would put me in touch with a ship captain who could take me across Lake Ontario to Canada.

He took hold of my elbow and led me into his schooner. He had red hair, and a strange, feminine, sing-song accent. His first words, which were mumbled at great haste, I couldn't understand. But his step was quick and sure, his back sturdy, his eyes blue as the lake water, and his hands strong. I could see that this man ate well.

The boat was about a hundred feet long. It had white sails hanging from three masts. He led me down into the hold, which smelled of fresh lumber. But there was none in there. There were saws of all sorts, and bags of nails and horseshoes and hammers, and four fine saddles and saddle bags. There was work going on, where this man came from. That much was clear to me.

He introduced himself as Captain Robert Wilson of Oakville, Canada West. He asked me if I had eaten recently. I had not.

"That's a good thing. I'll feed you when we get across the lake. But it's blowing out there, and I bet you haven't been out in rough water before."

I allowed that I hadn't.

"I'd advise you to see to it that nothing more goes into your stomach for the time being. I'm going to have to ask you to stay down here. Out of sight. Have you heard of the Fugitive Slave Act, my lad?"

I wouldn't have admitted it to a man who stole Negroes. But this man was different. He was saving me. He was about to sail me across Lake Ontario. "I know of it," I said.

"Then you have some sense of what they could do to me, for aiding and abetting in your escape. So until it's safe, stay down here in the hold. It won't be but an hour or so. If you absolutely must be sick in my schooner, please have the decency to use that bucket over there. I'm going up. Work to do. We'll set sail soon. You'll be a free man by the time you're eating supper."

I hoped that supper in Canada West tasted better than cornmeal mush, which I never wanted to eat again.

Up above me, I heard scraping, and heavy steps, and the jingle of metal on metal. There were two blankets in the hold. I rolled up one like a pillow, and stretched out on the other, and went to sleep. Quick, heavy, hard footsteps woke me up. I thought the slave catchers had found me. I bolted upright. The door to the hold opened. Light poured in, where before it had only trickled through cracks in the door. Down came another black man. Led by Captain Wilson.

"This is a first for me, gentlemen. Two of you in one trip. We are leaving in minutes. Keep your voices low, and use the bucket if you must."

My fellow traveler had brown, bulging eyes. He had a stutter. He recoiled, as if I, another black man, might actually spit on him. He had no shoes, and an open, running sore on the top of his left foot. He was a year or two my junior. He looked in worse shape than I was. I wondered how he had made it all the way north.

"P-P-P-Paul Williams," he said. "Come from Virginia."

"Langston Cane," I said. "Maryland. Though I was born in Virginia."

He drew his knees up to his chest, and commenced rocking.

"You're going to be all right, friend," I told him. "You're on your way to Canada."

"I'm so tired and sore I could lie down and die," he said.

"Then I'd have to lift you out of here, and I'm too tired for that, so do me a favor and stay alive, brother."

He smiled at me. His three front teeth were missing. It looked like a recent blow, for his gums were bloody. "Got nothing to eat, and nowhere to sleep, so I guess we got nowhere to go but up."

The door to the deck opened again. Down came a black woman. She was no fugitive. She was dressed to work. She was a strong-looking woman. I saw muscles in her neck. I'd never seen muscles in a woman's neck before. Her hands looked strong, too. She had a full bosom, and lean but full hips, and fast brown eyes. She was a few shades lighter than I am. She was a fine-looking woman and she knew it.

"You two are the sorriest-looking pair I've seen in weeks," she said. She had a throaty voice. I felt the faintest stirring in places long forgotten during my weeks of flight.

She told us her name was Matilda Tylor, and that she was a deckhand and the cook. "But I won't be feeding you. The captain says he's sick and tired of runaways throwing up on his schooner." Mattie leaned closer to us. "If he likes you, he'll feed you on the other side!" The cook scampered upstairs.

The trip took most of the day. I went up on the deck after we'd been sailing for an hour. It was cold out on the lake, and windy, and I couldn't see the other side. The water was blue and gray, and I didn't like it. It slapped the hull till I grew sick of the slapping, and then it slapped some more. I went back down in the hull and stretched out. I slept for an hour or two, and woke up feeling in desperate need of air. The lurching about was still bothering me. Up I went to the deck, and stayed there until the harbor was in sight.

"What's Oakville like?" I asked Matilda.

"I call it Nicefolksville," she said. "They'll nice you to death."

"What do you mean?"

"You'll see, brother. You'll see." With those words, Matilda walked over to the mast, her behind round and rolling. She was putting it on display for me. I watched her climb up the mast. Up, up, up, she went. Up to the top. I stood under her and attempted to ascertain, without appearing to do so, the color of her under-garments. I believe I detected the color gray, but then she came down so quickly and with such rapid leg movement that all I could notice was the rustling of her petticoats, which occasionally showed themselves as a leg bent into a right angle at the knee.

"Give it a try, brother. I'm just a woman, right? If I did it, it must be easy."

She didn't leave me much choice. Matilda had just done it and had surely done it a hundred times before and was watch-ing me right now. So I climbed that mast. I climbed thirty rungs. Looking down made me want to be sick, but I didn't want to make a fool of myself. I looked way off, rather than straight down. I looked out at Oakville drawing near. I saw a large creek snaking down to the lakefront. I saw a schooner under construction, another being unloaded, and horses pulling wagons to harbor. I saw vast patches of cleared land, and thick stands of trees. And then I looked down. Big mistake. The mast creaked. It swayed an inch or two, in the wind. My stomach heaved. It heaved, and heaved, and heaved, and all I could do was hold on to the mast like a baby to its mother, and tip my mouth down and to the side and hope that I didn't soil myself or anyone below with all the heaving, and tell myself that the schooner had been sailing for years and that its mast wouldn't likely topple now, at this very moment, with me monkeyed fool-ishly to the highest rung. I held on, since I had no intention of falling off the mast and cracking open my head on the deck below. Shouts rose up to me. "Get down. Get down from there. Are you a fool, man? Get down off my mast." I waited until my stomach ceased heaving, and closed my eyes, and climbed the thirty rungs back down to the deck. I wanted nothing other than a bed to put my head on.

"Matilda," Robert Wilson said. "Clean that up, please. You sent him up that pole in the first place. You know better than that. The man's never been on a boat before." The captain tossed me a rag. "Clean yourself up."

"Sorry about that," I said.

"You were doing fine until you had to keep up with her," Wilson said.

"Does she have a man?" I asked him.

Matilda was heading off to get a pail and some cleaning rags, and I thought she was out of earshot. But she wasn't.

"If you got a question about me," she said, "why, stranger, you can just ask me directly."

"I was just asking if you had a man."

"Not at this moment in time." She turned and walked off, and the captain winked.

Upon landing on the shores of Canada, Paul Williams made a sight of himself. Down on his knees, rolling in the water and sand and debris from the Oakville harbor, calling out, Lord Almighty, Lord Have Mercy, and so forth.

Personally, I was dirty enough, after four weeks of running, and I didn't care to get any of that sand or water on me. And as for the Lord — well, if it made Paul Williams feel better to think there was one, that was fine with me. But I think the Bible is just a scheme to keep Negroes from slitting their masters' throats. I read the Bible. It says, "He that knoweth his master's will, and doeth it not, shall be beaten with many stripes."

Oakville was a prosperous town, full of huge oak trees. They had so many oak trees that they made a business of cutting them down and sawing them up and sending them across the lake.

Paul and I helped Mattie and three deckhands and three men from shore unload the schooner. That took the better part of three hours. I was bone tired. And I was hungry. But I was in Canada, and I was free, so bone tired and hungry didn't matter. When we finished, Captain Robert Wilson asked us to walk with him to his home. I asked if he was a Quaker, and he laughed and said no, a Presbyterian.

It was slow going because of the mud on the roads. Captain Wilson had his trousers tucked smartly into boots that came almost to his knees, and he seemed not to mind leaping over a puddle here and stepping around oozing mud and horseshit there. We walked up a steep hill from the harbor. Navy Street, which we came onto, looked like a fairyland. Houses spaced neatly apart. Stone foundations, painted wood walls. Neat, small windows with many small, square panes of glass. Finely sculpted doors, brass doorknobs. Horse-drawn wagons pulled by steadily, drivers calling out to Captain Wilson, many in that same, sing-song, womanish voice with which he spoke. Where I came from, men didn't put such music into their talking voices. Up here, men and women chattered like birds. Many were out on the roads, dodging the potholes and mud, women hoisting up their skirts when necessary. I saw some black folks, too. Some looked our way, nodded gently, and kept at what they were doing. None of the Negroes seemed to lack employment. They carried buckets, drove horse teams, opened doors to sweep dust into the street.

Captain Robert Wilson lived close to the harbor, in a fine

two-story house that sat on a foundation consisting of slabs of gray-brown stone. Later, I would learn that it was shale, pulled from the bed of Lake Ontario. The walls were painted yellow. I tapped one as we stood at the door. "Pine," the captain told me, "cut down not two miles from where we stand." I noticed, as we were heading in, one or two gaps in the foundation. They were just big enough for a brown rat. The captain asked us to remove our shoes in a mudroom just inside the side door, walked us into what he called a guest room, which had a proper bed, and told us to put our things down, which took all of a moment, since I had but one bag, and Paul Williams had nothing at all.

He indicated that we were to clean ourselves in the washroom, down the hall. Paul whispered questioningly in my ear, "The man want us to wash wid water inside dese walls?" and I nodded. The captain, who must have heard, repeated that it was all right to clean ourselves in the washroom, and that it was meant for that. He said he would put some clean clothes out for us. He said he kept extra clothes around. We weren't to be bashful. The clothes were donated by church people in town. In fact, many of the extra clothes had been donated by colored people. So we weren't to be bashful, because the clothes had been no expense to Captain Wilson. When we were clean and clothed, we were to come out to the kitchen, where we would talk, and break bread. "You talk," Paul whispered, when we were left alone, "and I'll break de bread."

We made a mess of it. I had no experience with bathing inside a house. Also, I could not find the water, at first. There was no bucket on the floor, none in or near the tub, none left outside the bathing room. Finally, I noticed, up above my head, some thick planks holding up some sort of round container, made of brick. I climbed up on a chair and got a look inside — water. How was I supposed to get it down from there? At that moment, the captain knocked on the door. "Don't be shy. This is one of the first houses in Oakville to get rigged up like this," he said. "You must turn on the taps. See those taps attached to pipes at the end of the tub? Turn them. One is for cold water, the other hot. Be careful, though, with the hot. It will burn you. You must mix it with the cold in the bathtub." It seemed like a lot of trouble to me. The notion of just standing under the stars and splashing water onto oneself from a pail seemed far more sympathetic to my senses than all this work of tubs and brick containers and burning water from lead pipes. Also, it was difficult to catch the meager trickle that came from the pipes and to splash it on myself with the vigor necessary for a proper cleaning. Anyway, I did what I could, and mopped up the spilled water with my dirty clothes, and soon enough I was dressed and sitting in Robert Wilson's kitchen. Paul Williams, my friend, had skipped the bathing entirely.

I had imagined that a large, big boned, and confident man would have a wife of the same making. But she was a timid piece of work, with a pointed little chin and pale blue eyes cast downward, and no more hips or chest, it seemed, than a man. "Gentlemen," she said, as we took seats around the table. The captain's wife lifted a cauldron of beef and potato stew from where it hung suspended above a fire, and served it to us in large bowls. It is hard to do justice to the taste of that beef and potato stew. The potatoes were soft and ready to crumble, and the beef came apart readily in my mouth. There were bits of carrot, and onion, and all of it swam in a rich brown juice that I mopped up, following the captain's example, with fat chunks of bread that we tore, as needed, from a large, brown loaf. It was probably ordinary stew, but to me, after three weeks of flight, a lake crossing, a foolhardy climb to the top of a schooner's mast, and a few hours of work unloading the schooner, eating this first meal in freedom was an experience I shall carry to the grave. Now, in the twilight of my years, I remember Robert Wilson for many things, but I remember him most fondly for bringing us into his kitchen and eating with us on that first day of mine in Canada West. I ate three bowls of the stew. Paul ate four. We all had plenty of water, which tasted as fine and as pure as water has ever been.

Captain Wilson told us a few things as we ate. He said he expected us to make our own way as had the Negroes he had helped before us. We were free to spend the night, and to break bread with him in the morning. But after that, we were on our own. There was plenty of work in Oakville, if we wanted to stay here. There was work in the harbor, work in town, and harvesting work on nearby farms. He expected us to find work that same day or the next, and to make living arrangements through our employers or through other Negroes on the street, and he expected us to be upstanding citizens of Canada West from that point forward.

Captain Robert Wilson was up at dawn.

I met him in the mudroom, just inside the side door. Here, he left his muddy shoes and boots, and donned lighter shoes for inside wear.

"I didn't expect to see you up so early," he said to me. "Did you sleep well?"

"Yes, I did."

"Fine. My wife will fix you breakfast. Eggs, bacon, bread, coffee. She'll give you a packed lunch, as well. That ought to be enough to keep two enterprising young men going. If I were you, I'd head to the corner of Colborne and Dundas streets. Be there before eight o'clock. They're looking for men to work on the plank roads."

"Plank roads?" I said.

"Roads, made of planks, to help people driving teams of horses. If you ask me, it's complete nonsense. Plank roads will break down faster than they can make them. But no matter. They're offering work, and you should take it. Some of the men are being put up in tents and the like, north of town. I'd see about getting in on that. You can make some money and not worry about finding a place to live for a few weeks."

"Where does Mattie live?"

"Matilda? She lives with the Smith family. Has a room there. Works for them, when she isn't working for us. A number of the Negro women live with some of the better-off families. Do you have experience as a butler?"

"No."

"That's too bad. There's a Negro chap by the name of Christopher Columbus Lee working as a butler for the Chisholm family. That'd be a darn sight easier on your back than putting down plank roads. But given as how you haven't any —"

"I catch rats," I told him.

Captain Wilson scratched his reddish hair. He grunted, and opened the door. He looked at me with his eyebrows raised. "Can't say that'll get you far."

"I caught two in your schooner yesterday. Wasn't going to say anything. Just threw 'em overboard."

"Fiddlesticks. You were too busy losing the contents of your stomach to be catching any rats."

"I caught three in your house during the night."

"Let me advise you about something. I care about you Negro people. That's why I help you. I tolerate you considerably more than most people you'll run into. So listen to what I'm telling you. You won't get ahead, here, by exaggerating. People in Canada West don't like braggarts. They don't like a lot of talk. They like people who will do what they say they'll do. I won't judge you for talking up a lot of nonsense at six in the morning. I know you've been through a lot. But I'd hold my tongue until I had a sense of this place, if I were you."

I brushed past him, opened the side door, and pointed to the ground just to the right. He poked his head out the door and saw three brown rats laid out flat. I was thankful that they were a decent size. No less than three-quarters of a pound each. "You caught those?" He saw me nod. "Let's bury them quickly, before my wife sees them. You'll send her into a complete panic. How'd you catch them?"

"I pegged one with a stone, and trapped the others. You've never tried trapping rats in this house, have you?"

"No."

"I could tell. Your rats went for traps, this time. But rats are smart. They won't go for that, for long."

"Did you get them all?"

"Not a chance. You've got twenty rats in and around this house, at least."

"Can you get rid of them?"

"I'll make a deal with you. Give me one week to figure out this town, and to find myself a place to stay. During that week, you let me eat and sleep here. I don't need a lot. I won't eat you out of your house. One good meal a day will be enough. In that time, I'll clean out your rats. And then I'll be gone. And Captain Wilson?"

"Yes?"

"Let my friend stay here, too. He'll go work on those plank roads this morning, and he'll pay what you need for room and board. But give him a week to settle in. He needs it even more than I do. He's a little shaky. He spent half the night crying out in his sleep. I'm not complaining. If he hadn't been so beside himself, I wouldn't have been kept awake. And if I hadn't been kept awake, I wouldn't have thought about your rats. And if I hadn't caught those rats, I wouldn't — "

"That's quite enough. You've got your deal. Let's shake on it. What did you say your name was, again?"

"Cane. Langston Cane, the First."

"The First? Meaning?"

"Meaning that there will be a second. After I get to know Mattie better."

He let out a loud cackle. "Aren't you something. I've never met a Negro quite like you. Do you always talk this much?"

"Only when it's necessary."

"I'm off. Good day."

When he was halfway out the door, I said: "Captain Wilson?"

"What now?"

"I'm afraid I'll need money for arsenic. And where can I find a store that sells it?"

"Lumsden's Hardware. Go up Navy to Colborne, turn right, and you'll see it. But I'm not leaving you any money. I don't have time to explain all about shillings and pence and pounds and so forth. Get my wife to explain about British currency. Tell the man at Lumsden's to put it on my account. You're making me late. Good day."

Lumsden's seemed to sell everything. Eggs. Bread. Milk. Meat. Nails. Planks of wood. Paint. The men behind the counter — there were two of them — made me wait until all white people had been served. Then one of them said, "What'll it be, son?"

"Son?" I said, with enough force to turn heads. "Do you actually think I'm your son?"

"Shhh," he said. "Calm down. You'll disturb the customers."

Heads, indeed, were still turning our way. "I'm a customer. As for what it will be, I'd like a small container of arsenic, please."

I heard two people talking near the door. *I haven't seen him before, have you? No, he must be one of Robert Wilson's Negroes.*

"Arsenic? What is a Negro going to do with arsenic?"

"Just put it on Captain Wilson's account, please."

"Robert Wilson? Why didn't you say in the first place that you were in here on his behalf?"

"I'm not. I'm here on my behalf. But it's going on his account."

The man shook his head and handed me a small container of arsenic.

"Do I sign for this, somewhere, so that it goes on his account?" I asked.

"You can write, can you?" He burst into forced laughter. "Well, that takes the cake. A nigger who needs arsenic and knows how to write. Here, then, sign beside this entry." I signed the sheet, said, "Thank you, gentlemen," and left the store.

It took just four days to find a place to stay, and to rid Captain Wilson's home of rats. The captain was wrong about his wife. She was absolutely fascinated by the rat-catching process. True, she said, she would have screamed bloody murder if she'd seen one running wild through her kitchen. But she liked seeing them dead. She said that I was to handle them and dispose of the bodies, thank you very much, but she was most fascinated by my technique. I said I wanted the choicest bits of potato, beef, and fruit.

"We have apples and strawberries," she said.

I told her strawberries would be fine, with the other things. "Rats like good food," I said. "They like fresh food, and they like variety, just like people."

"You're pulling my leg," she said.

But she appeared to enjoy my explanations. She followed me about the house as I set down food here and there. "What about the poison?" she asked.

"Not till later," I answered. "First, you win their confidence. You feed them for two or three days, and get them used to the idea. Then you lace their feast with arsenic." The morning after I set out the laced feast, I found seventeen rats, belly up on the floor. I set them outside the side door, where the captain and his wife could admire them without feeling threatened. And then I plugged the holes in the house foundation. Captain Wilson offered to pay me. I told him that I hoped to render him many services over the years, but that he would never owe me anything.

Mattie helped me find a place to stay. The day after arriving, when I knew the captain was attending to business in town, I found the Smith home, knocked on the front door, and asked the portly white woman with the apron, who opened it, if I could have a word with Mattie.

"Mattie? You wish to see Mattie? Well, yes, certainly, come in, do come in, don't stand out there in the wind, come in and I'll get her." I could hear her calling out loud. "Mattie. You have a visitor. Mattie, you have a visitor, I say. No, I don't know who it is. A Negro. A man. A grown man. A grown Negro man. What did you say? What? Pardon?"

The woman returned to the door. "What did you say your name was?"

"Langston Cane."

"Thank you. Just a minute, again." She disappeared and then returned. "She says she'll be out in a moment. She's taking bread from the oven. Would you care for something? A glass of lemonade?"

"I'm parched," I said, having just learned the word the previous night, reading a volume by Charles Dickens in the Wilson home. "Positively parched. So yes, thank you, I would love a glass of lemonade."

The little woman ran off again. "Oh my God," I heard her shouting at Mattie. "He says he wants lemonade. Where am I to put him? What is this all about? Why are you making him wait like this? If you weren't making him wait, I wouldn't have to be fetching him lemonade. I've a mind to tell Mrs. Smith about this."

The good woman with the apron returned with the glass of lemonade and led me to a padded chair with armrests by a window. I had never before sat in such a chair. I sipped my lemonade. It was delicious. I saw bits of real lemon floating in the glass.

"I'm afraid it might not be terribly cold," the woman said. "Shall I get you some ice for it?"

"Sure. I would love some ice." I handed her back the glass. She took it, turned, marched off, and shouted out "Oh-h-h-h-h" when she was behind closed doors. "Now he wants ice. Get some ice for him, would you? You what? You won't? I am to get that man's ice, too? Are you about finished with that roast? You've been taking your time over it."

"What's your name?" I asked, when she brought back the glass, with ice.

"Wattle. Jane Wattle. I'm the maid here, and the assistant cook."

"The lemonade is delicious."

"Thank you. You're — you're not from around here, are you?"

"How did you know that?"

She leaned toward me. "You're the first Negro person ever knocked on this door."

Mattie joined us in the parlor. Jane Wattle disappeared without a further word. Mattie's eyes were clouded, and dark. "You look a fine sight more comfortable here than at the top of a schooner's mast," she said.

"So do you," I said. "I won't take up your time. I need your advice. About a place to stay."

"You could do what all the other newcomers do and get yourself a job building plank roads or picking fruit and see what your employers offer in the way of rooming."

"I could. Or I could get your recommendation. Somebody who has a room to spare, and wouldn't charge too much."

"I'll think about it."

"I'm at Captain Wilson's place for the rest of the week."

"I heard. He says you're quite something with your mouth."

"I'm good with my hands, too."

She grunted. She smiled. She didn't want to. She even covered her mouth with the back of her hand. But Mattie smiled. And, three days later, she left word that a bed was waiting for me in the home of Samuel Adams, a sexton at the Knox Presbyterian Church. It was a straw mattress, in the same room as Samuel himself. I took it. And I got a job nailing down planks on the nineteen-mile road they were building from Oakville to Stewart's Town.

The town of Oakville was a strange and active place. There were people coming in from Ireland. There were fugitives like me from the country of man-stealers. There were people moving in from other parts of Canada West. And they were all working. They were growing and picking pears and apples. They were growing grain and shipping out of the harbor. They were splitting timber and milling grain. They were building schooners to ship more grain. They were tearing down the trees they hadn't already torn down. And there was mud and dust and horseshit everywhere. On Colborne Road, the main east-west road running through town, you could step along a plank sidewalk by the storefronts. But just about everywhere else, if you were on foot, you had to look out for mud and horseshit. There were taverns and inns for the men building the plank road. There was talk of a railway maybe coming through town. There were more rats than I could possibly kill. There was all sorts of money passing through hands. Pence, shillings, and pounds, but American dollars, as well. There was beer and wine and whiskey, much to the disgust of some in the town. There were farmers, and there were blacksmith shops, and there was a livery business, and when the spring came, there was the subtle but pungent smell of strawberries in the fields. Children picked strawberries for the fun of it. Colored folks picked them for extra money, and for making jams. Farmers packed them morning, afternoon, and evening, and put them up on boxes to be drawn by horse to Toronto and to Hamilton. I didn't mind eating the strawberries, but I never picked them. Colored people had been bending over and picking things off farmers' fields for hundreds of years in the United States, and I sure as hell wasn't going to do it in Canada.

Oakville was a bustling town, and an easy place to make a living.

Matilda and I met again several months after my arrival in Oakville. She was on her way to the harbor, and I was going to see a man about his rat problem.

"Hello, fugitive, been up any mast poles lately?" she asked.

"I'm not a fugitive any longer," I said. "The name's Cane. Langston Cane."

"I know that. People are talking about you."

"How so?"

"That you're strange. That you been here months and have already walked away from all sorts of jobs."

"What people?" I asked.

"Colored people. They say you know a darn sight about rats. That you catch them better than any man in Oakville. What you got against some big black rat running free?"

"Where I come from, colored people don't mind killing rats. Colored people I know worry about their own black butts, and if they are going to swing free. Mine is swinging free right now. And I like having different jobs. Lots of jobs. I don't plan on working for anybody for any long period of time. That's why I like catching rats. I clean out a man's house or his barn, he pays me, and I'm free to go."

"People also say you ain't been seen in a church or in company of a woman."

"You could help me prove them wrong about never being with a woman."

"I'll think about it out on Lake Ontario. I'm heading out on Captain Wilson's schooner for a few days."

I caught malaria in the spring of 1851, not quite a year after arriving in Oakville. People also called it the fever, or ague. It hit the center of my bones, which I thought would explode. I had waves of nausea and a fever much worse than the common sort. I thought I was truly dying.

Mattie came in and looked after me when I got the malaria. She mopped my forehead when it poured with sweat, and put a cold cloth on my face when it was burning up. She forced me to drink broth, and sat by my side and rubbed my neck and told me how she had come to Oakville.

She had been living in Baltimore, as a slave. She'd fled five years before me. She told me I did it all the wrong way, butting my head this way and that, doing it without any planning. She said women weren't as strong as men, so they had to be smarter. She fled in a smarter way. She found out about some Underground Railroad conductors, who gave her safe passage most of the way to Rochester, where she'd been helped by Captain Wilson.

Oakville, Mattie agreed, was a strange and lovely town. Nobody beat up on you, or brought out a whip, or threatened to drag you back to slavery. But colored people were still made to feel like outsiders.

"The only talking that white people here want to do with me is about how wicked American slavery is, and how I must think I've died and gone to paradise, now that I'm in Oakville."

When my strength returned, I borrowed a horse and took Mattie north of town. We made our way into a forest and tore off our clothes. We went at it for quite some time. Later, I found bits of leaves in my hair, between my legs, and between my toes.

"Let's get married," Mattie told me, while we rode back to Oakville.

"Why?"

"It's what people do. We can go at each other in the peace of our own bed, in our own home, without having to do it in hiding from other people."

"I like doing it in hiding. Don't tell me you didn't like it, too."

"You know I did. But that doesn't mean I'd like it that way every day. Brother, I ain't lying down on the snow for you."

"Why marry? I just want to love you up and down, inside and out. Why don't we just enjoy this while we have it? We could be dead tomorrow."

"You're still thinking like a slave," she said. "You ain't gonna be dead tomorrow, and neither am I. We made it out of slavery, Langston. We've come this far, and nobody will crack our heads in Oakville."

We got married a month later in the African Methodist Episcopal Church in Oakville.

In the fall of 1851, I paid for horse and wagon fare to Toronto — a two-day trip — to attend the North American Convention of Negroes. There were about fifty of us Negroes at that convention, from Canada West and from the United States. We did so much talking that my head began to ring. We condemned slavery. We endorsed support for fugitive slaves to Canada. We talked about those tomfool plans that some colored people were making to go back to Africa. We talked about the trouble colored people had eating in taverns, staying in inns, and buying homes in Canada West. Some people talked about temperance and the worship of God and other measures to lift up the race. They nearly ran me out of the conference for arguing that we didn't need any lifting up and that if a man — colored or not — wanted whiskey, it was his own business. Nevertheless, the conference was worth attending. I heard about *The Voice of the Fugitive*, a newspaper from Windsor. After the conference, I started buying it whenever I could find it. I traveled to visit a colored community in Chatham. I didn't care for it. There were too many colored folks, too close together, each one making sure the other was praying enough. And they were all farming. I didn't care for farming. I didn't like the idea of bending down over growing plants and breaking my back to pick them. The whole thing made me think of the Virginia plantation where I was born.

I kept traveling. On weekends, I would go to Toronto, or Hamilton. I won't deny that I was roaming for other women, and that I found one, from time to time, who needed a man to warm her bed.

I had three jobs during Mattie's pregnancy. I helped build a plank road from Oakville to Fergus, hammering nails, sawing wood, carrying loads, and so forth. I got hired by a man hooking stone from the bottom of the lake. Shale was on the lake bed. People used it for house foundations, and for walkways and steps leading up to their homes. So I became a stone hooker, on weekends. At night, I helped homeowners by the lake get rid of rats. My rat-catching shoulder bag consisted of a bag of nails, a hammer, thin mesh wiring, various bits of fresh fruit and cheese, and so forth. And in my pocket, I carried a five-dollar ferret. People tried to pet his white-brown fur. They asked me what I called him. I told them he didn't have a name because he wasn't a pet. "This here," I said, "is a work ferret. He ferrets out rats for a living. That is our only business together. But I keep him well fed."

I became more demanding about the goods I would take as payment for rat-catching. I accepted flour, bread, meat, apples, pears, peaches, salt, sugar, potatoes, rice, greens, lettuce, and even baked pastries. I also took blankets, pots, a table, a winter coat, and boots — but these things I took only if we needed them, and if they fit. Stores in Oakville were starting to refuse to accept bartered goods as payment, however, and I started telling my customers that I couldn't accept them either.

The Voice of the Fugitive said colored people depended too much on others for their livelihood. That gave me the idea to write a little sheet of information and start selling it for a dollar to my rat-troubled customers. Mattie knew how to write, so she made copies for me. In the first part, I set out my reasons for eliminating rats. They spread disease, they were unsightly, they upset women, they contaminated food with their droppings, they chewed holes in your house, and, if cornered, they might bite. In the second part, I set out my own experiences catching rats in Virginia, Maryland, and Ontario. Said I had been catching black and brown rats for years. And, in the last part, I set out the techniques available for nabbing the rats. I talked about effective traps. I talked about setting out poison. I talked about the proper use of ferrets. I talked about smoking them out and pouring water down their holes. One spring, when the rats were particularly bad, I sold fifty information sheets.

In the winter, when it was too cold to hook stone and to lay down plank roads, I drove teams of horses. I drove for families and business people, such as the Chisholm family, and for Robert Wilson. I drove for farmers who wanted to move equipment to and fro and get things done that they couldn't do during growing and harvesting seasons. I worked when I could for a livery stable. In the morning, I would take five red-hot bricks from a fire and put them in a blanket under my feet. And when they started building the railway north of Oakville, I cut up and dropped off loads of wood for the steam engines.

I named our first son Langston Cane Jr. Before I left Oakville eight years later, we had two more boys. They, too, we named Langston. Mattie said, "As long as I get to call the first Senior, the second Junior, and the third Langston, and as long as you stick around to keep this roof over our head, we can call the boys anything you want."

Mattie grew heavier, and much older after the second and third births. Her hands were full, and from me she expected prompt and regular delivery of food and other necessities. "I know you're with other women," she said to me a year before I left. "I know, because of the way you don't look me in the eyes, and because of the way you don't rub up against me in bed any more, and because of the way that you seem to be doing a chore, forcing yourself to get through it, when we are doing it in bed. Don't leave me, Langston. Our boys need you. Colored women and men have been torn apart for as long as they've been on this continent, but it doesn't have to happen to us. Look at me, Langston. Look at me."

We joined the A.M.E. Church. I went, sometimes, to make sure the kids kept still in the pews. I didn't care much for the preacher, or for the others in the congregation. Matter of fact, I didn't care a great deal for black people in Oakville. They tried too hard to be like white people. They worked as long and as hard as they could. They didn't change jobs unless they had to. They didn't move their bodies or let themselves laugh in public or show any signs of wanting sex. They looked trapped, and they made me feel trapped.

In *The Voice of the Fugitive*, I read about colored people being seized in northern states under the Fugitive Slave Act and dragged back down south. I read about Negroes being beaten up and lynched on the eastern shore of Maryland, and about Frederick Douglass talking up a storm against slavery.

In Canada West, there was a lot of talk about the abolition of American slavery. Word went out among colored folks that some white man from the States wanted to round up black folks in Chatham and talk about setting free the stolen people.

His name was John Brown. He was tall and lean and gaunt and gray haired. A beard grew off his face like a violent crop. He walked so fast you had to double your step to keep up, and he talked like a church minister. He talked more like a black man than any white man I had met. He gesticulated with his hands and walked while he talked. He swore us all to secrecy in a one-room secret meeting place in Chatham in May 1858. We met on a Saturday and a Monday. The man didn't want to meet on Sunday, which he said was the Lord's day. We did a lot of talking — more than I cared for — but behind all this talk was a man burning to act.

He spoke with each of us individually. When my turn came, he said: "Are we agreed that slavery is a sin against God?"

"It's a sin against man," I said.

"God comes first. It's a sin against God, first, and man, second. Are you with me on that point?"

"I hear you."

"Good. We can work together. You're a man of intelligence, that is immediately apparent. But do not let that intelligence render you impassive. Will you join me?"

"I will hear out your plan."

"Your decision must rest on what is right. On the ineluctable course of action for a God-fearing man. Do you have a wife and children?"

"I do."

"Good. You are a serious man. Are you prepared to leave them, if need be?"

"I will consider it."

"I have fathered twenty children, many of whom have predeceased me. Each one to do so has taken a piece of me into the grave. But I have no fear of death. I am prepared to die tomorrow for the freedom of the American Negro. You must be, too, if you choose to join me."

I didn't hear many details at the Chatham meeting. Brown said he was going to strike a blow against slavery. He said he would free Negroes from the plantations and lead them in his fighting force. He moved many of the black men in Chatham to tears. They had never seen a white man speak with such passion about hard abolitionist action. My own eyes remained dry. John Brown had never lived on a plantation, and he didn't know colored folks. He assumed it would be easy to get thousands of Negroes to throw down their shackles and take up arms under his direction. Like I say, he didn't know colored folks. They would take one look at him and declare him mad.

Our Chatham meeting ended. John Brown went away. Over the next year, I often wondered what had become of his plan.

A month after meeting John Brown, I took a ferry to Niagara-on-the-Lake, one Saturday, and then paid to ride on a team of horses along a path up river to Niagara Falls. I had heard that a

Frenchman named Blondin would be doing stunts that day, and I wanted to see him. I met a colored woman on the boat, who was going with two friends to see Blondin, too. Her name was Jean. Young woman, straight back, full but slim butt, smooth skin, eyes unwrinkled, earthy laugh. This woman was from Hamilton. On the boat, I bought her tea and crumpets — white folks' snacks, but that's all they served. Her friends let us alone in Niagara Falls after we watched this Blondin fellow carry a man on his back while walking on a tightrope two hundred feet over the Niagara River. I couldn't take my eyes off him, with that man on his back out there. And I couldn't help thinking that people had been trying for centuries to kill black folks, so I sure wouldn't help them along by trying to kill myself on some thin rope over a raging river. Maybe that was the difference between black and white. Colored people had rubbed shoulders with death, and wanted none of it. This Frenchman named Blondin had obviously never been whipped within an inch of death, in his younger days. He felt the need to tempt the very fate that I had run from. I watched his every move out there. I put a dollar in a hat being passed around for his benefit. I made note of the fact that posters said he would be returning next summer for even more amazing stunts. And then I made off with Jean. She told her friends I would escort her back.

We got ourselves a room in an inn. And we went at it in the afternoon, and again after dinner, and again in the morning. We did it with her on all fours. We did it standing up, or with me standing, holding her from the waist down as we rocked. We did it on the bed, with me lying on my back, and Jean pumping up and down in a frenzy. And we did it long and slow and smoothly, in the usual way. We hardly talked. We laughed some, and shouted out, and let ourselves holler in the moments of ecstasy, and, finally, we took a wagon ride back to Niagara-on-the-Lake and the ferry back to Oakville.

Jean shared a home in Hamilton with some other young women. She had no family nearby. I started traveling from Oakville to see her, from time to time.

We had the longest and the wildest nights I have ever known. I did not love that woman, and I can't believe that I ever would, but now, in my final years, I can say that I never had that kind of sex with any other woman in my life. We humped in the morning, we humped in the afternoon, and we humped at night. We humped on weekends, or late or early in the day — whenever I could get away. We shoved aside food to hump in the middle of meals, and we humped at the height of her bleeding.

I made up some lie about living in a rented room in someone's house, and not being able to take her there. This went on too long. It went on until the inevitable happened. I seemed bent on ways that would ruin my life, and I didn't seem to have the power to stop it. I wasn't drinking. I wasn't fighting. I wasn't courting death over the Niagara River. But I seemed to want to destroy the conventions of my life. So we kept on, Jean and I, until she began to talk of marriage. She began to insist upon it. I said I couldn't do that. She shouted, and argued, and I shouted back at first, and then grew silent. Silent because I knew I would leave her soon.

"You seduced me," she said. "You have acted like my husband. You bought me food, helped with my rent, took me out, treated me like a wife. So marry me."

"I'm already married."

"That's a lie."

"I am married and have three children in Oakville. I will help you if I can, but I can't marry you. We are going to have to break this off. Take this. I have to go."

"Ten dollars. What am I to do with ten dollars?"

"I have to go now."

"Go then. Go. *Go.*"

Jean came after me a week later in Oakville. She served notice with the A.M.E. Church that we were married, and that she had learned I was married to someone else, and that she wanted my assets and money to support a child I'd left her with. I knew of no child.

I didn't tell Mattie. I could hardly look at her anymore. I played with my children more than usual. Langston, our third boy, was a year old. He had been walking since nine months. He liked to jump up and run into my arms when I came into our home. *I love you, baby,* I whispered in his ear. *I'm sorry for what's coming. But you'll make it. Look at those thick, fat thighs of yours. Look at your hand speed, the way you catch my nose so well. You'll make it without me, son. You'll have to.*

That same week, as if to save me, John Brown came to Oakville. He had heard of the work of Captain Robert Wilson in ferrying fugitives across the lake, and came seeking financial help and men for his mission. He asked to meet with the captain and with his two most trusted Negro associates. The captain summoned Paul Williams and me. The three of us met with John Brown in Captain Wilson's study.

Brown, who didn't remember me, asked the captain to close the study door. The captain complied, and produced a bottle of whiskey and four small glasses from a shelf behind his desk.

"Before our deliberations, gentlemen, may I entice you with a shot of fine Irish whiskey?"

Paul, a churchgoing teetotaler, shook his head. A shot of

whiskey would have done me just fine, as I liked how it warmed my throat, but rarely spent money on such luxuries.

"Mr. Wilson," Brown said, "would you mind putting the spirits aside until my departure? With no offense to you, or your hospitality. But I've come to speak of life and death. Of slavery and freedom. So I ask that you not trivialize this moment with such libations."

Captain Wilson raised his bushy black eyebrows. Most of his red hair had fallen out since I had met him nine years earlier. "As you wish," he said quietly, placing the bottle to one side. "Since this is my whiskey hour, and since you wish to rush the point, I will ask you to get to it."

John Brown began pacing the study. "Gentlemen, I am motivated first and foremost by the burning need to remove that which is utterly offensive to God."

"Meaning?" Captain Wilson asked.

"The bondage of men. It is a blight upon our great nation."

"Your great nation," Captain Wilson said. "We are on British soil, here."

"Correct," Brown said, "but surely we are not insensitive to the outrages of slavery. Canada West, after all, is only a quarter century removed from slavery."

"Mr. Brown," Captain Wilson said, "I beg you not to patronize me in my own country and in my own home. Your earlier entreaty notwithstanding, I am going to pour myself a shot of whiskey and drink that whiskey as I see fit, as this is my home and this is my whiskey hour and I have worked harder than you might imagine to allow myself that comfort."

"I wouldn't want the success of this meeting to turn on one shot of whiskey, so please, good man, go ahead. This is your home."

Captain Wilson downed one shot in a flash, and poured himself another.

Brown said he had a plan to strike at slavery in the heart of the United States. From men such as Captain Wilson, he would need financing for arms and for provisions for a small army of followers. From men such as Paul and me, he would need the stout hearts of those willing to die for the cause.

Spittle flew from Brown's lips. The study rang with his words. He scared the wits out of my friend, Paul. Captain Wilson asked how many men Brown had at his disposal, and how many arms they possessed, and how, precisely, they intended to topple the institution of slavery. Where would they strike, and how would they withstand the might of American gunpowder? John Brown danced around these questions.

My friend Paul bolted from the room. He'd been moving and itching in his seat since the conversation had begun. John Brown observed him run out, paused to consider the fact for a moment, and tried to continue. But Captain Wilson spoke first.

"I have heard enough. Cane has his own mind, so he will speak for himself. But I say no. Not on your life. I join your condemnation of slavery. But you speak in the absence of specifics. Rhetoric alone will not save you from American firepower. You're living in a fantasy, and you don't even know it. I believe you're mad. You won't have a cent of mine, and if you are finished, I will ask you to leave."

"I am but an instrument of God, and I ask that you do me the justice of focusing on my ideas and my project, rather than your perception of my state of mind. Mad or not, I have amassed support from men of means and from men who are prepared to die for what is right. In the final analysis, good Captain, God will not judge me on the grounds of madness. He will judge me for what I have done. Thank you for hearing me out, Captain. I have heard of your fine work helping fugitives escape to Canada. Carry on. I bear no anger or malice toward you. I wish you and your loved ones well."

"Fine. Let me show you to the door."

John Brown stepped outside. I nodded good night to the captain, and followed Brown into the warm August night. He told me where he would be staying, and indicated that he would be leaving at dawn.

He clasped my hands as we stood on the street. "Kiss your loved ones, and tell them you've chosen to strike a deed for God, and that you'll be back in due time, if He is willing."

Mattie had left me a note on the table. "The constable was here, asking for you. And the town has today served notice of suit. Please wake me. We must talk."

I wrote out a note for my wife. I said she would soon be hearing untrue allegations against me. Regardless, I explained that I was leaving. I was joining a man who had pledged to destroy slavery. I told her his name, and begged her to destroy the note and to keep the news a secret until the fighting had begun. I left her all the money in my possession, save thirty dollars. I kissed her cheek as I climbed into her bed one last time. Her back was to me, but I sensed that her eyes were open. She knew I was leaving. She had probably heard my quill scratching across paper.

I was not made for Oakville. I was not made for marriage. I was not made for church and children and unwavering employment. I was burning a hole in my own soul by leaving this woman and our children — the children she alone would have to feed and clothe and protect. I hated myself on the day that I left them. I hated myself more than Mattie or the children ever could. But I also felt free. Freer than I'd felt since running from Maryland nine years earlier. I felt intoxicatingly free.

I left before my wife and children woke.

We rode by horse and wagon to Buffalo, and rode on from there to Rochester, and from there caught a train to Philadelphia, and from there another train to Chambersburg, a small town in Pennsylvania, close to the Maryland border. All this took two days, and in that time, I didn't get to know Brown at all. He spoke only when he had to. He drove in the silence of the dead. He had no sense of humor. A very odd man he was. When we were short on food, he offered me more than half. In our nightly lodgings, he left me the more promising bed. If we met people, he unfailingly introduced me as his trusted and gifted aide from Canada. If thieves had attacked, he would have laid down his life in my defense. But, alone, pulled by two tired horses, or sitting on train seats, he preferred not to speak. He knew nothing of the pleasures of conversation. I sensed that he knew nothing of any pleasures at all.

In Chambersburg, we waited at length in the train station for someone to pick us up. I was hungry. Brown said he wasn't. I said I was going out to find something to eat.

"No. Wait with me. We are to be met soon. Patience, man. Mr. Douglass is sure to feed us."

"Are you talking about Frederick Douglass?"

"Would you kindly lower your voice?" he hissed. We were alone, save for the ticket master, in the one-room train station. I repeated my question, in a whisper.

"Yes," Brown said. "Do you know of him?"

"What do you take me for? An illiterate? Of course I know of him. Or do you think colored folks don't read the newspapers?"

John Brown turned on his bench and stared at me down the slope of his large, long nose. "I won't dignify that remark with a response," he said.

Frederick Douglass showed up five minutes later. He was a short, thick, scrappy-looking light-skinned man with kinked hair that shot from his head like an exclamation. His voice, however, was pleasant to the ear. He spoke with a familiar ease. He spoke naturally, which was refreshing after forty-eight hours with the Ascetic Personified. Douglass shook my hand and said, "Cane. I like that name. I hope, for your sake, that it's C-A-N-E and not C-A-I-N." He laughed heartily at his own joke. I liked the man.

Douglass had with him a large black man by the name of Shields Green. The four of us traveled in a horse-drawn coach to a house where Douglass and Green were staying.

"If I know Brown, he hasn't let you eat for the better part of a day," Douglass told me, with a clap on the back. "Come join us at the table."

I downed three bowls of soup, six chunks of bread, and four fried eggs. Brown limited himself to one bowl of soup, a piece of bread, and two cups of water.

Brown began talking as soon as the eating was done. He told Green and me that we were about to hear secret information. Then, turning to Douglass, Brown said that he had modified his plans. Instead of merely setting up mountain strongholds, he would attack the United States' arsenal in Harpers Ferry.

Douglass laughed and slapped the table. I sensed that I would rather have been working with him than with Brown. "You must have lost your mind."

Brown launched into explanations. Douglass said Brown

would be walking into a death trap. Harpers Ferry was on a spit of land squeezed in between the Potomac and the Shenandoah rivers, and enclosed by the Blue Ridge Mountains. Once Brown and his men had ventured into town, they would be sitting ducks for army soldiers.

Shields Green and I went to bed, and left the two men talking. In the morning, I awoke to find them drinking coffee and talking more. The four of us ate grits, sausages, and eggs. Brown tapped me on the arm and said, "Don't expect to eat this well at the farm in Maryland."

"What farm?"

"The Kennedy Farm, where we'll be getting ready for the raid."

The time came to go. Brown asked Douglass to join him. "Come with me, Douglass. When I strike, the bees will begin to swarm, and I shall want you to help hive them." I took that as a rare acknowledgment that Brown wouldn't know how to work with colored people.

Douglass turned him down. He said he had to be leaving, and that he'd best leave now. He had tears in his eyes. I wanted to leave with him. I wanted terribly to join him. But I could find no way to abandon Brown's mission honorably, so I held my tongue.

Douglass told Shields Green to make his choice. Green looked at Brown and said, quietly: "I believe I'll go with the old man." So Green joined us on the forty-mile trip south to the Kennedy Farm — a beaten-up two-story building within walking distance of Harpers Ferry. It would hold twenty-two men and a few women for the better part of eight weeks.

I wondered every hour what I was doing there. By the end of our stay, there were more than twenty men confined to the upper level of the dilapidated farmhouse. We couldn't get out during the day, for fear of being noticed by the neighbors. John Brown didn't want us to go out at night, either, but we ignored him. He couldn't hold twenty men in an attic all day and then keep them from blowing off steam at night.

We drilled and had military lectures during the day. We heard from John Brown about great revolts in history. Moses and the Jews. Hannibal in the Alps. The people of Haiti rising up against slavery. Nat Turner's revolt.

We learned how to strip and load our Sharps rifles. We held shooting practice when the neighboring farmers were away in town. We practiced jabbing pikes into trees. We ran on the spot and did stretching to stay limber. We ate upstairs and slept upstairs. "Holy John," as I dubbed him, frowned upon us going outside, and during the day we were allowed out only to use the outhouse. The men complained often. Damp sleeping quarters. Bland food. Boredom. No room to move about. The sense of being imprisoned. The absence of women. The lack of concrete details about John Brown's plans.

One of the first critics at the Kennedy Farm was Brown's son, Oliver. "I have a wife, and we want a family, and I want to know what we're getting into if I am to place my life on the line."

John Brown raised his hand. "Prepare yourself for war against slavery. What else need you know? You are either against human bondage, or you are not. The rest is idle chatter."

"My wife and future are not idle chatter," Oliver said.

"We need women around this place," said John Kagi, Brown's most trusted aide.

"All right," Brown said. He brought in his daughters, Annie and Diana, as well as Oliver's wife, Martha, to do cooking and housekeeping.

I could tell that Diana would bring me trouble if I dared look at her more than once. When I came near, she laughed too loudly, gesticulated too strongly, and spoke too enthusiastically to the other women. She was short and slender and looked deep into my face the first time I cast my eyes her way.

On the other hand, her sister, Annie, was the sorriest-looking woman I have ever laid eyes upon. Slim, of medium height, with long brown hair usually kept in a bun, and of the same calm gray eyes as her father. Sadness sprang from her like a smell. She kept her eyes lowered. I never heard her laugh. Annie was totally devoted to the cause, cooking, cleaning, lifting, sifting, and always on the look-out for strangers approaching the farmhouse.

Martha was a lovely woman, and Oliver was hopelessly in love with her. They held hands whenever John Brown wasn't looking. In the evening, they would escape into the darkness for hours at a time.

They sat with me under the stars one night, shortly after Martha had arrived. John Brown was on one of his many errands to Chambersburg, lining up the transport of rifles and pikes, so we felt free to talk.

"Langston," Martha said, "you're a man of experience. You have escaped bondage, we heard, and lived in Canada. You read and write well. So tell us. Is this an act of complete futility?" Martha held her husband's hand with both of hers.

"John Brown would say that no blow against slavery is futile," I said.

"Yes," Oliver said, "but what would you say?"

"I would say that I'd have to know exactly what your father has up his sleeve before I can judge its futility. You must make your own judgment. But don't throw your life away on a whim."

Oliver kissed his wife. She kissed him back. I cleared my throat and stood. "I think I'll move along now."

They laughed, and stood, and wandered off into the woods. I wiped my eyes. If I had been able to love like that, I would never have left Oakville.

I walked out under the stars. Someone stepped out from behind a tree.

"Langston. It's me, Diana. I'm so miserable. Walk with me."

I was conscious of my heart thumping against my ribs as we took the lane and then walked out onto the road. It was pitch-black except for the burning stars, but I knew my way, having been out here every night for two weeks.

"There's a hole up ahead. Come to the side," I said. She slipped her arm through mine.

"I'm frightened," she said. I stopped and turned to go back. "No, not of the night. I'm frightened of my father. And what he will do to you. To all of you. He has no love. He has no compassion. He'll think only of *justice justice justice* to the end — and that will be to the very end of your lives."

"I'm glad you're so sure of our victory," I said.

She giggled. "I've never held the arm of a black man before," she said. "You feel nice."

I shook my arm loose. "Let's go back."

"No. No. *No.* Walk with me a little, Langston. I've been watching you. You're older than the others. Wiser. You've been around. Have you been with many women?"

I tried to keep myself a full stride away from the woman, but she kept sidling up closer and touching my elbow.

"You've been around Annie and my father too long. They're so . . . austere."

"You're older than Annie."

"Yes, considerably. I'm twenty-six."

"Have you not been married?"

"Yes, I was. But my husband left me. He filed for divorce, and it was granted."

"I see," I said. We were still walking away from the farm. We walked a quarter mile before Diana spoke again.

"Aren't you going to ask me why?"

"No."

"It's because I'm barren. He left me for that. I can't bear children. So now I am to wait out the rest of my life, serving father. I won't do it. I'd rather die here with all of you."

"Why are you telling me all of this? What do you expect me to do? Do you realize what kind of position you're putting me in?"

"What? Because I'm a white woman, and you are a Negro? I wonder how my father, the Negro liberator, would take that, seeing his daughter arm in arm with a Negro man."

"He'd say, at the very least, that we were endangering the success of his project by walking out so far on the road. Shall we turn back?"

"No." She removed her arm and turned to face me. "I want to be loved. I haven't been loved for so long a time, and I live in a loveless house, and I have a loveless father and loveless sisters and I just want a little loving while loving is still possible. Love me, Langston. Love me now. Love me tonight."

"I can't do that," I said. "I'm sorry. Let's go back." I started walking back, so Diana was obliged to follow.

"You won't tell on me? You won't say anything?"

"Of course not."

"Are you married?"

"I was."

"Not any more?"

I said nothing.

"Do you have children?"

I continued walking back.

"You do," she said. "How many?"

"Three."

"It must be so difficult to think that you may never see them again."

"It wasn't so bad until you started talking about it."

"Boys?"

"Yes."

"All of them?"

"Yes."

"I bet you named one of them Langston."

"All of them."

"All of them!" She cried out in the night. She laughed like a fool. I had to put my hand around her mouth to make her be quiet. I felt her hot breath on my hand. I stiffened in an instant. I stepped back and turned away.

"You named all of your boys Langston?" she whispered. "What is it, with men? They all want boys named after them."

We were almost back. I told her I was going in. She grabbed my head and whispered in my ear. I got hard again. I went straight in. She let me go, and followed me inside several minutes later.

The next day, I caught her looking at me in the kitchen, while the men ate. I saw her bite into an apple. I watched her nibble all around the core. She had flashing blue eyes, and more meat on her hips than her sister, Annie. She brushed against me as she gathered the plates from the table, and splashed half a cup of water on my arm. Made it look like an accident. "Sorry," she said, and kept moving. I got hard again.

I didn't meet her the next night. Instead, I set out quickly to explore the area. I wanted to know where the roads led, and if there were paths that followed them, and if there were good hiding spots. If John Brown was going to play with my life, I wanted a few escape routes. For three nights, I walked for many hours, and as quickly as I could. I walked all the way to the Baltimore and Ohio Railroad bridge across the river from Harpers Ferry, and then wound back up through the hills of Maryland, looking at all times for places to hide and places to walk.

The following night, I headed north from the Kennedy Farm. Two miles north, under the light of the moon, I saw a barn several hundred paces off the road. I went to inspect it, and found that it had been abandoned. It was nothing but a shell. It did not look solid. There was no trace of recent activity.

I took Diana to the barn a week after she first approached me. She nibbled all along my face. She put her hands in warm places. She cried out, when we joined, and I smothered her mouth with mine. We joined and rejoined for half the night. And for a number of nights to follow. We stocked the place with provisions. Bits of food stolen from the kitchen. A blanket that nobody was using. Candles, and matches. Diana Brown loved her mouth, and loved to use it, for talking and loving. It was the most expressive, curious, exploring, and laughing mouth that I had ever encountered, and I wanted to survive John Brown's raid, if only to enjoy that mouth one more time.

It was two miles to the barn, and two miles back, and Diana whispered at me the whole time we walked. The only time she didn't whisper was when she was gasping with me in the barn. Tell me about this rat business, she would say. Tell me about Canada. Tell me about the women you've known. Tell me about your mother. Tell me about escaping from slavery. Tell me how you met my father. We rode each other like animals in the dark. And the more we made love, the less I felt prepared to die.

In the first days of October, we nearly had a rebellion at the Kennedy Farm. It started with a fistfight between Albert Hastings and Aaron Stevens. But it escalated into complaints about what we were doing there, and how they didn't like being pawns, and how John Brown had better spell out his plan or he was going to be losing some men right away.

John Brown sat down among us and began with a prayer. We don't want no more prayers, Captain, Dangerfield Newby told him. We want answers. Brown finished the prayer and raised his head and unveiled, finally, his plans.

The men were shocked. Raiding Harpers Ferry? Attacking the federal armory and arsenal? And then what? How would the raiders escape, after that attack?

Brown said that when we stormed the town, slave owners would be too cowardly to fight back. Slaves would flock to Harpers Ferry, and the raiders would supply them with pikes, and the swollen band would move through Harpers Ferry and into the hills of Virginia, where guerrilla bases would be established for further attacks. The raid on Harpers Ferry would attract such attention that more slaves would abandon their owners and join the raiders. The event would catalyze revolts throughout the South. The institution would be crushed.

"What are we going to eat?" I asked.

"Cane, you are too flippant for my liking," Brown said. "Have you not a serious bone in your body?"

"Eating isn't serious?" I said. The men all laughed, except Brown, who stroked his beard and stared at me. "You're going to be heading over the Shenandoah and into the hills of Virginia. You're going to have us, and a flock of runaway slaves, you say. So I say, what are we going to eat in those hills? Where are we going to sleep?"

Brown accused me of ridiculing a serious plan. He said provisions would be brought along in a wagon by his son Owen, once the raiders had established control of Harpers Ferry and the bridges leading in and out of town.

We talked for several hours. Several men said that Brown had misled them. He had led them to believe that they'd be freeing slaves — not storming a U.S. weapons manufacturing site. Brown countered that he hadn't been able to unveil his plans until they'd been perfected. And that he hadn't wanted to run the risk of information leaking out and destroying the entire project.

"We'll all die in there," Dangerfield Newby said. "You're sending us in there to die."

"We must not think of ourselves," Brown said. "We must think of the slaves. Who will speak for them, if we don't?"

"I don't mind dying if my death is a decent blow against slavery," Shields Green said. "I don't mind dying at all, as long as I get to take some of dem slave owners down with me. Maybe we will finish the job, or maybe we won't. But we can start it. And if we don't start it, who will? I say, let's take down Harpers Ferry and shout it to the whole world."

Brown offered his resignation, but who else had all the information? Who else had contacts with military suppliers and financiers? Who else had spent ten years establishing a network of support for this big moment? The men agreed uneasily to Brown's plan.

That night, Diana and I stocked the barn with bread, cheese, apples, and dried strips of meat. We also left extra clothes there, and blankets. John Brown was about to send the women away. Diana let me know that she had no intention of returning to her father's home. Not for now. We agreed that on the day of our attack on Harpers Ferry, Diana would split from the other women and hide in the barn with a horse and carriage. She would wait for twenty-four hours to see if I returned.

It was raining and cloudy on the night of October 16. We set out at eight in the evening, the men heading south and the women heading north. Martha Brown had to be torn from the arms of her husband, Oliver. She wailed, but he remained silent. His arms dropped. He started to cry. "I love you, Martha. I'll love you forever." She wailed again. Annie and Diana pulled her away.

Brown rode on a horse-drawn wagon, and eighteen of us men walked with him in silence. We walked for two and a half hours in the drizzle. There was no moon. Our rifles were hidden under capes. Owen Brown and two others remained behind with the supplies. They were to move into Harpers Ferry after we'd taken control.

The plan unfolded masterfully during the first hours. There were moments when I doubted my criticism of Brown. There were moments when I thought, This man *is* a genius. He's going to pull it off. He's going to bring down Harpers Ferry and get the hell out of here and people will be so impressed that they *will* flock to him. Crossing over the Potomac on the Baltimore and Ohio Railway bridge, we took a night watchman prisoner without a struggle. Exiting the bridge, we found the armory to our right, and the arsenal to our left. First, we took control of the armory with barely a struggle. We took the night guard prisoner, too. Brown directed Hastings and me to take control of the arsenal. That proved easy enough — there was nobody guarding it. A few twists with the crowbar broke the lock, and we were safely inside the weapons storage area. Brown dispatched other men to take control of the rifle works, which was a few minutes away on the Shenandoah River, and another two men to take control of the Shenandoah bridge, which we were supposed to cross later in our flight south into the hills of Virginia. A final group of men headed off into Jefferson County to take some plantation owners prisoner, and to free their slaves and bring them along for support.

After guarding the arsenal without incident for an hour, Hastings and I were replaced and sent to guard the Harpers Ferry end of the Baltimore and Ohio bridge. We stood there for an hour. Nothing happened. What was John Brown up to? Why was he spending so much time in the armory? A man approached us from the darkness.

"Halt," Hastings said. "You are our prisoner — "

The man turned and started running back. Hastings fired at him. The man fell forward, face down, arms splayed. Hastings reloaded. "I'll cover you," he said. "Go on out there and disarm him and finish him off if you need to."

I walked out toward the man. He was only thirty yards away. Drawing near, I heard him rasping and moaning. "Oh Jesus. Oh Lord. What have they done to me?"

"Throw me your gun, or I'll have to shoot you," I said.

"I don't have a gun. And you already shot me."

I walked to within arm's reach of the man. He was black. We had just shot a black man. I took the final step and kneeled by his face.

"You," he said to me. "You shot me? You, a colored man?"

"I didn't shoot you. Another man did."

"Why?"

"We're here to free the slaves."

"There's no slaves in town, damn it. The slaves are in the country. I'm no slave. I'm a free man. Why'd you shoot me?"

"I didn't shoot you."

"One of your men shot me in the back."

I drew a flask from my pocket. I wasn't expecting to need it so soon in the night. "What's your name?"

"Hayward Shepherd."

"What were you doing out here?"

"Just looking around. I'm the baggage man at the station."

"Have a sip of whiskey."

"First you shoot me, then you offer me a drink. Oh, man, I'm shot bad. Tell your friends that plugging a colored man in the back ain't no way to free slaves."

"Have a sip. Here." I tilted the flask toward the man's lips. Some got in his mouth. Some dribbled down his chin and onto the dirt.

"Shoot a colored man in the back. What kind of thing is that to do? I'll be hanging mad if I don't live to see my children. My boy and my girl were just sitting on my knee after dinner."

Somebody in the street shot at me and missed. I ran back to the cover of the bridge.

"Hastings, you shot that man in the back."

"He didn't obey my command."

"You shot him in the back, Hastings. He was going back."

"Got him good, did I?"

"You shot a black man, Hastings. A free Negro. His name is —"

"Don't tell me his name. I don't want to know. I'm sorry, he didn't obey, and I had to shoot."

I made Hastings lower his rifle, and I shouted out to a man on the street — probably the one who'd tried to kill me — that we were giving him two minutes to go fetch Hayward Shepherd and drag him to safety. The man walked out to help Shepherd back to the station platform.

"Let me plug the other one," Hastings said.

"Hold your fire, you fool. He's dragging a wounded man to safety."

"All right, all right. I'll let him go this time."

Why I didn't put down my Sharps rifle and walk back across the Potomac River bridge and leave at that moment, I don't know. I had no more fight in me. I suppose I never had any in the first place. Hayward Shepherd, colored man, father of two kids, was dying. We had shot him. One person was dead, or close to it, and that was enough for me. But I stayed. I don't know why. But I stayed. And things soon got bad enough that leaving was no longer a simple matter.

John Brown looked confused. He ordered us back to the arsenal, and then came to see us twenty minutes later, asking who'd given us the order to leave the bridge. We explained that it was him, and he nodded and headed off. He walked with an aide or two along the Shenandoah, presumably to check on his positions at the Shenandoah bridge and at the rifle works. He walked back to the armory. He walked back to see us, and then to see the men at the mouth of the Potomac bridge, and then back to the armory.

An eastbound train pulled into the station. Some of our men had it halted, and there was a great deal of discussion between Brown and the conductor. I didn't see what there was to discuss. Brown should have stopped the train, and ensured that everyone stayed inside it, and that was that. But no, Holy John had to discuss. He had to make his purpose known to the conductor. I could hear it all from my position in the arsenal. We weren't occupied at all, except for once, when a man from the town approached, presumably thinking he'd arm himself, and Hastings took a shot at him. The man turned and ran and Hastings said, "Cane, I have yet to see you use that Sharps." We went back to watching John Brown haggle with the conductor. It went on for hours. Our leader had brought us into a bloody rat trap, and here he was talking with a train conductor. To my astonishment, Brown let the train go at dawn. That was when I resolved to get out as soon as I could. But getting out was no easy matter.

I had to wait a long, long day. No food. No warmth. Nothing but the pungent odor of gunpowder in the air. Not long after Brown let the train go, church bells started ringing. They rang and rang and rang. People swarmed around the town. One man walked to within thirty yards of the armory and started shooting at it. Someone shot back at him, and he fell flat on his face. A group of militiamen arrived from the west, chasing Dangerfield Newby, Oliver Brown, and William Thompson — the three who had been ordered to guard the Shenandoah bridge. Brown and Thompson made it to the armory, although I don't know how, with musket fire all around their heads. Newby, who just the day before had been reading me a letter from his wife — a letter he'd had for months, and reread every day — fell on the cobblestones just a stone's throw from safety. At first I thought he had tripped. But he hadn't. Blood gushed from his throat. Hastings fired at the militiamen, downing one of them. The others ran back for cover.

"If you don't get in on this," Hastings warned, "I'm gonna report you to the chief, and we're gonna have to court-martial you."

I knew we were losing as the day wore on. Still no food, no contact any longer with John Brown or his men in the armory. It was freezing. I had been shivering all night. I thought of Diana waiting for me in that barn. Good-bye, Diana, I thought. I won't see you again. Good-bye, Captain Robert Wilson, and good for you for having that whiskey over John Brown's objections. Whiskey. Good idea. I had a sip from the flask, shared it with Hastings, who clapped me on the back and admitted that I was at least good for something and said, "Isn't this fun? Isn't this just the best thing you've ever done?"

While Hastings stood watch, I looked around the arsenal. Rifles and pistols and boxes of ammunition were stacked everywhere. At the back of the arsenal, I used a crowbar to break into an iron cage and smashed the lock of a cash box. I saw more bills in there than I've ever seen in my life. I grabbed a few hundred dollars and slapped the box shut and stuffed the money in my pocket and kept moving. Hastings didn't have to know about it. If I made it out of Harpers Ferry, that money could make the difference between life and death. I also found a window at the back of the arsenal. From the window, I could see the Shenandoah River. As I looked out at the river, I saw a body floating by. It belonged to John Kagi. He had been stationed at the rifle works. So it, too, had been overtaken.

I figured that I had a chance if John Brown could hang on to the armory until nightfall. People wandered near and took potshots at the armory. They seemed to have forgotten about Hastings and me in the arsenal. The mayor of the town — I knew, because I heard the people shouting — wandered into the thick of things and got himself shot dead.

Brown was totally hemmed in. He had lost control of the Shenandoah bridge, and he had lost control of the Potomac bridge, and I didn't have a clue what he was doing in that armory.

"Where do you think you'll sleep tonight?" I asked Hastings.

"Haven't a clue," he said. "I wish I was in that armory. There's more action going on over there."

"Don't shoot from here again unless you have to," I told him.
"Why?"

"Because everybody is focusing on Brown in the armory. We don't want to remind them that we're here."

"You got a point there. You're not so dumb, Cane."

A mob rushed into the Wager Hotel, which was between the Potomac bridge and the armory, and dragged one of our men into the street. It was Oliver Brown. He was dragged to the Potomac bridge, shot twice in the head, and thrown in the river.

The day went on, sometimes with sporadic shooting, occasionally with someone being felled in the street, but mostly with men shooting in the air and swilling beer and throwing their bottles up and shooting at them. Militiamen spilled into town. Townspeople milled about, shouted, laughed, swore about colored people, and grabbed women. A carnival had erupted in Harpers Ferry. Colonel Robert E. Lee of the United States army entered the town via the Potomac bridge. I didn't know his name until later. But I saw all the soldiers with him, and I saw the hundreds of townsfolk and militiamen flock to greet him, and darkness was falling, and I knew that this was my one and only moment.

I didn't say good-bye to Hastings. I didn't offer to help him. He didn't need my help. He was happy where he was. I moved to the back of the arsenal and removed my cape and Sharps rifle. I pulled on an old jacket lying in the cage near the cash box and took another fifty dollars. Thousands were there for the taking, but I felt I should limit my theft. I climbed out the back window and around the side of the arsenal. I walked, calmly, across the street. Nobody paid any special attention to me.

There were people drinking and shouting. One slapped me on the back and said, "Hey, boy, better get home."

I nodded and kept going. I walked up a street, took a lane to the right and followed it to the end. I ran past a house and down a long slope to the Potomac River. That took me ten minutes, crashing around in the bush. Luckily, a full moon shone. Down at the river, I walked upstream five minutes and found a boathouse and a rowboat. Nobody around. I rowed across the river — it was only fifty yards or so — and gained the Maryland side. Up the hills I went, through the trees, heading north and east to the best of my judgment. After an hour, I sighted the road that we'd come in on the night before.

I heard voices on it, so I stayed back, and followed it from well within the woods. I fell three times on my way. I hadn't slept, or eaten, for thirty-six hours. It was still dark when I got to the barn. I opened the door, and saw the candle flickering, and dropped to the floor. A figure emerged from behind a beam.

"Diana?" I whispered.

"Langston. I was so frightened! I was going to leave at dawn."

"Hold me," I said. She started putting kisses all over my face. "No, not that. Just hold me. I'm freezing."

"Come under these blankets," she said. She had a number of them, so one went under us, and several on top. She undressed me, and undressed herself, and pressed up close against me, and reached for food, which was there on the floor, and fed me cheese and apples and bread. We stayed like that for an hour. I told her what I knew. I said her father was doomed. I said we had to leave. We dressed. Diana got the horses ready. She said she'd kept them well fed all day and all night, so that they'd be in form for a long trip. She said her sister and sister-in-law had put up a fuss when she'd said she was staying behind. Finally, she had run out and taken her horses and buggy and left while they were packing in the kitchen. She assumed they must have left without her. They didn't know where she was. She asked me if her father was likely to die. I said he was.

We headed north. We agreed that if anyone stopped us, I was to be her slave, she my mistress, and I was driving her to her father's funeral. I got behind the reins, and we took off.

We put as much distance as possible between ourselves and Harpers Ferry. We rode through the last of the night and into the morning. We came to a town. I got out at the outskirts and hid. Diana proceeded into town, identified herself as a Quaker to the first sympathetic-looking person she found, and asked where she could find someone of her faith. She found a Quaker, explained that she was assisting a fugitive slave, and asked for help. They returned to get me. The Quaker gentlemen fed and sheltered our horses and us for the rest of the day and the night. The next day, Diana and I headed out in the horse and buggy, maintaining the pretense of Lady and Slave. We made it to York, sold the horses, and caught a train to Philadelphia, where we stayed together, in the most trying circumstances, for several months.

Diana was shaken by the fate of her father and of Oliver and Owen. News of their deaths came to us — as it did to the entire nation — very quickly. I made enough money to support the two of us doing construction work and catching rats.

When Diana left me to return to her family, I drifted out to California, and spent many years there before drifting back east, and it seems to me now that I've been drifting all my life, and that drifting is all that is left to me. I'm an old man now, old beyond my years. I have escaped death more than a few times. Yet with each escape, years have fallen off my life. I wish my wife and sons well, wherever they are. I stopped by Toronto, about a year ago, and paid a young man to travel to Oakville and to make some inquiries. I don't know what I would have done if he had found Mattie or my boys there, but they were gone. Long gone. Gone back to the States, apparently, at the close of the Civil War. I walked about Toronto for a day, remembering the time I'd come to attend a black abolitionists' convention. It seemed, then, that I loved my wife and children, but didn't know it. Didn't know it, or was afraid of it. Their claim on me felt suffocating. Nothing could have changed my mind, or made me think far ahead to a time in life when no one would want to have a claim on me. I was strong, when I was young, but I feared human ties. Now that I have none and no hope of any, I am but a shell of the man I once was. There's no point regretting what I've done. I had to live the way I was born. That ends my account.

Chapter 23

I DON'T BELIEVE ANNETTE SAID A WORD to me on the trip from Harpers Ferry back to Baltimore. Yoyo scribbled notes on a pad of paper. Mill stared out the car window. Annette slept. She had barely spoken to me since the afternoon before, when she said she wouldn't bother sleeping with me if I was going to be up late poring over the story of Langston Cane of Harpers Ferry fame. In Baltimore, I dropped off Yoyo, and then Mill, and was planning to join Annette inside her flat. But she told me not to bother parking the car.

"Just let me out," she said. "I want to be alone."

"What's wrong, Annette?"

"You don't know?" She turned in the seat to stare at me. She had on red lipstick again, and was wearing a red leather jacket.

"No, I don't, actually, unless it's because I was up late reading."

"I am not your tagalong toy. I do not exist for your amusement, when you're too tired to work."

"Who suggested that?" I said. "I invited you to come along. I was happy to have you. Why are we having this fight?"

"You didn't show me I was in any way special. You made me

feel like a tramp. Condescending to let me hang out with you, when you had nothing better to do. You shouldn't have invited me to Harpers Ferry, and I shouldn't have accepted."

"You knew I was going there to work."

"*Work*. Give it a break. You're investigating your family's history. Don't get me wrong. I think that's great. But it doesn't preclude making a woman feel good."

"Let's go out tonight. I'll make it up to you."

"No. That's my point. You can't just make it up by being available when you're too tired to work."

"I'll come see you soon, then."

"Don't bother. I'll come see you — if I have nothing better to do."

During the next two weeks, I dropped by Annette's apartment three times. I left notes. Got no response. I finally spoke about it with Mill.

"She's making you wait. A woman's way is a woman's way, Langston."

"I'm not so sure. She was mad after Harpers Ferry. And she hasn't responded since."

"I'll tell her to come over, and you can come over at the same time, and I'll stand you each in a corner of my living room and say, 'Okay, you two, kiss and make up.'"

"Thanks, Mill, but I'll take care of this problem. I've made an effort. Three times. I won't grovel. I groveled enough, after Ellen left me. Annette knows I want to see her. If she wants to see me, she'll come back."

"You're a young man, Langston. Wait a little longer."

"Pushing forty is young?"

"It's young enough, if you know where you're going."

I finished the first full draft of my family story. I spent two weeks cleaning it up, organizing it, paring it back, and digging through Mill's boxes, and visiting the Maryland Historical Society. I offered to show the draft to Mill.

She said, "Newspapers are the only reading I have time for." She did seem willing, however, to talk about what had happened to Langston Cane the First. "He stayed alive. You gotta give that to him. He shouldn't have messed with that white girl, but he stayed alive and he didn't kill nobody at Harpers Ferry."

I told Mill that I felt strangely connected to Langston the First. "I love the fact that he didn't fit in. I love him for his mixture of weakness and dignity."

"Don't make a hero out of him," Mill said. "He lived in hard times, but he was a regular man. But you're right about him not fitting in. If you ask me, the man had a loose chromosome that skipped a few generations and turned up in you."

She had a point.

I went out a few times with Yoyo. We hit some bars, visited jazz clubs, walked in parks. Fall was descending. It was mid-October, the season of John Brown's raid. Baltimore wasn't the place for me to stay. It was a great town — if you didn't get mugged or shot — but it wasn't mine. When I finished this book, I would try to sell it. And I would carry on with my life in a place where I was likely to stay. Where I was likely to meet someone. It was time for me to love somebody. It was the first time I could think of such a thing, without thinking of Ellen. And it was time for me to be a father. There was no denying that I had been a royal screw-up for most of my life. But my kids, if I was lucky enough to have them, wouldn't care about that. They would just care about being loved.

The *Toronto Times* published Yoyo's story about Harpers Ferry. His angle was that new evidence had been uncovered to the effect that John Brown had traveled to Oakville in the summer of 1859 to recruit troops and seek financial aid for his October 1859 raid, and that it now appeared clear for the first time that Brown had an extra man in his unit — a fugitive slave named Langston Cane, who had lived nine years in Oakville. The article generated a phenomenal amount of interest. Letters poured in to the newspaper. Historians and journalists contacted Yoyo and me. A publisher even expressed interest in looking at my novel. One evening, while I spoke about it with Yoyo, he produced a letter from Hélène.

"She says that if I come, I can stay with her. No promises, she says. But I would have a place to stay. Did you hear that, Langston? She wants me!"

"She said no promises, just a place to stay," I reminded him.

"What else is she going to say? Wait till I get there, and the night is cold, and her shoulders need rubbing. Wait till we've talked for seven days straight. Langston, I had that woman once, and I lost her. I won't lose her this time. Take me to Canada, Langston. When it's time for you to go, take me with you."

"How am I going to get you over the border?" I said. "They won't let you in if you say you're a visitor. You need a visa, if you're coming to Canada as a Cameroonian. And you're illegal here. If you try to cross the border, you could get arrested and deported."

"You worry too much, my friend. They don't stop every person they meet at the border, do they? We'll figure out a way. Take me. Take me with you, I say."

Yoyo was earning eight hundred dollars a week for cleaning houses, plus four hundred dollars for his weekly missives to the *Toronto Times*. He had been going like that for the better part of two months. He said he needed to save as much as he could before moving to Toronto. I showed him the manuscript. He read it the next day. "You have to get this published, my friend," he said. "You should have been sending it out in pieces for publication in magazines and newspapers. You have to learn to start making money, my friend. You need a little more of the African entrepreneur in you. Wake up, Langston. You have friends, right? You have contacts. You have all those people who called in response to my stuff in the *Times* about John Brown. I say, wake up, my friend, and make some money, and write another one. It's easy, writing, isn't it? Cleaning houses, that is hard work. Selling kebabs on the roadside and getting arrested and having to jump from police station windows — that is hard work. Writing is a snap. You can do it. I say, publish this one and write another."

A week later, I received a letter from Annette.

> Dear Langston,
>   Here you are running around all over Baltimore and Harpers Ferry trying to find out who you are and who your family is, and you don't even see love when it falls into your own bed.
>   I loved you from the minute I saw you. You seemed

unlike any man I'd ever known. Quiet, humble, but doing real things. And you stood up in a wonderful way for that boy on Pennsylvania Avenue. You didn't seem all full of yourself, like so many men I meet. And I have to say that you had a pair of lips on you that seemed just made for kissing.

I didn't want an elaborate and silly dating game. I have needs, just like you. Men and woman aren't that different. You must know how much I enjoyed making love with you. So, I figured, let's get all the sex out of the way, let's just do it from the start and enjoy it, and see if we can get beyond it to anything interesting, rather than the other way around, pretending something interesting is going on when you're just beating a path toward someone's bed.

But you really hurt me by ignoring me on that trip. I thought of that trip as a test. I thought, this man has things to do there, but if he really likes me, he'll make room for me. And you didn't. You hurt me, Langston. Good-bye.

I did the right thing this time. I wrote to Annette immediately. Told her I was sorry about Harpers Ferry, but hadn't attached the importance to it that she had. Perhaps that wasn't right, I said, but it didn't mean I wasn't interested in her. I told Annette that I had done pretty well everything I needed to do in Baltimore, except work things out with her. I asked to see her again, and mailed the letter special delivery.

I gave my landlady notice that I would be leaving in a month, told Yoyo that I had decided to help him get to Canada, and drove straight to Mill's house. When I said I had decided to leave Baltimore, Mill stared at me wordlessly. The pouches under her eyes seemed darker than usual. But when I went on to say that I wanted her to come with me to Canada, and that I would see to it that she was well taken care of, a light came on in Mill's face.

"Are you talking about driving? No airplanes at all, but a long car trip?"

"That's right. It'll be crowded in the car."

"Come over here, son." I walked to her chair. "Help me up." I gave her my hand. When she was standing, she let out a holler and shook her knees and arms, shook them as madly as one of her church cronies struck by a love bolt from Jesus, and said: "Langston, oh Langston, this is a homecoming that I have wanted for a long, long time." And she crushed me in a bear hug.

A few days later, Mill asked me to help her look through her personal boxes.

"Haven't I been looking through your boxes for the last several months?" I asked.

"No, you were looking through family history boxes. But I've got my own boxes. In another room. And I'm trying to find something."

"What is it?" I asked.

"Just start going through these boxes," she said.

She had me bring four boxes down from the attic. She said she was going to have to throw that junk out soon anyway. I picked through the first box — family photos, two pairs of old shoes, old railway tickets, a 1978 season's pass to the Baltimore Orioles, and so forth. Nothing doing. Same sort of junk in the second and third boxes. The fourth box was full of slips of paper.

"That's the box," she said. "Go through the papers slowly."

"What are you looking for, Mill?"

"My citizenship papers."

"American citizenship papers?" I asked.

"No. Canadian."

"You're a Canadian citizen?"

"I got some papers. I know I got them, somewhere. From when I was living in Oakville, back in the twenties. Dad got us all Canadian citizenship papers back then. He said they might come in useful one day."

I found them near the bottom of the box.

"Go get a pen and some paper." When I returned, she said, "Now start writing:"

> Dear brother,
>
> I'm coming to Oakville. I want to die there. Not that I plan on dying any time soon. But it's where you are, and it's where your boy Langston is soon going back to, and it's where Aberdeen Williams is. It's even close to where your other son Sean is, who, from what I hear, is going straightforward ahead in the lawyering business. I figure that if he's a lawyer, he's got as much mouth on him as your Langston does. Oakville is where my family is, so I'm coming up. Your son Langston has offered to drive me up to Oakville. I'll call you when we're leaving so you can get a room ready for me. You know I ain't getting on no airplane. I won't be flying but once in life, and that's when I'm going to meet my maker.

Mill had me seal the note and take it to the post office right away. She came along. But after I'd posted it, she made me stand at a counter and take down another dictation.

"Dear Aberdeen," I wrote for her. "Don't die on me yet, 'cause I'm coming up. To stay. See you soon. Love, Mill." That one went out by special delivery.

Mill asked Yoyo to clean her entire house. She wanted it so clean that a stranger coming in the front door and walking around would find it attractive. Yoyo replied that she would have to consent to let him throw out most of the junk in the house, and then paint it, and then clean every single room. They negotiated for two days about the price, but Yoyo wouldn't budge. He said it would take him ten hours a day for at least a week. Mill finally agreed to his demands: three hundred dollars to clear out the junk, four hundred dollars to paint the inside walls and the outside trim, and another four hundred dollars to clean the house to a state of perfection. It ended up taking Yoyo ten full days of work, but he didn't complain. Mill paid him in cash and threw in a hundred dollar tip.

Mill threw a party, and invited her church friends, Yoyo, my landlady, and me. When the party day came, I discovered a For Sale sign outside her house. Under that, I saw that it said Sold.

Mill announced that I was taking her to Oakville. Yoyo said I was taking him, too. I admitted that I hadn't yet figured out how to get him across the border. Annette stepped out from behind a door. "I'll help you figure that out."

Mill and Yoyo had to mail a few boxes of their possessions to Canada. There wasn't room for her luggage, and Yoyo, and Annette, and me, all in the Jetta. The only thing Yoyo insisted on taking in the car was his computer. Annette only packed a small suitcase — she didn't know how long she'd be staying. This would be a trial visit.

Mill got behind the steering wheel with fifty miles to go to the Canadian border at Niagara Falls. She said our family had been moving back and forth across the border for five generations and that she would know how to handle this crossing. We should all just hush up and leave the talking to her. The official at the Canadian border asked us what our nationalities were.

"Canadian," Mill said.

"Where do you live?"

"Oakville," Mill said.

"Where are you coming from?"

"Baltimore."

"How long you been there?"

"Just a week. We had a church reunion. We were at the African Methodist Episcopal Church, mister, and we had one thousand souls in the arms of Jesus."

The officer raised his eyebrows. "Are you are all related?"

"In the back there," she said, indicating Annette and Yoyo, "are my children. And this here is my nephew."

"This one is your nephew?" The officer studied me. "What is your name?" he asked her.

"Millicent Cane."

"And what is your name, sir?" he asked me.

"Langston Cane."

"May I see some identification?"

"You really got to see all that?" Mill said. "Okay, folks, get your ID out."

"Not everybody," the officer said. "Just yours, ma'am, and your nephew's."

I tendered my passport. Mill showed her seventy-year-old certificate of Canadian citizenship.

"I haven't seen one of these old certificates in years," the officer said.

"That's 'cause I was born a long, long time ago," Mill said. "But I'm a long way from dead."

The man laughed. "Have a safe trip home, folks."

Acknowledgments

MY FAMILY HISTORY inspired much of this novel. I couldn't have written it without help from my mother and father, Donna and Daniel Hill. When I began to research this novel, my father gave me more than twenty interviews — which I taped — about his and his ancestors' lives. Throughout the writing, my parents, my aunts Doris Cochran and Jeanne Flateau, and other relatives provided information about the black American side of our family.

I hasten to emphasize that this novel is a novel. Family stories have been altered or exaggerated, and almost all of this book is invented.

Many people, organizations, and books helped nudge this long project forward, and I am pleased to acknowledge and thank them.

The Canada Council and the Ontario Arts Council provided financial assistance.

Francine Landry and Terry Smith introduced me to the history of Oakville, and turned over the keys to their cottage in Haliburton, where I finished the book. Alvin Duncan spent many hours with me, giving interviews about the history of his family and of other blacks in Oakville. The Ontario Black History Society paid for a transcription of Mr. Duncan's interviews, and provided much support and encouragement.

Members of the Oakville Historical Society led me on a walking tour of historic Oakville, answered questions about the town's history, and opened up their library to me.

I consulted various books and documents about the history of Oakville, the most important being *Oakville and the Sixteen* by Hazel Mathews and *Oakville: A Small Town* by Frances Robin Ahern. At the Oakville Museum, I learned that Captain Robert Wilson had helped American fugitive slaves by hiding them in his schooner and sailing with them across Lake Ontario to Oakville.

Employees at the Maryland Historical Society suggested books and articles about the history of Baltimore and Maryland. Most helpful were *Slavery and Freedom on the Middle Ground: Maryland During the Nineteenth Century* by Barbara Jeanne Fields; *Black Marylanders, 1864–1868*, an unpublished University of Chicago doctoral thesis by Richard Paul Fuke; *The Baltimore Book: New Views of Local History*, edited by Elizabeth Fee, Linda Shopes, and Linda Zeidman; and *Baltimore: The Nineteenth Century Black Capital* by Leroy Graham.

As for John Brown's raid on Harper's Ferry, Virginia (now Harpers Ferry, West Virginia), I relied on the following books: *To Purge This Land With Blood* by Stephen B. Oates; *John Brown's Raid* by the Office of Publications, National Park Service, U.S. Department of the Interior; *John Brown of Harper's Ferry* by John Anthony Scott and Robert Alan Scott; *John Brown* by W. E. Burghardt Du Bois; and, most important of all, *A Voice From Harper's Ferry* by Osborne P. Anderson, a Pennsylvania-born black Canadian who took part in the raid and managed to escape.

I also wish to acknowledge *The Black Discovery of America* by Michael Bradley for its lively and detailed thesis. I sought information about the Underground Railroad from my father, from his book *The Freedom Seekers: Blacks in Early Canada*, and from Benjamin Drew's 1865 classic *The Narratives of Fugitive Slaves in Canada*. Details about rats were drawn from *The Rat: A World Menace* by A. Moore Hogarth.

Maged Soleman volunteered his time to organize the genealogical chart and to provide initial ideas and designs for the book cover.

Denys Giguère, Dan Hill, Karen Hill, Irène Léger, Bert Simpson, and Oakland Ross made detailed comments on early drafts. Mary Lynn O'Shea and Ruth Idler offered valuable advice, and Stephen Dixon and Paul Quarrington helped in many ways throughout this writing project.

I wish to thank my editor, Iris Tupholme, whose striking insights and suggestions made the final editing process pleasurable and exciting.

A Word About History

JOHN BROWN AND FREDERICK DOUGLASS, who played major roles in the American anti-slavery movement, are minor characters in this book. Their actual words appear in this novel in four places:

- when Douglass says, "John Brown's zeal in the cause of my race was far greater than mine — it was the burning sun to my taper light";
- when Douglass says, "I could live for the slave but he [Brown] could die for them";
- when Brown urges Douglass to join the raid and says, "When I strike, the bees will begin to swarm, and I shall want you to help hive them";
- and when Brown says, "I, John Brown, am now quite certain that the crimes of this guilty land will never be purged away, but with blood."

Also, Shields Green — one of the Harpers Ferry raiders — uttered this line when asked to join Brown's raid: "I believe I'll go with the old man." These words, too, have been revived in the novel.

I have attempted to provide a generally faithful rendering of

Brown and Douglass, and of their involvement in the 1859 raid on Harpers Ferry. However, I have taken many fictional liberties. Brown brought just one daughter (Annie) to the Kennedy Farm in Maryland to help prepare for the raid; this novel has him bringing Annie and a fictional daughter, Diana. In search of men for his raid, Brown did travel in 1858 to Chatham, Ontario, but to my knowledge he never made it to Oakville.

Hayward Shepherd, a free black man and an innocent bystander, was the first person to die in the raid. Words attributed to Shepherd in this novel are fictional. I don't know which raider actually killed Shepherd, so the task fell to the fictional Albert Hastings. To enhance the novel's historical flavor, I have used the real names of a few other raiders, but their fleeting words in this book are imagined. Langston Cane's involvement in the raid is entirely fictional.

In Chapter 11, Benjamin Curley, general secretary of the Central Committee of Negro College Men, encourages black Americans to enlist in an officers' training camp for World War I. His words, as well as details about officers' pay, are drawn from *Scott's Official History of the American Negro in the World War*, written and published by Emmett J. Scott in 1919.

As for Canada, a schooner captain named Robert Wilson did help fugitive slaves slip across Lake Ontario to freedom in Oakville. In this novel, specific events, dialogue, and diary entries involving Wilson are invented. On February 28, 1930, the Ku Klux Klan (led by W. A. Phillips of Hamilton, Ontario) burned a cross in Oakville as a warning to Ira Johnson, a black man who planned to marry Isabella Jones, a white woman. That event inspired a fictional scene in this novel.

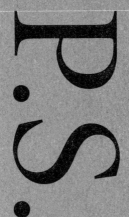

About the author

About the book

Ideas,
interviews
& features

Read on

Author Biography

LAWRENCE HILL is the son of American immigrants—a black father and a white mother—who came to Canada the day after they married in 1953 in Washington, DC. On his father's side, Hill's grandfather and great-grandfather were university-educated ordained ministers of the African Methodist Episcopal Church. His mother came from a Republican family in Oak Park, Illinois, graduated from Oberlin College and went on to become a civil rights activist in DC. The story of how they met, married, left the United States and raised a family in Toronto is described in Hill's bestselling memoir, *Black Berry, Sweet Juice: On Being Black and White in Canada*. Growing up in the predominantly white suburb of Don Mills, Ontario, in the sixties, Hill was greatly influenced by his parents' work in the human rights movement. Much of Hill's writing touches on issues of identity and belonging.

Lawrence Hill's third novel was published as *The Book of Negroes* in Canada and the UK, and as *Someone Knows My Name* in the USA, Australia and New Zealand. Published in translation around the world, it also won the overall Commonwealth Writers' Prize for Best Book, the Rogers Writers' Trust Fiction Prize, the Ontario Library Association's Evergreen Award and CBC Radio's Canada Reads. The book was a finalist for the Hurston/Wright Legacy Award and longlisted for both the Scotiabank Giller Prize and the International IMPAC Dublin Literary Award. In 2009, *The Book of Negroes: Illustrated Edition* was published with a new introduction from

Lawrence Hill

the author and with more than one hundred images, including early maps, documents, paintings, artifacts and illustrations to complement the novel.

Hill is also the author of the novels *Any Known Blood* and *Some Great Thing*. His most recently published fiction is the short story "Meet You at the Door," which appeared in the January–February 2011 issue of *The Walrus* magazine.

Hill's most recent non-fiction book, *The Deserter's Tale: The Story of an Ordinary Soldier Who Walked Away from the War in Iraq* (written with Joshua Key), was released in the United States, Canada, Australia, Japan and several European countries.

Hill has received honorary doctorates from the University of Toronto, Wilfrid Laurier University and the University of Waterloo. He has also won the Bob Edwards Award from the Alberta Theatre Projects, and he was named Author of the Year by Go On Girl!, the largest African-American women's book club in the United States. Hill won the National Magazine Award for the best essay published in Canada in 2005 for "Is Africa's Pain Black America's Burden?" (*The Walrus*). In 2005, the 90-minute film documentary that Hill wrote, *Seeking Salvation: A History of the Black Church in Canada*, won the American Wilbur Award for best national television documentary.

Formerly a reporter with *The Globe and Mail* and a parliamentary correspondent for the *Winnipeg Free Press*, Hill also speaks French and Spanish. He has lived and worked across Canada, in Baltimore, and in Spain and France. He is an honorary patron of Canadian Crossroads International, for ▶

3

which he travelled as a volunteer to the West African countries of Niger, Cameroon and Mali. Hill is also a member of the Council of Patrons of the Black Loyalist Heritage Society and of the Advisory Council of Book Clubs for Inmates. He has a BA in economics from Laval University in Quebec City and an MA in writing from Johns Hopkins University in Baltimore. Hill lives in Hamilton, Ontario.

&

An Interview with Lawrence Hill

You've described *Any Known Blood* as a loving but fictional tribute to your family. When did you first know that you would write it?

Just before my first child, Geneviève, was born in 1990, I felt that I should hurry up and interview my father about his life and our family history before I ran out of time. My father's health was already declining, as he had a painful terminal disease. Thankfully, he held up over the interviews, which I taped over the summer and completed just a few days before my daughter's birth. I knew as I was interviewing my father that I would mine, reshape and fictionalize at least some of the material for a novel.

What made you decide to develop the stories as fiction rather than non-fiction?

Never for a minute did I think about writing a family history. It was a novel from the first moment of conception, because I am primarily a novelist. I like the freedom of creating stories and characters, and I treasure the latitude novelists have to bend history and reshape the "facts" to tell a good story. I have written books of non-fiction, and I hope to write more. I am proud of them, too, and have worked very hard on them. But fiction is where my heart lies.

What was your family's reaction to their story being turned into a novel?

> " I like the freedom of creating stories and characters. "

5

An Interview with Lawrence Hill (*continued*)

Long before I first published a book, my parents used up all of their anxieties about having children who were artists instead of professionals. My father believed that the only way for a black male to transcend racism was to become a successful professional. By the time I started writing, however, Dad had come around to accepting that his children would make up their own minds about following their passions, and so my father and mother always supported my novel writing. They were positive about *Any Known Blood* but wary of how they and other family members were depicted, even fictionally. Certain stories from the lives of my parents and grandparents did enter into the story, but not without going through the creative meat grinder.

Although my father understood that this book was a novel, he was troubled by the depiction of a fictional sister—the character Mill—as a prostitute during the Second World War. "Larry," he said, "I know it's a novel, but did you have to make her a prostitute?"

"As a matter of fact, I did," I said, and that was the end of the conversation.

What aspects of the life of the fictional Langston Cane II mirror those of your great-grandfather, Daniel Grafton Hill I?

Daniel Grafton Hill I was the son of Richard Hill and Demias Crew, who were slaves in Maryland until Richard bought freedom for himself, his wife and their eight children in the late 1850s. Daniel

> **My father believed that the only way for a black male to transcend racism was to become a successful professional.**

was born in 1860—the last of nine children—and raised in Washington County in western Maryland. His mother died when he was just one, and his father did not have the means to raise all the children. I don't know what became of the other eight siblings, but Daniel was sent to live with Maryland Quakers. He studied at Storer College in Harpers Ferry, West Virginia, and then at Lincoln University in Pennsylvania. He went on to become a minister of the African Methodist Episcopal Church and to serve as minister at the Bethel African Methodist Episcopal Church on Druid Hill Avenue—the same church that is featured in *Any Known Blood*. Like Daniel Hill I, my character Langston Cane II is orphaned as a boy and raised by white Quakers before being sent back into his community to study and become a church minister. But those are the only similarities. I don't know much about the life of Daniel Hill I, and I was happy to invent a life for Langston Cane II.

What are some of the inherent difficulties involved in writing a work of fiction that incorporates real people and events?

The difficulty is respecting the broad lines of history, stamping the fresh face of fiction over the past, and being creative and lively at the same time. Historians will be happy to jump all over you if you get your facts wrong, but readers will drop your book in the trash can if you can't captivate them. Somehow, one has to mine history and then jack it up with dramatic tension, and make it worth reading. I believe ▶

“ I believe that fiction, well done, is a fabulous way to introduce readers to history. ”

An Interview with Lawrence Hill (*continued*)

that fiction, well done, is a fabulous way to introduce readers to history. I love speaking to students of all ages and trying to infect them with the history bug. I love telling them stories about the trials and triumphs of blacks in Canada. Part of my job as a novelist is to write the colour—and by that I mean human drama and struggle—back into history.

Oakville, Ontario, was in fact a relatively minor player in the Underground Railroad. What made you choose it as one of your backdrops?

I'm a bit of a nut for museums and local histories, and I am always curious to see how people examine and represent the past in their own backyards. When I moved to Oakville in 1990, I found that the Oakville museum had a black history exhibit, with information about a local schooner captain named Robert Wilson who had ferried fugitive slaves across Lake Ontario in the 1850s. The idea caught my imagination immediately. I found a black resident named Alvin Duncan, who was already an old man. He was born in Oakville, and so were his parents, and his grandparents had arrived there as fugitive slaves.

Alvin was a gold mine of information. For decades, he had collected newspaper clippings and photographs about the history of blacks in Oakville. He had great stories to tell, such as being turned away from an air force recruiting station during the Second World War because a medical examination had ostensibly revealed that his heart was located on the wrong side of

> **" Part of my job as a novelist is to write the colour— and by that I mean human drama and struggle—back into history. "**

his chest. Alvin was the first to tell me about the Ku Klux Klan coming to Oakville to try to protest the pending marriage between a black man and a white woman. My conversations with Alvin influenced the shape of *Any Known Blood* and inspired the creation of the character Aberdeen Williams.

How did your parents' active involvement in Canada's human rights movement influence your novel?

Like Dorothy Perkins in *Any Known Blood*, my mother worked for the Toronto Labour Committee for Human Rights and conducted tests to prove that employers, landlords and restaurant owners were discriminating against black people. While my mother was in the community gathering proof that discrimination existed, my father was working on his Ph.D. at the University of Toronto. He subsequently became the first director, and later the chairperson, of the Ontario Human Rights Commission. Both of my parents wrote books about the history of blacks in Canada, and their other significant contribution was to co-found, with some friends, the Ontario Black History Society in 1978. Aspects of their early life in Toronto—such as the barriers they encountered renting apartments because they were a mixed-race couple—transformed into fictionalized scenes in the novel.

How have your experiences working in Africa affected you and your writing?

I have travelled five times to Africa, three times as a volunteer with Canadian Crossroads ▶

> **❝** Aspects of [my parents'] early life in Toronto ... transformed into fictionalized scenes in the novel. **❞**

9

An Interview with Lawrence Hill (*continued*)

International. In the 1970s and 1980s, I spent about two months each in Niger, Cameroon and Mali. These trips changed my life completely and opened up a creative vein that I have mined ever since. My first published short story, called "My Side of the Fence," was set in Niger. Every one of my three novels to date has had scenes set in West Africa. My latest novel, *The Book of Negroes*, begins in Africa—in the country now known as Mali—in the mid-1700s, and it returns to Africa as the story unfolds. Almost all of my work touches in some way on fundamental and universal questions of identity and belonging. And all of these questions take me back, in one way or another, to Africa.

Do you feel that your work and that of other black writers has made a difference to Canadians' awareness of black history?

It is human history that interests me, and understanding it—including the things that black people have done and the ways that they have been treated. It reflects back on all of us. It is important for writers to explore history through their works and important for all of us to understand how our leaders have behaved toward our citizens—Japanese Canadians, Black Canadians and others who have faced discrimination—and to see the ways in which racism has limited and diminished our country.

With your interest in the past, have you been inspired by any particular historic figure?

" Almost all of my work touches in some way on fundamental and universal questions of identity and belonging. "

I suppose that Muhammad Ali was the first public figure to influence how I saw myself and how I saw the world. As a person and a writer, I like to imagine that I am standing on the shoulders of all the people who have gone before me on this earth. I try to leave behind the worst of their thoughts and actions and to be inspired by the best. Ali inspired me because he rose above his profession to state—with his own beautiful language—why he would not fight in Vietnam. Long before it was remotely popular to do so, he galvanized and inspired the anti-war movement in the United States. Muhammad Ali became my first hero. If I can accomplish with my writing a tiny fraction of the things Ali did to make this world a better place, I will be proud of my work.

❧

“ Muhammad Ali became my first hero. If I can accomplish with my writing a tiny fraction of the things Ali did to make this world a better place, I will be proud of my work. ”

An Excerpt from *Some Great Thing*

HIS SON WAS BORN in 1957 at the Misericordia Hospital in Winnipeg, before men had to start watching their wives give birth. Asked about it years later, Ben Grafton replied, "What's a man to do in a place like that, except grow all bug-eyed and wobbly and make a shining fool of himself?"

On that windless January night, Ben Grafton didn't enter the delivery room. He didn't consider it. He waited until Louise was "finished," poked his head in the door and shouted "atta way Lulu!" Wearing a blue woollen cap that stopped short of his huge brown ears, he followed two nurses who took the infant to the nursery. Ben Grafton was not invited. Nor was he self-conscious. He was a forty-three-year-old railroad porter who had coped with all sorts of nonsense in the past and had long stopped wondering what people thought of his being this or that. They turned to tell him he couldn't stay in the nursery. He said he wanted to look at his little man.

"So cute, this little baby," one nurse cooed, turning the brown face toward Ben.

Ben touched a tiny cheek. He didn't understand all this hospital nonsense. Why couldn't the nurses just leave the boy with his mother? Or with him? But he wasn't going to raise a ruckus. He was going to take it calm and easy. But then something happened. The nurse crossed the baby. With her thumb. She actually touched his forehead and made a sign of the cross. Then she started mumbling a prayer. "Hey," Ben said.

The nurse continued.

"No praying." Gently, but firmly, Ben poked the woman in the ribs.

She turned on him, eyebrows raised. "Please," she hissed.

"No praying," Ben repeated.

The woman's jaw dropped. The nurse beside her stared at Ben.

"That's right," Ben said, eyeballing both of them. "This little man is a Grafton. And Graftons don't go in for devils and angels and heaven and hell. This little man will believe in humanity. Humanity and activism. You can leave him here till his mother wakes up but I don't want any more of those rituals. Is that clear?"

The praying nurse nodded, the other one blinked. Neither spoke. They lay the baby in his bassinet. Ben backed out of the nursery but watched through the window. He stayed there for an hour or so. He had some thinking to do. Thinking about a name. A good one. This child was destined for great things. No ordinary name would do.

❧

❝ This little man will believe in humanity. Humanity and activism. **❞**

From Lawrence Hill's Essay "Is Africa's Pain Black America's Burden?"

IN THE 1970S, as a teenager, I took a solo trip from my home in Toronto to visit family in Washington, DC, and foolishly asked my grandmother, May Edwards Hill, what she thought of the black operatic characters Porgy and Bess. May, born in 1896 and raised in a prosperous family that fitted proudly into the ranks of what was then called "the talented tenth"—America's elite, university-educated blacks—tore a strip off me for even mentioning the characters popularized in the 1935 folk opera by George Gershwin, a white composer. The disabled Porgy, who wheeled himself about on a cart, and Bess, an unfaithful lover, were lowbrow Southern blacks who, despite poverty and suffering, loved each other and lived with gusto and passion. Even as fictional characters, they nauseated my grandmother.

"We have enough stereotypes to combat as it is," May muttered, "and they just bring shame down on all Negroes with their cavorting around and their immorality." Her complaint reflected one of the most troubling paradoxes about black identity in North America. For four hundred years, we've been seen to be less than human. And so, to compensate, we must be more civilized than the civilized. We place unreasonable expectations on ourselves, such is our desire to succeed in the world and to be accepted as equal by those who dragged us across the Atlantic Ocean.

By the age of ten, I was well versed in black

> 'We have enough stereotypes to combat as it is,' May muttered.

history and entranced by accounts of how my white, civil-rights-activist mother and black, graduate-student father formed a union against all odds, married in the American South in 1953 and decamped that very week to spend the rest of their active lives fighting for human rights in Canada. Dad's own father and grandfather had combined their work as ministers in the African Methodist Episcopal Church, disseminating the social gospel in the black communities they served. Stories had filtered down through the generations about my great-great-grandfather purchasing freedom for his wife, his children and himself in Maryland in 1860. "How did he get the money?" We speculated about it at the kitchen table. "Probably stole it," came one response, with a cackle. But when the laughter subsided, we were quietly warned: "If you don't fight racism, you become part of the problem."

Stories abounded in my family about W.E.B. Du Bois, whose essay collection *The Souls of Black Folk* stands out as one of the seminal works of African-American literature of the twentieth century. Du Bois, who was born in 1868 and lived to the age of 95, became the first black to obtain a Ph.D. from Harvard University in 1895 and went on to become one of the architects of the National Association for the Advancement of Colored People (NAACP).

In 1900, Du Bois coined a phrase that spread like a grass fire and became a mantra among observers of race relations in America: "The problem of the twentieth century is the problem of the color-line." And in ▶

'If you don't fight racism, you become part of the problem.'

From Lawrence Hill's Essay "Is Africa's Pain Black America's Burden?" (*continued*)

September 1903, Du Bois published "The Talented Tenth," one of his most famous essays. In it, he argued that only the elite of the African-American population could pull the rest of the black population up by its bootstraps and that education would save the black people of America.

For people like me, being black and having access to a good education carried certain obligations. It wasn't good enough to get A's in school—you also had to ball up your fists and charge into battle if anybody used the word "nigger." In the workplace, it wasn't good enough to merely succeed professionally. You had to change the world, too.

So what happened to this forward-looking, educated, socially engaged, black middle class? They were a powerful force for social change, leaders and supporters of civil rights movements, eloquent speakers and writers for the plight of North American blacks, and for Africa itself. Africa needs them now, but are they interested in Africa?

This essay, in its totality, first appeared in the February 2005 issue of *The Walrus*.

❧

❝ For people like me, being black and having access to a good education carried certain obligations. ❞

Further Reading

Bound for Canaan: The Triumph of the Underground Railroad, by Fergus M. Bordewich: This is an excellent account of the people who fled along the Underground Railroad and the "conductors" who risked their lives, as well as those of their families, to help them.

Cloudsplitter, by Russell Banks: This novel is about John Brown, his raid on Harpers Ferry and his tortured family relationships.

The Freedom-Seekers: Blacks in Early Canada, by Daniel G. Hill: Written by my late father, *The Freedom-Seekers* contains stories and background on the history of black people in this country.

Kipligat's Chance, by David N. Odhiambo: Set in modern-day Vancouver, this gritty, engaging novel from a promising young African-Canadian writer is about an immigrant from Kenya who must deal with the ghosts of his past and struggle to overcome poverty and self-abuse.

Narrative of the Life of Frederick Douglass, an American Slave, by Frederick Douglass: This is a classic memoir about a man who fled slavery and became a powerful and respected advocate for freedom.

The Refugee: or the Narratives of Fugitive Slaves in Canada, collated by Benjamin Drew: First published in 1856, this book is a compilation of interviews that the American ▶

abolitionist Drew conducted with black men and women who slipped across the border into Canada to escape slavery.

Their Eyes Were Watching God, by Zora Neale Hurston: This novel celebrates a free-spirited black woman who takes up with another man without bothering to divorce her husband. First published in 1937, this novel later came under fire from Richard Wright—the most famous Black American writer of his day—for offering "no theme, no message, no thought." How wrong he was.

Underground to Canada, by Barbara Smucker: I especially like this wonderful, short novel for young readers because the fugitives in the tale are clever, independent children.

ᥫ

Web Detective

www.nationalgeographic.com/railroad
This interactive site allows you to take on the role of a Maryland slave in the 1850s, following the Underground Railroad to freedom.

www.oakvilletrails.com
On the home page, click "Information Stations," then select "Early Village" for links to an essay ("The Underground Railroad") and a photo panel.

www.pbs.org/wgbh/aia/home.html
This is a companion site to the PBS series *Africans in America* and chronicles the history of racial slavery in the United States.

www.archives.gov.on.ca/english/on-line -exhibits/index-black-history.aspx
Explore black history in Ontario through this excellent site.

www.buxtonmuseum.com
This site celebrates the Underground Railroad and early black settlement in Canada.

www.olivetreegenealogy.com/can/ont /fugitives.shtml
Read fourteen real-life accounts of black fugitives in Ontario from an 1856 book compiled by Benjamin Drew.

To receive updates on author events and new books by Lawrence Hill, sign up today at *www.authortracker.ca*.